D0472811

THE
GARMENT MAKER'S
DAUGHTER

HILLARY ADRIENNE STERN

Published by Hillary A. Stern
www.hillaryadriennestern.com
ISBN 978-0-9982416-1-6

Copyright © Hillary A. Stern, 2011, 2016

Visit Hillary A. Stern's official website at www.hillaryadriennestern.com
for the latest news, book details, and other information

Cover Image © Unravel2 by Andrea Benson, www.andreabenson.com
Ebook Formatting by Guido Henkel, www.guidohenkel.com

All rights reserved. No portion of this book may be reproduced in any form without
permission from the publisher, except as permitted by U.S. copyright law.

This book is a work of fiction. Any references to historical events, real people, or real
locales are used fictitiously.

Printed in the U.S.A.

For my daughters
Julie and Lena,
who always inspire me and
whom I love more than words can express.

There is nothing I would not do for those who are really my friends. I have no notion of loving people by halves, it is not my nature.

Jane Austen, Northanger Abbey

PART I

CHAPTER ONE

SEPTEMBER 1917

DANIEL COWAN KNEW WELL WHAT IT WAS LIKE TO BE SURROUNDED by people and still feel lonely. But it wasn't loneliness he felt as he wended his way through the crowds on the deck of the S.S. Pretoria. Instead, he perceived his solitariness as conferring a kind of freedom. For once, he had an opportunity to be who and what he chose, unlimited by anyone's prior knowledge. On this ship, no one knew about his past, nor did they care. They were concerned only with their own uncertain but hopeful futures.

He was headed for the ship's bow hoping to catch his first glimpse of land although rumor had it that they wouldn't reach Ellis Island and the Port of New York until the next day. Twenty-two years old and gangly, with wheat-colored hair, guileless blue eyes, and gold-rimmed glasses, he stood at least a head taller than most of those around him. Even stooping a little, as was his habit, he had an excellent view of his surroundings.

The deck was more crowded than he'd seen it in the two weeks they'd been at sea. The re-emergence of the sun, after three days of heavy wind and rain, no doubt had something to do with that. To his right, people lined the rails that ran along the sides of the ship from stem to stern. To his left, the upper-class decks rose like tiers on a wedding cake. Everywhere in between was filled with the tops of people's heads, making the deck appear as impenetrable as a tree-covered mountain. Any movement from one part of the ship to another would require determination and patience. Daniel had both.

He forged a serpentine path, detouring around clamorous families who had staked out pieces of deck as if they were the front parlors of the homes they'd left behind. Darting children cut in front of him, forcing him to pull up short to avoid tripping over them. But he didn't mind. With every delay, his anticipation

1

grew. There was a current of excitement in the air and he felt it charging through him.

The sound of a crying child caught his attention. It came from a little boy planted like a small, stubby rock in the midst of streaming people. Daniel had never been able to pass by any creature in need and he was tempted to help. But even before he had taken a step in the toddler's direction, a young man about his own age came along and scooped the child up in a big hug. Relieved, he resumed walking.

By now, he had come within fifty feet of the bow. It was even more crowded here with people jockeying for a spot that would afford an unhampered view. Searching for a way to get closer to the rail, his attention was arrested by the sight of a young woman perched on a box as still as a statue.

She was immersed in a book and clearly oblivious to the people around her as she rapidly scanned one page after another. Seeing her so completely absorbed, Daniel realized how he must often have looked to others—there, but not there—his mind, his self transported to a place and time created entirely by words on a page.

He tried to make out the title of the book. But a young girl who stationed herself directly in front of the reader with her hands on her hips suddenly blocked his line of sight.

"Lena," the girl said loudly. There was no reaction.

"Lena," she said again, louder. Still no response.

The girl cupped her hands around her mouth, took a deep breath, leaned in, and yelled. "Lena!"

Watching, Daniel could see it all play out on the young woman's face. The abrupt collision of the real world with the one in her head and her obvious irritation when she realized who had interrupted her.

"What is it?" she said warily.

"Are you deaf? I've been saying your name over and over."

"I didn't hear you."

"You mean you pretended not to hear me so you could keep reading." The young girl said.

"What is it?" Lena said with practiced patience.

"You have to come back with me. We'll be arriving in New York any minute and we have to get our things ready. Don't you even care that we're almost there? Don't you care about anything besides that book?"

At the mention of the book, Lena's annoyance seeped away and her gaze softened. Daniel knew that she was back again in the world in which she'd been lost only a few moments before. Her mouth curved to reveal a generous smile. It transformed her face, softening her angular cheekbones, punctuating her pointed chin with a dimple, and bringing balance to her wide-set eyes.

"It's a wonderful story," she said, her voice passionate, her face animated. "You must read it. It's about a woman named Hodel who falls in love with a man named Perchick. He's a revolutionary fighting to overthrow the Czar. And Hodel wants to fight alongside him. So they decide to get married and –"

"What kind of crazy story is that?" the younger girl interrupted. "A woman fighting? And the two of them deciding to get married without the help of a matchmaker? The whole thing sounds stupid."

Daniel watched Lena struggle with the urge to make some retort, her face an easy read. But she reconsidered and instead smiled. "You're still young," she said. "You'll feel differently when you're older."

"Well, maybe I am younger than you," the girl said, thrusting her chin forward. "But at least I'm not a dreamer."

As Lena's smile vanished, Daniel recoiled inwardly at the barbed words. Variations of those same words had been hurled at him many times. He wanted to tell the rude young girl that reading was a gift, that books were to be treasured, and that there was nothing wrong with being a dreamer. While he debated whether to thrust himself into the conversation, Lena responded.

"Yes, I know. You're not a dreamer. In fact," she said with the barest hint of a smile, "I can barely imagine you ever having any dreams at all."

Daniel had to stifle himself to avoid laughing out loud at the way Lena had turned the girl's insult back on her without the youngster even realizing it. But at that moment, his presence was detected.

"What are you looking at?" the young girl demanded.

Heat flooded his face and he knew he was turning red as he always did when he was flustered. He opened his mouth to apologize for staring, but no words came to mind. So, he looked down and his glasses slipped down his nose. Hurriedly, he adjusted them. By the time he raised his head, they were no longer paying him any attention.

"Come on," the younger girl said.

"Alright, I'm coming."

He watched them as they wove their way into the crowd, a mixture of emotions swirling inside him. Chief among these was regret that he'd not spoken up in defense of Lena. Here he was dreaming of taking on a new identity but still allowing his old one to determine his actions. He would not let it happen again.

He resumed his journey toward the bow and almost at once, off in the distance, he saw another female. Someone he'd been dreaming about ever since he'd conceived of this journey. She was just as beautiful as he'd imagined. As the ship steamed forward, her outlines became clearer, the draped garb, the raised torch, the crown on her head.

A grin monopolized his face and he found himself wanting to share the moment with someone. Around him, fathers were hoisting children onto their shoulders so they could see the fabled statue. Next to him, two sisters stood, their arms around each other's waists, their faces rapturous. On his other side, an elderly couple trembled shoulder-to-shoulder, whether in fear of the unknown future or in delight it was hard to tell.

A hand clasped his shoulder and he turned to see a gleaming smile creasing a worn olive-skinned face and twinkling dark eyes. It was Martelli, the dapper little Italian man who slept in the bunk directly opposite his. *"Bella, no?"* Martelli asked. He gestured toward the statue. *"Signora Liberty e bellisima no?"*

Daniel grinned. "Yes, very bella," he said.

He looked back at the Statue of Liberty. He had been dreaming of this moment for so long. Now, he just had to pass the immigration inspection and be admitted into the United States. Everyone knew that America was the land of new beginnings and no one needed a new beginning more than he did.

CHAPTER TWO

THE WIRY FUZZ OF A WOOL BLANKET AGAINST HER CHIN TICKLED Lena awake and she rolled over onto her side, luxuriating in the roominess of a real bed all to herself after weeks of sleeping in a narrow bunk. In the silent darkness of Yosef's boarding house room, it was hard to tell what time it was, but she was too keyed up to fall back asleep.

She didn't want to disturb her brother, so she distracted herself with a daydream of the type she indulged in far too often. She would get a job, of course. But, she would also go to school. She imagined taking classes in all kinds of subjects, everything from botany to philosophy to literature. In her fantasy, she found one particular subject that enthralled her and began studying it in depth. There was a handsome and brilliant student in the same department who shared her passion and they began doing research together. One day, they made an amazing, world-changing discovery. They were jointly nominated for the Nobel Prize. They would—

The sound of Yosef stirring brought her back to the present. Her eyes had adjusted enough for her to make out his bear-like form in the wing chair he'd insisted would be fine for the night. Guilt flooded her. As soon as she'd seen that his room had only one bed, she'd tried to talk him into allowing her to sleep on the chair. But he had shaken his head and said she needed to get some rest "after all she had been through." She knew that this comment, along with the crushing hug he'd given her at Ellis Island, was his way of acknowledging how difficult the last few months had been for her as their father's sole caretaker until he succumbed to tuberculosis. She knew, too, that Yosef's reluctance to say more was not because he was unemotional but, rather, because he didn't trust himself not to be overly emotional.

There had been times growing up when Yosef, six years her elder, had been the only one around to watch over her. Their mother had died during an outbreak of influenza when Lena was three years old. Their father had put in long days at his tailoring shop in Lublin. The grandmothers and aunts who might have helped were back in the tiny shtetl where their parents had grown up. Without family nearby, the burden of caring for Lena had fallen mostly on Yosef and he'd generally been good about it.

Of course, growing up, they'd had their moments. Once, he'd made something for dinner that had been completely inedible and insisted that she eat it anyway. When she'd complained, he'd yelled and she'd started to cry. Even then, she'd known he wasn't really upset with her, just with himself. As if a young boy should be expected to know how to cook. And there had been other times too when he hadn't been as gentle as he might have been. But she'd always seen the love behind whatever front he put on. And they'd always been close.

Yosef was still sleeping, but she couldn't lie still any longer. She pulled her valise from beneath the bed and removed her black skirt and white blouse. After dressing, she bent again to close the suitcase, but paused to retrieve one last but very important article, a soft white handkerchief. She held it tightly and brought it up to her face to breathe the lingering scent of her mother's perfume, a woody and floral fragrance with just a hint of lemon.

Because she'd been so young when her mother died, most of what she thought she remembered about her were actually things that had been told to her—how thrilled her mother had been to have a daughter, how she had danced with Lena in her arms, and how she had entertained her with stories while she hung the wash on the line.

She did have a few memories that were really her own, but these were elusive and insubstantial, like the yeasty smell of the bread that her mother had baked every Friday in preparation for Shabbat and the muffled sounds of her mother going about her housework while she drifted into her afternoon nap.

Her only clear recollection had to do with the handkerchief. As a small child, she'd gone around with what seemed to be a perpetual cold. It hadn't been anything serious, probably just an allergy. But whenever her nose got too frustratingly stuffy or messily runny, there was her mother at the ready, pulling her handkerchief out of the pocket of her apron, kneeling so that her face was level with Lena's, cupping her chin with one hand, and gently wiping her nose with the soft cloth.

The handkerchief worked like magic. No matter how dirty it became, no matter how many times it was laundered, it still came out pure and clean. Time and again, it blossomed in her mother's hand like a soft white lily to clean her messy face, wipe away sloppy tears, or press gently against her knee when she scraped it. The fabric was both strong and soft at the same time. And without fail, it made everything better. The handkerchief was the only object she could really remember her mother holding and touching her with. And it was easily the most precious thing she owned.

An hour later, she hurried to keep up with Yosef as they departed for the factory where he worked. A bleak dawn was beginning to permeate the sky, but the light had not yet penetrated to street level. Boarding houses and apartments were jammed tightly against each other on either side of the street. Their fronts were darkly forbidding, with facades barred by metal fire escapes from which laundry fluttered like flags of surrender.

At the first corner, they turned left onto a much wider and longer street. Here, horse-drawn carts hugged the curb. Merchants pulled away tarps to reveal fruit and vegetables, spices and grains. As they continued to walk, dawn arrived and along with it came customers in great multitudes. The street filled with a cacophony of sounds as vendors hawked, livestock squawked, children whooped, mothers yelled, horses snorted and still more carts rumbled down the already clogged street. Lena pulled up her skirt's hem to protect it from the horse droppings as she listened to Yosef's description of his workplace so she would know what to expect.

According to her brother, the Northern Shirtwaist Company was owned by Jack Gordon, an immigrant from Russia, who'd started out working for someone else but quickly branched into business for himself. Gordon had built his business by being tough, thin-skinned, and stingy. He trusted no one, including his own family members, who he hired to help him run the business because he trusted outsiders even less.

"You don't really have to worry about Gordon," Yosef said, as they crossed the street toward a white brick building on the corner. "He mostly stays in his office on the tenth floor. It's his brother-in-law Max Horowitz you have to watch out for. He's in charge of the sewing floor and he's a real *gonif*. But if he likes you, he'll leave you alone."

They followed a group of young women into the building and joined the back of a crowd waiting for the elevator. Hearing the muffled sound of the car landing, Lena prepared to move forward. But when the operator pulled the inner and then outer grates open, the interior was large enough to accommodate only perhaps twenty people. It was not until the lift had made two full trips that she and Yosef were able to board.

Penned in on all sides, Lena's heart thrummed anxiously as they ascended creakily to the seventh-floor, where Yosef had started before moving up to the higher-paying cutting room on the eighth floor. The elevator opened onto a narrow hallway and she and Yosef moved along with the others like herded sheep.

At the end of the hall, the doorway to the sewing room was blocked by a man whose shoulders were broader than the frame. Max Horowitz was bald with bulging lidless eyes and a thick neck. Even without Yosef's warning, Lena would have known he was someone to be wary of. Just before they reached him, Yosef quickly whispered in her ear.

"Lena, just for today, let me do all the talking. Don't say a word no matter what. And one more thing. I forgot to tell you. In America, I go by the name Joe."

"What?!" Lena said.

"Shh!!"

Max Horowitz was affectless as Yosef inquired as to whether there were any job openings. The only sign that he'd heard anything was the slow shifting of his stare from Joe to Lena. Under his scrutiny, she felt the weight of the power he wielded. After a minute, his eyes shifted back to Joe.

"Vi alt iz di?" (*How old is she?*) Horowitz asked.

"Zib'tzn," (*Seventeen*) Joe answered.

"Iz das ir ershter arbet in America"? (*Is this her first job in America?*)

"Yoh." (*Yes*).

"Does she know how to work the machine?"

Yosef nodded. "Our father was a tailor and she operated his machine many times." He put a hand on Lena's shoulder and added, "She's a quick learner."

Horowitz shifted his eyes back to Lena but said nothing. As the silence and the scrutiny continued, she felt a strong urge to say something. Her father had always encouraged her to speak her mind.

"Listen to me, Lena-la," he would say. "Women are just as smart as men. Didn't Eve eat from the tree of knowledge even before Adam? Don't let anyone treat you like you haven't got a good head on your shoulders. Just because a woman must occasionally wield a dishrag doesn't mean she has to be one."

Now, seeing the expression on Horowitz's face, Lena thought she could tell him a thing or two about how people back home praised her precise stitchery and how sometimes, when Papa's old machines broke down, she was able to tinker with them and get them to work again. But, remembering Yosef's cautionary words, she held her tongue. She slipped her hand into her pocket, curled her fingers around the handkerchief, and concentrated on keeping her emotions from showing.

Abruptly, Horowitz nodded. "Alright. I'll try her out." He looked back at Yosef again and spoke rapidly. "Five dollars a week to start. If she breaks a sewing needle, I deduct ten cents. And for every shirtwaist she ruins, I deduct twenty-five cents. She messes up too much, she's out of a job."

Yosef nodded and Horowitz stepped aside, leaving room for Lena to enter. She gave her brother a quick last glance, received an encouraging smile, and took her first steps into the sewing room. Her breath caught in her throat at the sight before her.

The room was filled with row after row of sewing-machine topped tables wedged against each other, perhaps three hundred in all. The rows spanned nearly the entire width of the room. At the far end, they butted up against large, filmy windows that admitted dim light. A narrow aisle on the near end, afforded the only means of access. Above the tables were thick black electric cords strung like clotheslines from one end of the room to the other. Dangling tentacle-like wires connected the lines to the sewing machines below. It was a far cry from the cozy tailor shop where Lena's father had plied his trade.

Horowitz pointed to an empty chair in the third row. "Sit there," he said. "Sophie will show you what to do."

Taking her seat, Lena examined the black iron sewing machine. With relief, she saw that it was not terribly different from the one her father had used.

By now, the room was filling up—with some men, but mostly women and a few girls, some no more than eleven or twelve years old. The workers filed along the narrow aisle and squeezed down the rows, chatting and laughing up until the moment they took their seats. As the aisle began to empty, the noise of machine wheels whirring and bobbins clacking up and down took over the room and Lena began to feel foolish sitting idle in the midst of so much industriousness.

Waiting for "Sophie" to arrive, Lena snuck a glance around her. A group of very young children sitting in a circle of chairs at the front of the room puzzled her until she saw one little girl reach down and pick up some fabric. The child held it in the air, studying it. Then, with a pair of tiny scissors, she began to snip at the threads that dangled unfinished from the material. It dawned on Lena sadly that these little ones were Northern's youngest workers.

A woman squeezed behind her and slipped into the seat to her left. Lena tried to catch her eye and was rewarded with a quick shy smile.

"Sophie?" she ventured. The woman shook her ahead, bent over her machine, and began to oil it with a small, spouted can. Thinking it couldn't hurt for her to do the same, Lena reached for the oilcan nearest her. Suddenly, she felt a jolt against her chair.

"*Oyfshtey!*" (Stand up!")

The angry Yiddish caught her by surprise and she twisted around to see a stout girl with wiry brown hair. She stared down at Lena with flaring nostrils and brows that joined each other across the bridge of her nose.

"*Oyfshtey,*" the girl repeated. "*Dos iz meine shtool.*" (This is my chair.)

Lena glanced around. Horowitz was several rows away, working on another girl's machine. If he'd heard anything, he gave no sign of it. Maybe that was for the best. She twisted around in her seat again and tamped down the temptation to answer in the same tone she'd been addressed.

"Are you Sophie? Because Herr Horowitz said -"

"I'm not Sophie and I don't care what Max said. All I care about is the fact that you're sitting in my chair. Get out."

Lena felt sure she was sitting in the seat she'd been assigned. "Maybe we should ask Mr. Horowitz what we should do," she suggested.

"What?" The girl shouted at her over the din of the machines.

"I said, maybe we should ask Mr. Horowitz," Lena shouted back.

"Oh, so now you're telling me what to do?"

"No, I—" Lena stopped mid-sentence and thought furiously. Obviously, she couldn't disobey Horowitz. She'd never had any trouble standing her ground, but getting into a fight on her first day also didn't seem prudent. Maybe if she tried again to explain. She started to rise, but a slight pressure on her arm made her pause. Her neighbor on the right had arrived.

"Tsuhalt," the new girl said softly. She smiled at Lena, displaying dazzling white teeth against bright red lip color. "If Horowitz told you to sit there, you should stay there." She turned her attention to the wire-haired girl. She was still smiling, but there was no longer any warmth behind it and her eyes now gleamed with something less than amiable.

"You will have to find another seat, Anna," she said.

Anna's scowl deepened. "Stay out of it, Sophie. It's none of your business. Now," she glared again at Lena, "for the last time, get out of my seat."

Lena glanced back at Horowitz. He was still preoccupied with the malfunctioning machine. She turned back to Anna and shook her head slowly.

Beside her, Sophie was through being pleasant. "Let go of the chair, Anna," she directed. "And leave the new girl alone. You've been late to work every day for a week and now it's going to cost you your seat."

"It's none of your business," Anna repeated. "Stay out of it."

"But it is my business," Lena said. "And I don't want her to stay out of it." She glanced at Sophie, saw confirmation in her eyes, and looked back at Anna. Suddenly, with surprising stealth for such a large man, Horowitz loomed over them all.

"What's going on here?" he said.

"She's sitting in my seat," Anna hissed, giving the back of Lena's chair a little tug.

Lena kept her tone neutral. "I'm just sitting where you told me to sit."

Horowitz looked from Lena to Anna and back again. Finally, he turned to Sophie. "You say what happened."

Sophie shrugged and met Horowitz's stare with a cool gaze. "The new girl didn't do nothing wrong," she said.

"Alright then," Horowitz said. "You," he pointed at Anna. "Sit over there." He indicated an empty seat at the end of the row against the window wall. "Sophie, you show the new girl what to do."

"But that's not fair," Anna said. "It'll take me ten minutes just to get in and out of that seat. I've been working here for five months already. I earned this seat."

Horowitz shrugged. "It's that seat or no seat," he said. Then he turned and walked away.

"Shmuck," muttered Anna. She gave Lena's chair another shove. "You'll pay for this. And you too, Friedman," she added shooting Sophie a venomous look. She squeezed down the row, bumping into the back of every seat she passed.

Watching Anna's retreating back, Lena murmured. "Wonderful. My first day and already I've made an enemy."

"Well," Sophie said breezily, "one enemy and one friend. So, you're even. Anyway, don't worry. Anna's a nasty bitch who's been getting on my nerves for a long time. She deserves what she got."

Lena stared at her new co-worker, unsure which was more shocking, Sophie's language or the way she looked. With her jet black hair piled on her head and her obviously rouged lips and cheeks, there was a vivacity to her that made her stand out in the crowded room like a peacock in a coop full of chickens. Clearly, this was someone she needed to know better.

Taking in the expression on Lena's face, Sophie's shoulders shook as she laughed, her smile assuring Lena that she was not laughing at her but, rather, inviting Lena to laugh with her. Which Lena did, until a severe glance from Horowitz silenced them both.

"We'd better get to work," Sophie said. She reached into a basket on the floor beside her chair, pulled up a bundle of white cotton material loosely tied with a string, untied it, and demonstrated how the various pieces of fabric needed to be joined together to produce a single shirtwaist.

"What do we do with them when we're done?" Lena asked.

"Put them in that basket on the table behind your machine. Tony Marulo comes by once an hour to pick up the finished goods and bring more material. But keep track of your own count," she warned. "They're always trying to cheat us."

Lena reached for a bundle from the basket at her feet, and got started. Within a short time, she had mastered the process and deposited her first shirtwaist in the basket behind her machine. Then she reached down and grabbed another bundle. Even before her basket of finished shirtwaists was full, a door at the front of the room burst open and a tall, olive-skinned boy, his arms loaded with fresh bundles of fabric, skittered in. Then Tony Marulo quickly began weaving his way down each row, passing out new material. When he reached the back of the room, he reversed himself and, holding one long arm out like a rod, gathered finished shirtwaists with the other, slinging them over the waiting limb.

Hours passed. Sharp-edged pangs bounced against Lena's empty stomach. The constant up and down motion of the sewing needle, like a vertical pendulum, became mesmerizing. Tony Marulo's periodic crashing entrance was the only relief from the endless sameness of the morning. After a while, she barely even noticed Tony as he came around with new supplies of material. Finally, a shrieking whistle sounded, followed immediately by the scraping of chair legs. Lena stood up slowly, her back stiff and her neck tight. Edging out of the aisle, she followed Sophie to the women's cloakroom.

There, amidst the peg-lined walls where, Sophie explained, in winter, they would stow their coats and capes, workers stood in groups of two or three or four and ate their lunches. Sophie led the way to an uncrowded corner and Lena pulled her lunch out of the paper sack Yosef had handed her on their way out that morning.

"Is that all you've got?" Sophie asked, seeing Lena's roll. "Here. Have one of my cookies. I'm watching my figure anyway."

Lena looked at her doubtfully. Sophie's figure seemed full in all the right places and tiny everywhere else. But maybe limiting her cookie intake was how she kept it that way.

"Thank you."

"Don't mention it. I remember what it was like to be a greenie myself."

"A greenie?"

"A greenhorn. You know, a newcomer."

"Oh," Lena nodded. "Have you been in America long?"

"Six months. I came with my aunt and uncle. What about you? Did you come with family?"

"No, but my brother was already here. Yosef," Lena hesitated before trying out the unfamiliar sound, "I mean Joe works in the cutting room."

"Your brother changed his name, huh?" Sophie asked knowingly. "Me too. Mine was *Tzeitel*, but when the immigration officials asked me, I said it was Sophie."

"It fits you," Lena said. "You seem very American."

"Well, I do go to the movies a lot. And I read the fashion magazines. And I go to the dances at the Settlement House every Saturday night."

"Settlement house?"

"It's where I met my Jake. He was on the dance floor waltzing with some blond when I arrived. But as soon as I saw him, I said to myself, that guy is going to be waltzing with me next. We've been together ever since." Sophie pursed her lips mischievously.

"He doesn't know it yet, but one day soon we're going to be married."

"Married," Lena said, shaking her head in wonder. "And you decided it without your parents' approval and without a matchmaker being involved. I knew America would be like this."

Sophie laughed. "I don't think my parents would approve of Jake. They always wanted me to marry a scholar or a rabbi or at least a butcher, so I'd always have meat on the table. Jake isn't any of those things. He isn't book smart. And he sure isn't religious. I'm not sure he even believes in God. And he doesn't earn much working for that labor union he's so devoted to. But he's, oh, I don't even know how to describe him."

As Sophie talked on, a mini-fantasy bloomed in Lena's mind. She was standing at the edge of a dance floor. Suddenly, she saw a man with curly hair rather like the hero of the book she'd read on the ship. He noticed her and smiled. Then, somehow, she was dancing with him and, as they danced, he asked her if she would join him in his fight for the rights of the people. She was just about to answer him when the whistle sounded. She hurried with Sophie to join the line of workers making their way back to their seats.

How she wished she could talk to Sophie while she bent over her machine joining shirtsleeves to cuffs. She could listen to her talk about Jake and life in America and movies and Saturday night dances for hours. But she had learned during the morning shift that there was no talking, no humming, and no breaks of any kind while working. For the next six hours, the whir of sewing machines, the clanking of hundreds of peddles, and the plinking of the needles were the only sounds in the room. By the time the whistle blew again at seven p.m., she was so tired she barely had the energy to push her chair back and fall in line behind Sophie as they snaked their way toward the exit.

Outside, Lena spotted her brother and brought Sophie over to introduce the two of them. He laughed as they told him about the seating incident and invited Sophie to join them as they headed for home. They walked three abreast down Broome Street and Lena felt the tension of the long day begin to melt. Exhaustion set in and she was content to merely listen to Joe and Sophie chatting as they walked without bothering to chime in. As they approached Joe's boarding house, she saw an elderly woman standing on the sidewalk. Garbed all in black, and with beady eyes and a sharp nose, she resembled an angry crow. She waited until they were nearly there, then waggled a finger at them.

"Ha! Last night it was one woman and today it's two! Well, I won't have it. I run a clean boarding house and I'm putting an end to this business right now."

"But Mrs. Yelnow," Joe said, deploying the smile that never failed to charm, "This is my sister. And this other lady with us is just a friend. She's not coming up to the room with us."

The crow shook her head back and forth. "No," she said. "No sisters, no friends, no girls in the rooms no matter what. I won't have this place turned into a whorehouse."

"Now Mrs. Yelnow," Joe cajoled. "We'll start looking for a new place right away. Just give us a few days."

"I'll give you no days. Either she goes or you both go."

Joe turned to face Lena and lowered his voice. "I don't think she's going to change her mind. Maybe we can find a hotel room or something for tonight."

"What?" Lena was appalled. The thought of searching for a new place to sleep after she'd just spent twelve hours bent over a sewing machine made her feel nauseous. Unfairness always infuriated her and the woman's implacability made her head pound. She felt her mouth tighten into a line and struggled to keep her emotions in check.

"Yosef—I mean, Joe—it's nearly 7:30 and we haven't eaten yet. I'm starving. And exhausted. You must be too. Anyway, it's just a misunderstanding." She turned to the woman. "Let me explain—"

"I've already said all I have to say," the old lady told her. The expression on her face, like she had just inhaled an unpleasant odor, only fueled Lena's fury.

"That's not fair," she fumed. "You're being—"

"Lena." Joe squeezed her shoulder. "I think we better look for someplace else for tonight. There must be a hotel—"

"But Joe, she thinks I'm a, a..."

"What's all this talk about a hotel," Sophie interrupted. "Lena can just stay by me tonight. Our boarder just left, so there's an empty bed right in my room."

Lena whirled around. The offer was generous, if impetuous. She had, after all, known Sophie for less than a day. And, although she was touched by Sophie's kindness, she wasn't ready to leave Joe so soon after their reunion. Besides, the idea of letting the old bird win when she was being so unjust didn't sit well.

"You're being very kind," she said to Sophie, stalling for time while she weighed the alternatives. "But you hardly know me. And shouldn't you ask your aunt and uncle?"

Sophie waved her questions away. "So, we just met. I already know you better than I ever knew Anna and she sat next to me for three months. And, more important, I know you're a good person."

She tilted her head to one side, casting her eyes down in modesty. "I don't like to brag, but I have this gift. I can always tell if someone is a good person. My mama used to say that I could spot a *mensch* from a mile away. So, come home with me." She grinned. "I promise it'll be fine with Aunt Sarah and Uncle Lou."

Lena looked at Joe. From his expression, she could tell that he wanted her to accept Sophie's offer, though she also knew that, if she preferred, he would search for a hotel that could accommodate them both. She took a deep breath. Not every just battle was worth pursuing. Especially on an empty stomach.

"Thank you," she said to Sophie. "I really appreciate it."

Sophie shrugged. "It's good for me too. I've missed having a sister around these last couple of years." She laughed. "Of course, if my sisters ever heard me say that, they'd be amazed."

Joe left them standing out on the sidewalk, while he went to retrieve Lena's suitcase from the room. The crow retreated to the top step of the building's entrance, from where she continued to eye Lena and Sophie suspiciously.

Sophie leaned over and whispered in Lena's ear. "I don't really have anything to say, but if you look in the old lady's direction and laugh, I bet it'll make her crazy."

Just the suggestion made Lena laugh and, right on cue, the old lady's nostrils flared and her mouth twisted to one side. Though Lena knew it was childish, she couldn't help feeling a measure of satisfaction from this tiny victory. She just hoped Sophie was right about her aunt and uncle not minding a last minute overnight guest.

CHAPTER THREE

IN THE SPARSELY FURNISHED OFFICE OF LOCAL 25 OF THE INTERNA-tional Ladies Garment Workers Union, or "ILGWU," Jake Bren-ner was in the midst of an impassioned argument. He was con-vinced that the time was ripe for a general strike by the shirtwaist makers. He just needed to persuade Abe Gunther, president of the Local, and Rose Schneiderman, its secretary.

Jake was first vice-president of the Local, which represented the nearly 100,000 shirtwaist makers in New York. He had a wiry energy that was reflected in his unruly brown hair and a ten-dency to act first and think about the consequences later, which had twice resulted in him getting his nose broken. He stopped pacing and stood, arms crossed over his chest, opposite his two colleagues.

"I'm telling you," he said, "the timing couldn't be better for a strike."

Abe was sitting behind his battered wooden desk. With his gaunt face, Van Dyke beard, and pince-nez glasses, he looked more like a professor than a labor leader. But, despite a fondness for philosophy, Abe was as practical and hardnosed as they came.

And then there was Rose, perched on the edge of her own ad-jacent desk trying, as always, to play the mediator. Surely, Jake thought, he could make her see why the time to strike was now.

"Look," he said. "It's the height of the shirtwaist production season. And the Progressives took every seat in the last election except the Mayor's office. So, we might even get a little political support for a change. Plus, we've been getting incredible public-ity ever since Catherine Carter was arrested."

He was referring to Catherine Graham Carter, heiress to a multi-million dollar fortune. Three days ago, she and a few other members of her Society Ladies Trade Union League had joined the wildcat picket line outside the Dearheart Shirtwaist Company. Mrs. Carter had been taken away in a paddy wagon after she'd pointedly told a police officer who was threatening the strikers that he was paid to serve the public, not Dearheart's owners. The newspapers had had a field day with the story. And Jake wanted to take advantage of the attention it was bringing.

"I don't know," Abe said. "It's hard to get people to walk a picket line when temperatures start to drop below freezing. Folks need their coal money. They aren't going to let their families freeze to death waiting for the manufacturers to cave in to our demands. The union's money situation isn't good right now. Maybe in a few more months—"

"Right," Jake said. "We don't have as much money as we could have a few months from now. But a few months from now we won't have Catherine Graham Carter sitting in prison."

"Maybe Jake's right," Rose said. "We've already got wild-cat strikes going on at Dearheart, J. Cohen, and Grand Shirtwaists. So, there's some momentum."

"Exactly," Jake said. "That's exactly what I'm saying." Abe still looked unconvinced but he wasn't saying anything, so Jake continued. "There's a lot of anger out there, Abe. Our members know the manufacturers have been jerking us around for the last six months pretending to negotiate."

"They know? What do they know?" Abe said. "These are women and girls, Jake. Do you really think they know what will happen when the manufacturers send hired muscle to the picket lines to rough them up? Do they know that half the police are on the manufacturers' payrolls and will look the other way? Do they know we can call a strike in the morning and their jobs will be filled by the afternoon with the newest crop of greenhorns fresh off the boat?"

"They're not idiots, Abe," Jake said. "If they didn't know all that before, they learned it two years ago during the last general strike. They know a strike isn't a walk in the park. But they also know they don't have much to lose. They're already risking their health working in those fume-filled firetraps. And if we get support from the National office and from some of the other locals, we can make it work financially."

Now, he was on a roll. "Local 25's ready to explode," he said. "Dammit, Abe. Come on. The timing is right. You know it is." He slammed his palm on Abe's desk for emphasis, wincing as pain shot up his arm.

The wince didn't escape Abe's notice. "You're pretty fired up tonight," he said. "Those goons really got to you, didn't they? How bad are you hurting?"

Jake shrugged. "They worked me over pretty good." "They" were four thugs who had tailed him as he was walking away from the Dearheart picket line the day before. They had followed him halfway to the union office, then hustled him into an alley, where they had bruised three of his ribs and left him with a nasty welt on his left cheek as well as a few cuts and bruises on his forehead.

Rose spoke gruffly from her perch. "You should get yourself to a doctor, Jake." Although Rose tried to project a tough image with her severely-parted dark hair and mannish jacket and tie, she had a motherly streak she could never suppress completely.

Jake shook his head. "I don't need a doctor. Anyway, it wasn't the goons who got to me." He hesitated. "I went to Maria Ferregetti's funeral yesterday." Maria, a twelve-year-old shirtwaist worker who had worked for Dearheart, had been badly burnt two weeks ago when a fire had broken out on the workroom floor. For several critical moments, the workers had been trapped in with the fire while they'd waited for a management representative to come down from an upper floor and unlock the door. The incident had been the impetus for the current strike at Dearheart.

"She was only twelve, damn it," he said. "I'm getting sick of going to funerals for children. That was the second one this month."

Silence greeted this announcement. Jake knew that Abe and Rose had each gone to their share of funerals too. It was part of a union official's job. Abe had told him more than once not to get so caught up emotionally in the lives of individual union members that he lost sight of the bigger picture of what they were trying to accomplish. But Jake couldn't help how he felt. Especially about the youngest of the workers—the children. Poor little Maria should never have been in that factory in the first place.

Right now, though, the most important thing was to persuade Abe that the best time for a general strike was right now. He tried again to make Abe see that.

"I'll tell you what," Abe finally said. "You meet with the union reps at each factory and find out what they think about calling a strike in the middle of winter. If there's really as much enthusiasm as you say, we'll call for a general membership meeting at the Cooper Union Hall."

Jake nodded. He was confident about the level of support he would find when he talked to the reps. Once he reported back,

Abe would have to agree to call for a general meeting. Even as Abe and Rose were reaching for their coats, his mind was whirring and clicking with plans.

After his colleagues were gone, he stretched out on the office sofa. He had a furnished room in a boarding house, but found his present surroundings more comforting. Besides, the leather, cracked though it was, soothed his sore muscles. His bruises hadn't bothered him that much during the day, but now he was beginning to really feel them. It was just as well he had canceled on Sophie tonight. She would have gone crazy if she'd seen him looking like this.

Sophie. He had to figure out what to do about her. He didn't see himself feeling ready to get married any time soon and he didn't want to mislead her on that subject. But he didn't want to end things either. He'd been with her longer than he'd ever been with a girl before. Or maybe it was more accurate to say that Sophie had stuck with him longer than any girl ever had before. She'd hung in, despite all the dates he'd called off at the last minute for union business. She'd been patient, too, when he was distracted by organizing issues and too preoccupied to pay her much attention. And she was fun to be around. He knew that he had a tendency to be too serious sometimes, too intense. Sophie was just the opposite. Not only did she make him laugh but, when he was with her, he discovered a light-hearted side of himself that he didn't even know he had.

A few weeks ago, they'd gone out to dinner in Chinatown and then strolled all the way up to 60th Street where they'd passed the Harmonie Club. Even from outside they could hear that a party was going on, a wedding apparently, given the "just married" sign attached to the Packard parked out front. Sophie had proposed crashing the party.

"It'll be easy," she said. "The bride's family will think we're with the groom's family and the groom's family will think we're with the bride's family."

Jake was amused by the plan, mostly because he liked the idea of sticking it to some rich employer spending big bucks on a bash for his daughter while his workers subsisted on starvation wages. Still, there were obvious drawbacks.

"Won't someone from the bride's side eventually ask someone from the groom's side who we are?"

"Don't be silly. They'll all be too busy being polite or getting drunk to bother asking. And just think how much fun we'll have. We can dance all night long."

So they'd run laughing up the limestone steps, strolled into the marbled lobby, and walked casually into the mahogany paneled dining room. They'd danced to the music of a sixteen piece band and laughed it up with the best man and generally had a fine time, made finer by the possibility that their fraud could be discovered at any time. Yes, he thought, Sophie was a kick to be around.

As for the physical side of their relationship, well, he had no complaints. God had been generous to Sophie. And Sophie was generous with God's gifts. But marriage? He had little enough time for Sophie as it was. Working for the union wasn't a nine-to-five job. His evenings were filled with meetings and visits to the homes of union or prospective union members. Weekends were for organizing workers, talking to them after church or synagogue or wherever he could persuade them to give him a few minutes of their time. Weekdays were for planning and negotiating and trying to get the ear of anyone—lawmaker, newspaper reporter, philanthropist—anyone who might be sympathetic to the workers' plight.

It was a poorly paid, frustrating, sometimes dangerous job. And he loved it. More importantly, his union brothers and sisters depended on him. He would not let them down. He gave the work everything he had and, at the end of the day, he had little left to give anyone else. Sophie might be passionate about him, but would she always be willing to come second—especially when she spent a lot more of her time thinking about movies and dancing and parties than she did workers' rights?

He thought of his own childhood. His father, a baker, had worked long, hard hours. His mother had done the same, getting up at 3:30 every morning so she could make his father breakfast before he left for the bakery. She went to bed at the same time as his father too, just after supper was over and the dishes washed and put away. Between rising and retiring, she worked non-stop, cooking, laundering, mending, and cleaning house. The only times she slowed down were when she gave birth—six times in all. And even then, her time in bed seemed less to do with the birthing process than with the fact that each infant born after Jake died within the first hours its life. Only Jake had overcome his sickly beginning.

After each baby's death, neighbors took turns bringing food to the house and Jake was told not to bother his mother. He didn't bother her, but he did peer in at her from time to time. Most of the time she was sleeping. But sometimes he would see her reading a book. He hadn't even known that she knew how to read. His father, of course, went to work as usual. People still needed their bread.

If Jake's mother was unhappy in between these episodes, it didn't show. Or maybe it did but no one saw it. Certainly not Jake, who was twelve years old the day he came home from school to find his mother gone and all her clothes gone with her. At school the next day, Jake heard the rumors. An itinerant tin peddler had come through town the day before. He had been seen lingering at Jake's front door, conversing with Jake's mother. The peddler's wagon had been spotted the next day on the road to the next town over. There had appeared to be another person, a woman, sharing the driver's bench with him.

Once the shock wore off, Jake tried to make sense of his mother's leaving. It seemed obvious that if she'd really loved him, she wouldn't have left, except that he didn't know what he'd done wrong. His father cloaked himself in a silent sorrow that left no room for discussion. Jake stuffed his sorrow into some inaccessible part of his brain and metamorphosed directly from shock to anger.

He quit going to school and started working at the bakery where he could release his pent up emotions by punching and pounding dough. The first time he accompanied his father to work, nothing was said between them, but his father paused momentarily outside the door of the bakery and briefly rested his hand on Jake's shoulder. They worked together for the next four years until, shortly after his sixteenth birthday, his father had a heart attack and died. With nothing to keep him there, Jake left the village he'd grown up in and went to Kiev where he managed to get a job as an apprentice to a master baker. It was while working in Kiev that he was introduced to the concept of trade unionism.

The other baker apprentices, most several years older than him, were just beginning to rebel against the guild system that all but enslaved them to the master bakers. After work, they crowded around tables in the bars and talked about workers' rights, brotherhood, and the power of unity. They drank beer and argued strategy late into the night. The evenings always ended the same way.

"All for one and one for all," someone would call out. Then they would each put one hand into the middle of the circle, layering them, hand over hand, each hand gripping the one beneath.

"Solidarity forever," someone else would call out.

"Solidarity forever," they would all respond.

Finally, Jake felt that he belonged to something real and true. Something that was bigger than just himself. Something that would ensure he would never be alone again. The union became his home, his family, and his religion. Eventually, he worked his way to a leadership position. This distinction gave him the honor of being arrested along with the other union leaders during one of the many government crackdowns. On a train headed for a prison in Siberia, he waited until the guards weren't looking, and jumped off the moving train as it slowed for a curve. He hiked through the countryside, made his way to the port city of Murmansk, and snuck on board a steamer ship headed to America. Once there, he'd found a new home in the ILGWU, where Abe Gunther had taken him under his wing.

Now, as he lay on the sofa with his hands linked behind his head, he thought again about Sophie and about marriage. He thought of his mother reading in her room and his silent father. He definitely wanted to be a father at some point. He thought he would be a pretty good one. As for marriage—once he took that step, it would be forever. He would never leave his wife and children as his mother had left him.

He sighed and turned on his side. Exhaustion was beginning to set in. He ought to get up and get the blanket he kept stowed in the closet. He ought to at least turn out the lights. But he was just so damn tired. Maybe if he slept on it, the question of what to do about Sophie would be clear in the morning.

CHAPTER FOUR

DANIEL WOKE AT 5:00 A.M. AND QUICKLY SHUT HIS ALARM CLOCK SO as not disturb the two youngest Glickman boys who slept in the cot across from his. He retrieved his glasses from atop the small chest of drawers beside his bed and got dressed except for his shoes, which he carried with him and put on in the hall outside the Glickman's apartment. His rooming situation wasn't the most convenient but it was the best he could afford for the present.

He had found Glickman's as well as his job at Kresge's Wholesale Fabrics by pursuing leads given him by the Hebrew Immigrant Aid Society. The Society maintained a table in the cavernous Great Hall at Ellis Island that Daniel, caught up in the euphoria of being admitted to the United States, hadn't even noticed at first. Fortunately, the gentleman manning the table noticed him just as he was heading for the exit.

"Psst. Ich vil sprechen mit zi." *(I want to talk to you.)* The man, portly with a bulbous nose and a creased, sweaty face, thrust a cigar into his mouth and puffed on it while Daniel approached.

"Du bist Deutche? (*Are you German?*) " the man asked.

Daniel shook his head. "Ich bin Polishke." *(I'm Polish).*

"*Du bist a Yid?*" (Are you Jewish?)

"*Yoh.*"

The man nodded and took a few more puffs on his cigar and continued speaking to Daniel in Yiddish. "You need a place to live in New York City?"

"Well," Daniel said uncertainly, "I thought I would go to a hotel or an inn for the first night or two, just until I found something."

The man shook his head dismissively. "The hotels in New York are expensive and they all have bedbugs or fleas or both. How much money do you have?"

Daniel hesitated. The ship had been awash in talk of those who preyed on new immigrants. The man puffed on his cigar as he waited for Daniel's answer. His eyes, as he studied Daniel, were narrow and knowing.

Finally, he took the cigar out of his mouth and sighed. "Look boychik," he said, "it's good that you're being careful. You don't know me from a hole in the wall and there's lots of people in New York who'll pretend to help you while robbing you blind. But I'm not one of them. You see the sign?" He pointed to the wall behind him. "So, *nu*, can you read?"

Daniel nodded.

"Alright. Look, the Hebrew Immigrant Aid Society exists to help people just like you. I only asked how much money you have so I can find accommodations you can afford for a few days until you find a job. You got a job waiting for you?"

"No," Daniel said.

"I didn't think so. You got more than twenty-five dollars with you?" That was the minimum amount of money needed to enter the United States.

Daniel shook his head again.

"Then the best thing for you would be full board somewhere." He stuck his cigar back in his mouth, pulled out a sheaf of papers and began looking through them, shaking his head and muttering to himself as he went. Finally, he slammed a paper down on his desk and snatched his cigar out of his mouth.

"I found you something, boychick," he said, looking triumphant. "Oy, you're a lucky guy. I know this place and it's a good deal. Just five dollars a week for a bed, plus breakfast and dinner daily. And the Glickman's will treat you fair. You won't do better. Here." He pushed the paper over to Daniel.

"Now," the man rewarded himself with a long drag of his cigar and blew the smoke out slowly, "you got any skills? Can you sew or cut patterns? You know how to lay brick? Cut stone?"

Daniel shook his head after each question.

"Well that's alright. You'll find something. You don't have the build for construction work. But you got long legs. So you can move fast. There's lots of places that need runners. Try Marshall's or Miller's or Kresge's. Tell them you want *arbet*. In English you say "work.""

"Verk," Daniel repeated.

"That's close enough." The man turned over the paper that had the information about the room for rent and wrote something on the back. "Here you go. I don't know if any of these places are hiring, but at least it's a start. So," he pointed to a doorway a few feet away, "Go out through that door and get on the ferry to the city. You can walk to the Glickman's from the city dock."

"Thank you." Daniel said, bobbing his head and putting the paper with the information in his pocket. "I appreciate the help very much." He started to move away, but the man spoke again.

"Wait, boychik. Before you go, here's one more piece of advice." He handed Daniel a flier. "You want to do good in America, you got to learn English." He pointed to the headline on the flier. "See? You go to night school. It's free and they teach you how to speak English good."

"Free?" Daniel had been trying hard not to come across like a country rube, but now he couldn't keep the amazement out of his voice. "And anyone can go?"

The man grinned and nodded. "Yes, anyone, even you. Especially you. Listen, locations are on the flier. They're all over the city. The sooner you get started the better." He stuck his cigar in his mouth and sat back in his chair.

Daniel stared at him, speechless. Because going to school in America was his dream, the thing that he'd planned to work towards, once he got admitted to America, once he'd found a place to live and a job and learned to speak English and saved some money. Questions darted in his brain like moths bouncing off a light bulb. He wanted to know everything about these classes—where they were given and when they were offered and what he had to do to get admitted. But the man had already looked past him at the people who had lined up behind him. So, he ducked his head again in thanks, slung his sack over his shoulder, and moved away holding tight to the flier.

At the Glickman's, he'd enjoyed his first real bath in weeks followed by a good meal and a decent night's sleep. The next morning, he started out to look for "verk." At the third place on his list, Kresge's Wholesale Fabrics, he was directed outside and around the corner to the warehouse, a vast clapboard space presided over by a red-headed leprechaun of a man named Fletcher who stood on an elevated platform consulting a sheaf of papers and shouted directions at scurrying workers.

"Verk?" Daniel asked hopefully, looking up at him.

Fletcher cocked one eyebrow at him. "*Du bist a Yid?*" he asked.

"Yoh," Daniel said, a little surprised.

Fletcher snorted at the expression on Daniel's face. *"Ich visn a bisl Yiddish."* (I know a little Yiddish.)."

Fletcher looked down at the papers in his hand and nodded. "It's your lucky day. One of the "shleppers" just quit. Be here at 7:00 a.m. tomorrow."

The next day Daniel learned exactly what a shlepper did. Kresge's bought fabrics from manufacturers and re-sold them to clothing manufacturers. The fabric arrived wrapped around 12 foot long wooden poles, yards and yards and yards of it. It was Daniel's job to transport the fabric to Kresge's customers.

Hefting the first bolt onto his shoulder, Daniel staggered under the weight, the bulky cylindrical roll tipping forward and back as he tried to balance it while maintaining his footing. He couldn't imagine how he would navigate the city streets with just this one on his shoulder, never mind the five that Fletcher expected him to carry.

An hour into that first day, his back and arms were aching from the effort to keep the bolts from falling off his shoulder. Still, he moved about the city as fast as he could, following the rough directions that Fletcher had mapped out for him. Within a week, he knew how to get to almost any address Fletcher gave him.

Leaving the Glickman's apartment, he drew in a deep breath of the cool dawn air as he walked quickly through the still dark streets to Meltzer's Dairy Restaurant. Meltzer's was a tiny alley of a place, barely wide enough to accommodate the skinny counter that took up the entire right side of the restaurant and the single line of wooden tables that hugged the left. But nobody who worked there seemed to mind how long he sat at the counter and nursed a single cup of coffee.

As soon as the counterman put his coffee down, Daniel pulled from his back pocket the card with the English alphabet that Mrs. Levy had given to him. Although the shapes of the letters were completely different than the Yiddish alphabet, he was finally beginning to feel that he could match up the letters with the sounds they made. Pronouncing the sounds correctly was a different story. He struggled to make his mouth pronounce the "W" for which there was no comparable sound in Hebrew, Yiddish, or Polish. No matter how hard he tried, it kept sounding the same as the "V." Still, he refused to be discouraged.

After he'd studied the alphabet awhile longer, he pulled out the pamphlet that Mr. Howard, his citizenship teacher had given him. It was a copy of the United States Constitution including the

Bill of Rights printed in Yiddish. Mr. Howard said that reading it was the best way to understand what it meant to be a citizen of the United States.

The words were formal and the ideas presented complicated, so he read slowly. As he began to understand, his coffee grew cold and his awareness of his surroundings faded. The way the government was organized was brilliant, especially the way that power was spread between the President and the Congress and the courts. The idea that people had rights that could not be taken away was astounding. He couldn't wait to get to class so he could learn more about this remarkable document.

That night, propelled by eagerness, he hurried up the wide stone steps to the entrance of the high school where night classes were held. He held the door for a dark-haired girl wearing a blue wool coat. She passed quickly in front of him, acknowledging his courtesy with a murmured *"danke."* As he followed her into the building, something tickled at his memory.

It came to him a split second later. She was the girl from the ship. He stared at her rapidly receding figure. Her hair was plaited into one long thick braid that came to the middle of her back. Below it, her coat was belted at the waist. And below that there was a suggestion of an appealing round bottom. He quickly shifted his glance away, faintly ashamed for having even noticed such a thing.

What a strange coincidence it was, running into her here. Although, not really. After all, many immigrants took advantage of the free classes. But that he should reach the front door just as she was entering the building. It was like fate was giving him a second chance. She turned in the door of a classroom and he had an impulse to follow her but didn't want to be late for his own class. Maybe it would be better to talk to her afterwards anyway. That way, he would have time to think of something to say.

By the time his class was over and he'd finished asking Mr. Howard about the Constitution, she was nowhere in sight. Outside, he scanned the departing students, a patchwork quilt of coats, hats, scarves, and capes. She did not seem to be among them. He should have tried to leave quicker. What if she didn't return next week? What if he never saw her again? But, at that moment, he spotted her. She was already halfway down the street. He jogged down the stone steps and started after her. Despite his long legs, he wasn't gaining much ground on her.

"Tsuvartn (Wait)!" The word was out of his mouth before he had time to think. She didn't react.

"Lena!"

That stopped her in her tracks and she turned around, a quizzical expression on her face. *She has no idea who I am*, he thought, disappointment flashing through him. But then she smiled. And it was exactly as he remembered—wide and generous.

"Oh," she said. "*Vos makst du?* (How are you?)"

Flustered, his response caught in his throat. Her expression became uncertain and her smile started to fade. "You were on the ship weren't you?" she asked. "Or, I'm sorry, maybe I'm mistaken—"

"No. Yes. I mean, you're not mistaken. I didn't think you'd remember. I'm Daniel Cowan."

"I remember you." She looked pleased. "Now I can finally apologize. Judith was very rude to you. I should have said so at the time and made her apologize."

"It's alright," he said, blushing at the memory.

"Well, I did feel badly afterwards."

"She wasn't very nice to you either,"

Lena nodded. "She's not a very nice little girl in general. But the only way my aunt would let me make the crossing was if I traveled with her family. So I had to put up with her. What about you? Who were you traveling with?"

"No one. I came by myself."

"Lucky," Lena said with a little laugh. "Was someone from your family already here waiting for you?"

Daniel adjusted his glasses before answering. "No, no one was here waiting for me."

"So you're the first then. Do you expect others will follow soon?"

He shook his head and to his relief, she stopped asking him questions about the subject he least wanted to discuss. But now he needed something else to say. Trying to keep the conversation going was like trying to construct a house for which he hadn't any tools. He looked down, his blond hair falling in front of his eyes and his glasses slipping forward on his nose.

"Well," she said, "it is nice to see you again."

He looked up quickly and pushed his glasses back with his finger. He couldn't let her leave yet. "I noticed you back at the school. Are you taking a class?" *Stupid question, he thought, but at least she was still standing here and talking to him.*

She nodded and let out a deep sigh. "Tonight was my second time. But English is much harder than I thought it would be."

He decided not to mention that he was not finding the language difficult but, rather, stimulating and himself well up to the challenge. Instead, he said, "My teacher told us that it is important to practice speaking it as much as possible."

She laughed. "So, we should be speaking English right now. Is that what you're saying?"

He blushed again, hoping she hadn't taken his comment as criticism. "No, but I would be happy to practice with you. I might be able to help you with the things you're finding difficult. There's a place we could go that's quite nearby."

"That's very kind of you. I guess I could come for a little while."

"You mean right now?" he stammered.

"I thought that's what you meant."

"Oh, yes." He bobbed his head in confirmation. "Now is very good. So, then we should go. It's this way."

Later, Daniel would barely remember the walk to Meltzer's or how they were seated or who took their order. All he knew was that, somehow, he was not sitting in his usual place by himself at the counter but, instead, at one of the little wooden tables where they both ordered tea and he explained to her that in English, an "e" at the end of the word usually meant that the vowel in the middle had a long rather than a short sound.

After a while, she said. "How do you do it? How do you remember all of those rules—spelling rules, grammar rules? Yiddish is so much easier."

"After a while, English will seem easy too."

"I hope so."

She smiled and, again, the transformative effect was remarkable. But this time, it was the effect on himself of which Daniel was most aware. Like the sun had just broken through an overcast sky, instantly flooding him with light and warmth and happiness. He completely forgot what they had been talking about. To cover up his confusion, he cast about for a new subject.

"By the way, are you taking the Citizenship class as well?" he asked.

She shook her head. "I don't think I could handle another class. What about you?"

"Yes. I had that class tonight."

"What kind of things do you learn about?"

Daniel didn't know where to begin. "Well, we've been learning about the laws and about the Constitution and the Bill of Rights. Do you know what that is, by the way? Because I didn't. It's a whole list of things that people in America have the right to do and none of them can ever be taken away." He pushed his glasses back with one finger, but the motion didn't slow him down. He was too excited.

"And we've been learning about politics too. Did you know," he said, "that anyone can vote in this country? Only citizens, of course, but all citizens, not just rich ones or landowners. And, by the way, voting doesn't cost anything. Not only that, but did you know that anyone can become a mayor or a governor? Even a foreign born citizen can be elected."

He was rolling now, gathering energy and enthusiasm as he went. "Mr. Howard says that that's how change comes about in America. Through elections. The people that are elected make all the laws. So, if people want the laws to change, they have to elect people who will make those changes happen."

Lena's eyes sparkled and the beginning of a smile played around the corners of her mouth. "Perhaps," she suggested, "the laws will change for the better when Daniel Cowan is elected?"

Daniel blushed. Had he been that obvious? He saw that she was studying him as if trying to decide something. Probably, he thought, she was trying to decide just how crazy he was.

"Mr. Howard says women should be able to do everything men can do. He says, by the way, that one day soon women will have the right to vote."

"They should have it already," Lena said, her expression serious again. "Last night I went to a meeting of the League of Suffragettes and told them I would join their organization. It's ridiculous that only men have the right to vote. Women should be able to do everything that men can do. Don't you agree?"

"I do," Daniel said.

"And I –" Lena began.

The waiter was back, standing beside their table with a bored expression. "Anything else?" he asked.

"More tea?" Daniel said, half-directing it to the waiter and half-directing it to Lena.

"I'd like another cup," she said. Daniel nodded at the waiter and he ambled away again.

Daniel grinned. "By the way, I never order a lot," he said. "But since I come so often, I try to at least tip well so that they'll let me sit undisturbed."

Lena smiled again as she contemplated him. "You're very smart," she said as if it were an indisputable fact.

He felt his neck grow warm and looked down, then busied himself with pushing his glasses back up while she continued.

She continued. "I mean, you've been in this country exactly as long as I have but your English is so much better. And you've already learned about the Government and who can stand for election. I think your parents would be very proud of you if they could see how well you're doing."

He knew he should say something in response to this, but didn't really want to talk about his parents. He didn't even want to think about them. And he especially did not want to think about what they or anyone else in his family would have to say about how he was doing. He could just imagine how they would react to his taking night classes and dreaming of college and thinking he could be elected to something someday.

The more he thought about it, the more agitated he became. "My parents," he began, as he desperately tried to think of something innocuous to follow that phrase. But it was no use. The bad memories came flooding in so fast that when he continued, it was without thinking. "Who cares what my parents would think?"

The minute the words burst out, he was furious with himself. What had gotten into him? And what must she think, hearing that he didn't care what his parents thought of him. Now if he didn't elaborate, she would think he was an ungrateful and disrespectful son. But there was no way to explain unless he told her everything.

He looked back up at her expecting to see disapproval or at least disappointment. But he saw none of those things. He saw only a readiness to listen. She was not judging him, he realized. Not at all. And suddenly, he wanted to tell her everything. But he didn't know how or where to begin.

"I can imagine what you are thinking," he said slowly. "But my parents... well, I'll see if I can explain." She nodded and he continued.

"Growing up, I was very different from my brothers. They were all much older than me, but quite close in age to each other. And they all had dark hair and eyes. Even their skin was several shades darker than mine. I assumed that I took after my mother.

"I understand," Lena said. "I don't look much like my brother either."

He shook his head. "It wasn't just that." He took a deep breath. "Have you ever lived on a farm? It involves hard, physical, dirty work and my brothers weren't just good at it, they loved it. I was so much smaller than them, I could never work at their pace."

"It must have been hard being so much younger than the others," Lena said sympathetically.

It was, he thought. And I wanted to be like them. At least, I thought I did. But maybe, I really wanted someone to be like me. He continued.

"My brothers thought about farming all the time; talked about it all the time; debated when to do the planting and when the crops would reach their peak. I tried to be interested, but all I really wanted to do was escape to my room and read."

Lena nodded sympathetically. "I love reading too."

I could stop right here, Daniel thought. And she would still have a good opinion of me. But he went on. "The only thing that we put our work aside for was Sabbath. On Sabbath, we went to the synagogue together as a family. It was my favorite time of the week.

"Mine too," she said. "I especially liked hearing the bible stories."

He nodded in agreement. "When my oldest brother, Avram, turned thirteen and attained the age of adulthood, he was called to the *Torah*. It was a very important day in our family." *He could still picture his mother laying out everyone's good clothes; his father strutting as they walked into the synagogue.*

"The rabbi summoned Avram to stand beside the sacred scrolls. He called Avram by his full name including the name of his father and his father's father, according to Jewish tradition. 'Avram, son of Moishe, son of Yitzhak'. I was very young then, only four, but I still remember." *From that day forward, he'd started imagining the day it would be his turn to cause his father to strut and his mother to beam with pride.*

"As each of my brothers came of age," he continued, "he was summoned to the *Torah*: 'Reuben, son of Moishe, son of Yitzhak.' Then, 'Aaron, son of Moishe, son of Yitzhak'. It was always the same. They were called by their own name and the name of their father and his father before him."

He was lost for a moment in remembering. "Their father," he repeated, as much to himself as to Lena. He caught himself and looked at her. *She must know what's coming he thought. Why did it take me so long to see what seems so obvious in the retelling.*

"When I turned 13 and it was my turn to be called to the *Torah*," he said slowly, "I was so excited. I couldn't wait to make my father and mother proud of me finally. I could hardly sit still beside my father. I could barely keep myself from twisting around in my seat to look for my mother in the women's section. But then the moment came and the rabbi called my name.

"At first, I thought the rabbi had made a mistake." He paused. Even now, part of him still wanted to believe the rabbi had made a mistake. "Of course, I had never heard him make such a mistake before. But still I thought, he must have made a mistake. He called me Daniel, grandson of Lazar. He used my mother's father's name, but not my father's name or my father's father's name."

As he said the words, the memory came rushing back to him vividly—the shock of being called by his maternal grandfather's name rather than his own father's; his horror at the rabbi's mistake, horror that turned first to anguish, when he looked at Moishe and saw the coldness on his father's face, and then to numbness, when he looked for his mother and saw that she was weeping.

He glanced at Lena, realized that he hadn't said anything for a few moments, and willed his voice steady despite the sharp tightness in his throat. There was really no need, he thought, to go into detail about what else he had heard later that day. Still he felt that he should finish and tell her everything. She might as well know the worst about him. Might as well know who or, rather, what he was. So, he continued in a voice deliberately emotionless so that she would not be needlessly shocked.

"Later, hours after we left the synagogue, they told me. Thirteen years earlier, there was a pogrom in our little shtetl, our little community." He suspected she must know about pogroms but he told her anyway. "They happened from time to time. The local Polish peasants would get drunk or riled up or angry about something and take it out on our village. Our farm was on the outskirts of town. This particular time, when they came riding through the area, they stopped first at our farm."

He looked at Lena. For her sake, he would finish quickly. "My mother was home alone that day," he said quietly. "Four or five of them came to the farm, but my mother was alone." He took a deep breath, "I was born nine months later. So, you see," he said, speaking in a ragged rush, finishing the story aloud as he always finished it in his head. "I am the product of hate, not love. And no one has ever been proud of me for anything."

He stared at the table. It was out, but now that it was, he was already regretting it. Whatever made him tell her? He couldn't bring himself to look at her. He couldn't bear to see the expression that must be on her face.

She spoke gently, softly. "It's not your fault," she said.

"Yes, well..."

"Daniel," she said. "Listen to me. It wasn't your fault."

He nodded and looked around for the waiter. "I should probably get the check."

"Wait." She reached over and touched his hand. "Daniel, look at me. All of that, everything you just told me, it's all in the past. It has nothing to do with who you are now. This is your new life in your brand new country. Nothing that happened before matters anymore. Certainly not things that you had no part in and no control over."

Her words seemed to wash something from him, like a wave of clean ocean water carrying debris away with the tide. She'd heard everything he'd said and it didn't matter to her. As depleted as he'd felt when he'd finished telling his story, he now felt himself re-charging, filling with adrenaline pumped excitement.

"Yes," he said, leaning forward and planting his fists on the table. "That's exactly what I've been feeling. That this is the beginning of my new life." He sat back again, took a deep breath, and let it out slowly. "I feel like anything is possible in this marvelous country. Do you think everyone who comes here feels that way? Do you feel like that?"

She laughed, giddy and seemingly caught up in his elation. "Yes. I do," she said.

A little shyness crept back into Daniel's voice and he asked. "Do you really think I'm smart?"

She nodded. "I really do."

They smiled at each other until the waiter appeared, startling them both.

"Anything else?" he asked them. Daniel looked at Lena, but shook her head.

"Thank you, no," Daniel told the waiter. With a swift motion, the waiter tore off the top page of his pad and left the bill on their table.

Daniel picked it up, glanced at it, and reached in his pocket. When he looked up again, Lena's arm was extended and there was some change in the palm of her hand.

"What -?" he said.

There was a mischievous look on her face. "Did you mean what you said before about men and women being able to do all the same things?"

"Yes," Daniel said slowly.

"Well, then, you won't mind if I pay for the tea tonight." Her voice was light. For a minute, he wondered if she were just teasing him and trying to light his mood after what they had just been discussing.

"You can't be serious," he protested. He had never been out with a girl before but he knew enough to know that the man was supposed to pay for everything.

"At the suffragette meeting we talked about why men are expected always to act one way and women another. If men and women are equal, why should the man always be the one to pay?" she demanded, the amused expression still on her face.

"Because—because," Daniel desperately tried to think of a good reason for why the man should pay. He did believe that men and women should be able to do all the same things, but somehow, that didn't seem to include this situation. Yet, he couldn't think of why it shouldn't or why he wanted so much to be the one to pay tonight.

He looked up at her. Her eyes were full of laughter. "It's just tea," he said. "Please let me pay."

She wagged a finger at him playfully. "If we're going to be friends, we have to take turns."

Friends? Daniel thought. *Was that what he wanted them to be?*

"I'll pay this time," she continued, "and you can pay next? That's what friends do. They take turns."

"Next time?" Daniel asked. She nodded and he began to fill with an unfamiliar feeling that could only be hope.

She knows everything about me, he thought, and she's still willing for there to be a next time and, please God, a time after that. And even if we start out as friends, we don't need to stay that way. So, there was good reason to hope. And, still later, his hope only increased during his walk back to the Glickmans's as he played and replayed the evening in his mind.

CHAPTER FIVE

LENA HAD BEEN LIVING WITH SOPHIE FOR SIX WEEKS, LONG ENOUGH to know that the walk to work was not going to be a peaceful one. She was sure her roommate was going to try again to convince her to attend the shirtwaist makers' rally. Never mind that she'd already told Sophie that the rally was a distant fourth on her list of priorities for that evening, well behind her suffragette meeting, her English class, and her meeting with Daniel. Nothing she'd said had staunched the flow of her roommate's arguments. As they reached Broome Street, Sophie linked her arm through Lena's and brought it up in a chatty tone, as if they had never discussed it before.

"So, you'll come to the rally with me tonight?"

"You know that I can't."

"Your English class. And your suffragette meeting. But this is important too. It's our chance to hear directly from the top union officials."

"And a chance for you to finally introduce me to your Jake," Lena said. She didn't add that she would have met Jake weeks ago if he hadn't canceled his last five dates with Sophie.

"Meeting Jake is not the point," Sophie said. "This rally will probably decide whether we go on strike or not."

"That's what you said about the last rally, and the one before that."

"You didn't come to those either."

"And I obviously didn't miss much."

"But Jake said this one will be different. Decisions will be made."

Lena was dubious. She and Joe had talked about the union and she generally believed that workers had a better chance of getting employers to improve conditions when they banded together. But Local 25 didn't seem to be a particularly successful union. If Sophie's Jake was an example of what the rest of the union's officials were like, the union's failures were probably due to poor leadership.

"Well, if you won't come to the rally for yourself," Sophie said, "then come as a favor to me. I've done a lot of favors for you."

Inwardly Lena groaned. Sophie had just made the one argument she couldn't counter. Her roommate had done so many favors for her that she'd lost count, beginning with standing up for her at the factory on her first day and taking her in when Mrs. Yelnow kicked her out, an arrangement that had become semi-permanent when Joe suggested it would give them a chance to save up some money. And she never would have eased into life in America so quickly if it weren't for Sophie, beginning with their shopping trip to Macy's where they had picked out Lena's new American clothes.

Afterwards, back at the apartment, Sophie had unplaited Lena's hair and arranged it into an elegant and sophisticated pompadour. Lena had been so happy with the results that she would have looked at herself in the mirror for quite some time if Sophie hadn't insisted that they show off her new look by going out. So they had gone to the Strand movie theater, another first for Lena, where they'd seen Florence Lawrence, the Vitagraph girl, in "The Broken Oath".

Favor after favor, in just a few weeks, Sophie had become the sister Lena had always longed for. In some ways, she was even more than that. She was Lena's source of information for, not just all things American, but all things female, things to which Lena, growing up with only her father and her brother, had never before been privy.

"I'll come to the rally tonight," she said. "But Sophie, do you really care about the union? Or is it only your Jake that you care about?"

"Of course I care about the union. We owe our very jobs to the union."

"You mean the jobs that pay us barely enough to get by?"

"Well, if you've got suggestions for what the union should do, then I suggest you speak up when you come to the rally."

Twelve hours later, Lena was less enthusiastic about going to the rally than ever. But Sophie didn't seem to notice. She explained that she was leaving to meet Jake at the union office but would stop at home before the rally so she and Lena could go together. After she left, Lena looked around for her brother, hoping he would be able to restore her good humor. But, he turned out to have already made plans to dine with some friends before the union meeting.

"I can change my plans if you want," he offered.

"No, don't change anything. I'll just see you at the rally," she said, thinking it was just as well. No sense taking her mood out on Joe. She would be better off just hurrying home as quickly as possible and using the time before the rally to review her homework.

She set a quick pace and kept it up even on crowded Hester Street, weaving her way with single-minded determination through the maze of shoppers and pushcarts. Just before reaching Ludlow, she detoured temporarily into the street to circumvent a crowd gathered to watch an organ grinder. But as soon as the sidewalk was clear, she took a sideways leap onto the curb, resumed her pace, and abruptly collided with another person.

The impact threw her off balance and she stumbled backwards. She tried, but failed to find her footing and, reflexively used her arms to break her fall. Her handbag slipped from her grasp and flew through the air, spilling its contents and landing a few feet away. Once she'd caught her breath, she saw her change purse, key, and handkerchief strewn on the ground.

"*Klutz!*" she sputtered. "Why you don't watch where you are going?"

She struggled to her knees and, reaching for her handkerchief, clutched it before tucking it into the pocket of her coat. Of all days for someone to accidentally run her over. She was already in a bad mood. But, as she grasped her bag and change purse, it occurred to her that it might not have been an accident. Sophie had told her that thieves sometimes knocked women down, then grabbed their money. Well, she worked too hard to let anyone take anything away from her—even if she only had a few cents in her purse.

"Let me help you," a male voice said.

"I don't want your kind of help," she spit back.

"My kind of help?"

Lena flashed angry eyes up at her attacker. But maybe she'd been too quick to jump to assumptions. The eyes that met hers looked more concerned that criminal. She was just about to accept his offer, when she noticed a purplish bruise beneath one of his eyes. And there was a scar on his forehead too, perhaps inflicted by another one of his victims or a police officer trying to haul him off to jail. So he was a thief after all. She snatched her hand back.

"Let me alone, she hissed. Thinking of her nearly empty change purse, she added, "I would be a waste of your time anyway."

"How would helping you be a waste of my time?" he asked, one eyebrow raised and the other furrowed in obvious amusement. This just infuriated her even more.

"Go away," she said, as she stuffed her change purse into her bag. From the corner of her eye, she saw him suddenly drop to his knees. The nerve of him. He was still going to try and grab something.

"Go away," she said again.

"You go away," he answered, irritation creeping into his voice. "You're not the only one who dropped things when you knocked into me."

Lena stared at him in astonishment. "I knocked into you!" She slowly stood and looked down at him.

He met her gaze with cool eyes. "At least you admit it." He began picking up papers splayed all over the ground.

"I'm not admitting anything," she said defiantly, though a tiny bit of doubt was beginning to form in her mind. "You thought you could rob me so easily, but I'm not going to let you."

"Rob you?"

He was so obviously taken aback, that the dusting of doubt she'd begun feeling moments ago became more substantial and she glanced down self-consciously, brushing the dirt from her coat. The more she thought about it, the more foolish she began to feel. The collision had been at least partly her fault. And, apparently, she wasn't the only one who had dropped things in the process. He hadn't actually tried to steal any of her things. So, she could hardly blame him for being angry at being called a thief. She snuck a glance at him as he moved about intent on gathering up his papers.

Before she could turn away again, he looked up at her and a wry smile spread across his face. "You know," he said, "I've been in a good number of fights, but it's pretty rare for someone to knock me down without me at least getting a swat at them. And most of my opponents have been a little tougher looking than you."

She smiled back, grateful for his attempt to bring levity to the situation. "I'm sorry. Here, let me help you."

Methodically, they collected papers from the ground. Twice, Lena risked a quick look at him. Each time, she quickly looked away when he looked back at her. She peeked a third time and he grinned. For the first time, she didn't look away.

As they continued to gather the material on the ground, she tried to observe him whenever she thought he wasn't looking. His eyes, she noticed, were an extraordinary shade—gray but with a hint of another color, either blue or green, she couldn't decide. The longer she looked at them, the harder it was to tell. And his hands looked strong, capable, and sure. Just looking at them made her feel safer. Yet looking at him made her heart beat wildly.

When the last paper had been picked up, she handed her stack to him and they stood facing each other. Despite the flutter in her stomach and her racing pulse, she wished there was some reason for the encounter to continue but could think of none.

"Well," she said.

"Well," he said. "Thank you. For helping me pick up my papers I mean, not for knocking them down."

His eyes met hers and lingered, the intensity of his gaze changing and growing more thoughtful and more serious. She found that she could not look away and would not have even if she could. He smiled, slowly this time, not the quick boyish grin from before, and she felt her insides become warm and liquid. She wanted to say something, but her mind stubbornly refused to suggest words. Feeling foolish, she began turning away.

"Wait," he said. "Are you going to be at the union rally tonight?"

She turned back around and nodded. "Yes, I agreed to go," she admitted

There was that slight lift of his brow again, which had infuriated her but now seemed like an invitation to share a joke. "You don't sound very enthusiastic about it," he said. "Don't you think the union deserves your support?"

"I suppose. But I heard there may be a strike vote. Striking is very hard on workers."

"That's true," he acknowledged. "But sometimes a strike is the only way we can change things. The power to withhold our labor is the only weapon we have."

"But it's a power that should be used only when all else fails," she said. Now that they were debating, she felt more like herself again. This was almost like discussing issues with Daniel, although with Daniel, she'd never felt quite as alive as she did now.

"Words are powerful too," she said. "Before resorting to striking, we should try talking to the factory owners."

"Talking only works when the other side is willing to listen. At this point the factory owners refuse to even talk to the union."

"They refuse to talk? That's ridiculous."

"Well," he said, "they want the union to agree to a set of preconditions before they'll talk and that's almost the same thing."

"What kind of preconditions?"

"The want the union to agree that non-union members can be paid more than union members."

"What's wrong with that?" But before the words were even out of her mouth, she realized exactly what was wrong with that. "Oh, I understand. If non-union members are paid more than union members, then no one will bother to join the union."

"You catch on quick," he said smiling. "And now it seems that you and I are in agreement about the need for the rally. I'm glad we're both on the same side. I already know how tough it is to have you as an opponent."

He smiled and there was something about his smile and his pleasure at their being on the same side that made her incredibly happy. What a funny turn of events, she thought. Now, Sophie wasn't the one who only wanted to go to the rally because a certain man would be there.

"I'm glad we're on the same side too," she said.

"Shall we shake on it? After all, we workers have to stick together. One for all and all for one." He put out his hand and, looking down, she slowly laid her palm against his.

As he closed his hand around hers, she felt a tingling sensation that quickly spread to every part of her, making her feel dizzy and shaky and short of breath. It felt as if his hand holding hers was the only thing tethering her to the ground. She wondered if any of what she was feeling was apparent to him and glanced up. His smile had faded and been replaced by a serious, searching look.

"I suppose I should introduce myself," he said. "I'm Jake Brenner."

Lena stared at him. The shaky feeling in her stomach turned into a sick feeling. "You're... Sophie's Jake?" she asked.

"You know Sophie?"

"I'm her roommate." The sick sensation grew more intense. She felt light headed and would have looked for a place to sit down if she didn't have a desperate desire to get away as fast as possible. She realized that he was still holding her hand down and she gently extricated it.

"Her roommate?" he echoed.

"Yes." She began to babble, scarcely knowing what she was saying. "I've heard so much about you, I should have guessed who you were. Sophie—Sophie said she was meeting you at the union office."

"Oh, yes. We'd planned to meet there but then I told her I'd just come by her apartment. She must have forgotten." His voice dropped a bit as if he was talking to himself. "Or maybe I'm the one who forgot."

"Well, I think she's probably waiting for you," Lena said.

"Yes." Jake nodded his head. "I better get over there and meet her." He looked down at the fliers in his arm and seemed to be concentrating on something printed there. When he glanced back up, he had a puzzled expression, as if he was trying to figure something out.

"I guess I'll see you later then," he said, "at the rally."

Lena nodded. She felt, at that moment, incapable of uttering another sound. He turned and walked slowly away. She waited, knowing she should probably go too but not able to move.

He paused to look back at her. For a moment, it seemed as though he might say something. Hope hovered stubbornly inside her even though she knew it was wrong. But he said nothing. Instead, he abruptly turned and walked briskly down the street.

CHAPTER SIX

AFTER HELPING AUNT SARAH CLEAN UP FROM SUPPER, LENA WENT TO her bedroom to wait for Sophie. She sat at the dressing table, braiding and re-braiding her hair. There was no reason to be nervous, she thought. She'd done nothing wrong. Sophie would probably laugh when she heard the story of how she and Jake had finally met.

But each time she went over it in her mind and pictured Jake's gray-blue-green eyes and remembered the feel of her hand in his, her nerves failed her. Because, although the accidental meeting had all the ingredients of a funny story, nothing about it seemed amusing at the moment.

The bedroom door blew open and Sophie hurried in.

"I'm sorry. I know I'm late. Are you ready? Good. Jake and I had some kind of misunderstanding. I thought I was supposed to meet him at the union office and he thought we were meeting here. By the time he got to the office, there was barely enough time to hand out fliers."

Sophie was shrugging out of her sweater as she talked and pulling on her coat instead. "Wear something warm," she said. "It's getting cold outside. Let's hurry."

Lena opened her mouth to speak, but Sophie grabbed her arm, saying, "Come on. It's going to be a mob scene," after which she hustled Lena out the door. It was all Lena could do to keep up. She realized she would have to postpone telling Sophie about her meeting with Jake.

The Great Hall of the Cooper Union was filled to overflowing when they arrived. Vast as a cathedral, the ceiling was traversed by a series of arches supported by thick round columns and some people had climbed partway up these pillars to get a better view. There was a constant din that rendered normal conversation impossible. Lena momentarily forgot her troubled thoughts as she became caught up in the palpable energy and excitement.

"Come on," Sophie shouted. "I can't even see the stage from back here." She elbowed her way through the crowd, leaving Lena no choice but to follow. They made it only as far as the rear of the seating section. But Sophie seemed satisfied now that they were at the very front of the standees. She craned her neck, searching the hall.

"I don't see Jake yet," she yelled to Lena, "but I'll point him out to you when I do."

Lena cleared her throat. Now was the obvious time to tell Sophie that she already knew what Jake looked like. But before she could say anything, someone stepped from behind the curtain on the stage. It was Jake. And, suddenly, Lena found it impossible to speak at all.

"That's him!" Sophie said, flashing her a huge smile as she linked an arm through Lena's and pulled her close. Lena smiled back weakly, but Sophie was already looking back at the stage.

Jake held up both hands, signaling the crowd to quiet. After a few moments, there was a perceptible decrease in the sound level and he began.

"Ladies and Gentlemen," he said, "I know it's late. I know you've had a long, day and are anxious to go home and put your little ones to bed." There were murmurs of agreement and some grumbling too. But Jake held up his hands again.

"It's for those little ones that we're here tonight. We're here to fight for your right to put food in the mouths of your children. To be able to keep them in school, instead of having them go to work at the tender age of six or seven."

He was right, Lena thought, remembering the children who sat in the corner of the sewing room floor snipping the dangling threads from the shirts. At their age, she had spent her mornings in school and her afternoons playing with friends.

Jake continued. "We've been trying to talk to the factory owners, to reason with them, and make them see our side of the story. But they won't even talk to us."

It was ridiculous, Lena thought. The owners slammed the door to negotiations with the same arrogance that Horowitz displayed when locked the door each time he left the sewing room floor. There were murmurs of dissatisfaction around her and someone nearby muttered, "Those bastards." A man in the row in front of her shook his fist in the air and shouted, "Let them talk to this."

But Jake was not done. He took a deep breath and Lena could see the taut muscles along his jaw. He began slowly, picking up speed and volume as he went on.

"They've said 'no' to us again and again. 'No' to living wages, 'no' to workers' safety, and 'no' to compromise. They've said 'no' to every reasonable offer we have made, and, so my friends, I tell you. The time has come for *us* to say no. No to tyranny. And no to slavery. No to working 12-hour days. No to being fired merely because we stay home sick, when the reason we're sick is because we're breaking our backs for them. It's time for us to say no to anything less than each of us absolutely deserves for the sweat and the blood of our hands and our hearts."

The crowd was on their feet and roaring by now. Lena could hardly hear Jake's last few words as he spread his arms wide and exhorted them, "My friends, if you share my sentiments, then please welcome the president of the International Ladies Garment Workers Union Local 25, Mr. Abe Gunther."

The crowd exploded with applause. As Jake stepped back and Gunther walked on stage, Sophie turned eyes that could only be described as shining to Lena and squeezed her hand. Lena smiled back, but her heart was pounding and she had to work to keep her mouth from trembling until Sophie turned back toward the stage.

Jake was amazing she thought. She'd never known anyone like him. He made her want to throw herself into fighting for the union, to work by his side, and help him in any way she could. Even now that he'd retreated to the far side of the stage, Lena couldn't stop looking at him.

Abe Gunther started to speak and his style was as different from Jake's as two men's could be. Lena had to strain to hear him at first. But there was something akin to poetry about the cadence of his speech and he soon weaved a spell over everyone, so that even the children were hushed.

"The choice is yours," he said. "Though the battle is hard, it can be won. And victory will come if we are strong. So where does our strength lie? It lies in our commitment to each other. We must be brothers and sisters in this battle. We must be each other's keepers. We must be ready to lend not just a hand but also our hearts and minds."

He told them that if they decided to strike, they would forego wages for an indeterminable amount of time, spend hours walking on picket lines, risk permanent loss of their jobs, and face harassment from strike breakers and scabs.

But if they voted not to strike, the factory owners would be emboldened. Not only would there be no chance for any improvement in working conditions and wages, they would very likely lose the small gains the union had achieved to date. When he was done, there was applause and quiet murmuring, but none of the intensity that Jake's words had brought forth.

After Abe Gunther, there was a parade of other speakers. As the hour grew late, the crowd became restless. A woman near Lena holding a baby squeezed in the direction of the exit. A few others followed in her wake.

They were losing momentum, thought Lena. At this rate, there would be no one left to vote if the time for a vote ever came. The endless talking, talking, talking was killing the energy and spirit with which Jake's words had infused the room earlier. Something had to be done to put an end to it.

"Enough talking," she muttered, scarcely realizing she'd spoken out loud.

People nearby turned to look at her and she sensed approval in their nods. One of the men said, "That other feller what spoke earlier—now, he knew how to talk."

"Which feller?" said another.

"Don't know his name," the first one said.

"Jake Brenner," Lena told them, her heart beating faster as she said it.

"He knew how to get the crowd going," said the first man. "They ought to bring him back up there and call for a vote."

"They should just call for a vote now," said the other. He cupped his hands around his mouth and yelled, "Vote now!" The first man joined in.

Lena looked at Jake. Had he noticed? She cupped her own hands around her mouth and added her voice to those of the two men. "Vote now!" But the people on the stage still seemed oblivious. Someone needed to get their attention. She grabbed Sophie's arm.

"Come on," she said.

"Where are we going?"

"Follow me." She inched her way through the crowd toward the stage, reached the steps, and started up. As she and Sophie ascended, Jake caught sight of them, his face registering confusion.

"What—?" he started to ask.

Words spilled out of Lena. "There's been enough talking. They want to hear from you. They *need* to hear from you." Jake hesitated, but she willed him with her eyes to see that she was right and said, "Go!"

Jake strode to the podium, reaching it just as the last speaker stepped away. His eyes swept the room from side to side. He held up his hands until the crowd quieted down again. Then he spoke.

"There's nothing more that needs to be said. You know from your own experience how they lock you in, and never let you rest or stretch your muscles or even relieve yourselves. They treat you like thieves, like cattle, like machines. You're replaceable if you falter, disposable if you're sick.

"How many more have to die in workroom fires or from exhaustion or from cotton fibers that destroy our lungs. It will never change unless we make it change." He brought his hand to his palm in a chopping motion. "No more. Now is the time for change. Strike now! Strike now!" He thrust his fist in the air. The effect on the crowd was electric.

"Strike! Strike! Strike!" The voices of the crowd rose louder and louder and became a chant. Jake looked at her, or was he looking at Sophie, with eyes that burned with intensity. He walked over and reached a hand out to each of them, leading them to the center of the stage where he turned them toward the audience and raised their hands toward the ceiling. Abe Gunther joined them, grasping Lena's other hand, while the rest of those on the stage joined at either end, making a chain of W's across the stage.

Over and over, Lena shouted the word "strike", until she was hoarse. And all the while, she was keenly aware of being connected to Jake, as if a current was passing between them.

The crowd surged forward. The stage became pandemonium. In the jostling and mayhem, Lena was broken away from Jake. He was mobbed by enthusiastic union members while she found herself a sudden celebrity, her hand pumped vigorously over and over. Somehow, Sophie made her way over and spoke in Lena's ear. "I told Jake to meet us at Katz's Deli after the meeting. Let's just go straight there."

Outside the hall, Lena was still in a daze, the cold air numbing rather than invigorating. Her teeth chattered and her stomach felt like jelly. She thought she might be sick.

The tiny vestibule at Katz's was thick with the after-rally crowd. Here, as earlier, Sophie squirreled her way to the front with Lena in tow. At the entrance to the dining room was an agitated looking man with a gaunt face and thinning brown hair holding a sheaf of rumpled paper menus. He scanned the crowd and called out, "Any twos? I got tables for two's only. Everybody else got to wait."

Sophie held up her hand and yelled. "Hi Harry, it's Sophie. We're gonna be three, Harry. You got anything for a three?"

"Sophie dahling, if I get a three it's yours. But I got nothing but two's right now."

Behind Harry, waiters scurried by shouldering trays loaded with platters of bagels, lox, and eggs. The air was redolent with the tantalizing aroma of fried onions. She heard snatches of Yiddish conversation—women gossiping, men cracking wise, and waiters shouting orders to one another in the sharp, bossy tones of siblings. She felt her tension start to ease now that she was away from the union hall and in a place that felt so much like home.

"Sophie," Harry yelled out after a bit. "I got a three. Is the thoid poison in your party here yet?"

"He's here," Sophie blithely lied. "He's just in the bathroom, right Lena?" Lena gave Harry her most innocent, wide-eyed look and nodded. That seemed to do the trick. Harry signaled them to follow him with a jerk of his head and led them on a serpentine trail through the restaurant. Behind his back, Sophie squeezed Lena's hand.

The path ended at a booth where Harry dumped three menus onto the table and hurried off to reclaim his post. Lena and Sophie slid onto the benches facing each other.

"Well," Sophie said, as soon as they were sitting. "For someone who didn't even want to come to the union meeting, you sure had an impact. I still can't believe you ran onto the stage like that. Whatever made you do it?"

Lena laughed nervously. She didn't know how she could possibly explain what she didn't really understand herself. Now, she thought. Now was the time to tell Sophie about her earlier meeting with Jake.

But, suddenly, Sophie jumped up and waved wildly, "There he is! Jake! Over here!"

He was striding towards their table. Lena's stomach clenched and she found that she could only breathe in small sips. As Jake came near, Sophie reached out and grabbed his arm, pulling him down onto the bench beside her.

"Finally," Sophie said. "I've been wanting to introduce you two for so long. Jake, this is my best friend Lena. And Lena, this is my Jake." She slipped her arms around Jake and pressed herself against him, so that he was forced to raise his arms in the air to accommodate her and they hung momentarily akimbo, until he lowered one around Sophie's shoulders and let the other fall to his side.

"Hello," Jake said. And then, after a beat, "I'm pleased to meet you." His eyes bore into Lena's and somehow she understood. Neither of them would say anything about their earlier meeting. Though this afforded her some immediate relief, it also made her feel somehow guilty to know that she was now adding conspiracy to whatever other transgression she might be guilty of.

"I'm happy to make your acquaintance," she managed.

Sophie looked from Jake to Lena, threw back her head, and laughed. "*Nu*, so formal? Between the two of you, you just set the union hall on fire and now you're acting like the King and Queen of England?" She looked at Jake through narrow, puzzled eyes. "Jake," she said, "you do know that Lena is the one who came on-stage with me, right?"

"Of course," Jake said. He looked at Lena and smiled tightly. "That was, uh, very helpful."

Lena worked to make her voice come out sounding normal. "Of course, it was my pleasure. I've heard so much about you. It is nice to meet you. Finally."

Jake looked down. He seemed to be studying Sophie's hand in his. Slowly and deliberately, he curled his fingers around her hand. "I'm glad you were both there tonight."

"So," Sophie said animatedly, looking first at Jake and then at Lena like they were planning a prank together, "the strike is on. What do we do now?"

"Well," Jake said. He took a deep breath and became business-like, "tomorrow morning, we'll be organizing teams of picketers and trying to raise money to help carry us through for as long as the strike lasts."

"I'm ready to picket," Sophie said, as if she were accepting an invitation to a party. "Lena, you'll picket too, won't you?"

"Of course. I'll do whatever I can," Lena assured her. "But, you know, right now, I'm feeling a little headache coming on. All the excitement I think, or maybe I'm just tired. I should probably go home before it gets worse. Will you both excuse me?" It wasn't a lie. Her head was pounding and she felt a desperate need to get home as quickly as possible.

"But Jake just got here." Sophie protested. "Make her stay, Jake. Tell her it's too early to leave. After all, we needn't wake up as early as usual if we're not even going to work tomorrow."

Jake shook his head. "I'm sorry, Sophie," he said. "I'm tired too. Maybe it would be better if we all just went home."

Sophie looked from Jake to Lena, puzzled and disappointed. "I've waited such a long time for you to meet each other and now both of you want to go home before you've even had a chance to get to know one another?"

It was hard not to hear the hurt in Sophie's voice. But Lena wasn't sure how much longer she could keep up the pretense of smiling and acting as if her heart hadn't grown so large that she was aware of every beat. For Sophie's sake, she would try a little more.

"You're right, Sophie," she said, trying to keep her voice steady. "Of course, I can stay a little longer."

Across from her, Jake spoke soothingly. "Yes, of course, we'll all stay a little longer." He turned to Lena with an expression that was serious and thoughtful and, when he spoke, his tone was grave, full of caution. "I've heard so much about you but none of it did you justice. Now I can see that you are as good a friend as Sophie said you were."

Lena understood him perfectly and silently agreed. Whatever she'd imagined she'd seen in his eyes this afternoon and whatever she'd felt when he'd held her hand in hers, none of it mattered. She was Sophie's friend. And Jake was Sophie's guy.

The rest of the evening passed with painful slowness. By the time they were done and walking toward the exit, Lena had what felt like the worst headache in her entire life. Outside the restaurant, the night air had turned bitter and she pressed her legs together, shivering with cold and exhaustion.

"Good night, Lena," Jake said. She nodded, heard Sophie say something to Jake in a low tone of voice, and watched her kiss him goodbye.

Then Sophie linked her arm around Lena's, and she let herself be led in the direction of home. But as Sophie prattled on, Lena heard nothing. She was lost in imagining how it would have felt if she had been the one who had kissed Jake goodnight.

CHAPTER SEVEN

"I MISSED SEEING YOU LAST WEEK," DANIEL SAID TO LENA AS THEY SAT at their usual table at Meltzer's.

"I missed coming but it was the same night as the rally."

"I thought you might have gone to that," he said, not mentioning that he'd waited until the school was completely empty the previous week before going on to Meltzer's by himself. "So, are you on strike now?"

"I am," she said. "I haven't worked in a week."

He shook his head. "I'm sorry to hear that," he said. "It seems like the employees suffer so much more from a strike than the employers do. The manufacturers just go to Ellis Island and hire replacement workers as soon as they get admitted to the country. I think it would be much better if the union's leaders spent their time working through the political system instead of calling for strikes." He'd meant to empathize her plight, but Lena looked upset.

"Political changes take time." she said. "The power to withhold our labor is the only real weapon workers have against the power of the employers."

"It isn't the only weapon," Daniel said. "Laws can be weapons too. Mr. Howard says that laws can be passed that force employers to pay higher wages and make working conditions safer."

"Well, right now laws like that aren't being passed. Meanwhile, the politicians are looking the other way while the employers make slaves out of us."

"But workers can band together and can elect politicians who are in favor of labor protections."

"Elections take time," Lena protested. "Meanwhile, children are going hungry. The strike can force change to come about quickly."

"Or it can drag on for months," Daniel said.

Lena looked at him through narrowed eyes. "You sound like you're anti-union."

"I'm not anti-union," Daniel said, dismayed at the turn the conversation had taken. "I didn't mean to sound so negative." But Lena was still looking at him a bit defiantly as if challenging him to present another argument against the union so she could knock it down. Didn't she know he could never be against her? And why, he wondered, *was* he sounding so anti-union and anti-strike? Why did he have such a tight feeling in his stomach? He realized that it was because he was afraid. Not for himself, but for Lena.

If there was such a thing as a peaceful strike, he'd never heard of it. Back home, even the most peaceful protest by workers was put down with overwhelming force by the police and the Cossacks. During the revolution of 1905, when the Assembly of Russian Workers had gone on strike, nearly one hundred workers had been killed and another three hundred had been wounded.

Strikes here seemed no different. Only two weeks ago, a strike at a Massachusetts textile factory that had erupted into violence. In the ensuing melee, two strikers had been killed; one had been shot and the other, bayoneted. The newspapers had covered the story thoroughly with graphic photographs of the police on horseback charging the strikers and of the faces of the thuggish strikebreakers as they attacked the defenseless workers. The pictures had made him sick. He wished he could be sure that Lena would keep far away from any picket line, but he thought he already knew her well enough to know that she would never hang back and let others carry the banner. Still, he couldn't let her think he was against the union or against her.

"I really hope the strike is successful," he said. "I hope the employers give in quickly and that you're back at work in no time."

She smiled. "I know you're not hoping we fail. I shouldn't have accused you of that."

"No. It was my fault. I spoke without thinking."

"Change of subject?"

"Change of subject," he agreed. "Was it very hard for you in class tonight since you missed last week?"

She laughed. "It's always hard. That's why I am so glad to have you for a friend."

She took out her book, opened it and pointed to a paragraph. "Can you help me understand this part?"

"Of course."

He bent his head over the page and she bent hers too. He couldn't help noticing that her hair smelled like fresh lemons.

CHAPTER EIGHT

"LOOK AT HIM," ROSE SCHNEIDERMAN SAID TO ABE GUNTHER AS SHE pointed at Jake who, having slept on the office sofa again, was folding the blanket he'd used. "He sleeps two hours and he's ready to go. Tell me, Jake, what are you taking? I'll have some too."

Abe shook his head. "If we could bottle it and sell it, we'd all be rich. The truth is, he thrives on this stuff."

Jake rolled his eyes to let them know he'd heard them and was ignoring them on purpose. None of them had been getting much rest. The work involved in getting the strike up and running had been overwhelming.

They divided the necessary tasks amongst themselves. Abe communicated with union headquarters and coordinated assistance from the other locals. He was also the chief negotiator. He'd managed to get the owners of Dearhart Shirtwaists to come back to the table, but nothing had been agreed upon. Indeed, Dearheart was trying to back out of demands it had accepted under previous agreements. All the other manufacturers were standing firm too.

Rose managed the finances, reviewed requests for loans from union members, and approved expenditures for supplies. She also coordinated the assistance provided by the Ladies Trade Union League. The League's membership of wealthy matrons was eager to help anyway it could and the publicity they brought was good for the cause.

Jake was in charge of day to day picketing operations. He did his best to provide protection from the thugs employed by the manufacturers and even hired his own muscle when he deemed it necessary. Every day, he spent some time walking alongside picketers, trying to bolster the spirits of those manning the thin-

55

ning lines. And nearly every day, he visited City Court, bailing out picketers who'd been jailed on trumped up charges. He was also spearheading the publicity campaign. Unfortunately, after the first week, most of the newspapers relegated the story to their back pages.

But these were just the jobs they did during the day. At night, Jake visited the homes of union members, gauging their support for the strike, enlisting picket volunteers, and building up morale. Worker dedication to the strike was still strong, but when he stood in his member's homes, he was well-aware of the empty coal boxes and unheated apartments. Still later, back at the office, he, Rose, and Abe spent hours hashing and re-hashing strategies to see if there was any detail they were overlooking, any gambit that might make the manufacturers more willing to concede.

Thinking about the newspaper coverage, Jake tossed the blanket onto the sofa angrily. "I can't get a single newspaper to promise to cover tomorrow's rally."

"Calm yourself, Jake," Gunther said in his soft voice. "They may not want to commit themselves, but they'll show up if the rally is big enough."

Jake strode over to Abe's desk. He didn't want to calm himself. He wanted to grab the newspaper reporters by their throats and shake them.

"We've dropped out of the public eye," he said. "We need to do something new to get their attention. Picket where we'll be noticed. I was thinking about it last night after you two went home and I finally had an idea."

"Did it come to you in a dream," Rose asked, "or did you just stay up all night?"

Jake ignored her teasing and plowed on. "Just listen. Now, the way I see it, the strike has slowed down production, but it hasn't stopped it completely. Every day, the manufacturers fill a few more jobs with greenhorns fresh off the boat.

Abe nodded. "We know. There's nothing we can do about that. So, what's the big idea Jake?"

"We hit 'em where it hurts most," Jake said. "We organize a boycott by the public. Picket outside the department stores. People support us by not buying from stores that sell shirtwaists. It's that simple."

Abe nodded. "A secondary boycott. It's been done before, but it's risky. Sometimes it breeds more anger than support from the public."

"But it's worth a try," Rose said. "We're getting so little publicity now."

"Exactly," Jake said. "I bet I could get a lot of volunteers for those kinds of picket lines and it would generate some great publicity too." He looked levelly at Gunther. "What do you say, Abe?"

Abe nodded slowly. "All right. Let's give it a trial run. Start organizing something and we'll see how it goes."

Jake whirled around feeling triumphant and headed back to his desk. He was so distracted by excitement that he nearly collided with Sophie who had just arrived at the office. She was wearing a kerchief tied around her head from which wisps and tendrils of black curls charmingly escaped. And she was toting a picnic basket. She looked like a voluptuous red riding hood.

"You're a sight for sore eyes," he said. "I didn't even hear you come in."

"I brought you some lunch. I know how busy you are. I thought maybe you wouldn't have time to go out and get something."

"That was sweet." He smiled at her and she grinned back.

Putting her basket down, Sophie said, "How are we doing, Jake? How's the strike going?"

"It's going okay." Jake half sat on the edge of his desk. Rose might not see it, but he was weary. "Some of the picket lines are getting a little light, but we're working on some new strategies to beef them up."

Sophie moved closer to him and tipped her head up, looking at him through long, dark lashes. "I want to be on the picket line," she said. "I really do. I'm sure Lena does too. Just tell us where to go."

"Where is Lena today?" Jake asked, trying to make it sound casual.

Sophie shrugged. "She's studying. That's all she ever does these days, study for her night school classes."

"Why don't you go to class with her?"

Sophie laughed. "I'm not exactly the studious type."

Jake grinned, unsurprised by this confession, "What type are you?"

She reached out and pulled his arms around her waist. "What type do you think I am?"

"Hmm. How should I answer that?"

"As long as you say I'm your type, it doesn't matter."

His type, he thought. What was his type anyway? He thought of Lena, intense and opinionated, with her frank gaze and sensual mouth. And, then there was Sophie, sexy, fun-loving, and loyal. Before he could say a word, the telephone on his desk gave a shrill ring. Saved by the proverbial bell, he thought.

Gesturing to the phone, he said, "Listen honey, I would love to keep talking to you, but things are kind of hectic around here."

The phone rang again and he grabbed the receiver and said, "Hold on a minute. He pressed the phone to his chest. "I better get back to work. I've got about a million things to do."

"I know. That's why I'm here. To help. Just tell me what to do. Tell me which picket line to join."

Jake rubbed his jaw with his free hand. He was hesitant to put Sophie on a picket line. They could be rough places. Dangerous even. Just the other day, a scuffle had broken out on one of his picket lines. He was sure it had been started by a bunch of hired union busters, but somehow the only ones arrested had been strikers. Even worse, one of his people had come out of it with a broken arm and three broken ribs. On the other hand, shielding Sophie from the strike effort was hardly fair or consistent with the union's credo of one for all and all for one.

"The picket lines are fine today," he said. "Wait a few more days and, when we set up picket lines in front of some of the stores, we'll need truly dedicated people like you to walk them. For now, just spread the word to all your friends and neighbors not to buy shirtwaists.

"Spread the word?" Sophie laughed. "Now you're talking about something I'm really good at."

"Good." He grinned back. "Now go." He leaned forward and gave her a quick kiss.

"That the best you can do?"

She tilted her face up expectantly. He cupped her chin with his hand and kissed her. She tasted like fresh raspberries.

"Now go," he said again, but more gently this time. Sophie flashed him another smile and sashayed out the door.

Watching her leave, Jake felt better than he had for weeks. He'd seen little of her since the night of the rally. After saying goodbye to her and Lena outside of Katz's, he'd spent the entire walk back to the office as well as several nights on the sofa trying to sort out his confused feelings about Lena.

It wasn't just that he was attracted to Lena. And it wasn't just that he'd enjoyed debating the merits of the strike with her and the spirited way she'd challenged him or the way he could see the wheels of her brain clicking when she processed some new piece of information. Crazy as it seemed, he had decided that his confusion had something to do with the way he'd felt when he touched her hand. Like he was more alive than he'd ever been in his whole life.

At first, he'd thought it was just his imagination. But then at the rally, when she'd joined him on stage and they'd held their clasped hands aloft, the feeling had returned. And he didn't know what to do with it. So, he tried pretending that it didn't exist. When that didn't work, he decided it didn't matter. So what if he was attracted to Lena? He was a man and only human. Just because he was with Sophie didn't mean that he wasn't going to notice other women.

What mattered was that he wasn't going to do anything about it. At least not while he was still with Sophie. If there was one thing he'd learned at twelve when his mother took off, it was that, no matter who else came along, you didn't just up and leave the people who loved you. You didn't abandon them. Because the confusion and the pain of being left like that was something you never got over.

Now, thinking of Sophie with her mischievously slanting eyes, he reminded himself how she brought out the lighter side of him. Maybe this weekend, he would take a break from everything that was going on and take her out. He was itching to feel the syncopated rhythm of one of his favorite ragtime numbers and to really let loose on the dance floor. Maybe that would get all this pent-up tension from thinking about Lena out of his system.

CHAPTER NINE

A SHIVER RAN DOWN LENA'S BACK AND SHE WAS GRATEFUL FOR THE printed strike signs that covered her front and back, giving her an extra layer of insulation. At five in the afternoon, it was almost dark and very cold. So few customers were approaching Stewart's Department Store that she wondered whether it was worth it to continue picketing, although they'd committed to staying until six p.m.

It was hard to tell if picketing the store had done any good. Earlier in the day when there had been more customers, most of them had simply ignored the strikers. Those that acknowledged their presence seemed more offended than moved. Some of the elegantly turned out female customers even sniffed distastefully.

In the morning, when the picket line had been flush, there'd been a certain camaraderie among the strikers. They'd walked in a big oval, chanting solidarity slogans. A group of women from the Ladies Trade Union League, including Catherine Graham Carter, had arrived midmorning to hand out paper cups filled with hot coffee. A few of them had even joined the picket line. A photographer from the Herald Tribune had taken pictures of them waving their arms in the air and shouting, "Solidarity Forever!"

But now the league ladies were long gone and most of the picketers had left too. The five remaining tried to stretch the picket line out by leaving big spaces between themselves. Every so often, somebody would realize that the circle had shrunk again and they would spread out once more.

Lena's feet were so cold that all she could think about was being someplace where she could pull off her boots and soak her feet in steaming water. Walking in front of her, Sophie looked pretty done in too. The wooden handle of her picket sign was resting on her shoulder and she looked more like a sentry than a striker.

Down the street, Lena saw a trio of men approaching and her breath caught in her chest. Jake had not yet visited their picket line. Sophie had been looking forward to his presence all day, while Lena had been both longing for and dreading it. The thought of having to pretend that she felt nothing for him but friendship was nerve wracking.

But as the men drew closer, she could see Jake was not amongst them. All three wore denim overalls and workman's jackets. The one in front was the biggest, with an unusually large head, abundant red hair, and a pig-like face so fleshy that his eyes were slits. He stopped a few feet away and his buddies installed themselves just behind him on either side.

"Yer in my way," the leader growled at Lena. "I'm tryin' to get into this store and yer blockin' my way."

The picketers had been coached about this sort of confrontation. They'd been warned that strike busters might show up, pick fights, hurl fake accusations, and generally try to get a rise out of them. They had been instructed on how to respond.

"This is a lawful strike," she said. "We are peacefully marching on public property."

"Oh yeah? Well, it ain't lawful to block someone's way. So youse better move." He took a step toward her and she took a step back.

"Hey, Red," said one of the other men, "I don't think she takes you serious, do you?"

Red shook his head slowly. "I don't think so, but she better. Cause I don't like it when someone's blockin' me."

Despite her intention, Lena's voice quavered. "I am not in your way. The door is right there."

"Don't you shake yer head at me, you little kike," Red growled as he advanced closer.

At that moment, Sophie gave a shriek. Lena whirled around. Sophie was sitting on the ground massaging her ankle.

"Get up!" Red snarled at Sophie. "Get up and get outta here or I'll move you myself."

"I can't," moaned Sophie. "I think I broke a bone." She rubbed her ankle and groaned.

Clever, nervy Sophie, Lena thought, knowing her friend well enough to tell she was faking. She hurried over, hoping Sophie's ploy would be enough to make the thugs back off. But Red followed right on her heels and just as Lena knelt to look at Sophie's ankle, he grabbed Sophie's arm.

After that, everything seemed to happen at once. Later, Lena wouldn't even know if she'd been hit intentionally or whether her face was just in the wrong place when Red tried to jerk Sophie to her feet. The blow to Lena's jaw sent shockwaves of pain racing through her entire face and head. Everything around her melted into blurriness then faded to a misty gray as she struggled not to lose consciousness.

By the time her vision sharpened again, Red was holding Sophie tightly. Sophie's arms and legs flailed as she fought to free herself from his grasp. One of Red's henchmen was advancing towards Sophie's captive body, his arm pulled back as he readied his punch. Lena glanced around wildly. Not far away was Sophie's abandoned picket sign. She ran over, grabbed it, and with all her strength, swung it, catching Red on the back of his knees.

Startled, he loosened his hold on Sophie just enough for her to squirm away. Recovering, he spun around and stared at Lena, seething and breathing like a bull getting ready to charge. Sophie jumped onto his back, but she might as well have been a flea for all the effect she had. Red's lip curled. He reached up, took hold of Sophie's wrists and flung her away like a rag doll. Then he balled up his hand and walked slowly toward Lena.

Before he could reach her, Jake appeared and cut him off, fists flying, launching a powerful punch to Red's gut. He followed this with a crashing blow to Red's jaw that spun the big man around until he dropped.

The clattering sound of hoof beats filled the air as the police arrived. Lena felt her arm being grabbed roughly. Dazed, she offered no resistance as she was pulled along. From the corner of her eye, she saw Jake twisting in a policeman's grasp.

"Don't worry," he yelled to her as he wrenched himself free, "we'll get you out as soon as we can." Then he turned around and took off, the officer in hot pursuit.

Get me out of where, Lena wondered, as she was shoved through the back door of the paddy wagon. She was aware of Sophie being pushed in next to her and the door being slammed. In the dark, the smell of urine was overwhelming. The wagon started with a jolt and she almost fell, a movement that triggered a shot of pain so terrible she felt a wave of nausea. Fighting the impulse to vomit, she grabbed the bars on the rear window of the wagon and saw Red nod at one of the police officers before sauntering off with his buddies. The officer nodded back, glanced around, and strolled down the street, swinging his club.

Minutes later, the wagon stopped. The door swung open and a beefy officer pulled her out. She and Sophie were propelled into the station and through crowds of people that swirled around them. Some of their fellow picketers were there, as well as some of the ladies from the Ladies League. There were even a couple of reporters. And many more police.

Bulbs flashed in front of her. People shouted but she was in too much of a stupor to comprehend what they were saying. The crowd was so thick they were forced to stop. A man wearing a fedora with the brim pulled low and shielding his face, pushed his way through the crowd and appeared before them. Disoriented as she was, Lena recognized Jake immediately.

"Are you alright?" he asked in a hoarse voice.

"Back up," barked the officer holding Lena's arm. "Make way."

"Goddamn it, you can give me a minute," Jake said. "I just want to see if these women are all right. They're entitled to medical care for God's sake."

"I said back up," snarled the policeman.

"I'm okay, Jake," Sophie said in a subdued voice. "But I'm not so sure about Lena."

Jake's worried eyes searched Lena's face. "My God," he said in a whisper. "What did they do to you...." He reached a hand toward her cheek.

Lena felt her legs buckle and would have fallen if not for the police officer's iron-clad grip. "Here now," he said. "Keep it moving, keep it moving. You'll have time to speak to yer lawyer when yer in front of the judge."

Lena found her footing and managed a small smile. "I'm okay," she said. "I'm tougher than most of your opponents, remember?" And then, she was moving again, pushed through the crowded room until she was shoved into a cell and heard the door clang shut behind her.

CHAPTER TEN

JAKE WASTED NO TIME IN GETTING BACK TO THE OFFICE TO SEE WHAT he could do about arranging to get Lena and Sophie out of jail. Rose had already called Aaron Carey, the union's lawyer. Carey, a small, wiry guy wearing a trench coat, who looked more like a gangster than a lawyer, was waiting in the office when he arrived. Jake shook his hand and got right to the point.

"Can we go over there right now and get them out?"

"*I* can go over there right now and see what *I* can do. But I think it would be better if *you* stayed here and waited." Carey replied.

"What the hell are you talking about? I'm not staying back here and sitting around while they're stuck in that hole."

Carey glanced at Rose and then back at Jake. "Look, it's not going to help if you go over there and end up punching some police officer in the nose. From that scowl on your face, I'd say that's not out of the realm of possibility. Why don't you stay back and I'll bring the girls here when we're done, probably in a couple of hours."

A dozen reasons why he should go to the jail with Carey sprang up in Jake's mind, but one look at Aaron's unyielding face, and he knew this was one argument he would not win. He watched Rose hand over the bail money. Carey folded the money and slipped it in his pocket. Then he touched his hand to the brim of his hat in goodbye and left the office.

Watching him go, Jake knew that Carey had a point. His insides were churning with fury. And the person he was angriest at was himself. How could he ever have been so stupid as to let Lena and Sophie walk a picket line? And why, if he was going to allow them on a picket line, did he put them on one with minimal protection? He'd been so sure that being in such a visible place would be a form of protection.

He saw Lena again in his mind as she had looked at the police station, her cheek battered and bruised. He'd wanted to take her in his arms right then and there. As for the cop who was man-handling her, Carey was right, he'd wanted to punch that jerk right in the smacker.

And what about Sophie—thank God she hadn't gotten hurt too. He wondered if she'd seen him reach his hand toward Lena's face. He didn't think so. But he couldn't be sure, couldn't be cer-tain his feelings hadn't been obvious to her because right now he felt like his emotions were written all over his face. And he needed to get them off his face because Lena and Sophie were best friends.

He knew that women had a code about these things. A girl didn't go out with the guy who'd broken her best friend's heart. Nor would he want to do anything to hurt Sophie. Until he fig-ured out how to let Sophie down gently, he didn't dare start any-thing with Lena. Assuming, of course, that Lena was interested. He thought the feeling was mutual, but he really couldn't be sure.

Restlessly, he walked over to the sofa where someone had left the day's newspaper. He sat down on the sofa, picked up the pa-per, and tried to focus on the words in front of him.

From her seat at her desk, Rose said, "One thing's for sure, to-day's events will bring some publicity."

"Uh, huh." He turned the pages without knowing what was on them. He stood up again and walked over to his desk. But in-stead of sitting in his chair, he just stood looking down at it.

"Sophie will be okay, Jake," Rose said. "Aaron will take care of her."

"I know." He reached for the telephone, changed his mind, and spun around to look at Rose. "I'm going down there."

"But Aaron said—,"

"I'm not going to go in the building. I'm just going to wait for them."

"It might take hours."

"Well, I'm not going to get anything done here today. Besides, I don't think it'll take that long. I'll try to stop back in later."

Rose nodded, defeated. Jake ignored the look on her face and strode out the door.

Lena heard footsteps coming down the hall in the direction of their cell. From the expression on Sophie's face, she'd noticed too. They'd already been taken from the cell once before and escorted along the mazelike corridors by a prison guard who had delivered them to the courtroom where they'd met Aaron Carey. They'd had only seconds to talk to him before being called to stand before the judge. Afterward, the same guard had returned them to the cell. But Carey had told them as they'd left the courtroom, that this time it would be only until he paid the bail money set by the judge. Then they would be released.

Now, a different guard than before swung open the cell door and motioned with his head for them to exit the cell. He led them back through the endless hallways until they passed through a security gate into the now nearly empty police station where Carey was waiting to escort them out of the building.

It had been late afternoon when they had first arrived. It was now nearly eleven o'clock at night. They walked out of the bright lights of the station and into the night where a flight of marble steps led down to the dark and empty streets. Or nearly empty.

In the light of a lamppost, Lena saw Jake. His hands were hidden in the pockets of his long topcoat; his face was shadowed by the brim of his fedora. Sophie caught sight of him too, ran down the last few steps, and flung herself into his waiting arms.

Lena forced her shaky legs to keep moving next to Aaron Carey. As she reached the bottom of the steps, Sophie and Jake parted.

"Are you alright?" Jake asked her in a quiet, controlled voice.

"I'm alright. Just a little tired, that's all."

Jake extended his hand to Carey. "Thanks for everything."

Aaron waved him off. "I'll let you know when I hear from the District Attorney. With any luck, they'll drop the charges and neither Miss Friedman or Miss Rothman will ever have to set foot in that building again. Ladies," he said, tipping his hat at Lena and Sophie. Then he turned and walked down the street.

"Let's get you two home," Jake said, offering them each a bent arm. "There's a certain Aunt and Uncle and brother who are pretty anxious to see both of you."

Following Sophie's example, Lena slipped her arm through the circle made by his crooked elbow. But having done so, she couldn't think what to do with her fingers that wouldn't involve touching Jake. Sophie was resting hers on Jake's forearm. Lena let her hand lightly touch the fabric of his coat, but her fingers were shaking.

Jake looked down, noticed and frowned. "You're trembling. You must be freezing. Here." He stopped and shrugged out of his coat, then stood facing her. Lena's chest constricted and she avoided looking at him as he reached around to drape his coat around her shoulders.

Turning to Sophie, he said, "You must be cold too." He undid his suit jacket and slipped it off, settling it around Sophie.

Lena crossed her arms, trying to shrink into the warmth of Jake's coat, grasping the lapels and pulling them close around her. Still, she could not stop herself from shaking.

At last, they reached the entrance to their building. Home, Lena thought, refuge, safety. All she could think about was getting inside, getting away. Carefully she removed Jake's coat before he had a chance to help her off with it and handed it back to him.

"Thank you," she said.

Jake shook his head. "Don't thank me. It's because of me that you were both some place you never should have been in the first place."

"No," she said. "We belonged on that picket line today. It was our turn."

"Lena's right," Sophie agreed. She reached up and put her hands on either side of Jake's face. "What happened today was not your fault."

Lena left them standing there and hurried up the steps to the door. But as she stepped into the darkened vestibule, she couldn't stop herself from turning to look back one last time. She could see Sophie's back, her body pressed tightly against Jake, her head tucked under his chin. And, she could see Jake, looking over Sophie's head at the doorway of the building, his eyes searching. She longed to step back over the threshold and make eye contact. But, instead, she swallowed hard and slowly started up the steps.

CHAPTER ELEVEN

DANIEL SAT ACROSS FROM LENA IN THEIR USUAL TABLE AT MELTZER'S. It was their eighth week having coffee together. Two months of sharing coffee and conversation and stumbling over a new language together. Two months of talking about their plans for the future and sharing bits and pieces of their pasts. And in all that time, he'd said nothing, done nothing, to let her know how he really felt about her. That was going to change tonight.

He'd given the matter a great deal of thought. He'd even gone so far as to ask Fletcher for advice while sharing a beer with the diminutive dispatcher one night after work. Not that it helped. Fletcher had just rolled his eyes and said, with the thick Irish accent that Daniel still had trouble understanding, "Eight weeks 'n ya still 'aven't so much as kissed 'er? Go on w' ya." But, of course, you couldn't just kiss a girl without saying or doing something first to let her know how you really felt. He pushed his glasses back, cleared his throat, and looked around for their waiter.

"It's my turn to pay tonight," Lena reminded him, reaching for her purse.

"You should at least let me pay until the strike is over," Daniel protested.

Lena shook her head. "You need every penny you can save for going to college. Anyway," she said, as she dug coins out of her purse, "I may not have many more opportunities to do this if they don't dismiss the charges and I have to go to back to prison."

"You won't have to go. You didn't do anything wrong. You'll see. Everything will work out."

"You have a lot more faith in the legal system than I do," she said.

They left the restaurant and paused just outside the front door. This was where they ordinarily parted and Daniel was aware of his heart hammering in his chest. He heard Fletcher's voice in his head and cleared his throat.

"Would it be alright if I walked you home?"

Lena looked surprised. "It's not out of your way?"

"No. Not at all."

"Alright then."

On Delancey Street, there was a chill in the air. Lena hugged her notebook tightly to her chest with criss-crossed gloved hands. Daniel walked with his bookbag slung diagonally over his jacket, his bare hands jammed tightly in his trouser pockets and a gray, wool scarf wrapped round his neck. From Delancey, they would turn onto Ludlow. He had exactly five blocks to muster up his courage. Better get the ball rolling, he thought.

But it was Lena who broke the silence. "I forgot to ask—did you finish the application? For City College?"

"I did it yesterday. And took it to the post office right away."

"Daniel, that's wonderful." Her eyes lit up. "Will you tell me the minute you get an answer?"

He laughed. "I will if it's the answer I'm hoping for."

"It will be. I'm sure of it."

They turned onto Elizabeth. It was much quieter than Delancey and seemed like a better setting for what he wanted to say. But now that the moment had come, he hesitated. Nothing ventured, nothing gained, he'd told himself earlier today. But the opposite was true too. Nothing ventured, nothing lost. Two months of coffee's together. He couldn't dismiss the fact that there was a lot at stake.

In the dark, he wondered what she was thinking and whether she could sense his racing thoughts. She must, at least, suspect the reason for his offering to walk her home. Before he had anticipated, she stopped and turned towards him.

"Thank you for walking me home," she said.

For a moment, the meaning of her words didn't register. But then he realized that they had reached her apartment. He cleared his throat.

"Before you go in, there was something I wanted to ask you."

At that moment, the door to her building opened and a woman came bursting out. She ran up to them, grabbed Lena's hands, and pulled her into a ring-around-the-rosie dance.

"I've been waiting for you to come home," she said. "I've been going crazy. The charges were dismissed! It's all over. We're free. The charges were dismissed!"

Laughing, Lena brought the dancing to a gradual stop. "Sophie, stop. I can't understand what you're saying."

"The charges against us were dismissed. Aaron Carey is a genius. We don't have to go back to court!"

"Are you sure? Are you absolutely certain?"

"I'm one hundred percent certain. Aaron Carey is a genius, the judge is a genius. America is full of geniuses!"

"That's wonderful! Better than wonderful," Lena said.

"We have to celebrate," Sophie said excitedly. "This Saturday night." She spun around and faced Daniel, "You have to come too. Help us celebrate our victory. Our freedom! Will you? Oh," she laughed, "you must think I'm some kind of crazy person. We've never even been introduced. I'm Sophie Friedman, Lena's roommate."

"Oh, yes," Lena murmured, "Excuse my bad manners. Daniel, this is Sophie. Sophie, Daniel Cowan."

"Very nice to meet you," Daniel said.

"Nice to meet you too," Sophie said. "I've heard a lot about you. You're a genius too. At least, that's what Lena's always saying. You will come won't you? On Saturday night?"

Daniel glanced at Lena. She looked surprised, but that didn't necessarily mean she was against the idea. And there was the fact that she'd talked about him to Sophie. She'd called him a genius. That had to be a good sign.

Sophie was waiting for his answer, so he nodded. "Yes, I'd like to come. Thank you for inviting me."

Sophie clapped her hands. "It'll be the most wonderful celebration. We'll meet here and then we'll paint the town. What's a good time?" She looked from Lena to Daniel. "How about eight? Does that sound alright? Then we're all set. Saturday night at eight."

With both Lena and Sophie looking at him, Daniel realized there was no reason for him to linger any longer. The moment he'd been waiting for all night had somehow slipped away.

"Well, until Saturday then," he said.

As he walked away, he could hear them talking animatedly behind him. They probably weren't watching him anymore. But, just in case, he tried to infuse his stride with a confident air. Once he turned back onto Delancey, he slowed his pace and took stock. Things may not have gone exactly as he'd planned but he *was* going out with Lena on Saturday night. Of course, it would have been better if he'd been the one to ask her and if it were just going to be the two of them. Then again, maybe being part of a celebratory group would be good. The main thing was that Lena would have an opportunity to see him in a new setting. With any luck, she would realize that he had more to offer than merely grammatical advice.

Yes, he thought, as exuberance began to bubble up in him, this celebration on Saturday night might be just the chance he'd been looking for. He felt almost heady with excitement. He let the grin that had been welling up in him break out. He couldn't stop grinning. He had no idea what was going to happen on Saturday night, but, for now, he was going to enjoy this feeling. And tomorrow, he would just see what Fletcher had to say about the fact that he, Daniel Cowan, had a date.

CHAPTER TWELVE

SATURDAY NIGHT. LENA SAT ON HER BED WATCHING SOPHIE WHO was stationed in front of the dressing table putting the final touches on her make-up. She caught her friend's eyes in the mirror and shook her head. Sophie held her lipstick mid-air and sighed.

"For the thousandth time, I'm sorry it turned out to be just the four of us. I didn't know everyone else was going to back out of our celebration. I didn't know Aunt Sarah would have a cold and Uncle Lou would be staying home to keep her company. And I thought Joe would be back by now."

"He would have been if he wasn't so good at selling gloves," Lena said. "His new company is so happy with him, they've expanded his territory to include the whole state."

"Well, I didn't know that was going to happen. And, I'm sorry that I invited Daniel without asking you first. I was just so excited when I found out about the charges were dismissed. But I'm sure it will all work out."

Lena stood up and walked over to the washstand. "I just don't think it's a good idea. Now that it's just going to be you and Jake and me and Daniel, I'm afraid he'll think it's a date."

"I don't see what the problem is. You already go out with Daniel once a week."

"I keep telling you that those aren't dates."

"Well, why don't you date him? You're always talking about how smart he is and how kind. And he's quite nice looking in his own way. I'd give anything for such blue eyes and long lashes."

"Then you date him. Just don't do it on the nights we have class."

Sophie shook her head and clusters of shiny, fat curls bounced up and down. "It's too late to do anything about it now. Aren't you going to get ready?"

Lena sighed. "I haven't got anything to wear."

"That," Sophie said, "is no problem at all."

Daniel checked his watch. It was two minutes before eight o'clock, and he had just arrived at Lena's building. With one hand, he fingered the inside of his new paper collar. The skin on his neck was still a little tender where the barber had shaved him.

In his other hand, he held a square brown florist's box with the corsage he'd bought. It was a white orchid, which the shop clerk had said would match anything Lena wore. He was as ready as he was ever going to be. It was time, as Fletcher liked to say, to either piss or get off the pot. The door to the Friedman's apartment was opened by a short, round, very bald man with a beaming smile.

"You are?" the man asked.

"Daniel Cowan."

"Exactly what I thought. And I am Lou Friedman, the Uncle."

"Lou," an unseen female voice called. "Who's at the door."

"It's Mr. Cowan," he called back. "Come in, come in," he told Daniel. He walked backward into the apartment. "No need to wait out there. Welcome to my harem."

The Friedman's front door opened into a large kitchen, and Lou waived Daniel over to a large rectangular dining table flanked by four straight-backed chairs.

"The girls are still getting ready," Lou said. "You know how they are. Have a seat. God only knows how much longer they'll be." He grinned conspiratorially at Daniel.

"I see none of the others have arrived," Daniel said.

"Others?" Lou raised his eyebrows. "I don't know about any others coming besides Jake. Sarah," he said to the short, round female version of himself who had just entered the kitchen, "this young man is Daniel Cowan. Mr. Cowan, this is my wife. Sarah, Mr. Cowan seems to think there are going to be others joining tonight's festivities in addition to himself and Jake."

"It's a pleasure to meet you Mr. Cowan."

"It's nice to meet you too."

Sarah Friedman shook her head at her husband. "What others are you talking about? There are no others coming. For heavens sake, Lou, how many escorts do two girls need?"

"Well," Lou said, " if Mrs. Friedman says there are no others than she should know. After all, the women plan these things. We men are just along for the ride." He grinned again.

Daniel nodded his head slowly. So it was just going to be him and Lena and Sophie and her escort. The evening was getting off to a magnificent start.

At 8:05 Jake was still in his apartment. He was not in a good mood. He'd been uncomfortable with the idea of this celebration from the moment he'd heard about it. His only hope was that there would be enough other people in the group that he wouldn't have much contact with a certain female.

Distracted, he put on his blue pinstripe, forgetting that the vest had gotten tight. Once it was on, he could feel the seams pulling along his sides but there wasn't time to change. He grabbed his hat and headed out the door.

When he got to the Friedman's, he saw that he was not going to find any refuge in numbers. Only one person was sitting with Lou in the kitchen and that person was a slim, bespectacled, awkward looking fellow. Uncle Lou made the introductions and confirmed his suspicion. The evening's party would be composed solely of himself, this fellow, Sophie, and Lena.

"So, Cowan," Jake said, "how do you know Sophie?"

"Oh, I don't really know her. I just met her the other night when I walked Lena home."

"Really," Jake said. "So, you're a friend of Lena's?"

"We attend night school together."

"So you're a classmate of hers?"

"Well, we're not actually in the same class. But we were on the same ship coming over from America."

"So you met on board the ship?" Jake asked, starting to lose patience.

"Not exactly."

Jake stared at Daniel. He had no idea what kind of game this beanpole was playing, but he was tired of it. To hide his annoyance, he turned to their host.

"So, Lou," he said, "how are things in the grocery business?"

From the bedroom, Lena started as she heard Uncle Lou's hearty voice welcoming Daniel into the apartment.

"Sit still," said Sophie. "I'm almost done with your hair."

"What are you doing? It looks fine." More than fine, actually. Thanks to Sophie, she had undergone an amazing transformation. The peach-colored dress Sophie had lent her made her skin glow and her eyes look like brown velvet. Her hair was twisted into a French roll at the back, while in front, a combination of waves and curls becomingly framed her face.

"This is the final touch," Sophie said. She wound a narrow peach ribbon around Lena's head and tied it in a small bow that peaked out through the curls near her right temple.

From the doorway, Aunt Sarah surveyed them both. "Beautiful," she exclaimed. "You both look gorgeous."

There was the sound of the apartment door opening and closing again and Lena's heartbeat quickened as she realized Jake must have arrived.

"Come on," Sophie said. She reached for Lena's hand and led the way out of the bedroom.

Walking into the brightly lit kitchen, with Aunt Sarah beaming from her spot over by the stove, Uncle Lou smiling like a benevolent Buddha, and Jake and Daniel sitting at opposite ends of the table, Lena felt like she had entered onto the set of play. All the actors were in place; only she didn't know her lines.

Her eyes compulsively sought out Jake's. He returned her look and held it for just a moment. But it was enough. Damn him, she thought, for having the effect on her that he did. Damn herself for allowing it. She was grateful for the distraction of Daniel, who jumped to his feet. He was fingering the inside of his collar with one hand and holding a florist's box out to her with the other.

"This is for you," he said.

She took the box and opened it. Nestled against a swirl of pink tissue paper was a beautiful white orchid corsage.

"Daniel, it's lovely. Thank you."

"You're welcome. I –"

From across the room, Jake cleared his throat. "Well, if everyone's ready," he said, "we should get going."

Startled, Lena looked at him and then smiled reassuringly at Daniel. "I just need a pin."

Aunt Sarah quickly came to her rescue. "Let me help you with that."

She attached the flower to a spot near Lena's shoulder. Dipping her head, Lena could see the soft, satiny petals, snowy white, unfolding against her dress. Her first corsage. How sweet of Daniel. Just wearing it made her feel more sophisticated. For the first time since the evening had begun, she felt a touch of excitement instead of the dread she'd been enduring all week long.

There was a flurry of handshaking between Uncle Lou and the men and hugs for the girls from Aunt Sarah. Then Jake strode out the door at such a brisk pace that Sophie had almost to run to keep up with him.

Outside, the cold December night air felt fresh and clean. The crescent moon was as sharp as the blade of a scythe and the plentiful stars sparkled in the sky like so much confetti. The hardest part of the evening was over, Lena thought. She'd seen Jake, greeted him, and watched him escort Sophie out the door. And she was feeling alright. Maybe it was the dress or the orchid or the stars or the darkness but her trepidation had disappeared and a frizzon of anticipation had taken its place.

She stole a sideways glance at Daniel. He looked very nice tonight. If she wasn't mistaken, he was wearing a new overcoat, double-breasted and just slightly flared at the waist. It flattered his slim build and long legs. The high, starched collar of his shirt gave his jaw a square, clean look. He'd gotten his hair cut too. It was parted neatly in the middle and, in the soft glow of the street lamps, it gleamed golden. Maybe Sophie was right about him after all. Maybe the only reason she hadn't thought of him romantically before this was because they'd never done anything together except homework. Maybe tonight was a chance to see him in a new light. At a minimum, it might help to take her mind off of Jake.

By now, they had walked farther south than Lena had ever been before. They crossed Canal Street, walked another block, and with an abruptness that was astonishing, were suddenly in what seemed like a foreign country. Every shop-sign, broadside, and billboard was covered with the hash-marks of Chinese lettering. In storefront windows, brown roasted ducks hung by their necks and whole leathery pigs were displayed on platters. Chinese people crowded the sidewalks. They bargained with shopkeepers in a language filled with twangs and pings and scurried down alley-like streets with their purchases. Intoxicated by the exoticism, Lena didn't know where to look first.

On a street narrow as a pathway, Jake led them down half a dozen steps into a tiny room, crammed with patron-filled tables. Lena and Daniel compressed themselves against the wall to avoid getting in the way of the waiters who bustled by burdened with trays of silver-domed platters. Pots and pans clanged in the background, a percussive background for the dissonant, foreign speech of the waiters and the noisy chatter of the restaurant customers.

Sophie laughed at Lena's astonished face. "I told you this would be fun," she said. "Now, you have to promise to taste everything. And we have to let Jake order, because he knows everything that's good here."

Lena nodded helplessly. Of course Jake could order. She wouldn't know the first thing to say if a waiter came to her. A party of four rose from a table toward the rear and edged their way to the front of the restaurant. When they had squeezed past, Jake led the way to the vacated table.

Almost immediately, a short Chinese man arrived armed with a pad and pencil. Jake told him what to bring, but none of it meant anything to Lena. She wondered whether he had ordered anything with pork or shrimp, both of which were prohibited in Judaism. Although she'd been raised in a liberal household, her family had still followed certain traditions. Some of these had already gone by the wayside. Since arriving in America, she'd not been able to avoid violating the prohibition against working on the Sabbath as Northern Shirtwaist, like every other company, required its employees to work a half-day on Saturdays. But eating non-Kosher food was a different thing entirely. She knew Sophie didn't care and Daniel had told her long ago that his bar mitzvah had been the last religious rite he'd participated in. Now, she needed to figure out for herself what parts of her religion she was going to hold onto and what she could let go of while still holding fast to her memories of her father.

She recalled a time when they'd gone on family holiday to a place with a lake. Joe had jumped into the water without hesitation while she had stood at the lake's edge testing the temperature with her toe.

"Lena-la," her father had said. "in a way, the lake is like life itself. To really experience it, a toe dip is not enough." Then he'd walked with her deeper and deeper into the water until she'd gotten used to it. For the rest of the holiday, she'd practically been a mermaid.

As the waiter returned with a huge round tray of food, she made up her mind. She would dive in. She felt sure that her father would not just have understood, he would have approved. As the waiter whisked lids off platters releasing tantalizing aromas, she felt suddenly giddy. This was going to be fun. Not only was she going to taste every new food Jake had ordered, she was going to go along with every other wild and crazy idea Sophie had.

Daniel watched the waiter set down a variety of platters. He was not opposed to trying new things, but he really had no idea what anything was. There was one plate with bite-size pieces of something, maybe chicken, along with what looked like peas and carrots. Another held large, red claw-like pieces of something. A third platter held yellow-brown, eggy pancakes. There were also four small bowls filled with mounded white rice. At least that was something he recognized.

Opposite him, Sophie's boyfriend nodded his approval. *He* seemed to know what he was doing. He'd ordered all the food without even bothering to ask anyone what they liked. In fact, he'd barely said a word to anyone since they'd arrived at the restaurant, as if the rest of them were merely props for his evening out.

"I know it may all look a little strange," Sophie said after the waiter left, "but wait until you taste it. Jake," she said, "tell them how your friend Ja Ling taught you to order."

Jake sat back and put his arm around Sophie's shoulders. "It's just the usual stuff," he said. "The best thing to do when you're eating foreign food is to eat like the natives do. What's your practice Cowan?"

Daniel looked up startled. "I don't really have any practice, but that sounds fine."

"So you haven't had a chance to sample Chinese food yet?" Jake asked.

Sure, Daniel thought. The minute I got off Ellis Island, I asked where the nearest Chinese restaurant was. But he kept his musings to himself and merely shook his head.

"Well, then," Jake said, "the thing to do is to try everything." He spooned a good amount of food onto his plate from the platter with the bite size meat, then handed it across to Daniel.

"Here you go, Cowan. Have a try." There was something in the tone of his voice or perhaps the look in his eye that held a distinct challenge.

Daniel hesitated. The prudent thing would be to take a small amount to taste. But Jake's eyes were still on him and he quickly transferred a few spoonfuls to his plate before passing the platter to Lena. The ritual was practiced three more times. Jake took hearty helpings of each of the remaining dishes and Daniel matched him spoonful for spoonful.

As Daniel picked up his fork, Jake's voice interrupted him. "Chopsticks, Cowan," he said. "If you're going to eat like the natives, you may as well go all the way."

In his hand, Jake held two wooden sticks, which he somehow maneuvered so that they opened and closed like pincers. Daniel picked up the set of sticks nearest his plate and held one in each hand. He glanced surreptitiously over at Jake, who was instructing Sophie on their proper use. Copying them, he tried to get the two sticks to open and close. When he finally managed to grip a piece of food and maneuver it to his mouth, he felt immensely successful.

Beside him, Lena was giggling as she looked at her chopsticks, which were parallel from end to end. "Don't make fun of me," she pleaded. "I'm going to starve unless someone gives me a fork."

"Here, I'll help you," Daniel said. He captured a piece of meat with his chopsticks and steered it carefully in the direction of Lena's mouth. She opened her mouth, but just before he could put it in, the meat dropped to her plate.

"Thanks," she said dissolving into laughter. "With help like that I'll be dead of starvation in no time."

"Give me another chance," he said. He grasped another piece of meat and slowly carried it to her mouth. "There," he said smiling. "I saved you." *These chopsticks were turning out to be a pretty good thing after all.*

"Help me, Jake," begged Sophie. "I'm not getting anywhere with these things."

"Sure, " Jake said. "But—hey," he shrugged, "I just thought it would be fun to try the chopsticks. We don't have to actually use them the whole time." He put his pair down and picked up his fork. "These work fine too."

Leaving the restaurant after dinner, Daniel was the last to climb the stairs back to the street. He saw Sophie grab Jake's hands and squeeze.

"I know what's we should do now," she said. "Let's go dancing!"

"Dancing! Where could we go?" Lena.

"Oh you silly Lena," Sophie said. "There's dancing every Saturday night at the Settlement House."

Jake shook his head. "I'm not so sure I'm up for dancing to-night."

Sophie turned to him in astonishment. "You don't want to go dancing? Who are you kidding, my darling?"

Lena turned to Daniel. "What do you think?"

He hesitated, not wanting to be a party pooper. Obviously, Jake was an experienced dancer whereas he had never even seen women and men dance together. The look on Lena's face decided him.

"Sure," he said slowly. "I guess dancing would be fun."

CHAPTER THIRTEEN

As they entered the Henry Street Settlement House, Lena heard a band playing in the next room. Her heart started to race. Sophie led the way to the edge of the dance floor and Lena stood between her and Daniel watching the crowd wriggle and hop to the syncopated beat of the band.

"It's the Cincinnati Two-step," Sophie said. She grabbed Jake's hand and they joined the couples out on the dance floor.

Watching them dance, Lena couldn't help imagining how it would feel to have Jake's arm around her waist pulling her close to him. She felt a flutter in her stomach and forced herself to look away. She didn't even know why she still felt this way about him. Jake had been acting so strange all evening, rude to Daniel and barely acknowledging her. He'd been acting like the old Jake. The one she'd disapproved of before ever meeting him. Perhaps, tonight she was seeing the real Jake. Perhaps she'd only imagined the Jake she'd been mooning over.

She watched the other couples on the floor. The beat of the music was contagious and she was itching to join them.

"What do you think?" she asked Daniel, trying to sound like she would fine either way.

He looked at her, looked out at the dance floor and looked back at her again. Swallowing noticeably and taking a deep breath, he nodded. "I guess we can't look any sillier than anyone else."

On the dance floor, Daniel stood for a moment, watching the movements of the other couples.

"Daniel? Are you ready?"

He nodded, then placed his left hand lightly on her waist and held his right hand in the air, meeting hers, palm to palm. He was nothing if not a quick study.

"You're doing fine," Lena said as he concentrated on steering her through the crowd. In fact, she thought, Daniel really was doing fine. Like a stutterer whose halting speech disappears when he starts to sing, Daniel on the dance floor was, despite his intense concentration or maybe because of it, almost smooth.

Daniel felt like he was flying. And not just around the dance floor. Never had there been an evening like this. The Chinese dinner, which had started on a tense and awkward note, had somehow transformed into a wonderful time. He couldn't remember when he had laughed so much in his entire life. And Lena had laughed too.

The only moment that had spoiled it was when the bill came. That jerk—Sophie's boyfriend—had paid without even giving him a chance to pitch in and then practically stalked out of the restaurant. He'd accepted Daniel's money later when they were outside, though Lena probably wasn't even aware of it. But Daniel decided to forget it.

Now, he was dancing and, if he wasn't mistaken, not doing too badly at it. At least, Lena didn't seem to mind. And any activity that gave him an excuse to keep one hand on her waist and another holding her hand was fine with him.

The two-step was followed by something the bandleader called the cakewalk and that was followed by another fast paced number. Afterwards, they were both ready for a break and Daniel led Lena back to the edge of the dance floor. By now, the cool night air was just a memory. It was hot in the crowded noisy hall, but it was a different kind of heat than the one Daniel most often experienced as it crept up his neck. And it wasn't in the least bit unpleasant. A minute later, Jake and Sophie joined them.

"Isn't this fun?" Sophie demanded. She turned to Lena. "Aren't you sorry you didn't come sooner?"

"Yes, very," Lena said.

Sophie grinned triumphantly. "Hey," she turned to Jake and Daniel, "how about if you two bring us something to drink?"

While the two men moved through the crowd in search of refreshments, Sophie turned back to Lena.

"So, you and Daniel cut quite a rug out on the dance floor. You look good together."

Lena laughed. "Another hour and you'll have us married off."

"You could do a lot worse."

"You and Jake look good out on the dance floor too," Lena said, careful to keep her voice neutral.

Daniel and Jake returned and Lena gratefully accepted the cup of punch Daniel handed to her. The band was taking a break, so the four of them made small talk until the music began again. This time it was a waltz. She looked questioningly at Daniel.

He hesitated. "Would you mind if we sat this one out? I guess I shouldn't have worn new shoes tonight."

"Of course. I'm tired too." Lena said.

Next to her, Sophie said, "Why sit it out? Jake loves to waltz and I hate it. It's so old fashioned. You dance with Jake. You'll be doing him a favor, and me too."

Lena started to shake her head, but Sophie had already grabbed her hand and Jake's and was pulling them together. "There," she said. "Go dance you two. I want to talk to Daniel." With a little push, she directed them toward the dance floor.

The waltz was Lena's favorite dance. It might be old-fashioned, as Sophie said, but it still had a hypnotic, dreaminess about it that she loved. This one was starting out slow. Jake put his hand on Lena's waist and held her other hand in his and they began.

Lena glanced down at the dance floor. Her heart had quickened the minute Sophie had put their two hands together.

"Are you having trouble following my lead?" Jake asked softly.

She shook her head. Jake was a far stronger lead than Daniel. With Jake there was no sense of following, only the sense of being so caught up that his movements automatically became hers.

"Don't look down," he encouraged. "You're doing fine. Look at me."

No, Lena wanted to say. But, despite herself, she lifted her face and let her eyes drift up to meet his. Once they did, she could not look away. As he held her, there was nowhere to move but with him, in the slow, rhythmic one, two, three of the dance. With eyes that never wavered from her own, Jake led her about the dance floor. If only it would end, Lena thought desperately, or if he would say something. Then I wouldn't go on feeling this way. But Jake said nothing.

The music picked up speed and they began to move faster. They circled the floor, from one end to the other, shifting direction so fast she felt dizzy. Quicker and quicker, her heart kept the tempo. And the feeling of giddiness she'd had at the start of the evening returned and grew into recklessness. Faster and louder the band played, until the beat of the music was the beat of her heart. Her feet were flying; her hair was loosened. It came all undone and fell streaming behind her.

They changed direction, yet Jake's eyes never left hers. She felt as if she were going to burst into a million pieces like a firecracker and come floating down in tiny confetti pieces. There was no one but them on the whole of the dance floor.

And then... the music stopped. They stood staring at each other, breathing hard. Around them, people were clapping for the band. Still, Jake's eyes did not leave her face. The clapping died away. The music started again. It was a slow dance.

Jake pulled her closer and breathed in her scent. He held her soft warmth against him as he steered her slowly and easily around the dance floor. All night long, he'd had to put up with watching that beanpole act like he was with Lena. Now it was his turn.

He felt strong and vital and more clear-headed than he'd ever felt in his life. It was if a space he'd not even known existed within him had been filled. It felt completely right. He didn't want the music to end; he was barely aware of the music; he was only conscious of how wonderful it felt to have his arms around her. He pulled her closer. She pulled away, free of his touch, and stopped dancing.

"No," she said in a shaky voice. "We can't do this."

"What? Of course we can."

"No." She backed up a few steps, turned, and walked away from him and off the dance floor.

He opened his mouth to say something, anything that would bring her back to his arms. But it was too late. He thrust his hands in his pockets and slowly walked off the dance floor. The evening had gone on way too long. It was time to call it a night.

CHAPTER FOURTEEN

AND THEN, SUDDENLY, THE STRIKE WAS OVER ON TERMS THAT allowed each side to claim victory but in reality, changed little. Lena and Sophie went back to work. Joe decided he like selling gloves more than cutting fabrics and stayed with his new employer. Otherwise, everything was back to usual. But nothing was the same.

In the weeks since the night of the dance, Lena had not been able to stop thinking about Jake. She recalled the feeling of being in his arms, the look in his eyes when he gazed at her, the touch of his hand on the small of her back. Her guilty conscience made her feel as if her thoughts and emotions were obvious. But, so far, neither Sophie nor anyone else seemed aware that anything was amiss. And Lena was grateful for that. Because she wouldn't be able to bear it if Sophie knew how she felt about Jake.

As to Jake's feelings for her, she didn't know what to think. The more time went by, the more she doubted her memory and perceptions of that night. Sometimes, she wondered whether she had only imagined parts of it.

And then there was Daniel. The first time she saw him after the evening of the dance, she tried not to notice the way his eyes lit up when he spied her. She even briefly considered making up some reason she could not join him at Meltzer's. But in the end, she went and sat opposite him at their usual table. She let him pay the bill, since it was his turn, but reminded him that it would be her turn next time. And she tried not to see his disappointment when she declined his offer to walk her home.

Monday morning, the sky was overcast for the fourth day in a row. Rain had been forecasted all week but not a drop had fallen yet. There was just the ominous threat of it, a malevolent force waiting to be unleashed. As she and Sophie rounded the corner onto Greene Street, only a few workers were entering the Northern building, and Lena realized it was later than they'd thought. They both dashed for the door. As they waited for the freight elevator to slowly creak down to ground level, Sophie fidgeted impatiently.

"Hurry up," she muttered.

Lena peered through the metal grate up into the shaft. "It'll be here in a minute."

"We better not be late," Sophie warned. "Max is even meaner now than before the strike."

The lift landed with a thump and Buddy, the elevator boy, pushed open the accordion gates.

"Hey Lena," he grinned. "When are you gonna go out with someone who'll treat you good?"

Lena smiled. "As soon as your mother allows you to stay up past eight o'clock."

"Aw, you been hanging around Sophie too much," Buddy said with a mock scowl. "Why does everybody gotta be such comedians?"

When they reached the seventh floor, the lift settled and Buddy opened the inner and outer grates for them. "I still got Saturday night free girls," he said as they left. "Keep me in mind."

They hurried to the sewing room entrance where Horowitz stood waiting, his heavy-lidded eyes shifting like a lizard's from his pocket watch to the hallway. Once inside, they hung their purses in the cloakroom, hastened to their seats, and got to work.

At noon, Lena shut her machine and she and Sophie headed to the cloakroom where they joined their usual lunch group. Martha Hunt, a painfully thin girl who spent all her free time at the movies, was telling everyone about the new Mary Pickford flick.

"It's called *Poor Little Rich Girl* and Mary is so sweet in it," Martha said. "Of course, she looks just adorable."

Sylvia Degarmo, a tall, statuesque beauty who wore her long dark tresses unfashionably loose, asked, "But which is she—poor or rich? She can't be both."

"She's rich," Martha said, "but her parents ignore her because they only care about making money. The servants are very mean to her too."

Frannie Caputo, a diminutive red-head, sneered. "Typical rich people. None of them care about anything except money."

"That's not true," Sophie said. "The Trade Union League ladies are rich. But they care about a lot of things besides money. They were very helpful during the strike."

"When it didn't interfere with their tea," Frannie scoffed.

Sylvia shook her head. "Sophie's right. The Trade Union League donated a lot of money to the strike fund. And many of them are involved in the women's rights movement."

Sylvia was a dedicated suffragette. She'd even participated in suffragist hikes to Albany and Washington, D.C., which just went to show that women were as physically capable as men.

"Well, anyway," Martha said, "the movie was wonderful."

Usually Lena talked as much as anyone. But today, she just listened, glad to be among friends, and content to have a break from her own thoughts. She genuinely liked all the women, but particularly admired Sylvia. Sylvia, she thought, would never waste time mooning over some man. She wouldn't either. Instead, she would re-devote herself women's rights and to her original goals. She allowed a little daydream to blossom in her mind. She saw herself finishing night school and going to college while becoming a leader of the suffrage association.

Despite her resolve, once she was back at her sewing machine, her thoughts returned to Jake and she had to repeatedly force herself to turn to other subjects. Joe's birthday was coming up and she decided she would plan a small celebration. Perhaps Sophie and Uncle Lou and Aunt Sarah would join them. They could eat in Chinatown. Joe would probably like that. Thinking of Chinatown reminded her of Jake eating with his chopsticks and acting like a know-it-all. She'd disliked him intensely in that moment. And yet....

The rest of the afternoon passed in the same way. It seemed as if quitting time would never come. At long last, it was only a few minutes away. Tony Marulo burst through the door at the rear of the workroom carrying a box filled with pay envelopes. She could probably complete another two or three blouses in the time it would take him to get to her.

At seven p.m., the quitting whistle blew. She shut her machine and slowly pushed her chair back. Tony wasn't even halfway through distributing the pay. But it didn't really matter. No one could leave yet because Horowitz had not arrived to unlock the door. The telephone on Horowitz's desk began to ring and Tony looked up. *Ignore it, Tony, Lena thought. Just give us our pay."*

Two rows in front of her, Sylvia DeGarmo twisted around in her seat, looked at Lena, and rolled her eyes. Lena shook her head. Everyone just wanted to go home. As she debated whether to celebrate Joe's birthday at an Italian restaurant instead of a Chinese one, she heard an odd crackling sound that seemed to be coming from the far side of room. She saw Tony glance at the windows. He'd heard it too.

Suddenly, there was a loud blast as the window exploded. Bits of glass pelted down like shards of hail, clicking loudly as they hit the floor. Roiling clouds of fire quickly filled the empty frame. With fast successive booms, each of the other windows exploded.

Screams filled the air as the fire spread from the windows to the floor. The blaze tore through the workroom like a hot tornado. The sound of it was deafening; the roar filled Lena's ears, muffling the cries around her. She looked around frantically; dodged to avoid being trampled by her frenzied co-workers. Through the noise and flames and chaos, she caught sight of Sophie standing on a nearby sewing table. She quickly followed suit.

From atop the table, she saw a crowd of workers massed in front of the sewing room entrance. Frantic hands were pulling at the locked door. Desperate fists were pounding on the wood. They cried out. "Help! Help us!! "Let us out!"

The only other way out of the workroom was through the door that Tony Marulo used. Lena pivoted. Workers were already there. More rushed to join them. They pinned those closest to the door against it, preventing it from being pulled open.

She had to do something. The air was so hot. Her skin felt like it was burning. Even her eyes felt hot. The heat made everything look blurry and wavy. It was hard to think.

Something close by exploded and she looked down and saw fire rushing along the table towards her. The blaze raced. It engulfed sewing machines like sacrificial offerings. It turned oilcans into torches. She began choking on smoke and oil fumes. Tears streamed out her eyes. Air. She needed air.

A girl rushing by shouted, "To the windows!"

It was Sylvia DeGarmo with her black skirt billowing behind her and her black hair flying. Something in Lena clicked at the sight of her and she looked at Sophie and nodded. They both jumped to the floor and ran toward the glassless holes in the walls where the windows had been.

At the pane-less opening, Lena faced out and filled her lungs. A crowd quickly formed behind her and she grabbed the window molding to keep from being pushed over the sill. Far below, on the street, fire trucks were parked in a tight line. One truck was almost directly below her. From its rear, the firemen extended a ladder and angled it toward the building. They pushed it out until it would go no farther and then moved it against the building where it rested several stories below the sewing room floor.

Across the street, another group of firemen manned a bulky hose. But the water, like the ladder, reached only to the lower floors of the building. Still, the fire-fighters showered the bricks in a sweeping motion, as if hoping the damp would transfer by osmosis to the upper floors.

A third cadre of firemen had formed a circle. They were grasping a huge white tarp and stretching it tight. Behind Lena, the pushing and jostling stopped momentarily. A girl had climbed up onto the ledge of the next window over and was poised on the sill, her skirts gathered in her hand. It was Sylvia DeGarmo, standing straight and tall and seemingly calm despite the fact that the bottom of her long black hair was smoldering.

She turned away from the window and looked back into the room. Her eyes were wide and vacant and Lena's heart rose into her throat. Sylvia looked out again and Lena watched as she stepped off the ledge and plunged downwards for an agonizingly long time before hitting the fireman's tarp with such force that she tore right through it.

Lena gasped in horror. The sight of Sylvia falling shook her more than anything else that had happened up to that point. The pushing and shoving against her back threatened to catapult her out the window too. This scared her even more than the fire, which was now moving relentlessly back up the aisles towards the windows. Another girl climbed on top of the window ledge where Sylvia had stood a moment ago. Without looking back, she pitched forward into the air. Lena turned quickly away. She had seen enough.

"This way," screamed Sophie, as she pushed away from the windows and started toward the cloakroom.

Lena took a deep breath then followed her. The fire had not yet penetrated the cloakroom and about a dozen workers had taken refuge there. They were crouched, whimpering, among the coats and scarves. In the rear of the cloakroom, two shutters were nailed fast to the wall. Sophie rushed toward these and began to pull and yank at one of the shutters. Though Lena had no idea what was behind them, she followed Sophie's lead and tugged as hard as she could at the top edge of the other shutter. Anna Kutler, whose seat she had taken her first day of work, furiously pulled at the bottom edge. Together they pried the shutter loose, revealing a window leading to a fire escape. Lena and Sophie forced the window open.

Immediately, a crowd of girls stampeded over shouting, "Move, move, let me in!" They shoved out onto the fire escape. Lena was pushed all the way to the edge of the platform. She was now pinned against the narrow wooden railing that ran around the perimeter of the fire escape. It was the only thing between her and the yawning chasm that ended seven stories down.

She looked around for Sophie and spotted her on the far side of the packed fire escape. There was no way she could get over there. She glanced down and shuddered. She had always been fearful of heights. Now she shut her eyes. A vision of herself pitching over the railing and into the abyss formed in her mind. The sight of Sylvia plunging from the window replayed in her head.

The fire escape creaked and shuddered, setting off cries of fear, as more and more girls pushed their way onto the platform. Lena fought the panic that was rising in her throat, cutting off both breath and rational thought. In the center of the platform, girls were beginning to make their way down the rickety steps to the fire escape just below them. Even assuming she could make her way over to the steps, Lena didn't think she could manage to get down them. She imagined losing her balance, tumbling down, falling head over heels, and being trampled. She could not bear to be in the midst of the crowd any longer.

There was one spot on the fire escape that was not crowded—the staircase leading to the floor above. Slowly, she squeezed her way over to it and climbed up a few steps. Looking down momentarily, she spotted Sophie motioning to her to return to the platform. But she couldn't. It wasn't too bad looking up, but she could not bring herself to look down again. Nor could she entertain the thought of descending any steps. Instead, she began to climb up as fast as she could.

At the eighth floor fire escape, there was no opening into the building, just wooden boards covering the place where the opening should have been. So she kept going. At the ninth floor, neither boards nor window blocked her way into the building and she could see that the room was ringed with fire but the conflagration hadn't yet spread to the entire floor.

She put one leg over the windowsill. As she did, she heard a terrible screaming from below and she reflexively looked back out the window. Down on the seventh floor fire escape, the thin perimeter railing was bending outward from the pushing and shoving. Then, as she watched in horror, the entire fire escape started to pull away with a sickening, groaning, metallic sound. The girls on the stairway, caught midway between floors, froze in fear. The fire escape remained tenuously attached to the building for one more heartbreaking moment. Then it broke free and, still filled with a mass of screaming and crying girls, it plunged to the ground.

"Sophie!" Lena tried to scream but all that emerged was a primitive, animal sound.

There was a crashing sound in the room behind her and she whirled around. A chunk of ceiling had fallen in a corner of the room. Before she could react, another chunk of burning ceiling fell even closer to where she sat straddling the window frame. She swung her other leg over the sill, picked up her skirts, and started towards the opposite side of the room where she hoped she could find the door leading to the hallway and the elevator.

The smoke was thicker now and she began to have trouble seeing where she was going. Like a blind person, she put one hand out in front of her. Breathing had become a struggle again. She felt like she was suffocating but instinctively reached into her pocket, pulled out her handkerchief, and spread it over her nose and mouth as she stumbled forward. Her outstretched hand hit something solid and she fumbled for the exit. She found a knob, turned and pulled it, pitched herself through the opening, and shut the door behind her. Hysteria bubbled up in her. She was almost there. She needed only to get to the elevator.

She ran down the hall to the shaft and peered over the iron accordion gate. Far below her, the elevator was making its way up. It rose slowly, and creakily, and stopped at least two floors below her! She heard the sounds of the grates sliding open and could see the elevator shake very slightly as it filled up with people. Then the gates clanged closed and the elevator began to descend.

"Wait!" she screamed. "Don't leave."

Her words echoed in the empty shaft as the elevator went further and further down. She spun around and quickly reviewed her options. She could not go back the way she had come. She could not stay where she was. She turned back to the elevator shaft and stared down into the blackness. The elevator had begun its slow ascent again. It was coming closer and closer. She screamed as loudly as she could.

"Buddy, I'm up here. It's me, Lena. Please come and get me. Up here!"

Once again, the elevator stopped far below, tantalizingly out of reach. In despair, she heard the elevator gate slam shut again and the car again began its slow descent. She felt the heat of the fire at her back and willed herself not to turn around, afraid that if she saw what was there, she would lose what little ability to think she still had.

The only thing before her was the empty elevator shaft. In the middle of the shaft were the fat black elevator cables that connected to the top of the elevator car. Which would be worse, she thought, to stay where she was and burn to death or to try to reach the cables and, if she missed, be killed by a fall down the elevator shaft?

For a moment, she felt as if all of this was happening to someone else, as if she were watching it from afar. The clanking sound of the elevator brought her back to reality. Once again, she heard the elevator stop. It was not coming her way. She locked her eyes on the elevator cables. They were within reach, she told herself. She could do it. She took the handkerchief from her mouth, slipped it into her pocket, squeezed it for luck, and whispered, "Please, mama." Then, she leaped into the darkness and reached for the cables with both hands. Her palms burned as they slipped along the fat black cords but she hung on, trying to wrap her legs around them for added gripping power.

The top of the elevator broke her downward slide with a sudden jolt that sent shockwaves up her spine. For a moment, her eyes felt warm, her ears slightly clogged, and her head light as she fought nausea and the sensation that she was about to faint. With an effort, she forced herself to concentrate on remaining conscious as the elevator slowly descended.

A sudden thump and cessation of movement told her that the elevator had landed. Beneath her, she heard the sound of the accordion gate sliding open. The whole car vibrated lightly as it emptied out and she banged on the top, screaming. "I'm here, I'm here." Nothing happened. She heard the gate clang shut and, with a sudden jerk, the elevator started to move up again. She looked above her. Flames had burst into the shaft so that she was now moving directly toward swirls of red-hot haze. She screamed for Buddy to stop. But the elevator continued to rise.

Terrified, like a demonic toddler throwing the biggest temper tantrum of her life, she beat her fists and feet as hard as she could on the elevator roof and screamed at the top of her lungs, "STOP! STOP! STOP!" Then, just as suddenly as it had started, the elevator stopped. It hovered.

She screamed again as loudly as she could. The elevator started to move and she realized that it was going down. Exhausted, she lay limp on the top of the car. The elevator continued its downward course until the top of the car was even with the lobby of the building. Strong hands reached out and helped her off the roof of the car. She stumbled as she was set down gently on the floor and blinked rapidly, half-blinded by the light of the lobby after the blackness of the shaft

She glanced around but her eyes were still having trouble focusing so she squeezed them shut. Instantly, she saw again in her mind the swirling flames and felt herself moving upwards to be devoured by them. She opened her eyes and willed herself to see.

Firemen were herding workers, ash-covered and crying, toward the exit where police officers stood preventing distraught family members from entering. Relatives leaned over and around the officers and called for their sisters and mothers and daughters to answer them. They broke down sobbing when they got no response.

Lena couldn't stand it anymore. Walking unsteadily, she headed for the exit. The brightness of the day caught her by surprise. It felt like the world should have ended, but it was still there. A huge crowd of gawkers had gathered. Their necks arched backwards, their faces pointed at the windows of the burning building. The fire trucks were still in place, their useless ladders sticking up like vestigial appendages. The ground adjacent to the building was a cemetery of sheet-draped bodies. Which one was Sophie? Lena could not bear to look.

She turned her back on the devastation and began walking home, her pace slow, deliberate, her focus on heel, sole, toe, heel, sole, toe. She reached her building, walked up the stairs, went into the empty apartment, and then into her bedroom where she lay down on the bed, curled up in a ball, and started shaking. Her teeth were chattering so hard that it hurt her head and she tried clamping her jaw shut. But it didn't help. She reached for the wool blanket folded at the foot of her bed and pulled it around her but she still shook uncontrollably. She felt as if she was fighting to keep her body in one piece.

Suddenly, there was a pounding sound that she heard as if in a dream. It seemed to come from very far away and she couldn't quite figure out what it was. But the pounding got louder and she realized that someone was knocking on the door.

CHAPTER FIFTEEN

JAKE STOOD IN THE ENTRANCE, BAREHEADED AND SWEATING. HIS coat and tie were askew. He was breathing hard as if he had been running. His voice broke as he said, "Thank God you made it out of there!"

She started to sway. He caught her just before she passed out. When she came to, she was lying on her bed. She started to sit up and he slipped an arm around her back to support her. Then he reached into his back pocket and pulled out a flask.

"Here, drink some of this."

She took a sip. The alcohol burned the back of her throat and she choked a little.

"Try again," he coaxed.

Obediently, she took another sip and then another.

"Feel better?"

She nodded and sat all the way up. He went over to the wash-stand, took the towel that was hanging over the edge, and poured some water over it. Then he sat on the bed and wiped her face gently. The cool cloth felt good. It was only then that she realized how hot her face was. After a bit, he put the cloth down and waited.

"Can you talk?" he asked.

She nodded and the words began almost of their own accord. "We were waiting for our paychecks," she said. "We just wanted to go home."

She talked on and on, reciting the facts but not her feelings. She knew instinctively that she was not ready to re-live her emotions. She wasn't sure she ever would be. But she felt compelled to include every single detail of the fire as if it was too soon to figure out which parts were important and which were not. When she reached the part about the fire escape, she shook her head in bewilderment.

"It just pulled away," she said. "And I saw her. I saw Sophie. She was standing right near the stairs but she was still on the platform. It was separating from the building and she was still on it. And then the whole thing... it just went crashing down."

She paused and looked at Jake to see if he could make any more sense of it than she could. His eyes had filled with tears and his face was contorted. But he didn't say a word. So, she continued. She didn't stop again until she had told him everything.

When she was done, Jake sat perfectly still. She could see that he was lost to some inner turmoil, fighting some kind of battle with himself. The sight of his shoulders shaking was the first sign that he was losing the struggle. He covered his face with his hands and shuddered and then his whole body began to heave. Lena's heart broke for him, for Sophie, for all the women and men and children trapped by the fire, and for the immense tragedy of it all. She stroked his back gently, letting him cry for as long as he needed. After a bit, the sobs grew less. Finally, they stopped.

He uncovered his damp face and turned to her. The grief in his eyes was even more naked than his sobs. The rawness of his anguish broke through the shell in which she'd been ensconced and she erupted in sobs. He put his arms around her while she buried her face in his chest and cried. When she finally calmed down enough to pull away, his face was still wet with tears. She reached up to wipe away the wetness but he caught her hand in his, and pressed her palm to his cheek. She caught her breath.

Slowly, giving her plenty of time to say no, he moved her palm from his cheek to his mouth and kissed her hand. After that, he leaned forward and kissed her lips, softly at first and then again. His lips were soft but strong. As he kissed her over and over again, with increasing intensity, her hunger for him grew; so did her need.

He paused suddenly, pulling away and looking at her with questioning eyes. But she would not let him stop. She grasped his shirt and pulled him into a kiss. He leaned forward as she lay back down on the bed. His tongue, surprising at first, probed her mouth. It was questioning, but then sure and deft and oh-so-pleasurable, a sensation she had never imagined. She wanted so much for him to hold her. She wanted to feel safe. And, at the same time, she wanted to be taken away, transported somewhere where the nightmare she'd just lived through didn't exist. She undid the buttons on her blouse. She moaned when he kissed her breasts. She became aware of an empty space inside her that achingly and urgently needed to be filled. When at last he thrust inside her, the momentary searing pain felt somehow right.

But then, as he continued, that raw sensation faded and was replaced with a deeper more complex feeling; one that was satisfying, dizzying, and frustrating all at once. It was a feeling that intensified until rational thought, any thought, was gone and there was nothing but a pulsing rhythm that carried her to a place close to a frenzy. And then there was a bursting inside her that made her feel like all her body was filled with warm liquid.

Afterward, she started to cry. Looking confused, he rolled away to sit on the edge of the bed. But it was not regret that made her cry. She reached out and touched him gently on the back and he turned to look at her.

"It's alright," she said.

"I'm sorry," he began.

She shook her head and put a finger to his lips to silence him. "Don't be sorry," she said. "I'm not."

"But with the state you're in, I shouldn't have taken advantage."

"You didn't. Perhaps I took advantage of your state. Anyway," she paused, then forged ahead, wanting and needing to tell him. "I love you."

"I love you too," he said.

"You don't have to say that."

"But it's true. I think I've been in love with you since the first time I saw you."

"I wanted to believe that you felt something," she said. "But I wouldn't let myself. Because of Sophie."

At the sound of Sophie's name, Jake's face folded. "I still can't believe it. I can't believe she's dead."

"I know. I can't believe it either." Tears pooled swiftly and spilled down her cheeks. Jake lay back down and fitted his body next to hers. And after a while, with his arms around her, she fell into a deep, dreamless sleep.

CHAPTER SIXTEEN

THE SOUND OF A DOOR CLOSING WOKE LENA UP. WHEN SHE HAD drifted off to sleep, the room had been sliding from shadow to darkness. Now, it was daylight. She was alone in the bed and could hear voices in the kitchen: Aunt Sarah's and Uncle Lou's, and Joe's. Dear Joe! How she loved him. She listened for another minute but didn't hear Jake's voice. Momentarily disappointed, she quickly realized it was for the best. She would tell them all about her and Jake eventually. But for them to find out now, in the wake of Sophie's tragic death, would be unseemly.

She sat up and moving, discovered that her body ached all over. Her blouse was still open and she carefully re-buttoned it before walking into the kitchen. Aunt Sarah was stirring something on the stove. Uncle Lou and Joe were at the table reading newspapers. Joe noticed her first and, striding over, enfolded her in an embrace that was simultaneously fierce and gentle.

"Thank God," he murmured. "Thank God." A ragged sobbed escaped before he caught himself. Letting her go, he wiped his damp face with his hands and took a deep breath.

"You're alright?" he asked.

"Yes."

"You're sure? Because the whole time I was on the train coming back from Buffalo, I kept thinking—if anything happened to you—"

"I'm fine," she said. "Really."

She looked beyond him at Aunt Sarah, who was dabbing at her eyes with her apron, and Uncle Lou, who was nodding at her with a smile on his sweet face.

"I'm fine," she said. "But Sophie…"

"We know," Aunt Sarah said. "Our poor Sophie. It's a miracle that she wasn't killed. As soon as I make you something to eat, we're going right back to the hospital to see her."

Lena stared at her. "Sophie is -"

"At Bellevue hospital," Uncle Lou said. "In the critical care ward."

"She's alive?"

"Thank God," Aunt Sarah said.

"But in bad shape," Uncle Lou added, shaking his head. "Very bad." He looked at Sarah. "We really have to leave now. The doctor said he would talk to us at ten o'clock."

Aunt Sarah looked torn. She pointed her finger at Joe. "You make sure she eats something. And rests."

"Of course," Joe said.

"Well then…" Aunt Sarah bustled over, hugged her gently and caressed her face with the palm of her hand. "*Shayne Maidele*," she said.

From the doorway, Uncle Joe blew her a kiss. "We'll see you soon. You get some rest."

After they were gone, Joe shepherded her over to the table and she sank onto a chair. But when he put a plate of eggs and toast before her, it was all she could do to eat a bite or two. Afterward, she went back to bed, feeling more tired than she could ever remember feeling in her whole life. Yet sleep did not come easily. And as she lay there, all she could think was: *Thank God, Sophie's alive. But, oh God, what have we done?*

It wasn't until two days later that Joe gave in to Lena's pleas and deemed her strong enough for a visit to the hospital. Uncle Joe and Aunt Sarah had warned her of Sophie's condition, but nothing they'd said prepared her to see her friend's face so devoid of color it looked as though she were made of wax. Her arms, wrapped in bandages, were at her side. Her protruding hands looked waxen too. Aunt Sarah reached down and covered Sophie's hand with her own.

"Sophie dahlink," she said softly. "Wake up. Someone has come to see you. Lena and Joe are here with us today."

Sophie lay as still as before. There was no sign that she had heard or understood anything. Lena forced a swallow to ease the tightness in her throat.

"You look pale," Joe said to her. "I'm going to look for some chairs for you and Aunt Sarah."

Lena watched Sophie, saw the slight rise and fall of her chest. Please God, she prayed. Please, let her live and be fine and strong and back to the way she was. She was so engrossed in her thoughts that she didn't hear the approaching footsteps. The sound of Jake's voice broke her reverie and her heartbeat quickened as it always did when he was near.

"Lou." Jake seemed to be right behind her. "How is she today?"

"The same."

Jake walked around to the other side of Sophie's bed. Lena risked a quick glance and their eyes locked. His gaze was steady. She read no regret in them, only intensity of feeling, and knew that, despite the circumstances, nothing was changed between them.

"How are you feeling?" he asked her.

Before she could speak, Joe, returning with the chairs, answered for her. "I'm taking her to see a doctor later today."

"Good idea," Jake said. "And it's good that you're here to take care of her."

Aunt Sarah looked offended. "And she has us too, Uncle Lou and myself. "

"Of course," Jake said. "It's just that you're bound to be spending a lot of time at Sophie's side right now. Just as I will be. All I'm saying is that it's good Joe is here so he can take Lena to the doctor and take care of her when you're busy."

Aunt Sarah seemed mollified by this explanation and Jake turned his attention to Sophie. But Lena understood his message perfectly. Right now, his place was here, by Sophie's side. There would be time later to figure everything else out. After a few more minutes, Joe touched her shoulder.

"I don't want you to overdo it on your first day out. I think we should go home now."

She nodded and stood up. Joe walked over to Aunt Sarah and Uncle Joe and said something to them. He put a hand on Jake's shoulder.

"I'm sure we'll be seeing you here again," he said.

"I'm sure, you will. I'll be here every evening for as long as it takes Sophie to get well."

Lena looked at Sophie one last time, then turned away. Joe put his arm around her and shepherded through the ward.

CHAPTER SEVENTEEN

AS THE DAYS PASSED, LENA FELT AS IF SHE WAS LIVING IN A PARALLEL universe, one that was both the same and completely different than the universe in which she had lived before the fire. Things she'd been passionate about, like her English classes and suffragette meetings, failed to hold her attention. She knew she should probably look for a new job, but could not bring herself to peruse the want ads much less actually go out and apply for anything. She had no desire to read the endless articles and editorials about the fire.

She was aware that a day of mourning had been declared and that nearly half a million people, had marched down Fifth Avenue to honor the 148 victims. But she stayed away. And when a list of the dead was published, a group that included skinny Tony Marulo, the distributor of the pay envelopes, Sylvia DeGarmo, her fellow suffragette, and fierce Anna Kutler, whose seat she had taken the first day of work, she did not even look at it. Although the doctor said she'd suffered only scrapes and bruises as well as the slightest bit of smoke damage to her lungs, Joe insisted she take it slow until she was feeling completely well. He fussed over her like a mother hen. She didn't feel like she needed fussing over. She didn't feel anything besides exhausted.

Every morning, she accompanied Aunt Sarah to the hospital to visit Sophie. Every afternoon she took a nap but awoke feeling as tired as when she'd laid down. Every evening, Uncle Lou visited Sophie. He told them that Jake came to the hospital after work and sat at Sophie's side for hours.

Daniel made several attempts to visit before finally catching her home and awake. She sat with him at the kitchen table while Aunt Sarah made tea and she tried very hard to act like she felt fine to ease his obvious concern. When he asked when she thought she might be ready to come back to school, she changed the subject.

"Have you heard yet about your application to City College?" she asked.

"Not yet. But they've got it. I received a letter from them thanking me for applying."

She tried to smile encouragingly at him. But all she really wanted was for him to leave. She was really very tired. When he finally said goodbye, she went into her bedroom, lay down and cried.

Another day, Catherine Graham Carter, the heiress who had once joined the Dear Heart picket line and been carted off in a paddy wagon, came to visit. She told Lena and Aunt Sarah that if there was ever anything else she could do for them, they should just ask. A relief fund had been set up by the Ladies Trade Union League to provide funds for the survivors of the fire and the families of the victims and she gave Lena a packet of cash. Despite the money, Lena knew she needed to find a job. Several weeks after the fire, she finally forced herself to go job hunting. She returned home after two fruitless hours to find Aunt Sarah humming happily as she stirred something in a big soup pot on top of the stove.

"Lena!" Aunt Sarah rushed over and hugged her. "I have the most wonderful news. Our dear Sophie is awake!"

"Awake?"

"Yes," Aunt Sarah clasped her hands together. "It's a miracle, isn't it? It happened just today while I was sitting right there beside her. All of a sudden, I saw her eyes flutter and then she opened them. It was just for a few seconds and she couldn't say a word, but she knew who I was." Aunt Sarah shook her head and paused to dab at her eyes with the corner of her apron. "It's just... it's just..."

"A miracle," Lena murmured.

From the table, Uncle Lou's tone was more sober. "It's wonderful news, of course. But we have to remember that the doctors say her injuries are very severe. She still has a long way to go before. And even if she leaves the hospital eventually, she'll never be able to walk again."

"Don't be Mr. Pessimistic," Aunt Sarah said frowning. "First, the doctors said she wasn't going to live. Well, she lived. Now, they say she isn't going to walk. But if I know my Sophie, she'll not only walk again, she'll be dancing before you know it."

"From your mouth to God's ears," agreed Uncle Lou.

A vision of Sophie as she had looked the last time Lena had seen her—pale, unresponsive—flashed through her head. She tried to conjure up a new vision based on what Uncle Lou and Aunt Sarah were now saying. A Sophie who was bedridden or wheelchair bound. What kind of life would that be? And what would it mean for her and Jake, she thought, hating herself for even thinking about that.

"Does Jake know about Sophie yet?" she asked.

"Yes," Uncle Lou said. "I stopped off at the union office on the way back from the hospital just now and told him. He dropped everything and went rushing over there."

Lena nodded. Of course that's what Jake would do and what he should do. She suddenly had a desperate desire to see him and talk to him.

"Anyway, it's a miracle that she survived," Aunt Sarah said, her smile back on her face. "And if there can be one miracle, there can be more. Sophie will walk again. You'll see." She turned back to the stove and resumed humming.

Lena excused herself and went into the bedroom. She closed the door behind her, sat on the edge of her bed, and stared at the empty cot across from her. She had prayed for Sophie to live and she had meant it. But she had only imagined two possibilities—one unthinkable and the other, Sophie as she had been before the fire. She had never considered what would happen if Sophie lived but never fully recovered.

CHAPTER EIGHTEEN

LENA WAS HALFWAY UP THE STAIRS THAT LED TO THE UNION OFFICE when it occurred to her that Jake's co-workers might find her visit strange. But it was too late to turn back and her need to see him was too great. She pushed open the door hesitantly and saw a woman seated at a desk talking on the telephone. Otherwise, the office seemed to be empty. The woman hung up the phone and noticed her.

"Can I help you with something?"

"I'm looking for Jake Brenner?" she said, making it a question.

From a sofa in the middle of the room, Jake suddenly popped up. He stared at her in surprise while, Lena, startled by his sudden appearance, stared back.

"Hello," Jake finally said.

"Hello," Lena said. She glanced at the woman still sitting at her desk, then looked back at Jake. "I, uh, was wondering if you knew... I mean, of course you know, so maybe you can tell me, how Sophie is doing?"

"Of course." He sprang to his feet.

They stood looking at each other across the sofa for several seconds, not speaking. The woman at the desk looked from Lena to Jake and back to Lena again. She grabbed her pocketbook.

"I'm dying for a cup of coffee," she said. "Anybody else want one?" Without waiting for an answer, she strode to the door and left.

In two quick steps, Jake crossed the room and took Lena in his arms. "Is everything alright?" he said. "I've missed you so much."

"I've missed you too. I wanted to see you, but..."

" I know." He took her hand and led her around to the front of the sofa, sitting beside her. "How have you been?"

"Alright." Since he still looked concerned, she added, "Really." There was no need to tell him that she was still feeling tired so much of the time.

"You know about Sophie," he said.

She nodded. "I haven't seen her yet, but Aunt Sarah told me. How was she when you saw her?"

"I don't know," he said, shaking his head. "I feel like she's broken on the inside even worse than she is on the outside."

Lena glanced down and then looked back up. "Aunt Sarah believes Sophie will recover completely. But do you really think she'll ever leave the hospital?"

"The doctors say it's possible," Jake said, but his voice lacked conviction. When Lena was silent, he made his voice more upbeat. "Hey, if the doctors say it, it must be true. Me? I think anything's possible."

"Anything?" she asked.

"Are we still talking about Sophie?"

Lena glanced down again. "I feel so guilty."

"Look at me," Jake ordered her. "We didn't do anything wrong. I didn't plan to fall in love with you. It just happened. And when we were together, we both thought she was... gone."

"I know. And I don't regret anything," Lena said. "I didn't plan to fall in love with you either. I tried to stop myself and I would never have done anything about it if I hadn't thought, well, you know. But now, everything is different. Now-."

"Now we have to be patient," he interrupted her. "When she gets better, we'll figure everything."

"What if she never gets better?" Lena said, again hating herself for even asking.

Jake took a deep breath. "She will get better."

Lena was silent. She wanted to believe him. Now he was the one who looked grave and she forced herself to smile, "Anything's possible," she reminded him.

"Anything," he agreed. He put his hands on either side of her face and kissed her gently. "Absolutely anything." He kissed her again. "The possibilities are endless."

She slipped her arms around him and gave herself over to the indescribable pleasure of kissing him. While he was kissing her, anything did indeed seem possible.

But later, walking by herself back to the apartment, her optimism began to ebb. A fine drizzle was falling. The weather matched her mood. She wondered what the chances of Sophie getting better really were. If Sophie didn't get better, Lena didn't see how Jake could ever leave her. She sighed. Jake had said to be patient and she was trying to be. But it wasn't easy. Because there was something she hadn't yet told Jake.

She was late. She'd already missed one menstrual period. In a few days, she would have missed two. Of course, the trauma of the fire could have thrown her system off. But, with each passing day she felt a little more desperate, a little more panicked.

She had told no one yet. If her worst fears were true and she was pregnant, she didn't want that to be the reason for hearts to be broken or friendships to be betrayed. If it was true, it was the result of impulsive and, in retrospect, unwise behavior and she didn't want the news of it to cause still more impulsive and unwise behavior.

The rain was starting to come down more heavily, but she didn't bother to hurry. The water streaming down her face would be a good alibi for the tears she could no longer hold back. She reached into her pocket, found her handkerchief, and pulled it out. The smoke from the fire had blackened it so completely that, even now, after several washings, it was tinged a pale dove gray. It was not as soft as it had once been either. The fire had stripped it forever of its silken sheen. But the fabric was as strong as ever. The threads that made it up were still tightly woven together. And, as she wiped away her tears, she drew comfort from this as well as strength.

CHAPTER NINETEEN

DANIEL LEANED FORWARD, ARMS CROSSED ON THE TABLE, AND CON-centrated on the book propped up in front of him: an introduction to the work of Sigmund Freud. It was challenging material, but at least he could read without interruption now that he had his very own apartment. He glanced around with satisfaction. The newspaper listing had called it an "efficiency" and it was certainly that. He could sit at his kitchen table and reach his ice-box, sink, and hot-plate with no difficulty at all. The only other furniture, a bed and small chest of drawers that doubled as a wash-stand, were a stone's throw away. But tiny as it was, he was glad to have it, even though he'd had to take a second job as a door-man to afford it.

The sound of knocking startled him. It was Mrs. Calivarri, the landlady, from down the hall. A corseted bulldog of a woman, she'd grilled him the day he moved in with questions about every-thing from his employment to his bathing habits. Now, she smiled at him obsequiously when he opened the door.

"Good evening, Mr. Cowan," she began. "I'm sorry to bother you."

"That's alright. Is there something I can do for you?"

"Well," she held out an envelope. "I found this in my mailbox. I guess the postman put it there by accident." She waited as if daring him to challenge her, adding, "You know your mailbox is right next to mine."

Daniel nodded. "I know, Mrs. Calivarri." He reached for the envelope and she reluctantly let him have it.

"I noticed that it was from a college," she offered.

Daniel's eyes were glued to the return address and he nodded without looking up. This was it, he thought excitedly. This was the letter he'd been waiting for these last few weeks.

"Thank you, Mrs. Calivarri," he said as he began to close the door.

"It's important news maybe, Mr. Cowan?"

"Um, well, yes. It could be."

"That's what I told my husband," she said, pleased with herself. "I said to him, this is an important letter for that nice Mr. Cowan. And I thought I should bring it up right away."

"Yes, thank you Mrs. Calivarri. I really appreciate it."

Again he tried to close the door and again she interrupted him.

"Of course, important news can be good and it can be bad. I thought this was important, but I didn't know if it was the good kind of important or the bad kind." She waited expectantly.

"Yes, well. Thank you again Mrs. Calivarri. I'd ask you in but I've got an appointment and I must get ready."

Mrs. Calivarri's disappointment was plain. But Daniel firmly closed the door and hurried over to the kitchen table. He ripped open the letter and read it.

Dear Mr. Cowan,

We are pleased to notify you that you have been accepted for admission to the City College of New York. Additional materials will be mailed to you shortly. We look forward to having you as a member of our community.

Very truly yours,

John Robertson
Dean of Admissions
City College of New York

A slow smile spread over his face. This was it. The first step along the path he'd laid out for himself. He was really doing what he'd previously only imagined.

He couldn't wait to tell Lena because this changed everything. He'd wanted to court her for a long time now. If he was honest with himself, almost from the minute he'd seen her at night school. But, in the beginning, he'd been too shy. And, then, after he'd finally gotten the courage, the timing hadn't seemed just right. She'd seemed distracted. There was the strike, the commotion on the picket line, and her arrest.

Then, after the fire, he'd seen that she needed time, that she was shaken to her core, and that she'd come to see the world as even more unpredictable place than she'd previously believed. But he thought he could help her with this; could be a steady ship in the storm. Now, with his college acceptance in hand, he could do more than tell her, he could show her that he really was that steady ship and that she would be safe with him because his future was bright.

That night at Meltzer's, he waited until the waitress had taken their order and left, then cleared his throat.

"I'm so glad you felt well enough to come to class tonight."

"I almost didn't."

"But now that you did, it'll be easier next time." He smiled encouragingly. She smiled back and he saw her shoulders relax as some of the tension went out of them. Now, he simply needed to find some way to tell her all his news.

"I'm sorry I didn't come to see you again last Sunday," he began.

"That's alright."

"But I had a good reason."

"And what might that be?" she asked obligingly.

"Well," he said, wanting to be casual and sophisticated but unable to suppress his excitement, "I couldn't come last Sunday because I was busy moving into my own apartment."

"Daniel!" She smiled and his heart soared. "Your own apartment! Tell me all about it."

"It's very small," he said with a laugh. "More like a big closet than an apartment. But I don't have to share it with anyone. No more tip-toeing around sleeping boys."

"That's wonderful. I'm so happy for you. I know how much you've been wanting this."

"I had to take a second job to be able to afford it," he admitted. "You're looking at the newest doorman at the St. Regis hotel. Only on Sundays, though."

"The St. Regis. Isn't that where President Taft stayed when he came to New York last year? What's it like?"

"Boring for me mostly. Just holding the door for a lot of wealthy ladies and gentlemen."

"Are they grateful and say thank you? Or do they take you for granted and ignore you?"

"Some of them treat me like I'm part of the door frame. But others are kind and say a word or two. I haven't seen anyone really important yet. But one of the other doormen told me he once held the door for John D. Rockefeller."

"Rockefeller. Imagine that," Lena said shaking her head.

"Maybe you can come by one Sunday when I'm on duty," he suggested. "I'll hold the door open for you and you can feel very grand."

She hesitated for a moment before saying in a low voice, "Maybe."

Their coffee arrived and Daniel, anxious but wanting to choose just the right moment, waited until the waiter left before saying, "I saved the best news for last."

He reached into his pocket, pulled out the letter, and handed it to her. He wanted to see her expression when she read it. He was not disappointed. When she looked up, her face was glowing and her dark eyes were luminous.

"You did it," she said. "You got yourself accepted to college." She smiled and he enjoyed anew the transformation this brought to her face. The effect on his emotions was equally transformative.

"I can't believe it," she said. "I'm so happy for you."

He took a deep breath. The moment was right. She was still holding the letter and he reached over, took it out of her hands, placed it on the table, and then took her hands in his.

"Lena, you and I have been friends for a while now," he began.

"Daniel-"

"No, just listen," he continued. "Let me say this. You and I have been friends for a while and I've gotten to know you very well." He paused to take a deep breath. "I think you're wonderful. I have for a long time now."

"Daniel, I really..."

"Please let me finish. No matter what, I need to tell you this. Now, I may not have a lot to offer right now but it's not always going to be that way. I'm going to make something of myself. I've got my own place now and two jobs and I'm going to get through college and then law school after that. I think it's safe to say that I can offer you a good future. So I guess what I'm trying to tell you is, well, I hope we can be more than just friends from now on."

"Oh, Daniel," Lena sighed.

In those two words and the length of her sigh, Daniel felt his heart sink. He steeled himself for what he sensed would follow.

"Daniel, I'm not going to be coming back to class after to-night."

He stared at her. "What are you talking about?"

She gently eased her hands away from his. "I'm going away. I'm leaving New York City for good."

"But why? Where are you going? What's going on?"

She shook her head. "Please don't ask me to explain. I'm going because I have to. I don't mean to be so mysterious but I really can't explain any more than that."

"Are you in some kind of trouble? Because whatever it is, I'll help you."

She bit her lip. "This isn't just a mistake on my homework. You can't fix this Daniel." She looked into his eyes. "I'm going to have a baby."

"A baby!"

She nodded and looked down.

Daniel stared at her bent head while he tried to make sense of her words. At first, it was as if the words themselves had no meaning, so devoid was his brain of intelligent thought. And then thoughts started coming too quickly, in jerky bits and pieces of information that flew at him in no particular order as the full meaning of her words began to sink in.

He was shocked. There was no getting around that part. Beyond that, his feelings were a jumble, except for one thing. Nothing she'd said had changed how he felt about her. And right now, looking at her, her whole body trembling slightly, all he wanted to do was gather her up in her arms.

"Lena," he said, feeling helpless before her obvious distress. "It's alright. Everything will be alright."

She looked up and he saw that her face was streaked and that her eyes were still full of tears. She opened her mouth to say something then shook her head, giving up even the effort.

"It's alright," he repeated. "You don't have to tell me any... any details if you don't want. But," he leaned forward, "that's no reason for you to leave town. To the contrary, you're going to need your friends more than ever. And your brother, does he know? Surely, he's told you the same thing."

"Joe knows," she said in a broken voice.

"And what does he say?" Daniel demanded.

"He doesn't want me to go."

"I thought so." He took a deep breath. "Can I ask you a question?"

She nodded.

"Does," he hesitated, "does the baby's father want to marry you?"

Lena's eyes were bleak. She shook her head. "That isn't going to happen. There are... reasons."

Daniel thought about this new information. She wasn't going to marry the father of her baby, so maybe she didn't love him. And if she didn't love the guy who'd done this to her, then there was still a chance she might come to love himself. Besides, he reasoned, she would need him now. More than ever.

"Marry me," he said, knowing as the words shot out of his mouth that it was exactly what he wanted.

"What?"

"Marry me." He searched her eyes, willing her to see how serious he was. "I'll take care of you. And the baby. That way you won't have to leave. You can stay near your brother and you won't ever have to worry about anything."

Lena's eyes filled with tears again. "Oh Daniel. That's very kind of you, but..."

"I mean it. I know my place is too small, but we could get a bigger place. I could ask Kresge's for a raise or ask for more hours from the St. Regis."

"No," she said softly. She shook her head slowly back and forth. "I'm not going to do that to you. You have a wonderful future ahead of you and I'm not going to let anything get in your way. You have to go to college and then law school. You can't do that with a wife and baby to support. It's very, very kind of you to offer, but no."

"We can make it work," Daniel told her, as she continued to shake her head no. He thought fast, trying to come up with answers to her objections. "I'll still go to college. I'll just work the extra doorman hours around my classes."

"Daniel, college is going to be hard enough. You don't need a wife and baby around to slow you down."

"But..."

"No," she said in a way that sounded very final. "Thank you. But no."

Daniel was quiet. It was obvious that he was not going to convince her of anything right now. And he couldn't really blame her. After all, he might be a prospective college student but, right now, he was just a shlepper and a doorman. His mind racing, grasping for a solution, he switched tracks.

"Where will you go?" he asked.

"I'm going to a town called Liberty. I'll be working for the owners of a small hotel."

"Liberty?"

"It's in the Catskill Mountains. It's supposed to be a beautiful area and good for one's health."

"But how did you find a job so far away?"

"I went to Catherine Graham Carter for help."

"The lady from the Trade Union League?"

"Yes. She told me when she visited that if she could ever be of any assistance to me, I need only ask. I doubt she actually expected me to do it though."

"It must have taken courage to go to her."

"It did. I stood on her doorstep for a long time before I got up the nerve to ring the bell. And Daniel," she smiled a little, "you should have seen the look on her butler's face when he opened the door and saw me standing there. He wanted to send me around to the servants' entrance. When I told him that I was there to see Mrs. Carter, he asked if I had an appointment."

"Did you?" he asked.

"No. But I told him that she had invited me, which was sort of true. Anyway, he made me wait outside while he asked Mrs. Carter, but then he came back and let me in. The house was so beautiful and elegant. I felt very out of place."

"But," she continued, "Mrs. Carter was wonderful. I didn't want to deceive her so I told her about my condition and she never said a word or even looked disapproving. I said that I needed a job and that it had to be away from the city. She remembered that her former cook had left the city with her husband to open this small hotel."

"Good for you," he said although it was the opposite of what he wanted to say. "It sounds like a very good situation."

"Really?"

He ignored the fact that his heart was breaking and said firmly, "Yes. It's going to be fine. After all," he tried to make his voice lighter, "it's not so far away. And just think of all that fresh air."

"Yes, that part will be wonderful."

"Will you write and tell me when you get settled?"

"If you really want me to."

"Of course I do."

The waiter brought the bill and Daniel stared unseeingly at the numbers. He still couldn't believe that this was the last time they would be sitting together like this. Was he supposed to simply let her get up and walk out of Meltzer's and out of his life? He had never felt so powerless.

Outside the restaurant, he couldn't stop shivering even though the air was unseasonably warm. Everything about the moment seemed magnified, so that, as a woman rounded the corner and passed them, he noticed the clicking of her heels against the pavement and the crackly sounds of the shopping bags dangling from her hand as they crushed against each other.

"Can I at least walk you home?" he asked Lena.

"I think it would be better if you didn't," she said. She put out her hand and he took it in his. He wanted to hold it forever, to keep her beside him by sheer force of his desire.

"I know I don't have to wish you good luck in college because I know you'll do well. And I'll be so proud of you. You're really—," her voice broke and she didn't finish the sentence but only said, "Good bye Daniel."

"Goodbye," he said, forcing the word out of his throat.

She turned and walked away and he watched her go. When he could see her no longer, he instinctively felt that he must start to walk in order to resume breathing. He thrust his hands in his pockets and took long, deliberate strides, his heels hitting the pavement with precision and force. He focused only on walking this way, as if it were the only thing he cared about at that moment. His right hand in his pocket brushed against the letter from the college, and he curled his fingers around it tightly, crushing it. Then he turned and, maintaining his speed, strode hard in the direction of his new apartment.

CHAPTER TWENTY

Jake looked up from his desk at the sound of the office door opening. As soon as he saw it was Lena, he felt his spirits lift. Beauty and brains. How the heck had he ever gotten so lucky? He couldn't wait for Rose to leave so he could take Lena in his arms.

As if she'd read his mind, Rose stood up, grabbed her coat from the back of her chair and announced, "I guess I'll go and get a cup of coffee."

He wondered whether Rose knew or at least suspected that something was going on between him and Lena. Well, Rose might or might not say anything to him about it later, but he was sure she would never say anything to anyone else. Right now, he was just happy to see her go.

"There's no need for you to leave," Lena told her. She turned to Jake. "I just stopped in on my way to visit Sophie and I was wondering if you would like to come with me."

Jake was bewildered. They'd made it a point never to visit Sophie at the same time, much less together. "Are you sure you want to visit Sophie right now?" he asked.

"I'm sure."

"Alright," he said. The wheels of understanding tried to churn in his brain, but like mismatched gears, nothing was clicking. He walked over to get his coat. By the time he'd put it on, Lena had already started toward the door.

Outside, she began walking briskly in the direction of Bellevue. Jake longed to move closer and put his arm around her. But, he restrained himself. At times, the city could be a very small town. He knew a lot of people and a lot of people knew him—and Sophie.

"Is everything alright?" he asked cautiously.

"Fine."

He couldn't keep the frustration from creeping into his voice. "Do you really think visiting Sophie together is such a good idea?"

"Yes." she said shortly. "I think we should have done it a long time ago." She hadn't yet looked at him or broken stride.

Jake risked grabbing her elbow. "Lena, slow down and talk to me."

She glanced over at him. "What do you want to talk about?"

"Well," he began, then stopped. Obviously something was very wrong, but it was clear he was going to have to wait until she was ready to tell him. He fell silent, following her lead.

Lena broke the silence first. "I found a job today."

"You did—that's wonderful," he said warily. "Is it in a union shop?"

"No."

"What? Look, I know you've been desperate to find work, but how can you go with a non-union shop. Especially after everything that's happened?"

"It's not in the trades. It's in a hotel," she said tersely.

"Oh, a hotel, that's great. What will you be doing?"

"A little bit of this and a little bit of that," she said.

"Which hotel is it?"

"I don't think you know it."

They had reached the front entrance of Bellevue and she pushed through the heavy front doors.

"Lena," he touched her shoulder. "Stop. Look at me. What's wrong?"

She looked at him, but her affect was neutral. When she spoke, her voice was flat.

"Let's go see how Sophie's doing," she said. He followed helplessly as she forged ahead.

Sophie was lying still in the same bed she'd been in from the beginning. A nurse was re-arranging her blankets as they approached.

Lena waited until she was done, then asked, "Please, can you tell me how she's doing?"

"She's doing better every day," said the nurse with a fixed smile.

Lena went to stand on one side of Sophie and Jake automatically went to the other.

"Sophie," Lena said gently.

Sophie's eyes fluttered open. "My two favorite people," she said in a weak voice.

Lena smiled. "You're looking wonderful today."

Sophie said nothing, but the smile on her face faded a bit.

"You are," urged Jake. "How are you feeling?"

"Like dancing," Sophie whispered.

"And you will," Jake said with forced enthusiasm.

"Yes," Lena said. "You have to be patient."

Sophie made no response to this, and there was an awkward silence, while Jake searched for something to say. But, Lena beat him to it.

"I have something I must tell you, Sophie dearest, although it isn't easy for me."

For one brief instant, Jake had this crazy feeling that Lena was about to tell Sophie about the two of them. She'd been acting so strange, he felt like he didn't know what she might be capable of saying or doing.

"I got a job," Lena said.

"That's wonderful," Sophie said "What kind of job?"

"As a chambermaid."

Sophie nodded sleepily, her energy already seeping away.

"In a hotel." Lena paused, then added, "In the Catskill Mountains,"

The look in Sophie's eyes as they flashed back open matched the shock Jake was feeling. He shot a look at Lena. "What did you say?"

But Lena didn't, wouldn't look at him and when she spoke it was to Sophie alone that she directed her words. She reached down and took Sophie's hand.

"Dearest Sophie, I won't be able to visit you every day for a while. But I'll write to you."

Sophie frowned. "It's too far away," she whispered. She looked at Jake imploring. "Tell her Jake," she begged.

"Sophie's right," Jake said woodenly. His throat felt painfully engorged, like something had suddenly swelled up in it. The Catskill Mountains were hours away by train. What the hell could she possibly be thinking to be accepting a job so far away? Unless she wanted to get away. But why? What had he done that could cause her to want to leave him like this?

Lena was still focusing solely upon Sophie. "So, dear, darling Sophie, this is goodbye for a while."

Sophie's eyes filled with tears. "What about Joe?" she asked, though speaking at all was clearly a huge effort by this time.

"I've already told him and he understands," Lena assured her. "Please try to understand too. I have to do this. And now," she patted Sophie's hand. "now, I really must leave." She bent over and kissed Sophie's forehead.

Pulling away, she kept her head down as she moved around the bed and walked past Jake and toward the exit. He watched her, too stunned to move.

"Lena, wait!" he called.

He heard Sophie say softly to him. "Are you leaving too?"

"No. I'll be right back, I promise."

Then he went after Lena. Out in the hall, he caught up with her in a few quick strides.

"What the hell is going on?" he demanded.

"I'm leaving," she said grimly, without breaking pace.

"But why?"

"Isn't it obvious? Don't you see that it's not going to happen?"

"What are you talking about?" He grabbed her by the arm, spinning her around to face him. "Just stop for a minute. What are you talking about?" he repeated.

"Us. We're not going to happen," she said without visible emotion. "It's impossible."

"Why? Why is it impossible?"

"Because of Sophie," she said wearily as if explaining for the tenth time to a child why he couldn't have a piece of candy. "I'm not going to do it to her. I can't."

"Listen," he said. "There's no need to decide anything right now. Let's just wait a little while until Sophie's doing better. Then, in a few months, we'll explain to her that what happened between us wasn't something we planned, that it was just something that happened. We'll talk and we'll work it out."

Lena shook her head stubbornly. "I can't wait a few months," she said.

"Why not?" Jake demanded.

Lena looked down. "I just can't, that's all."

"Are you—are you pregnant?" he asked hesitantly.

She shook her head. "No."

"So, what's this about then? Are you saying that you love Sophie more than you love me?"

"No! Never!" Lena's eyes flashed. And for a moment, he saw in them the passion that matched his own.

She shook her head and said fiercely, "I love you more than anything or anybody. I always will. But I have to live with myself too. And I couldn't. Not when the price for having you is Sophie's destruction." She looked deeply into his eyes, searching for something. He only wished he knew what it was.

"You *know*," she said. "You know it would kill her if you left her now. I couldn't live with that. And I don't think you could either. I couldn't love a man who could."

Jake stared at her. What was she talking about? All he wanted to do was love her. Now she was saying she couldn't love him if he did? That was crazy. And why was she leaving? Why did the women he loved always leave him? Why did the man always have to be the one left to carry on, as his father had been when his mother had taken off? As he, himself, had been when his mother had taken off.

Lena took a deep breath than continued in a softer voice, "My father always taught me that you can't build happiness on someone else's misery."

Jake shook his head. "What the hell does that mean? What about our misery? Is it fair if we're miserable?"

"Fair?" Lena said. "You want to talk about fair? Well, none of it's fair. Is it fair that hundreds of people, who other people loved, are dead because of a fire in a factory? Is it fair that Sophie will be crippled for the rest of her life? Life isn't fair. I learned that a long time ago."

She started walking again, but he caught up with her and stepped in her path, forcing her to stop yet again. He stared at her hard but saw nothing in her face that explained her actions. She said she loved him, but words were cheap. She obviously didn't mean it. Not if she could leave him like this. He would never have left her. But maybe women were different, he thought. Maybe they meant something different when they said they loved you. His mother had often told him that she loved him too. Right up until the day that she'd left.

So, maybe Lena meant something different when she'd said she loved him. Or maybe she didn't really love him at all. Actually, it didn't matter which it was. It wasn't what a person said or felt, it was what they did that mattered. And if leaving him was what she wanted to do, then, to use the phrase she'd brandished at him just moments ago, she wasn't the woman he'd thought she was. Anyway, one thing was for sure. He wasn't going to let himself be hurt again.

He made his own face purposely expressionless. He wouldn't waste either sorrow or anger on this person that he now saw he didn't really know. She stepped around him and started moving toward the exit again. He didn't try to stop her. What was the point? Instead, he turned around and started walking back to where Sophie lay waiting for him.

CHAPTER TWENTY-ONE

LENA WALKED WITH JOE INTO THE POLISHED GRANITE CONCOURSE OF Grand Central Station and, looking around, was a little overwhelmed. The vast terminal was indeed grand, with its hundred-foot ceilings, curved stone staircases, and immense windows. It made her feel very small and a little lost. Joe steered her to a corner, set her bag on the floor, and smiled reassuringly. Since the day she'd told him about her pregnancy, he'd been a rock. Instead of recriminations, he'd given her a long, protective hug and focused all his attention on her well-being. He'd approved of her plan to leave the city, but been distressed they would be separated by so many miles.

"Maybe I can find some work near you," he'd said.

Lena smiled at him. "And what would you find to do in the Catskill Mountains? It's mostly farmland. There's not much demand for garment cutting and no big department stores for you to sell gloves to."

"You think gloves are all I can sell?" Joe said. "Wasn't it you who said I could sell anything? Maybe I can sell tractors or seeds to farmers. Anyway, I could learn to do farm work if I had to."

"Well, you don't have to." She made herself sound confident. "I'll be fine."

"I guess so. And, don't forget, I'll be visiting at least once a month."

Despite her bravado, as they waited for the train to be announced, she tried to keep her thoughts unfocused, afraid that if she acknowledged what was happening she would fall apart. When Joe touched her shoulder and nodded, she knew it was time to board. He walked her downstairs to the platform, where a porter relieved him of her bag. Suddenly, she felt a desperate wish for everything that had led to this moment to be undone.

Hot tears filled her eyes as she hugged Joe. He gave her arm a squeeze.

"I'll be up to see you soon," he reminded her.

"I know," she said, clinging to him. Was it only ten months ago that she'd thrown herself into his arms with excitement over their reunion?

"Come on," Joe said, patting her back. "Rothman's don't cry."

She nodded and took a deep breath.

"See you soon," she said.

As the train pulled away from the station, she waved through the window of her compartment until she could no longer see him. Then she fished around in her suitcase for the copy of *Anna Karenina* that Daniel had left for her as a going away gift. But it was no use. She was too distracted to read and, closing the book, she looked out the window instead.

Faster than she would have imagined, the view changed from densely-built high-rise apartments to single-story flat-roofed warehouses and then to sporadic structures of indeterminate natures. Soon there were no buildings at all, just the Hudson River, the occasional passing boat, groves of trees that obscured the water, and grazing deer who looked up startled when the train hurtled past. She was passing into unknown territory.

As the railroad traveled northwards, the sky clouded and the river took on an icy, gray look. The fast sinking sun became hidden by mountains. Lena felt the drop in temperature even through the thick glass of the train window and, shivering, she pulled her shawl tighter.

Her thoughts turned to her new employers. Mrs. Carter had told her they'd purchased the hotel after Mr. Grossman was advised to move to the country for health reasons. She also knew that they had one child already and another on the way. Other than that, the Grossman's were an unknown quantity.

Lena knew you couldn't tell anything about a person just from their name. Still, the word "gross" in Yiddish meant big, so "Grossman" literally meant big person. She conjured a comforting image of Mrs. Grossman as a fat, jolly, motherly type, like a younger version of Aunt Sarah.

On the other hand, the last landlady she'd encountered hadn't been anything like Aunt Sarah. What if Mrs. Grossman was like Joe's mean old landlady? And what about Mr. Grossman? What if he was another Max Horowitz? She knew it was no good thinking this way, but now that she'd begun, it was hard to stop. Her anxiety mounted until the wall of denial she'd been hiding behind cracked and worries popped into her mind fully formed like caption screens at the flickers. What was she doing? Why was she going off to live with people she didn't know in a town where she had no friends or acquaintances? What if her pregnancy made her feel too ill to work? And how would she be able to take care of an infant while working? She struggled to regain control. Her time would be much better spent reviewing the story she'd conjured to account for the absence of her husband—a slightly embellished version of the tale she'd told Mrs. Carter when she'd asked for her help.

She'd realized early on that it would be easier to keep the lie going if she invented a husband who was dead, rather than one who was merely absent. So, she'd presented herself as a war widow, a story Mrs. Carter had accepted without question. For the Grossman's, she was prepared to provide more information, including her husband's name, Abraham (father of the Jewish people), and an explanation for why her maiden name was the same as her married name (she and her husband had been distantly related). If pressed further, she would either invent details on the spot or feign grief too great to talk. The important thing was that the story be one she could live with forever because she was determined that her child would never be known by that ugly word—bastard.

The door to the train car slid open and the conductor stepped through. "Next stop Liberty," he intoned.

This was it, she thought. Hopefully, Mr. and Mrs. Grossman would be nice people. Hopefully, Grossman's would turn out to be a place she could stay for some time. And, hopefully, everything would work out fine. That was a lot of hopefully's but hope was all she had and she was going to hold onto it as long as possible.

Twenty minutes later, holding on was all she could think about as she experienced her first ride in a horseless truck courtesy of Sam Grossman. He sped along the narrow road, with one hand on the steering wheel and the other on a stick that grew out of the floor. At unpredictable moments, he pushed the stick or pulled it, causing them to lose momentum and then lurch forward again. As they careened around curves and jolted over bumps, he resumed the welcome speech he'd begun at the depot.

He'd been waiting for her when the train pulled in standing beside a wood panel truck with Grossman's painted on it. An apple-faced man in overalls and a workman's jacket, he'd shaken her hand with such warmth that she'd felt instantly at ease. Her comfort level increased when, after introducing himself, he immediately added, "Call me Sam."

But her equilibrium was now seeping away as they drove perilously close to wood fences and stone walls. Gripping the car door with one hand and clutching her shawl with the other, she was both terrified and mesmerized by the way the road unfurled just seconds before they drove over it.

"I hope the train was comfortable," Sam said, turning to smile at her, his eyes crinkling at the corners.

"It was fine," Lena said, a gasp escaping her as they flew over a bump. "But do you think you could perhaps go just a little slower?"

His face changed from sunny to remorseful so quickly it was almost comical. "I'm sorry. I forgot myself." He shook his head. "My wife is always telling me to drive slower on these roads. Is that better?" He reduced his speed a little and Lena's heart followed suit.

"Much better, thank you."

He shook his head again. "Sorry about that. It's just that I know this route so well. I think I could drive from the station to the hotel blind-folded."

"Why do you drive it so often?"

"I transport the guests. They mostly come by train. I ferry them to the hotel at the beginning of their stay and take them back when they leave. In the summer, I make the trip at least a half-dozen times every week, sometimes more.

"Then you have many people staying at the hotel?" she asked.

"Once we open for the season, we're nearly always fully booked. It's been like that right from the beginning, just like my wife said it would be. It was her idea to come up here, you know. Well, of course, it was my doctor's idea first. Then, once we got here, my wife said there were probably a lot of other people who needed to get away to the country for their health and that we ought to open a hotel. She said once word got out about her cooking and baking, we wouldn't have to worry about having enough business. And she was right. She always is."

Lena pasted a smile on her face, then looked away. A woman who made all the decisions and believed she was always right? That didn't sound very promising. She remembered Joe's boarding house owner again and shivered.

"Are you cold? Would you like a blanket?" Sam asked.

Lena shook her head. "No thank you." She didn't even want to think about what acrobatics Sam would employ while driving to retrieve a blanket for her.

There was a break in the wall of trees on Lena's side of the truck and in the distance she saw a small white farmhouse, it's front porch illuminated by a light glowing over the front door. For just a moment, she let a mini-fantasy bloom in her mind in which she lived in a place like that. In the summer, she would relax on the porch enjoying the fresh air. In the winter, she would sit before a fireplace and read while sipping her tea. She would -

"So, what do you think?" Sam asked, his voice cutting into her daydream.

"Oh, I'm sorry...."

"I was just asking what you thought of the place." He gestured toward the farmhouse with the front porch. "It may not look like much from here, but it's bigger than it seems. We've added rooms every year. My wife says if we build it, customers will come. And, of course, she's always been right."

Lena stared at him in surprise and looked back at the house again. As the road curved and the side of the building became visible, she saw it was much larger than it had initially appeared.

"It's lovely," she murmured.

Sam grinned as he turned the automobile down a dirt road.

"When we found it, it was practically falling down and the grounds were completely overgrown. But I've always been handy with hammer and with my wife in charge of the garden, the weeds never had a chance."

As they drew up in front of the hotel, the front door swung open. Standing on the threshold was a girl, perhaps fifteen or sixteen years old. Sam jumped down from the truck and walked around the front to help Lena out. As he did, he called to the girl.

"What are you doing Bess? It's cold out here. We won't get in any sooner by you freezing yourself to death." He shook his head, but he was grinning affectionately at the girl. "My wife." he said. "Thinks she's invincible."

Lena could barely hide her shock. Of all the images she had conjured during the long train ride, this diminutive female had not been among them. She didn't even look old enough to be married, much less the mother of one with another on the way. Bess held the door open until Lena and Sam were inside, then spun around and hurried down the central hallway.

"Come on," Sam said. "It's always warm in the kitchen."

As soon as Lena entered the brightly lit room she could see why. On one side of the room, a fire blazed in a large brick hearth. On the other side, there was a huge cast-iron oven where Bess stood stirring an enormous white-enamel pot. In the middle of the room, was a large, round, claw-footed table surrounded by six wood chairs and a high-chair containing a miniature version of Sam who stared at her curiously.

"This is David," Sam said, tousling his son's hair and sitting beside him.

Bess scurried over, took Lena's coat and shawl, and pointed to one of the remaining chairs. "Sit," she said. She tied an apron around her waist and hurried back to the stove.

Moments later, she brought Lena a steaming, hot bowl of soup. "Eat," she said. The bowl was filled with hearty pea soup, thick with chunks of carrot and tender slivers of meat. No sooner had Lena finished it then a plate of stuffed cabbage was set before her. And that was only the beginning.

Despite Sam's entreaties, Bess never joined them. Instead, she flitted back and forth from the stove to the table and back again bringing food for Lena, Sam, and little David. It wasn't until she set down a plate of cookies and poured three cups of hot tea that she finally took her son from his high chair, sat him on her lap, and looked at Lena over the top of his head.

"So, your trip was good?" she asked.

"Very good. Thank you."

"That's good." Bess nodded, then fell silent.

"Thank you so much for dinner," Lena ventured. "Everything was delicious."

In response to this, Bess attempted a nervous smile. It dawned on Lena that Bess, too, had been harboring anxieties about her coming here. She smiled as warmly as she could and was pleased when Bess's brow un-furrowed and her eyes softened. Later, after she'd helped with the dinner dishes, Bess showed her upstairs to her room, a small, cozy space with a braided blue rug, a patchwork-quilt-covered bed, and a light oak dresser adorned with a graceful oval mirror.

"I hope the room is alright," Bess said, her forehead puckered again.

Lena smiled reassuringly. "It's better than alright," she said. "It's perfect."

This time, they smiled at the same time.

Lena adjusted to life at Grossman's quickly. Together with Bess and Sam, she worked to get the dining room, twelve guest bedrooms, and common areas ready for opening day. The three of them made a good team as they laundered bed, bath, and dining room linens, cleaned and aired the rooms, washed dishes and polished cutlery, and tended the vegetable garden.

Lena's concerns about how she would take care of her baby while working were assuaged when she saw how Bess simply planted David where she could keep her eye on him, gave him a toy to play with, then went on with her business. When he tired of playing on his own, Bess made whatever she was working on into a game, giving him seeds to plant in the garden, dough to knead in the kitchen, or letting him hold the basket while she collected eggs from the chickens.

To help Bess and to prepare herself for things to come, Lena began offering to feed David, change his diapers, and give him his daily bath. One evening at dinnertime, David toddled over to her, looked up with big brown eyes, and held out his arms to be lifted him into his high chair. Lena's heart melted on the spot.

Bess looked up from her cooking and smiled. "I think he wants his Aunt Lena to pick him up," she said. From then on, she was "Aunt Lena." And when Joe began his monthly visits, the Grossmans adopted him too.

Most evenings, after David was in bed, the three adults sat in the kitchen, Sam reading in the corner rocking chair and Lena and Bess sitting at the table, knitting and sipping tea. Sometimes Sam turned in early. Then, the women's conversation became intimate. They discovered that they had much in common. There were the obvious things, like their pregnancies, and the less obvious ones. Both women harbored big ambitions; Bess dreamed of creating a grand hotel and Lena still nurtured hopes of college and a career. Though Bess's plans seemed more plausible, she refused to let Lena get discouraged.

"You can do a correspondence course," she said. "Sam's cousin did that and now he's a lawyer."

"Maybe. At least it's a possibility."

One evening, when they were in the kitchen after Sam had retired for the evening. Lena took a bite of one of Bess's pastries and said, "Your ruggelach are the best I've ever tasted. How did you learn to bake so well?"

Bess shrugged. "I can't even remember a time when I didn't have a mixing spoon in my hand. The women in my family have always been known for having a way with food. Did your mama like to cook?"

"I never really knew my mama. She died when I was just a baby."

"I'm sorry," Bess said, flustered. "I had no idea."

"It's alright," Lena said. "My papa was really wonderful. And Joe has always been so good to me."

"Still, it doesn't seem fair," Bess said. "First, you lost your mother so young, and then your father. And now your own baby has lost...." She looked down and started knitting furiously. "Mrs. Carter told us what happened," she said. "It's just so sad."

Lena swallowed. "Sam seems very excited about the new baby," she said, forcing a light tone into her voice.

Bess didn't look up. She tried to hide it but couldn't disguise the fact that she was tearing up. In a low voice, she said, "I don't think I've told you yet how sorry I am about your husband."

"Bess, I -" Lena hesitated. It was one thing for her not to volunteer the truth about her pregnancy, but to lie to Bess's face after all they'd shared didn't feel right. Bess had even confided how, during the hotel's first year, she had regularly hid in the cellar to escape the guests. She'd said that not even Sam knew she'd done that. It felt wrong to repay Bess's candor with lies.

On the other hand, telling her the truth might be a terrible mistake. Bess and Sam might be shocked, even disgusted. They might not want their children to be around her. Even if they kept her on as an employee, she didn't think she could stay if they disapproved of her. And there were other concerns too. The more people who knew her secret, the more likely it was that other people would find out... that her child would find out.

Bess was struggling to contain her sorrow over Lena's "loss." But as sad as Bess was at this moment, Lena knew if she continued to withhold the truth from her, the person who would suffer the most in the long run would be herself. She would never really be able to let down her guard around Bess, would never really be able to be herself. She'd told herself that it was simply the price she had to pay to protect herself and her child. But, she couldn't really imagine Bess and Sam judging her badly or doing anything harmful to her or her baby. And, if she was wrong about that, then she might as well find out now.

"Bess," she began, "there's something I need to tell you. And if you don't want me to stay on after you hear, I'll understand."

"Don't want you to stay! What are you talking about? We love having you here."

"Wait. Just let me talk for a minute."

"Alright. But I'm sure everything will be fine, or as fine as it can be given your loss."

"That's just it." Lena shook her head. "I never really had a husband."

"I know." Bess nodded. "Mrs. Carter told us that you lost him very early on. It's like you never even had a chance to be husband and wife. I'm so sorry."

"No. You don't understand. It's not that something happened to him. It's that I never was married." Bess stared at her confused until slowly her eyes widened and her mouth opened into an "O."

Lena pressed on. "So, if you want me to leave, I understand. I could stay until you find my replacement or I could leave before that. But if I could just stay until I find someplace else to go..."

Bess shook her head vigorously. "I don't want you to leave." She reached over and touched Lena's arm. "I'm glad you told me. But please don't say anything more about leaving. This is your home now. And it will be your home for as long as you want it to be." She looked down at her knitting, suddenly shy again. "I hope that will be for a very long time."

Lena's throat swelled with emotion and she couldn't speak. She'd never really been one to believe that her late parents were able to intervene from heaven on her behalf, but it did seem unusually fortunate that, for the second time in only a few months, she'd found someone she could love like the sister she'd never had. Even when she could talk again, it was hard to find the right words.

"I don't know what to say except thank you," she said. "And I don't know how to thank you enough."

After this confession, it seemed only natural that Lena would tell Bess about Sophie, Jake, the fire and everything that had followed. By the time she was done, Bess was staring at her transfixed.

"Did you ever tell Jake about the baby?"

Lena shook her head. "I couldn't. He would never have let me leave if he'd known. And I wouldn't have had the strength to leave either. Do you think I did the right thing?"

Bess nodded. "You did the only thing you could at the time."

The confirmation lifted another weight from Lena. She hadn't realized how much she'd needed to hear that.

"But, more important than what *I* think, how do *you* feel now that some time has passed?" Bess asked.

It was not an easy question to answer, Lena thought. A day rarely passed without her thinking of Jake. Sometimes, she felt angry at him, unfairly perhaps, for not coming after her. Surely if he'd wanted to, he could have found her. She'd told him that she was going to work at a hotel in the Catskill Mountains. Was his love so fleeting that he could not even take the trouble to make sure she was all right?

Other times, her anger gave way to doubt. Perhaps Jake had never really loved her as much as she'd thought. Perhaps she'd only convinced herself that he loved her because she wanted it to be true. The night that they'd spent together, he'd been in complete shock; his actions motivated as much by that as anything else. Perhaps all his words after that had been just a way of letting her down gently.

Still other days, she remembered how she'd felt when he'd held her in his arms. Then, she felt certain that he loved her just as she'd thought. Sometimes she let herself envision a future in which they could be together, a full blown fantasy in which Sophie recovered fully and, along the way, fell in love with a handsome doctor. In her dreams, Sophie would break the news to Jake and Jake, free of any restrictions, would suddenly appear at Grossman's to propose marriage to her. At those times, she felt a yearning for him that was as strong as it was frustrating. The memories were not enough. She wanted him. She needed him. She could not imagine ever not needing him.

But always, at the end of this daydream, she remembered the look on his face when she'd told him she was leaving. He'd tried quickly to hide the shock and hurt, but she'd seen it and it had torn her up. She could deal with anything except the idea that he was under the mistaken impression that she did not love him. If only there was some way for her to know that he wasn't sad and that he didn't hate her.

She looked up and saw that Bess was still waiting, but she shook her head. "I don't know how I feel, but what does it matter? The baby is the only thing that matters now."

Bess nodded. "We'll help you. You won't be alone in this. We're here for you."

Lena's eyes filled with tears. She reached over, grasped Bess's hand, and hoped her friend understood just how much her kind words meant.

May 1st came and with it opening day. The hotel quickly filled to capacity. For Lena, it felt odd to have her home filled with strangers. She had no idea how friendly or formal to be towards the newcomers.

She took her cue from Sam and Bess. Sam's ability to put everyone around him at ease made him a natural born hotelier. And though Bess hadn't yet completely gotten over her shyness, she still managed to make everyone feel cared for through the loving care she put into everything that came out of her kitchen. Together, they inspired an affection from their customers that soon extended to Lena. After a while, the hotel guests seemed less like strangers and more like family.

Mrs. Moscowitz, installed in room four for the entire season, clucked over her growing roundness every time she saw her, made predictions of the baby's sex, and offered suggestions for everything from how to avoid having a colicky infant to toilet training. Old Mr. Kaplan, also a full-season guest, called her "dahling" and thanked her profusely for remembering that he liked prune juice in the morning and stewed prunes every evening.

In July, Sam found a cheap used piano, carted it back to the hotel in his truck, and installed it in the dining room. The night it arrived, Mrs. Moscowitz settled down at the keyboard and played while the guests took turns singing. After some coaxing, Sam took the floor and sang *Down Where The Swannee River Flows*. He even went down on one knee just like Al Jolson. Afterwards, Joe, who was visiting, delighted everyone by performing a rendition of another popular song, *I Love A Piano*. He wasn't half bad.

With the days so full, the operating season sped by. Fortunately, Lena continued to feel well despite her advancing pregnancy. The same could not be said for poor Bess, whose morning sickness seemed to get worse the hotter the weather got. Bess didn't let it stop her though. She was there in her kitchen like clockwork, from five in the morning until eight o'clock at night.

September arrived and, with it, Rosh Hashanah and Yom Kippur. To Lena's surprise, the guests did not abandon Grossman's for the holidays. Instead, they observed the days of awe at the hotel, with a rabbi who came from Monticello to lead services in the dining room.

But as September turned in October, the weather grew much colder. The trees around the hotel burst with intense color and the sweet-crisp smell of snow was in the air. At the end of October, Sam ferried his last batch of departing guests to the station. The next morning, Lena walked out of her room and felt at loose ends. The warmth and vitality, the life and heart of the hotel were missing. Bess had told her she would feel like this. Like she was living in a ghost town. She'd said that it would take a while to get used to being able to walk into the kitchen at mealtimes without having to worry about bumping into a waiter.

It was comforting to know that they would all be back again next year. Meanwhile, there was plenty of work involved in closing the hotel down and not much time to do it if they wanted to be done before the babies arrived. Both Lena and Bess were due in less than a month, which meant anytime according to the doctor. Now, every repair inside and outside the hotel that they'd been too busy to get to during the season had to be taken care of. Sam boarded up the windows of the guest rooms for added insulation. Lena and Bess repaired tears in curtains and soaked stains from tablecloths. Together, they harvested the remaining vegetables from the garden and Bess canned what they didn't eat.

One lucky week near the end of the month, temperatures soared to summer-like highs. Lena, standing in the field in back of the hotel hanging damp pillowcases and sheets out to dry, enjoyed having a good excuse to be out of doors. She picked up the last sheet, clipped it to the clothesline, and took a minute to massage her aching back.

A gentle breeze caused the line of wash to bounce a bit. On a day like today, she thought, it wouldn't take long for the linen to dry. She would return in a little while to take everything down and, perhaps just this once, because her back hurt more than usual, she would ask Sam to carry it in for her. She started back to the hotel, but a sudden twisty twinge deep in her stomach made her pause. It passed and she started walking again. Halfway back, she felt another twinge, stronger than the first. And by the time she reached the back entrance to the kitchen door, she'd felt one more. It might be a false alarm, she thought, but she'd feel a lot better once she found Bess.

PART II

CHAPTER TWENTY-TWO

1922

DANIEL FINISHED HIS COFFEE AND PUT THE EMPTY MUG IN THE SINK. He would like to have had another cup, but it was nearly 7:30 a.m. and if he dallied any longer, he might get to work late. Not that he was in any rush to see Henry, his co-worker. But that was a different story.

In the five years that had passed since Daniel had moved into his own place, he'd finished college and gotten a scholarship to New York University Law School. He'd also parlayed his experience at the St. Regis hotel into a better paying position at the Wolcott on forty-third and Madison. Not only was the salary enough for him to stop working as a *shlepper*, but the hours were regular and didn't interfere with his classes, though it was still a challenge to find time to do all the required reading.

He closed his Corporate Law textbook and fitted the hefty volume into his leather satchel along with his Constitutional Law book. There was barely enough time between the end of his shift and the beginning of classes to grab a bite to eat and get downtown to NYU, much less stop off at his apartment to pick up his books.

As he approached the Wolcott, he saw Anthony, the night doorman helping Mrs. Hancock into a taxicab. The Wolcott had permanent residents in addition to overnight guests and, after three years, Daniel had become familiar with many of them. A few even knew that being a hotel doorman wasn't his ultimate ambition and would inquire about how he was coming along with his law studies. Julie Danvers, for example, who had graduated Smith a year ago, always stopped to chat with him.

In the hotel office, Henry was busy chatting up Annie Watson, the pretty blond bookkeeper with whom he had been flirting for at least a month. So far, she seemed to have resisted his charms.

"Hi Daniel," Annie sang out.

Henry whipped around. His beefy face grew larger as he displayed a wide lipped toothy grin. "Hey, buddy," he said. "So you made it in to work. I thought you might still be tired after Saturday night."

Inwardly, Daniel groaned. He'd taken Henry's sister out mainly to get his co-worker off his back but also, admittedly, because a guy could get awfully lonely doing nothing but working all day and going to school at night. For the same reason, he never discouraged Ms. Caliveri's attempts at matchmaking. But at least she understood that a pretty face wasn't the only thing that interested him.

"Daniel took my sister out this Saturday," Henry told Annie. "Seemed like *she* had a pretty good time." He made his voice into a falsetto. "Daniel is such a gentleman. Daniel is so smart. He says even girls should go to college." He guffawed. "Like my parents would let my sister go to college."

"They should," Daniel couldn't help interjecting. "There's no reason women shouldn't go to college."

"That's right," Annie said. "Women are just as smart as men."

Daniel smiled at her. "In some cases," he said with a quick glance at Henry, "even smarter."

Anthony sauntered into the office. "Hey you guys mind? I'd like to go home sometime in this lifetime."

"Sorry," Daniel said. He turned to Henry. "You want to be inside first?"

Henry shrugged. "Sure."

Around mid-morning, Daniel switched with Henry and took up the post at the reception desk in the lobby. It was a quiet morning. The phone hardly rang and only a couple of guests stopped by with requests. Daniel wished he could use the time to review his reading for that evening's classes, but attending to personal business was not permitted.

At noon, Henry annoyed Daniel by eating his lunch in the lobby, rather than in the office as he was supposed to. As soon as Henry had wolfed down the first bite of his sandwich, he started in. "So, Danny boy, you gonna take out my sister again?"

"I don't know Henry. I've told you before that I really don't have much time for dating."

"I know, I know. You gotta study. You always gotta study. But man," Henry exclaimed. "Ya can't study all the time. Besides," he added, "if ya get married, then ya wife can cook ya meals and clean ya clothes. Then ya got even more time for studying."

"Don't you listen Henry? I've told you before. I'm not looking to get married until I finish law school and have a real job."

"Aw. Why don't you just admit it. Ya just didn't like my sister. Have you ever met a girl ya did like?"

Once, Daniel thought. *Once I met a girl I liked a whole lot. But I had nothing to offer her. I won't make that mistake again.* To Henry he said, "There've been a few."

"Like that Julie Danvers, I bet," Henry said. "I seen the way you look at her. Ya think she's gonna go out wit' a doorman? Rich girl like her? And you not even an American yet? Man, I'd have a better chance wit' her than you, being I'm a regular citizen and all. That is if I was interested,– which I ain't. It's a good thing her old man's loaded, cause she sure don't have it in the looks department. I mean, I like blonds, but ya gotta admit, she's kinda horsey looking with them big teeth and all."

Daniel felt his face flushing as it always did when he was angry. He could have told Henry that he did enjoy talking to Julie. That she was very bright, well read, articulate, and liberal minded. But that he wasn't interested in her romantically, though he couldn't say exactly why. As for Julie's feelings, Daniel suspected she might have a slight crush on him but he also had no doubt that someday she would meet a suitable young man at a debutante ball and that he would become nothing more than a dim memory. But none of that was Henry's business, so he kept it to himself.

"Henry," he said instead, "you don't know what you're talking about, so why don't you just stop talking."

Before his co-worker could respond, there was a pinging sound that signaled the arrival of the automatic elevator and Mr. Stimson from room 416 appeared. Louis Stimson, an attorney with a thriving law practice, was not only one of Daniel's favorite tenants but also something of a hero to him. Stimson had made a side career out of taking on cases that he felt were morally worthy and providing his services at no charge to the litigants.

A month ago, the New York Times had carried a story about how Stimson had argued before the United States Supreme

Court defending a law that limited the hours in a day a laundry-woman could be forced to work. Stimson had won the case and now, the decision was being used to support laws limiting working hours in other industries as well. To Daniel, it was the perfect example of how the law could be used to change working conditions on a permanent basis and a large scale.

"Good morning, Daniel," Stimson said. "Or I should say good afternoon."

"Good afternoon, Sir."

"Good afternoon, Mr. Stimson," called Henry from where he was sitting.

"Oh, Henry. I didn't see you sitting there. Good afternoon." Stimson turned his attention back to Daniel. "So, I must ask you, have your ears been burning?"

"Sir?"

"Your name came up the other day when I was having lunch with my old friend Hayden Planter."

Daniel's eyebrows rose in surprise upon hearing the name of his Constitutional Law professor. "I didn't realize you were friends with Professor Planter, Sir."

"Yes, we've been friends for years. We went to law school together. He's seems quite fond of you Daniel. Couldn't stop talking about how brilliant you are, how you're one of the first, maybe *the* first night school student to be invited to write for the law review. That's quite impressive."

"Thank you, Sir." Daniel said, filled with both pleasure at Stimson's words and annoyance at the knowledge that Henry was close enough to hear every word.

"You know, Daniel. Perhaps we should talk a bit about your future. What hours do you work on Sundays?"

"Nine to six, Sir."

"Well, then, why don't we get together this Sunday at 7. Have dinner and a little chat. "

"I'd like that, Mr. Stimson."

"Fine then. I'll meet you right here, in the lobby."

"Thank you, Sir. I'll be looking forward to it."

Stimson nodded. "Until Sunday, then." He glanced over in Henry's direction. "Good day, Henry."

The minute Daniel closed the door behind Louis Stimson, Henry was on his feet.

"At it again, eh, Danny-boy?" he asked. "Trying to hobnob with the big wigs?"

Daniel shook his head wearily. "Louis Stimson is one of the finest lawyers in the country. He does more for the rights of the working man than practically anyone. If I could work for someone like that, I could really do some good."

"Sure," said Henry sarcastically. "And if I could have tea with the Queen of England, I could do some good too."

Determined to ignore him, Daniel said, "Done with lunch Henry?"

"I'm done. You gonna stick around and have lunch here, or do you have an appointment with the President?"

"I'm going to eat my lunch in the office as usual," Daniel told him.

"Right," Henry said. "Just stay away from Annie. I got dibbs on her. But she's probably not educated enough for you anyway."

Daniel shook his head. He was not going to let Henry ruin this moment for him.

On Sunday evening, Daniel waited in the Wolcott's lobby and tried to decide where to stand. Too near the front entrance and he would only get in the way of Andrew, the weekend evening doorman. Too near the elevator and Mr. Stimson might feel pounced upon. He moved around the lobby, sat for a few moments on one of the sofas, felt uncomfortable, and stood up again. The elevator doors opened but instead of Louis Stimson, Julie Danvers emerged.

"I didn't think you worked on Sunday evenings," she said with obvious delight as she walked over to him. "Is it a special occasion or have you changed your hours?"

"No. Actually, I'm not working tonight. I'm here because I have an appointment with Mr. Stimson. A dinner, that is," he clarified.

Julie's face registered surprise, but she hid it quickly. "Of course. I should have realized," she said. "You're not even wearing your uniform. Oh, but dinner with Mr. Stimson." She looked thoughtful, then with dawning awareness, she smiled. "How marvelous," she said. "That's a wonderful opportunity for you, isn't it? To work for Louis Stimson? I can't imagine any better first job for a lawyer."

Daniel blushed, hoping that Mr. Stimson wasn't somehow overhearing this. "Well, I don't actually know exactly what Mr. Stimson wants to talk to me about."

"Of course it's about a job," Julie said. "You surely don't think he's taking you to dinner just to discuss the mayoral election."

"No," Daniel admitted. "Still, I don't want to presume anything."

"Well, of course, you're right not to presume. But I'm sure that's what it is. You've done so well in your studies. My father always says that Louis Stimson snaps up all the brightest, most promising law school graduates and leaves none for the rest of the firms in the city."

Daniel blushed at the compliment, though he knew this last statement was not exactly true. Julie's father, James Danvers was, like Louis Stimson, a prominent attorney, but of a very different ilk. A partner in one of the city's largest and most prestigious white shoe law firms, Daniel guessed that James Danvers would never consider hiring a law school graduate with the last name of Cowan or Goldstein or Goldberg, no matter how promising or bright he might be.

But Daniel didn't bother to point that out to Julie who, for all her intelligence and innate kindness, seemed either blind to her father's prejudice or determined to ignore it. Anyway, it was nice of Julie to think so well of him. And it felt good to have someone other than himself excited about this dinner with Stimson.

"I'm afraid your opinion of my abilities is way too high," Daniel said. "But thank you anyway."

"My opinion is exactly right," Julie said. "Will you tell me how your meeting turns out?"

"If you like. I only hope that you won't be too disappointed if it turns out to be nothing like what you're thinking," he said.

Julie shook her head back and forth quickly. "Oh no. You could never disappointment me."

Daniel felt himself starting to blush and he pushed his glasses back with one finger. "Well," he said with mock seriousness, "for the record, just in case he asks me, I'm going to tell him I'm for Roosevelt for mayor."

"Oh, yes," Julie said. "Roosevelt's the best man for the job. My father thinks he's the devil himself, but Mr. Stimson is one of his biggest supporters." She paused. "Good luck Daniel."

There was a pinging sound and they both turned in the direction of the elevator. Louis Stimson himself stepped out.

"Miss Danvers," he said, smiling warmly. "How very nice to see you. And Daniel," he thrust out his hand and they shook, "I'm glad to see you too."

"It's good to see you, Sir," Daniel said, while Julie inclined her head in greeting.

Stimson looked from Daniel to Julie and back again. "I'm sorry," he said. "I didn't mean to interrupt anything."

"I was just going," Julie said quickly.

"Then please give my regards to your parents," Stimson replied.

Julie nodded. "And mine to Mrs. Stimson. Good day."

Louis Stimson waited until Julie had left the building then turned to Daniel. "Well, shall we go Daniel?"

"I'm ready when you are, Sir."

The restaurant was elegant with white tablecloths, heavy crystal glassware, and weighty silverware. Tables were set far apart from each other, lighting was subtle, and the atmosphere was hushed. The waiters were deferential, to Mr. Stimson for obvious reasons, and to Daniel sitting opposite him, by extension.

Stimson ordered first, and Daniel told the waiter, "I'll have the same." The first course was soup, pale and creamy with bits of seafood that he couldn't identify until the waiter removed the bowls and asked whether they'd enjoyed the chowder. After that, the waiter put a big plate in front of first Stimson and then Daniel with an enormous slab of steak and a fat baked potato. But the food didn't matter. What counted was the conversation.

"So, Daniel," Stimson said, "let's get to the reason I invited you to dinner. What are your plans for the future? What kind of a lawyer do you see yourself becoming? What are your ambitions?"

"Well, Sir, I hope you don't think I'm being cheeky but, basically I'd like to be doing the kind of things I read about you doing. Defending labor laws before the Supreme Court, taking on cases that can lead to real change."

Stimson looked at him intently for what seemed like a very long time and Daniel did his best to hold up under his scrutiny. Finally, Stimson said, "Those kind of cases don't always pay very well. Don't you want to make a lot of money? That's what most young men seem to aspire to."

"I'm not going to say that money is unimportant to me. I'd like to earn a decent living," Daniel said.

Stimson nodded, stuck his fork into a chunk of steak, and said casually, "You'll have to do better than that if you want to be able to support a girl like Julie Danvers."

"Excuse me Sir?" Daniel stammered. He wondered whether Stimson throwing out such an outrageous comment was a test of some kind. "Miss Danvers? She's just a, well, I'm not even sure I would use the word friend and she's certainly not more than a friend."

"Is that what Miss Danvers thinks?" Stimson asked.

Thinking of the expression on Julie's face when she'd said, "You could never disappoint me" and a little embarrassed at the personal nature of Stimson's questions, Daniel felt himself redden slightly as the back of his neck grew warm. "I don't know what Miss Danvers thinks, Sir."

Stimson laughed. "Good answer son. Any man who says he knows what a woman is thinking is a fool." He turned serious again. "Miss Danvers' father is a fine man and a good attorney, but he has some very particular ideas about who his daughter should socialize with. So, consider yourself warned."

Daniel nodded. "I understand." He paused and then, knowing this was his one chance to impress Stinson, he added, "But, frankly Sir, if Miss Danvers were—ah—interested and I were equally inclined, I would not be dissuaded by outdated attitudes even if they belong to the lady's father."

Stimson arched one eyebrow. "And what if I share those attitudes and think Mr. Danvers is quite correct?" he asked.

Daniel considered the question. Now, he was more certain than ever that Stimson was putting him to some kind of test. The stares, the personal questions, the probing were all the tools of a skillful attorney. What Daniel had to do was to show Stimson that he also had the skills to be a successful attorney. He knew it was a bit of a gamble, but he waited a full minute before he answered Stimson. Then, having decided that there was no point in being anything but honest, for he would not want to work for Stimson if he weren't the man he appeared to be, Daniel gave the only answer he could.

"Sir, if I were to learn that you share those attitudes, I would be both surprised and disappointed."

The corners of Stimson's mouth turned up as he began to nod, slowly at first and then faster as his grin got bigger. "By God," he said pointing his fork at Daniel, "Hayden Planter said you were something and damned if he wasn't telling the truth. 'Surprised and disappointed' eh? Well, I may yet surprise or disappoint you, son, but not in this instance."

And from then on their conversation flowed uninterrupted until that magic moment when Stimson said, "Daniel, if you're interested, there's a part time position available for a law clerk at my firm. And, while I can't make any promises, there's every possibility that it might lead to a full time job if there's an opening at my firm when you're ready to graduate."

Daniel was sure that the feeling that came over him at that moment was something he would never forget. Later, back in his apartment, he burst with the desire to tell someone his good news. He imagined himself saying to Mrs. Caliveri: "Yes, it's true. I haven't even graduated yet and I have a job at Louis Stimson's law firm," and laughed as he thought how shocked she would be. It would be even more satisfying to tell Professor Planter, and to thank him for his part in making the job offer happen. But he found himself wishing there was someone else to share the news with.

Julie Danvers had asked him to let her know about the meeting. He could go back over to the hotel and hope to run into her again. But she might read more into his telling her than he meant. So, he decided against it.

He had a couple of friends who he could tell, fellow law students who might be envious but would still happy for him. But, if he was honest with himself, even telling his friends would not satisfy the urge he felt now. The truth was that, almost as soon as Stimson had made the offer, he'd known exactly who he wanted to share the news with and it was no use pretending that she hadn't popped immediately to mind. She was, in fact, always in the back of his mind so that, although he'd not seen her in nearly five years, he could conjure up a vision of her immediately, with those large dark, shining eyes that had once looked at him with admiration and friendship, if not love.

She'd written to him soon after leaving, to let him know where she was, as he'd asked her to do. But each time he'd tried to put pen to paper, something had stopped him. His news about getting into college hadn't been enough, so why would he think that news of his acceptance to law school would be. But this was different. This was a job. A job at a law firm. And not just any law firm, Louis Stimson's law firm. The impulse to tell Lena this news was so strong, it was overpowering. Still, he wondered what she would think when she saw his letter, after all these years. Perhaps she wouldn't even answer or would ignore him, feeling that he'd ignored her. There was no way to know.

And then he thought about Fletcher the dispatcher from his earliest days as a shlepper. There was no doubt in his mind what Fletcher would say. "Criminy man. Either piss or get off the pot." Maybe this time, he thought, Fletcher would be right.

CHAPTER TWENTY-THREE

1924

JAKE HELD HIS WRIST JUST BENEATH THE TOP OF THE CONFERENCE table and glanced at his watch. It was already so much later than he'd hoped the union's executive board meeting would last. Just that morning, he'd promised Sophie that, for once, he would make it home in time for dinner since it was their fourth wedding anniversary. She'd smiled knowingly.

"I'll wait to eat with you no matter how late it gets," she'd said sitting at the kitchen table in her wheelchair. "Anyway, a late dinner is romantic. We can light some candles and pretend we're in a fancy restaurant."

"Why don't we really do that?" he asked. "Why don't we go to a fancy restaurant and really celebrate?"

"Not this year. Maybe for our next anniversary."

"Are you sure? I can carry you downstairs like when we were newlyweds and I can have a taxi waiting to take us to someplace special."

Sophie looked down at the buttons on her housecoat. "And what about when we get there?" she said in a low voice. "You'll have to carry me into the restaurant and everyone will be staring and then we'll have to do it all again when it it's time to leave. I'd rather just have dinner at home this year."

"Well, if you're sure," he said, already knowing that she was. They'd had the same conversation or some variation on it for the last three anniversaries and her answer had always been the same: *Maybe next year.* He saw in her eyes her unspoken plea that he drop the whole subject.

He stood up and took his breakfast dishes over to the sink, then rinsed and stacked them on a dishtowel. From across the room, Sophie addressed him, a plaintive, defensive note in her voice.

"You don't need to wash dishes. I can do them. And, besides, Mary's coming today to help with the housework." Mary Brewster was a nurse from the Henry Street Settlement's Visiting Nurse Program who came twice a week to check Sophie's condition. Because of her smoke-damaged lungs and limited mobility, the doctors had explained that a close watch on her health could prevent small problems from developing into larger ones. Sophie, however, preferred to focus on the few household tasks Mary performed as if Mary was more of maid than a nurse. In fact, the housework mostly got done through the combined efforts of Aunt Sarah and himself.

Jake didn't mind helping with the housework. He just wished Sophie didn't feel the need to pretend things were other than the way they were. If she were able to be more honest about the housework and her abilities, then maybe he would feel like he could be honest too. As it was, the little fictions added up. And if they couldn't talk about the little fictions, he couldn't imagine how they could ever begin to talk about the big ones.

"When is Mary coming?' he asked as he removed his suit jacket from the back of the kitchen chair.

This morning. And Aunt Sarah is coming this afternoon to help me prepare dinner."

"What's on the menu?" he said, grinning.

Sophie shook her head. "You'll just have to wait until tonight to find out."

"Is it roast beef? With that special mushroom gravy?"

But Sophie only put her thumb and forefinger together, held them to her lips, and pretended to lock them up. "I'm not saying a word. Now go to work, so you can get everything done and come home to me."

Jake had promised he would. But a person could only control so much. He glanced again at his watch. It was 8:30 p.m. and the meeting had already consumed 5 hours. He took a deep breath and let it out slowly. Things had been so much easier back in the days when his involvement had been at the Local rather than the executive board. That was before he'd left the Local to fight a bigger war. The war to end all wars they called it. When he returned, his position with the Local was occupied and Abe Gunther was running for his second term as president of the ILGWU executive board. He immediately started trying to talk Jake into running for Second Vice-President. He didn't have to twist Jake's arm.

The election had been a dog-fight but, in the end, both Jake and Abe had won. It was pretty damn satisfying to know that people understood what you were trying to do for them and appreciated it. Appreciated you. Sometime in the future, when Abe was ready to retire, maybe it would be Jake's turn to lead. Not bad for a baker's son from Odessa. Unfortunately, the candidate that Jake and Abe had supported for First Vice-president had not won. Instead, the votes had gone to Gus Dyche, a big Irishman with a nasty temper and a foul mouth. Now, Dyche was holding forth in his usual loudmouthed manner.

"I say we can't afford to wait any longer," Dyche said. "The communists already have majorities on the boards of Locals 15, 23, and 25. They've threatened to call for midterm elections of the executive board. We've got to put the brakes on this now or we're going to lose control. We've got to take 'em down."

"'Take 'em down'" seems a little extreme," Abe said. "I agree that we've got to tackle the communist threat before they turn the union into some kind of Soviet satellite. But we've got a lot of members who are sympathetic to the communists and we can't afford to alienate all of them at once. We don't want to win the battle at the risk of losing the war."

"I'm not talking about losing any war," Gus said impatiently. "I'm talking divide and conquer. Look, I know some of you have a soft spot for the shirtwaist makers Local." He stared pointedly at Abe and Jake. "But that Local's one of the biggest sources of communist infection. I say we divide it up and limit its power. We can make every factory north of Union Square into its own local and limit Local 25 to everything below fourteenth street."

Dividing up Local 25 would go over like a cannonball, Jake thought. It was true that the shirtwaist makers' Local was, as Dyche suggested, a hotbed of communists. But he felt sure that if the Executive Board tried to break them up, the shirtwaist makers would simply quit the union. And maybe take a bunch of other Locals with them. He agreed with Gus that something had to be done. But he didn't think they'd tried enough other options to be resorting to such drastic action.

Jake understood guys like Gus. Once upon a time, he, too, had been in a hurry for action. He, too, had seen things as all right or all wrong. And, he, too, had been impulsive, even rash. He'd certainly rushed to volunteer for military service, enlisting practically as soon as war was declared. His motivation had been partly patriotic and partly, he admitted to himself, a desire to get away from everything and everyone. Not that he was sorry he'd gone. He'd met some amazing guys, witnessed some real acts of heroism.

But he'd seen other things too. Assigned to the First Division, he'd been among the first American combat troops sent to the front lines in France. For months, he and his fellow soldiers had fought to keep the Germans out of Paris. They'd succeeded but, along the way, he'd witnessed hundreds of terribly young soldiers, both allies and enemies, killed before they'd had a chance to live; children orphaned and alone who wandered about begging for food; and injured soldiers and civilians whose lives would never be the same.

The war had made him see that not everything was quite as black and white as he'd once thought. Most people were neither all good nor all bad. The guy kneeling beside you in the trenches could be a prejudiced bastard one minute and, in the next, he might risk his neck for your skin. A peaceful looking town could turn out to be a booby-trapped nest of bombs. Even your mortal enemy was probably just a young guy far from home who missed his wife and kids. He'd learned that rushing into action before studying a situation could come back to haunt you. It was far better to analyze and strategize. Fighting, he'd come to believe, was a solution of last resort, not first.

When he came home, he found that he wasn't the only one who had changed during the war. The country had changed too. The only thing that hadn't changed was Sophie. She was out of the hospital at last and living with her aunt and uncle. She had no use of her poor crushed legs and never would.

But she was wearing her love for Jake on her sleeve. In the wake of the cruelty and bleakness of the war, her warmth was a balm on his soul. Too, the thought of hurting Sophie in any way was unthinkable. After fighting for so long, he did not think he could ever bear to deliberately harm another human being, much less Sophie, who had already been so horribly and undeservedly hurt.

He'd never lost his affection for Sophie. She was a sweet, good-natured person. It wasn't hard for him to do the right thing and marry her. The toughest part was accepting that he would never have a child of his own. The doctors had been unanimous on that score. Sophie's many injuries had included a broken pelvis and severe abdominal bleeding. To repair these she had gone through extensive surgeries that had saved her life but scarred her internally. He and Sophie were still able to be intimate, but she would never bear children.

Jake knew that women were supposed to care about children more then men. He didn't know why he wanted a child so much. He didn't even care if it was a girl or a boy. But once he married Sophie, he put that dream into a compartment and resolved that, instead of taking care of a child, he would take care of her. A sudden noise snapped him out of his reverie. Gus Dyches was shouting and pounding his fist on the table.

"These commies are like a cancer. We need to cut them out before they spread their poison everywhere," he said.

Abe was as soft-spoken as ever, but Jake could tell he was losing patience with Dyche's heavy-handed approach. "You divide up Local 25 and they'll pull out of the ILGWU completely," he said. "Half the other New York Locals will go with them."

"I say we put it to a vote," Gus said defiantly.

"I second the motion," said Joe Bondor, one of Gus's cronies.

"Wait a minute." Jake said. "Dividing up Locals is against union by-laws. What good is a vote if it's unconstitutional? Anyway, Abe's right. We'll lose too many members. There are other ways to handle this."

"A motion's been made," Gus said loudly. "All in favor say aye."

There was a chorus of ayes.

"All against?"

A smaller chorus of voices said "no."

"This isn't right," Abe said. His voice rose to a higher register as it did when he was extremely upset. "You can't just circumvent the by-laws. I won't stand for it. I'll resign if this thing goes through."

"Go ahead and resign then," Gus said.

"You're always threatening to resign," Joe Bondor said, "but you never actually do. I dare you this time."

"You dare him?" Jake said. "What are you, five years old?"

"I dare you too," Alex Garvey, another board member, said.

Jake tried unsuccessfully to catch Abe's eye. "Abe," he warned. "Don't do it." Jake knew that Abe's health hadn't been good for a couple of years, that he talked of retiring often, and occasionally threatened to actually do it, mostly when he was fed up about something. But the union still needed him. Jake needed him.

"Fine," Abe said. "I quit. You're a bunch of lawless dictators. This kind of action makes you no better than the communists you're trying to get rid of." Abe stood up and walked to the door. "Good luck," he said and walked out.

Jake got up quickly and followed him out into the hall. "What the hell are you doing? This isn't the time to make good on that old threat to resign."

"I'm tired, Jake," Abe said. "Anyway, the vote went against me."

"In there maybe, but the membership voted *you* President, not Gus."

"The vote in there is what counts. I can't get anything done if the executive board is against me. Gus has the votes for now."

Jake stared at him, not believing what he was hearing. "So," he said. "you're leaving me."

"This isn't about you," Abe said.

"No, of course not," Jake agreed. "But you're abandoning the membership. Don't do it Abe."

Abe shook his head. "Go back in," he said slowly. "Go fight the good fight. I'm done for now. " He turned and walked down the hall.

Jake watched him walk away. He didn't believe Abe really meant it. He was just blowing off steam. Give him a little time and Abe would come around, he thought. Tomorrow would be a better time to continue this discussion.

When he re-entered the room, Gus was holding forth but stopped talking as soon as he saw Jake. As Jake made his way to his seat, he was aware of Gus watching him with narrowed eyes. Sitting down, he met Gus's gaze with an impassive expression, biding his time. With a triumphant look, Gus resumed discussing the breakup of Local 25. The meeting didn't last much longer after that. The rules of succession called for Gus to assume the presidency and the board voted to make it official before adjourning.

Outside, Jake took a deep breath of the night air. He thought about walking home to burn off some of his anger but thought of Sophie waiting and took a taxi. From the sidewalk in front of their building, he could see the lights were still on in the apartment. Not that he'd ever doubted Sophie's promise to wait up. He debated walking around the corner to pick up a bottle of wine to go with dinner. He'd meant to get some flowers earlier, but had never gotten around to it. At least he had a box of those chocolates she liked sitting in his top drawer, the gift already wrapped and beribboned by the salesclerk.

He tried to think of some topics they could talk about over dinner. He didn't want to think about, much less talk, about union business. But he had no little anecdotes to recount that might entertain her. He could ask Sophie about her day. As always, she would embellish upon the few things she'd had the slightest involvement in, leaving out anything that couldn't be made to sound gay and entertaining. It was the way their conversations always went and usually he didn't mind.

Tonight, he didn't feel up to it. He was tired, physically and mentally. It wasn't just the union meeting. It was... hell, it was everything. It was this place they were living with the flight of steps from the street to the front door that might just as well be a mountain as far as Sophie went. It was the goddamn wheelchair that couldn't even fit through the goddamn front door. Their apartment was Sophie's prison. And, somehow, even though he left it every morning and was away for ten, eleven, twelve hours each day, it felt like a prison for him too.

Or maybe it was his marriage that was the prison. Maybe all marriages were. They were all about choosing one door, which meant forever forsaking all others. Maybe that's why his mother had left his father all those years ago. For the first time it seemed believable to him that her leaving might not have had anything to do with him. But that didn't matter. Leaving was never the right choice.

On impulse, he pulled his wallet out of his pocket and flipped it open. From behind the bills, he slipped out a folded square of newspaper and opened it. He stared at the worn image. It was a picture of two smiling women with their arms around each other's waists. The caption read: **Charges dismissed against strikers.** Sophie was mugging for the camera, her jaw jutting forward, her grin impish. But it was Lena whose image the photographer had placed at the center of the photo.

It had been a little over six years since Jake had seen her. For four of those years, he'd been married. And, for all he knew, she'd gotten married too. He'd hated her for a long time after she left. But he'd never stopped loving her.

Enough, he told himself. Sophie was waiting. He should go in to her. It was the right thing to do. He re-folded the newspaper, tucked it back in his wallet, and put the wallet back in his pocket. Then he slowly mounted the stairs and let himself in the building.

151

CHAPTER TWENTY-FOUR

1926

"I TOLD YOU TO NOT TO CLIMB SO HIGH," LENA CALLED TO HER daughter, her tone more severe than she'd intended. But Rachel, seven years old and not easily ruffled, appeared unrepentant as she gazed down from her perch in the sprawling oak opposite Grossman's front porch.

"This branch is much stronger than the one you said I could climb up to," Rachel replied. Her gray eyes were wide with innocence and she stood with one arm casually encircling the tree trunk. Her long brown hair had come loose of the braids that Lena had painstakingly formed that morning and tumbled from her head like curly vines.

Lena sat back down in her rocking chair and took a deep breath. Life with her strong-willed daughter could be trying at times, but it wasn't Rachel's fault that she'd gotten up on the wrong side of the bed. Instead of criticizing her, she should be happy to have some time alone with her. It was a rare event these days.

In earlier times, Rachel had accompanied her throughout her workday, first as a snub-nosed infant in a Moses basket that she'd carried from room to room, and later, as a curly-haired toddler, using her chubby hands to "help" Lena make beds and empty trash cans. Those days had passed all too swiftly.

Now, Rachel spent most of her time running around Grossman's with Esty, Bess and Sam's daughter. Together they organized the hotel guests' children into games that inevitably involved Rachel as the Captain and Esty as the first mate or Rachel as the President and Esty as her Vice-President. It reminded Lena of her own childhood when she and Joe had passed the hours playing similar games.

Like Rachel, she had always been the leader and Joe had been her assistant, her brother being too good-natured to fight her for the top position. Together they had conquered imaginary worlds. How possible everything had seemed when she'd been seven years old. How few her possibilities seemed now.

This particular afternoon, Rachel was lonesome. Sam had picked Esty up from school and taken her to Monticello for a dentist appointment and Rachel's efforts to persuade David to play with her had been unsuccessful.

"He said he wasn't interested in doing stuff with little girls," Rachel complained as she followed Lena out onto the porch. "I told him that seven is not little and that if he played with me, I would show him the place that me and Esty use for hide and seek. But he still said no."

"Well don't take it personally. Twelve year old boys often don't want much to do with girls. Esty will be back soon. Until then, why don't you start working on your homework."

"I don't hardly have any homework."

"Well, what about reading a book then," Lena suggested.

But even before she finished talking, Rachel seized upon the idea of climbing the tree. She tackled it the way she did most things, her moves deliberate, confident, and quick. Lena watched her climb, torn between admiration for her daring and concern for her safety. Raising a child as adventurous as Rachel meant frequently trying to find the right balance between those. Lately, she'd been wondering whether she'd gotten the ratio wrong in more ways than one.

"Hello!" Rachel shouted, standing on tiptoes, leaning forward, and waving frantically at someone.

Lena jumped to her feet. "Stop that right now and come down from there."

"But I see Esty and Uncle Sam."

"I don't care if you see the President of the United States. Get down now."

"But –"

"Now," Lena said in a way that made clear she meant business.

As her daughter slowly descended, the old paneled wagon came into view. Sam stopped in front of the hotel and Esty jumped out. Rachel's best friend had inherited her mother's diminutive stature and her father's outgoing personality. She ran to Rachel and whispered something in her ear that made her giggle.

The two of them scampered off as Sam came around from the other side of the wagon.

"Esty," he called after them. "I think your mama would like to see you before you disappear." But the girls were either too far away to hear him or just pretending to be, because they gave no response and never broke stride.

Sam shook his head. "Those two are like peas in a pod."

"From the day they were born," Lena agreed. "How was your afternoon in town?"

"Productive. I got everything I wanted at the hardware store including the newspaper you asked for. Then I stopped at the post office and found, among other things, these packages for you."

He handed her two smallish brown parcels along with the New York Times. She saw right away that the top package was from Joe. Her crazy brother! He visited at least once a month, sometimes more if he had a salesmen's meeting in Gloversville where Hanson Gloves had its headquarters and, in between visits, he sent letters and gifts.

"Thanks, Sam." She started to get up but he waved her back down.

"Stay. Enjoy a few more minutes of peace and quiet."

"I won't be long."

He shrugged to show her that he didn't care and went inside. Pleased to have some time to herself, she tore the paper from Joe's package, revealing an elegant white box with the words "Hanson Gloves" embossed in gold on top. Inside was a small envelope nestled atop a pile of pale pink tissue. Feeling only a little guilty, she put the envelope aside temporarily and dove in to find a pair of beautiful cream-colored kidskin gloves. She tried them on immediately. The nap was so fine that she put the gloves up to her cheek to feel the delicate texture against her face. How sweet of Joe. She would wear them tonight to the Women's Voting Rights class she taught.

Pleased by the thought, she pulled the gloves off, put them back in the box, and read Joe's card. He wrote to say that he had a sales meeting in Gloversville in two weeks and planned to stop for a visit on his way back to the city. He would probably arrive at around dinner-time. And, if it was all right, he might bring along a fellow salesman who had expressed an interest in meeting her. She rolled her eyes at this last bit.

It wasn't that she had no interest in meeting a man. Sometimes in bed at night, after Rachel was asleep, she imagined herself, like the star of some romantic movie, meeting a handsome stranger and falling in love. But, so far, despite Joe's good intentions and the efforts of many hotel guests who knew "just the right guy," she hadn't met anyone in whom she'd been remotely interested. Joe, in particular, had awful taste in potential suitors.

She put Joe's gift aside and turned to the other package. She saw with pleasure that it was from Daniel. Judging by its weight, it likely contained a book in addition to a letter. During her first few months at Grossmans, she'd wondered whether she would ever hear from him again. She knew he'd been hurt by her response to his marriage proposal; perhaps too hurt to stay in touch. But he'd finally written her a couple of years ago and since then they'd kept up a steady correspondence. This time, he'd sent two books, *Winnie The Pooh,* and *The Sun Also Rises,* which had a letter tucked inside the front cover.

> *Dear Lena,*
>
> *I apologize for not writing sooner but when I tell you my news, I think you'll understand. First, a word about the enclosed books. The one by Hemingway is a debut novel and, I have to say, I was very impressed. The reviews have been mixed though, so I'll be interested, as always, to hear what you think. The book for Rachel was recommended by the store clerk, who surely knows more about children's books than I ever will. I hope she enjoys it.*
>
> *And now, for my news. About a month ago, my boss, Louis Stimson was appointed United States Attorney for the Southern District of New York. He offered me a position as an Assistant and I accepted it. I've been working like a demon ever since. If anyone can make a dent in ridding New York City of corruption, it's Stimson and I'm excited to be part of the effort. I have a feeling I'll be very busy for the foreseeable future, but will write again when I have a chance. Until then, my best to you and your daughter.*
>
> *Yours truly,*
> *October 10, 1926 Daniel*
>
> *P.S. Thank you for sending the picture of Rachel. She's looks just as I pictured her.*

Lena lowered the note to her lap and gazed off into the distance. A job as an Assistant United States Attorney. It sounded very impressive and she wanted so much to feel nothing but joy for Daniel. But it was just a tiny bit difficult not to also feel envious of him. He was on his way to realizing his dreams, while her own seemed less attainable than ever. She was not only envious of him, she was disappointed in herself.

Other women had managed to achieve their dreams. Elizabeth Arden had come to the United States as an immigrant and launched an entire cosmetics company from her kitchen. So had Helena Rubinstein, another immigrant turned into cosmetics entrepreneur. Susan B. Anthony had dreamed of women having the right to vote and she'd fought to make that dream come true. Now that women had that right, Lena extolled her students to use their votes to gain control over their lives. But how much control did she have over her own life?

Of course, Sam and Bess were wonderful. As employers, they didn't ask her to do anything they weren't willing to do themselves. And as friends, they were incomparable. But the work was endless. Each year since Lena had arrived, the hotel had sprouted additions so that now there were fifty guest rooms and Grossman's could accommodate two hundred people. The staff had grown as well. Lena now supervised five full-time chambermaids and two full-time laundry women. During the newly expanded operating season from the beginning of March through the end of December, she had barely a minute to herself. Nor was it any better during the two-month off-season when all the maintenance and repair work had to be accomplished. More importantly, no matter how valued Sam and Bess made her feel, the fact was that she was working for someone else's dreams, not her own.

Frustrated, she picked up the newspaper to look for articles about the upcoming elections to bring to tonight's class. At least her continued involvement in the women's rights movement was something she was proud of. Since most of her students read only the local weeklies, she'd decided to expose them to a wider variety of views on the upcoming elections. The New York Times would provide a different perspective. She was scanning the pages looking for pertinent articles when she came across something that made her heart leap into her throat. It was a headline and it read: Jake Brenner Elected President of ILGWU.

The words hit her with the force of a punch. Before she'd even fully processed them, her stomach muscles were pressing against her back as if sucked by a giant magnet. Her eyes pooled with tears and she fought for self-control, shocked by the depth of her reaction. It wasn't as if she never thought about Jake. She could hardly look at Rachel's gray eyes and unruly brown hair and not think of him. And there were times when she allowed her memories to surface and examined them with what she believed was the objectivity that only time could provide. But those times were different. Now, her throat throbbed painfully as if something sharp was caught in it. She debated not reading the article but instinctively knew that, if she didn't, she would obsessively wonder about its contents. She blinked her tears back and focused on the words.

The election had been close. The article talked about how Jake's victory represented a major defeat for the communist wing of the union. It gave some background about the union and some of the challenges the new president faced. And then came the part she'd been unconsciously searching for, a short biographical paragraph about Jake, which stated that the new union president was married to the former Sophie Friedman, a survivor of the Northern Shirtwaist Factory fire. Lena sat very still with this information. She wanted to control her reaction to it, rather than have it control her. After all, she told herself, it was her vindication. It justified all the choices she had made, including the decisions to leave Jake and never tell him about Rachel.

Logically, she thought, this should make her feel good. But, instead, she felt an overpowering bleakness. She didn't even know whether it was the past she was grieving or the present. Here at Grossman's, it was easy to forget the world outside, easy to forget that people's lives went on. But this article and the letter from Daniel comprised proof that they did, in fact, go on. Her life had gone on too, but not wholly the way that she wanted.

Minutes went by and she sat in the grip of inertia until she made an effort to pull herself together. She looked down at the pile in her lap, the package from Joe, the letter from Daniel, and the newspaper still in her hands. Maybe the coincidence of simultaneous learning Daniel's news and reading the announcement about Jake was the impetus she needed to do something about her own life. If anything was going to change, it was up to her to make it happen.

Her gaze was drawn to a picture in the newspaper. It was an advertisement for Chanel No. 5, the new perfume that had taken the country by storm. Coco Chanel was another woman who had made her dreams come true. Lena tried to imagine how it would feel to have your name emblazoned on thousands, maybe millions, of bottles of perfume that women everywhere craved.

A mini daydream blossomed in her mind. She saw her own name in flowing script splashed across the label of a bottle of perfume or embroidered on a label attached to the finest couture clothing. She imagined herself as the head of a business that sold all kinds of things with her name on them. It was thrilling. There was something magical about seeing your own name inscribed on an object. No wonder rich people monogrammed their towels and silverware. Perhaps she would embroider her name on her towels.

But, of course, her towels belonged to Grossman's. Well, she thought as she rose to resume her duties, maybe later, she would think of something else she could monogram.

That evening, Lena clasped her gloved hands together and smiled at the students in her Voting Right's class. Nearly twenty women, her biggest group yet, smiled back from the long rows of oak tables in the high school classroom. Most had been coming to the sessions ever since she'd begun offering them in September, but she was delighted to see several new faces.

Back in March, Lena had gone to Albany for an instructor training session sponsored by the National American Women's Suffrage Association. The session prepared her to teach classes on everything from the mechanics of voting to women's new political power as a voting constituency. Over the summer, she'd arranged for a meeting space in downtown Liberty and posted fliers advertising the weekly classes. Attendance had been sparse at first but had grown as word spread. The women in tonight's class looked at her expectantly.

"Good evening," she said.

"Good evening," they chirped back.

"Today, I want to talk to you about the influence of newspapers upon our political decisions. I've brought some examples with me to share with you. This first, is the Ellenville Journal which, I'm sure, all of you are familiar with."

"I'm familiar with the back page," joked Hedda Meade, who, at the age of 28 and with five children already, claimed only her sense of humor kept her sane. "Mr. Meade reads the sports every morning at breakfast time and all I ever see of the paper is the back page." The other women exchanged knowing nods and Lena smothered a smile.

"Well," she said, "if Mr. Meade has no use for the main news section, you might want to start reading it yourself." She opened the Ellenville Journal to the next to last page before continuing.

"The editorial section is usually close to the back of the main news section. That's where you'll find the newspaper's endorsements. Endorsements are how the newspaper tells its readers which candidates the newspaper believes are the best qualified."

Sally Warner, a sweetly demure young newlywed raised her hand.

"Yes, Sally?"

"I know I should probably wait until later, but I just can't hold off any longer. Your gloves are beautiful. Are they new? Did you get them in town?"

Lena smiled. "The gloves were a gift from my brother Joe. He's a glove salesman."

"And did they come like that with your initials on them?" asked a woman who was new to the class. "Because I'd buy them if they came with my initials."

"So would I," said Sally.

"Can you have your name on the gloves instead of your initials?" asked Hedda.

Lena hesitated. She wanted to make the sales for Joe, but she wasn't sure he could deliver the gloves monogrammed. Of course, she could just do the monogramming for him, just as she had done it for herself to satisfy her CoCo Chanel inspired longings. She thought of all the sales she could make for Joe by offering to do just that. And then she thought about selling monogrammed gloves to women other than the ladies of her class. She remembered the advertisement for Chanel perfume she had just seen. She could advertise too.

A little fantasy began coming to life in her mind. She saw herself with a little business all her own. She imagined a newspaper article about her: Lena Rothman, entrepreneur, businesswoman. It could happen. Especially if she had Joe's help. She realized that the women in the class were waiting for her, watching her with quizzical looks on their faces.

"Yes," she said impulsively. "You can order the gloves to come monogrammed. You provide your initials when you order them, and they come monogrammed in the embroidery thread color of your choice."

"How much are they?" Hedda asked.

Lena thought fast. "I'll have to check with my brother and I can let you know."

"I'd like a pair," Sally said.

"Me too," the new woman spoke up.

"The latest thing, huh?" Hedda said. "I'd like to wear them when I go to the voting booth for the first time. They'd be just the thing with my new coat and handbag."

"Well," Lena told them. "Let's finish the class and then I can take down everyone's name who wants to order the gloves."

In the end, nearly half the women in the class wanted the gloves. Lena couldn't believe it. Maybe the ability to sell gloves ran in the Rothman blood.

Joe arrived the following Friday and, thankfully, without the blind date to whom he'd alluded. As usual, Rachel attached herself to him from the moment he arrived. At dinner, she sat next to him and, the minute he put his fork down, she grabbed his hand.

"Come on, Uncle Joe. You promised you'd play with me after you ate."

"Uncle Joe is still eating," Lena said. "And so should you be. You hardly touched your food."

"I'm full already," Rachel insisted. "If I eat too much, I'll be too heavy to play horse with Uncle Joe."

"Oy" Joe grinned. "I thought *you* were going to be the horse this time, and I was going to climb on *your* back."

"You're too big to be the rider!"

"Well, if I'm going to be the horse than I need to eat a lot so I'll be strong enough to handle a rider like you."

"Rachel," Lena said, "Uncle Joe will come and find you after he's had dessert."

"Okay. But don't forget Uncle Joe. I'll be waiting for you."

"I know you will, bubbeleh."

Lena told herself to be patient. Joe would be around all weekend. At some point, she would have a chance to talk to him about her idea.

But it wasn't until Sunday afternoon that she found a chance to be alone with her brother. Passing through the dining room, she glimpsed him through the window sitting by himself out on the front porch. She pushed open the screened front door and stood, looking at him and smiling.

"How did you shake her?" she asked.

"Rachel?"

"Of course Rachel. How did you manage to get free?"

Joe laughed. "Cookies. Bess just took a fresh batch out of the oven and apparently, I'm no competition for chocolate chip."

160

"Does that mean you have time now for a walk with your sister?"

"I always have time for my sister."

"Then let me take off my apron and I'll be right back."

Joe nodded and Lena turned and went back into the hotel. Hurrying back to her room, she snatched off her apron, and picked up her new gloves. She slipped them into the pocket of her skirt, feeling a bit nervous. She was so excited about her idea and so hopeful, it was hard not to be anxious about what Joe's reaction would be. From the porch steps, they strolled around to the back of the hotel, veered off at an angle through the open meadow and, headed toward the gazebo. They settled themselves on the swing and Joe pushed his foot against the gazebo floor to give them a start.

"This really is the life," Joe said, looking out at the trees and the lake in the distance. "One of these days I'm going to stop all this traveling back and forth from the city and settle down in one place. Get myself a little place near here to call my own. Maybe even have a vegetable patch."

"You?" Lena laughed. "You'll never leave the city. You love it too much."

"You know me well," Joe grinned. He looked around again. "But it is beautiful here."

"It is," Lena agreed.

"You don't sound very enthusiastic."

"No. Of course, I mean it. It is beautiful here and I do love it but sometimes -"

"What?"

"I miss the city. I miss you, of course. And I miss living in a place that's separate from where I work."

"I miss you too. You could come back, you know."

"No, I can't," Lena said. "You know I can't."

"We could move to a different city," Joe suggested. "You and Rachel and me. We could start all over again in a new place. We did it once before."

Lena smiled. "But you love New York and you have all your customers and your friends there. Anyway," she shook her head, "I can't imagine taking Rachel away from this place. And I don't really want to leave either, it's just that -. I don't know."

"What is it?"

Lena thought about what had been bothering for the last few weeks, trying to put it in a way that Joe would understand. "I had so many dreams of becoming someone important. I wanted to invent things, to discover things, to do the kind of things people thought only men could do. And now look at me. I spend my days cleaning other people's messes. I'm nothing more than a maid."

"That's not true. You help run this hotel." Joe insisted. "And you're Rachel's mother. That's a very important job."

"But, what if that's not all I want?" she said slowly.

"What else do you want?" Joe asked gently.

"I have an idea," Lena said abruptly.

"An idea?"

"Yes." She took a deep breath. "Now, hear me out Joe. You know those new gloves you sent me?"

"Yes."

"Well, look." Lena took the gloves out and slipped them on. She held them out for Joe to see. "What do you think?"

Joe stared at the cuffs where Lena had embroidered her initials in a delicate script. He was silent. After a few minutes, she couldn't take the suspense any longer.

"I've already got orders for ten pairs with initials. And I bet I could get more orders if I tried. And, look at this." She pulled her handkerchief out of her pocket. On the corner of the white cotton, she had embroidered her name. "What do you think?"

Joe pursed his lips. "What are you suggesting?"

"That I sell them. I can do it right from here. I can put an advertisement in a magazine, get orders in the mail, embroider the monograms, and send the gloves on to my customers by mail. People order things by mail all the time. Why shouldn't they order from me?"

"And I would supply the gloves?"

"Exactly."

"And you would have time to do this in addition to working here at the hotel or are you planning to leave Grossmans?"

"I can do the monogramming at night. I'm always using that time to darn or knit anyway."

Joe's eyes began to twinkle. "You've given this quite a bit of thought, haven't you."

"I have. I tested them on the ladies from my women's rights class and they loved them. I didn't plan to sell them at first, but they all wanted them. Other women have started businesses.

Look at Coco Chanel and Helena Rubinstein. But if you think it's crazy..."

"I didn't say that. In fact, I think it just might be a great idea."

"Don't you just say that, Joe Rothman," she told him. "Don't you give me false hopes."

Joe shook his head. "I would never do that to you. I really think you've got a good idea. Why don't you do it? Put the advertisement in and let me know how it goes. If you get some orders, you'll be in business. "

In business! No words had ever sounded so exciting. "Oh, Joe." She threw her arms around him and kissed him on his cheek. "Will you help me figure out what to charge and go over all the details with me, so there are no surprises?"

"Bubbeleh," Joe said, "in business, there are always surprises. But let's see if we can keep them to a minimum."

"Can we go back and start working on it right now?"

"Whenever you want," Joe said. "I'm at your disposal."

"Then what are we waiting for?" Lena stood up. "Let's go, big brother."

Laughing, Joe let himself be pulled to his feet and together, they walked back to the hotel.

A few weeks after her conversation with Joe, Lena placed her first advertisement, three lines in Ladies Home Magazine. It was so small, she wondered whether anyone would even notice it, much less place an order. Within days, she received her first request. Soon orders were flying in so fast, she had to get help with the monogramming from some of the local townswomen. She enlisted Rachel and Esty to package and address the finished products.

One evening, nine months after placing her first advertisement, she walked into her bedroom, looked at the cluttered mess that filled the space, and felt overjoyed and overwhelmed. Every available surface was covered with boxes of gloves. It was the same in Rachel's adjoining room. No wonder her poor daughter had been complaining. Lena needed more space, she needed more time, she needed more help. It was impossible for her to keep track of and process the incoming and outgoing orders, supervise the ladies that helped her with the sewing, keep her payment books straight, and still do her work at the hotel.

There was a knock on her door and she sighed. She really hoped it wasn't one of her hotel staff members reporting some problem that required her attention or, worse yet, a guest come to present a complaint in person. Unfortunately, it was the latter, a gentleman with sleek black hair and startlingly bright blue eyes nattily attired in a dark pin stripe suit, a crisp white shirt, and blue silk tie. Hiding her annoyance at whoever had given him her private room number, she pasted a smile on her face.

"Good evening, Sir. What can I do for you?"

He smiled back, his teeth as white as his shirt. "Are you Mrs. Rothman?"

"Yes."

"I'm William Kerner, Mrs. Rothman. We haven't had a chance to meet yet, but I'm the new hotel business manager. "

"Business manager?"

"That's right. I'm in charge of all the accounting, bills, etcetera."

"Oh, you're the new bookkeeper Sam hired to replace Mr. Green."

"Business manager, book-keeper, same thing."

"I suppose," Lena said. "Well, how can I help you Mr. Kerner?"

"Actually, I was hoping to speak to Mr. Rothman."

"Joe? He's not here this weekend. Was there something in particular you wanted to talk to him about?"

"Well, it's about the Rothman Company."

"In that case, you can talk to me."

"I'd really prefer to talk to your husband."

"I don't have a husband, Mr. Kerner," Lena said crisply. "My husband passed away many years ago."

Mr. Kerner looked confused. "Then why did you say that Mr. Rothman is here on weekends?"

"Because -" Lena hesitated. William Kerner didn't appear to mean any harm. His face showed only curiosity and no ill will. Still, there was no reason for him to know all her personal business.

As if he had read her mind, he shook his head and said, "I'm sorry. None of this is any of my business. I guess I jumped to the wrong conclusion. You can see how I might have assumed you were married, since your little girl led me to your room. I'm very sorry for your loss and I apologize for my rudeness."

Lena nodded. After all, he wasn't the only one who had initially jumped to conclusions. "No harm done, Mr. Kerner. Now, was there something you needed to speak to me about? Concerning the Rothman Company?"

"Well, it looks as though a check meant for the Rothman Company somehow got mixed up with the hotel accounts. I've been going over the books. They were a bit of a mess when I first arrived. Anyway, I found a check for $3.00 made out to the Rothman Company that somehow got deposited in the hotel's account. Sam said I should talk to you about it. I can make out a check to you on the hotel account and straighten the whole thing out."

"That would be fine. Thank you very much." She started to close the door.

"Do you mind if I ask you a question?"

"No. Of course not."

"What is the Rothman Company?"

Lena hesitated.

"If you'd rather not say," he began.

"No," she shook her head. "It's just a little business I started."

"You," he crossed his hands over his chest and stared at her, "started a business."

"Yes. I sell gloves. Monogrammed gloves."

"You have a little glove shop?" He looked dubious. "In your hotel room?"

A vision of ladies shopping in the cluttered chaos that was her room at this moment flashed through Lena's mind and she almost laughed, but the skeptical look on his face brought her back to earth. Typical male. He couldn't even conceive of the idea of a woman running a business.

Brisk again, she said, "I sell them through the mail. I advertise in magazines and people send in their orders."

"You run a mail order business?"

"Yes."

"Do you sell many gloves?"

"Well, this month, I've gotten orders for over 200 pairs."

He was silent, his eyes searching her face so long she began to get annoyed. She knew what most men thought about working women generally, never mind women who went into business. Running a business was not ladylike, not feminine. It was obvious from the way he had questioned her that he was like every other man in this respect. Well, he could just take his opinion and –

"Amazing," he said in wonderment. "That's absolutely amazing."

Lena felt herself blushing. "Well, my brother is a glove salesman, so it's not as amazing as it sounds."

"I think that's just wonderful," he said.

"You do?"

"Oh yes, I think it's admirable. After my father died, my mother raised my sisters and myself and I know from watching her that that's no easy thing for a woman to do alone. And here you are doing your job here at the hotel and monogramming gloves in addition. Well, that's pretty impressive. Look, if there's anything I could ever do to help you, I hope you'll let me know."

"That's very kind of you. Thank you. And thank you for bringing the check to my attention."

"No thanks necessary. I was just doing my job." She nodded and waited for him to take his leave. He was looking at her intently as if he might say something more. But when he did speak, all he said was, "Good night, Mrs. Rothman."

"Good night, Mr. Kerner."

As he walked away, Lena closed the door, then turned around and leaned against it thoughtfully. So, this was the new bookkeeper. He was, evidently, good at his job. And it was certainly kind of him to say those things about her running her own business. It had been a long time since anyone besides her brother had been so complimentary. He was a little too well dressed to be a local. So he must have come up from the city. She wondered whether he was living in town or had a room in the staff wing. If he had a family, he would probably find it more convenient to live in town. Of course, she had no idea if he had a family or if he was even married. Bess would know, though. Maybe sometime tomorrow, she would catch up with Bess and ask her.

At five minutes to eight, Lena stood in her room before the full-length tri-fold mirror of her dressing table and examined herself.

"You look beautiful, Mama," Rachel said.

Lena smiled, uncertainly. She had planned to wear her best white shirtwaist and black skirt for her first date with Will Kerner. But Bess had pronounced both of these choices unsuitable and replaced them with a dress borrowed from a hotel guest—a sleeveless yellow shift that had a deeply scooped neckline, a dropped waist that skimmed her hips, and a bottom hem that barely grazed the bottom of her knees.

Lena generally liked the shift-style dresses that had recently come into vogue. And she didn't think herself a prude. But bare legs with bare arms and a bare décolletage added up to a lot of bare skin. She just hoped she didn't look foolish. She wasn't a flapper, after all. She touched the back of her upswept hair. The dress really called for one of the newer, shorter hairdo's, a bob or a crop cut. Long hair was so old-fashioned.

"You really think I look alright?" she said.

There was a knock and Rachel jumped off the bed and ran over to answer the door. Will Kerner stood there looking very debonair in a black dinner jacket, white shirt, and black bow-tie. His dark hair gleamed with pomade and he was holding a large bouquet of red roses in one hand and a smaller bouquet of pink and white carnations in the other.

He smiled down at Rachel. "Good evening, young lady."

"Good evening," Rachel said, her eyes wide.

He extended the smaller bouquet towards her. "These are for you."

Rachel's eyes grew even wider and her mouth formed into an "O" shape that gave way to a huge, delighted smile. "Really?"

Will chuckled. "Yes, really."

"Thank you! No one ever gave me flowers before."

"Then you better go put them in a vase with some water. Flowers need water to stay looking pretty, you know."

Rachel whirled around to face Lena. "Mama, do we have a vase for my flowers?"

"I don't have any vases," Lena said, amused at her tomboy-daughter's excitement, "You can go down to the kitchen and ask Sue for a water pitcher. That will work just fine."

"Better ask for two pitchers," Will said looking at Lena over Rachel's head. "Your mother will need one too."

Lena lifted her gaze from Rachel's face to Will's. For all his suaveness, there was something boyish about him, an eagerness to please and an openness that was endearing. She was glad she had decided to stick with the yellow frock.

Winter came and Will took Rachel sleigh riding, helped her build a snowman, and took Lena out to dinner several more times. Each time he called for her, he brought flowers or chocolates. He was courting her in the most gallant way and she found that she didn't mind a bit. He made a good impression on Joe too, who liked that he had a good profession, was kind to Rachel, and was a gentleman with Lena. Sometimes Lena thought that Will was, perhaps, a tiny bit too old-fashioned. But after so many years of doing things for herself, it was nice to have someone who wanted to do things for her.

Will could not do enough for her. He helped her with her business, assisting with the parts she liked least—the paperwork and the accounting. He analyzed orders to see what styles were the most popular so they could focus on those in the advertisements. He helped negotiate better advertising agreements with the magazines and tracked which ads brought in the most business. He had good business instincts and she appreciated his advice and the way they worked as a team.

Most valuable of all, was Will's encouragement. He was Lena's best cheerleader, endlessly telling her what a remarkable job she was doing, how much he admired her, and what a wonderful mother she was. Dinner out with Will become a weekly event and one that Lena looked forward to more and more.

For so many years, it had been necessary for her to be strong. She had stowed away the soft side of herself and forgotten what it felt like to be treated like a woman. Will made her remember. If there was a heavy box to be lifted, he insisted on lifting it. When the first storms of winter blew through, he told her that he wouldn't countenance the idea of her making the treacherous trip into town to check the mail for orders and shipments of goods coming in and out. She might slip on the ice or catch a cold. Besides, he said, he was glad to do it for her. If she wouldn't accept his help for her own sake, he urged her to let him for Rachel's sake. Her daughter needed a mother who was healthy and well.

One evening after everyone but she and Will had gone to bed, she was sitting at the kitchen table monogramming gloves while he sat beside her going over some paperwork. It was late and she was getting tired. She was thinking about stopping for the evening when she accidentally stuck herself with the sewing needle. Her eyes filled with tears and Will, noticing, took her calloused hands in his. Turning them palm up, he lowered his head and gently kissed each one. Then he slowly leaned toward her and kissed her on the mouth. His lips were firm and yet yielding, tentative at first, then stronger when he sensed she did not object. And with only a little surprise, she realized that she did not.

CHAPTER TWENTY-FIVE

1928

"SO," DANIEL SAID AS HE RETURNED TO THE TRAIN COMPARTMENT and took his seat beside Julie opposite Louis Stimson and his wife, "what kind of crowd do you think will be waiting to welcome the Governor-elect when we get to Albany?"

"Huge," Louis said. "Twice as many as came to see him off at Grand Central Station. Franklin has a lot of friends in Albany. The Roosevelt's home in Hyde Park isn't that far from there."

Julie brushed a spot of dirt from the skirt of her camel hair suit. "I just hope the reception platform they have us stand on is a little higher in Albany than the one at Grand Central. I didn't care much for the feeling that my foot could be grabbed by someone in the crowd at any second."

Louis laughed. "A little too close to the great unwashed, for your comfort, eh Julie? Just remember, those cheering minions are the folks who voted Roosevelt into office. They're who Daniel and I will really be working for in Albany."

Anna Stimson, who loved her husband but was not above bringing him down to earth from time to time, smiled gently. "I'm sure neither Julie nor Daniel needs to be reminded of that."

Stimson turned and looked sharply at his wife. But after a moment, he nodded and said in a mild tone, "Very true, my dear, very true." Turning back, he said, "I meant nothing by it. I said it to remind myself as much as anyone else."

Daniel wasn't offended. He'd been working full time for Stimson since graduating from law school six years ago and was used to his lectures. Besides, he owed too much to the man, not the least of which was this job in Roosevelt's labor department, to take hasty offense at anything Louis said. He turned to Julie to see how she was reacting. She was used to Louis too and looked serene, with only a hint of an amused smile. He was suddenly very glad to have her by his side.

There were times when being with Julie felt just right and this was one of those moments. He knew her joy over Roosevelt's election was equal to his own and exceeded only by her happiness over his appointment to the new administration. He gave her hand a little squeeze and she turned to him. The adoring look in her eyes made him instantly regret the hand squeeze. And this, in turn, made him feel frustrated with himself.

It had been three years now since his friendship with Julie had morphed into something more, the exact nature of which was still undefined in his mind. There was no doubt that he enjoyed her company enormously, respected all she'd accomplished, and admired the way she'd grown into her patrician looks. But he knew very well that it was possible to feel all those things for a woman and yet feel something more—a feeling as different from the fondness he felt for Julie as boiling water is from tepid.

Louis had been hinting to Daniel for quite a while that it was time for him to ask Julie a certain question. And while Julie herself never said anything about the subject, Daniel knew that no woman wanted to be courted forever. The problem was that he just wasn't ready to take the next step. He wasn't sure he would ever be ready. He also wasn't sure he never would be. So he continued to merely court her, lacking both sufficient reason to end things and sufficient strength to overcome what he considered the weakness of character that prevented him from committing to her.

In the corridor outside their compartment, a conductor passing by called, "Next stop Rhinebeck Station. Rhinebeck Station coming up."

"Not much further to Albany," Louis said.

As the train slowed, Daniel glanced out the window. The ride had afforded some beautiful views of the Hudson River. Now, his attention was caught by a magnificent view of peaks rising on the far side of the river.

"Louis," he said, "do you know what mountain range those peaks belong to?"

Louis laughed. "Better brush up on your geography, my boy. The Governor's staff works on behalf of the entire state of New York, not just New York City. Those are the Catskill Mountains."

"The Catskill Mountains?" Daniel said, startled. "I didn't realize Albany was anywhere near there."

"Well, we're only about half an hour from Albany right now. But I wouldn't count on having much time to go mountain climbing anytime soon."

"No, Sir," Daniel said. But his mind was racing. This was the closest he'd been to Lena in years. They'd been corresponding for some time now. It wouldn't be completely unreasonable for him to propose that he come for a visit now that they would be practically neighbors. His pulse quickened at the thought.

He glanced over at Julie. He'd told her about Lena one evening, relating the essentials in a casual way appropriate to a distant youthful experience. He was fairly sure he'd also mentioned that he occasionally sent Lena and her daughter books because they lived out in the country with little access to well-stocked libraries. But he couldn't remember whether he'd mentioned that Lena lived in the Catskill Mountains.

Julie was looking at him quizzically. "I didn't know you enjoyed mountain climbing. Is that something you did before you came to America?"

"No. I, uh, I just always wanted to try it."

"Well, then you should take advantage of your new surroundings," she said earnestly. "There's wonderful skiing in this area too. Lake Placid has some of the best slopes I've ever been on. My family used to go every year when we stayed at our lodge in the Adirondacks."

"Skiing." Louis said. "That was never my cup of tea. Skeetering down a steep slope on two skinny boards." He shook his head. "But you should try it Daniel. Take Julie with you. She can get you started."

"I'd love to," Julie said. "It would be great to get back on the slopes." Her face was glowing and, in her eyes, Daniel saw a level of emotion that begged to be answered in kind.

But he only nodded and said, "Maybe. But if there's not going to be enough time for mountain-climbing, I doubt they'll be much time for skiing either."

That night, Daniel escorted Julie to the first of several victory parties scheduled for the weekend. As he entered the hotel ballroom, he couldn't help feeling proud to have her on his arm. Julie was one of those women who had grown into her looks at the same time that she'd developed an impeccable sense of style. She was as glamorous as a movie star in beaded white silk and diamonds, her tall slender figure a perfect match for current styles. They moved through the crowds of tuxedoed men and gowned women and paused beneath crystal chandeliers to accept punch and hors d'oeuvres from liveried waiters. While Daniel still didn't completely feel like he belonged in this milieu, it was always easier for him to navigate it with Julie at his side.

After a few minutes, they found Louis and Anna. With apologies to the women, Louis bore Daniel away to introduce him to various people—so many, in fact, that Daniel's head started to spin. There was much backslapping, hearty hand-shaking, and mutual congratulations. Above all, there was boundless optimism. Though President Hoover and the Republicans had won big nationally, at least New York State had a Democratic governor who was finally going to do something for the average, hardworking citizen. Hope was running high among the Roosevelt crowd.

Suddenly, Daniel saw a particularly welcome face smiling at him from the other side of the room. It was Jim Kogan, his old buddy from the U. S. Attorneys Office. Along with Daniel, Kogan had been one of the first young attorneys Stimson had hired after his appointment. He was as different from Daniel as a person could be, short and chubby, as well as loud, outgoing, and brash. But Kogan was a great attorney and a hard worker and the two of them had hit it off both professionally and personally.

Two years ago, Kogan had gone home to Chicago and Daniel had not seen him since. He'd been looking forward to this moment ever since Louis had told him that he'd persuaded Kogan to join them in Albany. He made a bee-line towards his old friend as Kogan did the same towards him.

"Cowan, you old dog." Kogan grabbed his hand and pumped it. "I've been looking all over this place for you. How've you been?"

"Well. And you? You've put on a few pounds since I last saw you."

Kogan laughed. "There's a reason for that. But first, tell me what you've been doing since I last saw you."

"Cleaning up the city and keeping it safe from scoundrels like you, what else?" Daniel said. "Man, I'm glad to see you again. I couldn't believe it when Stimson said you agreed to come back east. What've you been doing with yourself?"

"Well," Kogan said, drawing the word out and looking around the crowd as if he were searching for someone. "There have been a few developments in my neck of the woods. Lucy," he called and waved his hand. "Over here." A petite and very pregnant brunette slipped through the crowd and came to stand at Kogan's side. "Lucy, I'd like to introduce you to a buddy of mine from my Assistant United States Attorney days. This is Daniel Cowan. Daniel, my wife, Lucy."

"It's a pleasure to meet you," Lucy smiled.

Daniel quickly hid his surprise and clapped his friend on the back. "Congratulations!" He returned Lucy's smile. "It's nice to meet you too. And best wishes. When did the happy occasion take place?"

Kogan answered the question. "About a year ago. I would have invited you to the wedding, except there wasn't one. We got married kind of spur of the moment."

"That's alright," Daniel said. He grinned at Lucy. "I didn't think any woman was ever going to be able to pin this guy down."

Kogan was beaming. "Well, not just any woman did. And, to answer your original question, it turned out Lucy's father was a lawyer and I ended up joining his firm. But what about you? Is there a Mrs. Cowan yet?"

Daniel shook his head. He thought about Julie and realized guiltily that he was relieved she was off chatting with Anna Stimson so he didn't have to introduce her to Kogan. His old friend would surely pump him for information and he didn't need Kogan's laser-like probing of his psyche at this particular time.

"So is married life the reason for your augmented presence?" he teased Kogan.

Jim's round face creased and he laughed. "It's all Lucy's fault. She cooks even better than my mother. And now that she's in the family way and eating for two, I seem to have followed suit. I'm telling you Daniel, if things keep on this way, I'll be lucky if I can keep from exploding altogether."

Just then the dinner bell sounded. He and the Kogans moved along with the crowd into the dining room. Jim and Lucy found their table and, after promising to catch up with them again later, Daniel excused himself. He passed Julie, still engaged deeply in what looked like a serious conversation with Anna Stimson, decided against interrupting them just in case the topic was the one he was trying to avoid, and continued on to his and Julie's table.

So, he thought as he took his assigned seat, Jim Kogan—married. He would have bet that Kogan would have remained a bachelor for a very long time. But, his old buddy seemed happy enough. Rueful, Daniel realized how much he'd been counting on the good times he'd planned on having with Kogan here in Albany. Rabblerousing evenings seemed unlikely with Lucy (and soon a little one) waiting for Jim to arrive home in the evening.

Julie still hadn't arrived, but Daniel's tablemate on his other side was already there and he introduced himself. The Hon. George Bingham was a state senator from Sullivan County. An affable man with a florid face and a booming laugh, he appeared to need nothing but regular nods and the occasional monosyllabic response to keep his chatter going. Daniel was more than willing to accommodate him. He just hoped that Bingham's affability would continue once the legislative session got under way.

"Cowan was it?" Bingham asked him after several minutes. "Don't think I've heard that name before. Though I know a family named Cohen. Cowan, Cohen. Not that different. Do you think they might be related to you?"

"I don't think so," Daniel said. "I come from a very small family."

"Oh—well, maybe not then. Nice people though. Industrious. They opened up a hotel in my county. There's a lot of them now."

"A lot of Cohens?"

"Well, that too. But, no, I meant a lot of hotels. They do good business. And they bring a lot of business to the area. Folks coming up for the weekend or sometimes the whole summer. Hardly a week seems to go by without some new hotel opening up. Ellenville, Liberty, Monticello, Mountaindale—they're full of them. In the beginning there was hard feelings about it all. County residents felt kind of invaded, run over, what with so many Hebrews descending on them. But I—"

"Liberty?" Daniel interrupted him. "Did you say that Liberty was in your district?"

"It sure is."

He felt his face grown warm. "Have you ever heard of a hotel called Grossman's?"

"Sure I have. That's Sam and Bess's place. Boy, you talk about business stepping up. Every time I turn around, that place seems to have grown another wing. They're good folks though."

"So you've been there?" Daniel asked.

"Not to stay over, but I've had dinner there. Say, how do you know the Grossmans? I thought you said you'd never been to the Catskills."

"That's right, I haven't." Daniel thought fast. "But one of my friends is a friend of the Grossman's and she told me about it."

"Well, you should come by one of these days. It's not so far from here you know. Just on the other side of the river. You can get there easy enough between the ferry and the train. Take you maybe two hours altogether. "

"Two hours?" Daniel was suddenly conscious that Julie was just at that moment taking her seat beside him. He lowered his voice. "Two hours?" he repeated. "I thought the Catskill Mountains were only about a half an hour from Albany."

"Well, the beginning of the range is probably only about half an hour away, but Liberty is more like two. Easy enough to get there by train though, now that they've built the Catskill Mountain Railroad.

Daniel tucked away the disappointment he'd felt on hearing that Lena was further away than he'd thought and turned to greet Julie.

"I'm sorry I didn't wait for you," he said. "but you seemed to be privately engaged with Anna Stimson."

"That's alright. And now it appears that you're engaged. Please don't let me interrupt."

"You're not interrupting. Allow me to introduce you. Julie Danvers, the Honorable George Bingham," he said.

Julie and Bingham exchanged "How do you do's" and then George Bingham was off and running again. But this time, Daniel didn't hear a word. While Julie supplied nods at appropriate places, all Daniel could think of was the fact that Grossman's was so much further away than he'd thought.

After dinner, Daniel joined the other men for brandy in a room adjacent to the main ballroom. Louis Stimson propelled Jim Kogan in his direction.

"Did you hear?" Stimson demanded. "Did you hear who's become respectable? Kogan finally beat you at something. He's gotten married and his wife is already in a family way. What do you think about that?"

Daniel smiled. "I think it's wonderful."

"And do you intend to take it lying down?"

"What am I supposed to do about it?" Daniel asked.

"Marry Julie and get started on a family. Before you know it, you'll be in the lead again."

"I didn't realize it was a competition," Daniel said.

"Everything is," Stimson replied grinning. "But seriously," he took a sip of his brandy. "When do you intend to do the honorable thing with respect to Julie?"

"What's this?" Kogan asked. "You've been holding out on me, old buddy. Letting me go on and on about Lucy without saying a word about yourself. I knew you wouldn't be unmarried for long."

"I'm still unmarried," Daniel said. Louis was looking at him meaningfully, so he added. "I know it's not fair to Julie to go on dating forever."

Louis nodded. "Fair is the least she deserves." It was the closest he'd ever come to reproaching Daniel on the subject and Daniel knew it was neither lightly said nor completely undeserved.

"I'll figure it out soon," he said.

"You do that," Louis said. Then he smiled. "Don't look so grim, my boy. It's only marriage we're talking about."

Kogan whooped. "Yeah buddy, it's only marriage."

Daniel returned their smiles, but his began fading almost as soon as it appeared. "*Only marriage,*" he thought. And Grossman's was *only* about two hours away. The one thing ought to have had nothing to do with the other. He finished his drink quickly and excused himself to get a refill. He had no desire to continue the conversation that Louis had begun.

The rest of the weekend was filled with receptions and parties. When it was over, Daniel put Julie on the train back to New York City. He knew she was disappointed that he hadn't said anything specific about when he would see her next. He was disappointed in himself for not figuring out what he wanted when it came to their relationship. But as the real work of governing the state of New York began, he had little time to think about Julie or anyone else.

The state's economy was in deep trouble. Employment levels were sinking and more and more people were out of work for longer periods of time. Governor Roosevelt ordered his staff to come up with ideas for getting people back to work as well as ways to tide them over while they were between jobs. Daniel was busier than he had ever been in his whole life.

And then things got even worse. If the beginning of 1929 had been bad, the ending was a disaster. A little over nine months after Daniel arrived in Albany, the stock market crashed and the national economy descended into a deep depression. Roosevelt made it clear that getting the people back to work and helping them manage until they found a job was his top priority. Daniel's main assignment was to develop some kind of system for providing compensation to those who'd lose their jobs through no fault of their own. He realized, however, that if New York State started doling out unemployment compensation but neighboring states didn't, people would start moving to New York just for the benefits and the state would be inundated. He thought Roosevelt should host a meeting with the Governors of the surrounding states and try to persuade them to adopt a similar unemployment compensation system. The idea was enthusiastically received within his department and Louis said he would bring it to Roosevelt's attention at the next cabinet meeting. Friday afternoon, Daniel sat in his office, waiting for Stimson to return with the Governor's verdict. When he heard his boss's voice in the hallway, he hurried out to meet him.

Louis looked grim. As soon as he saw Daniel, he shook his head. "Every time I think it can't get worse, it does. Unemployment in New York has hit twenty-five percent. The foreclosure rate is climbing so fast, we don't even have reliable statistics."

"President Hoover still doesn't get it." Daniel said.

Louis nodded. "Hoover's living in a bubble and he's surrounded himself with a bunch of incompetents who can't even calculate the national unemployment rate properly. Frances had to correct their figures for them." He was referring to Frances Perkins, who Roosevelt had appointed as the State Commissioner of Labor.

If the news hadn't been so awful, Daniel probably would have enjoyed the fact that Frances had had to correct Hoover's labor secretary. But nothing about the current situation was amusing.

"So," he asked, "did you have a chance to talk to Roosevelt about hosting a multi-state conference on unemployment compensation?"

"Yes, and he's very interested. He wants to talk to you about it this weekend in Hyde Park."

"Where?"

"You and I are invited to his family home, Springwood. You'll love it. The change of scenery will do you good."

"What do you mean it'll do me good?"

"I don't mean anything critical by it. We've all been working at a frantic pace, and you more so than anyone else. A body needs rest, my boy. Makes the brain work more efficiently. Kogan and I have wives waiting at home. But you've got no one keeping your dinner hot for you and no reason to leave the office. I know you've been burning the midnight oil."

Daniel looked down and made a pretense of checking his pocket-watch. He was not in the mood to discuss his lack of a wife.

"Any suggestions for how to prepare for the weekend?" he asked.

"Casual clothes, sturdy shoes, and a tennis racket if you play." Louis said.

"I meant with respect to presenting my ideas for the Governor's conference."

"Roosevelt wants to hear your ideas for topics that would be covered at the conference and learn more about the results of your research. We're expected in time for dinner tonight. I'll drive. Can you be ready to leave by 5 p.m.?"

"I guess I'll have to be."

Walking back to his townhouse later that day, Daniel realized how long it had been since he'd arrived home before nightfall. The picture Louis painted of him as practically a hermit was disheartening. Was that the way others saw him?

He opened his front door, bent down to scoop up the mail, and carried it upstairs into the bedroom so he could start packing. As he began pulling clothes from his drawers, he thought of Stimson's and Kogan's home lives. Among his colleagues, he was clearly the odd man out. Even his boss had a helpmate. There was no doubt that Eleanor Roosevelt made her husband's life and job easier. Some people called her Franklin's not so secret weapon.

Done with his packing, he checked the mail that he'd set aside. There were some bills, a letter from his old Constitutional Law professor, Hayden Planter; and a thick white envelope from Lena. He felt a surge of anticipation, as he always did, at the sight of her name in the return address, though he was a little surprised to see something from her as he'd not yet responded to her last missive.

He checked his watch. It was a quarter to five. He still had some time. He walked into the living room and, switching on the lamp beside his favorite wing chair, he sat down to read Lena's letter. Except that it wasn't a letter after all.

The honour of your presence is requested
At the marriage of

Lena Rothman

To

Will Kerner.

On Saturday, the twelfth of December,
At Grossman's Hotel, Liberty, New York

His first thought was that it simply didn't make sense. He stared at the embossed lettering on the vellum paper. Will Kerner? Who the hell was Will Kerner? He tried to remember Lena's last letter. He didn't recall anything in it to suggest an impending marriage. No mention of anyone courting her. Not even a reference to a gentleman caller or even a friend. Of course, his letters never mentioned Julie. But that was different.

Random thoughts flew through his head. If only he'd gone to visit Lena sometime during the last nine months as he'd originally planned. If only he'd answered her last letter. Then again, what difference would any of that had made? What did he think would have happened? That he would see her and she would be so impressed with who he was now that she would throw herself at him and beg him to marry her? Was that the fantasy he'd been harboring and keeping a secret even from himself?

What an idiot he'd been. A complete fool. Truly pathetic. What else did you call someone who still nursed romantic fantasies about someone who'd rejected them years ago? Anger surged through him. Thank goodness she was getting married. This was the best thing that could have happened to him. Now, he would have no choice but to abandon his ridiculous, no—insane—hopes. He would be forced to live the life that was actually in front of him instead of one that existed only in his imagination. After all, he didn't really know the Lena of today. Didn't know whether she would be someone he would be in the least bit interested in. A letter every few months was hardly the same as actually spending time in someone's presence. If he had changed over the years, and he liked to think that he had, so must she have.

Indeed, what did he really know of her other than the little she wrote in her letters. Speaking of which, he realized, their correspondence would now end. Married women did not exchange letters with male friends. Married women did not have male friends. And that hurt as much as anything else. Like a physical blow, it knocked the wind out of him. No contact with her anymore? Not even to know how she was doing? He should have answered her last letter. What had she said anyway? Perhaps there had been some hint of Mr. Kerner in it. Some mention that he'd missed.

He went over to his desk, pulled open the top left-hand drawer where he kept all of Lena's letters, and he removed the most recent one. It was full of news about her growing business, a few lines about how much she had enjoyed the copy of "Pride and Prejudice" he had sent her, and a comment about how quickly her daughter was growing up. But no mention of any man. Nothing to prepare him for the bombshell he had just opened.

He looked again at the wedding invitation. He wanted to rip it to shreds. Burn it. Roll it into a tube and hit someone with it. Do something to get rid of the emotions that were roiling him. The ones he had no right to feel anyway, especially given his relationship with Julie. Oh yes, Julie. The woman he'd been treating badly for months now. Barely keeping in touch with her and blaming the lack of communication on his workload.

Alright, he thought. Enough. It was finally time for this chapter of his life to be over once and for all. He would send a gift and a note of regret for his inability to attend the wedding. Once that was done, he would be done. He replaced Lena's letter and shut the drawer. Louis would be here any minute. He would use these last moments to look over his notes.

Upon arrival at the Governor's large and comfortable home, Daniel was relieved to hear that dinner would not take place until eight o'clock, giving him an hour and a half to compose himself and prepare mentally for the presentation on the Governor's conference. It had been a strain to keep Louis from noticing that anything was amiss during their drive. He didn't want to be similarly distracted before the Governor. The butler informed them that there was no need to dress. The Roosevelts preferred to be in-formal when they entertained at Springwood.

Just before eight, feeling more like himself, Daniel put away his notes and emerged from his room into the hallway. He heard the sound of another door closing nearby and looked up reflexively.

"Julie," he said in shock.

"Hello Daniel." If she was as surprised as he, she was hiding it well.

"It's wonderful to see you," he said quickly. "It's been so long. I'm... I know I've been remiss. You've written me and I haven't had time -"

"It's alright Daniel. I know you've been busy," she said as if she'd been practicing for this moment.

"No." He shook his head. "I mean, yes, I have been busy, but I still should have written. I'm very sorry."

Julie's smile was very small and very quick. "Apology accepted."

Daniel extended his arm. "May I escort you to dinner?"

She nodded. "Thank you."

"Have you been at Hyde Park for long?" Daniel asked as they descended the stairs. Now that he was over his initial surprise and awkwardness, he felt a familiar ease and pleasure in her company. He just hoped she felt the same.

"I arrived yesterday," Julie said. "Mrs. Roosevelt invited me so we could discuss Ladies Trade Union League issues."

"Are you staying the entire weekend?"

"Yes. And you?"

"I'm not quite sure. I guess I'll be here for as long as the Governor wants me."

"If you're lucky that will be for the entire weekend. Hyde Park is a very special place."

He nodded. "I'm already discovering that."

They'd reached the entrance to the dining room. He took a deep breath and turning to her said, "Notwithstanding my poor correspondence skills, I'm very happy to see you Julie. I've missed you."

Julie blushed. "I've missed you too."

"Then we'll have a chance to talk again?" he asked.

She nodded and he released her to find her seat.

It didn't take long for Daniel to succumb to Hyde Park's charms. His presentation to the Governor after dinner was an unqualified success and he was given the go-ahead to organize the conference. Afterwards, Roosevelt made it clear that he was to remain for the rest of the weekend. He even offered to give Daniel a personal tour of the area the following morning.

For the next two days, Daniel spent more time with the Governor than he had in all the rest of the time he'd worked for him.

When he wasn't with Roosevelt, he was with Julie, strolling the grounds of Springwood, viewing the Hudson from various vantage points, trying his hand at tennis under her guidance, and having tea with her and Eleanor at Val-Kill, Eleanor's private cottage.

Late Sunday afternoon, he stood on Springwood's rear terrace waiting for Julie so he could say goodbye. The view from the terrace was magnificent. The sun sat low in the sky and the clarity of the pre-dusk light made everything appear exceptionally vivid. Daniel didn't usually take much notice of nature, but the azure October sky, the undulating green lawns just beyond the terrace, and the copper, plum, and gold leaves on the surrounding trees dazzled him. He was struck by the feeling that, for the first time in a long time, he was seeing what was around him. He'd spent so many of the last months focused on work, that he'd forgotten there was a real world beyond the one that existed in his mind. There was. This was it. This sun, this sky, this terrace, this moment.

The door from the house opened and Julie walked out looking cozy but still elegant in a hip-length sweater and cloche hat, the low brim framing and flattering her eyes. A wave of gratitude spread over Daniel. He was so fortunate to have Julie in his life. He silently rebuked himself for the foolish and immature thinking that had led him to all but ignore this woman who was right for him in every way.

"There you are," he said, smiling and walking over to her.

"I'm sorry I'm late. I hope I haven't held you up."

He shook his head. "Don't apologize. I'm only sorry I have to leave at all. I was just standing here and thinking how right you were when you said this place was special."

"I'm glad you agree."

"It's been a wonderful weekend," he said. "It's been wonderful being with you." He reached for her hand. "I'd like it if we could spend a lot more time together."

Julie hesitated. "I suppose I may visit Albany if Anna Stimson invites me."

He looked deeply into her eyes. "And what if I invite you?"

Julie disengaged her hand and walked over to the low stone wall that bordered the terrace. She stood for a moment looking out, then turned to him with a wistful half-smile.

"It's alright, Daniel," she said. "You don't need to say that. I think I've always known how you've felt about me. I admit, I've wished things could be different. I suppose I still do. But that's not your fault. I think I'm not quite the right one for you. I already have a well-stocked library. You don't need to send any books to me."

So she did remember, Daniel thought. He walked over to stand beside her.

"You're wrong Julie," he said. "I don't know what you think, but Lena and I are just friends. And we're not even that anymore. In fact, she's getting married in a few months. Anyway, I don't want to talk about her. I want to talk about us." He reached for both of her hands and she allowed him to hold them while he gazed into her eyes.

"I may not have expressed myself in the past as well as I should have," he said, "but there's no one whose company I enjoy more than yours, no one whose opinion I value more, and no one who makes me feel as good about myself. I guess it just took being apart from you for me to realize how much you really mean to me."

"Daniel...." Julie began.

He put a finger to her lips. "Just let me finish and then I'll listen to anything you want to say. The thing is, now that I've come to this realization, I don't want to go for months without us being together. I'm not just asking you to visit me, Julie. I'm asking you to marry me."

She looked at him with tremulous eyes and he suddenly worried that he'd missed his chance and that she was about to turn him down. He didn't think he could stand it if she did. He didn't think he could bear losing both Lena and Julie in the same weekend. Before she could say a word, he leaned forward and kissed her. At first, there was a tentativeness to her response that he didn't remember. But after a while, her tentativeness melted away. And by the time they parted, he felt sure he'd convinced her of his sincerity. Still, he decided not to press her any further for the moment.

"You don't have to answer me now. I know you weren't exactly expecting this. You can let me know whenever you're ready."

Julie's eyes searched his and finally, she nodded. "Alright," she said. "I promise not to keep you waiting long."

As Daniel got into the car for the ride home with Louis, a slight hysteria or euphoria, bubbled up within him. One thing was for sure, conversation would not be lacking on the ride home. A grin slowly spread across his face as he anticipated his boss's reac-

CHAPTER TWENTY-SIX

1933

"I DON'T BLAME GLORIA FOR TAKING A JOB THAT PAYS MORE," JAKE said to Sophie as he rose from the dinner table and took his plate to the sink, "but she's going to be tough to replace after all these years."

"Can't you give her a raise?"

He shook his head. "There's no money. The union's practically penniless. Our membership is one tenth of what it once was and that's not going to change until people start working again. I'll be happy if I can just keep the union afloat until then."

"President Roosevelt will figure it out," Sophie said. "And so will you."

"Thanks for the vote of confidence." Jake did not want to worry Sophie, but hiring a secretary and bolstering the union's finances were hardly the only challenges facing him during his third term as President. There was the communist wing, which was still trying to take control of some of the locals. And then, there was a new, more sinister threat. Organized labor, the Mafia, the Mob—whatever you called it—the gangsters involved in it had already managed to infiltrate some of the other unions through a combination of bribery, force, and intimidation. He was not going to let them do the same to his beloved ILGWU. He may have won the election for President, but his battles were far from behind him.

The election itself had been tough. To win it, he'd needed every hand on deck. He'd even enlisted Sophie's help, bringing home tasks she could do right at the kitchen table. Sophie had dived into the effort with an enthusiasm he hadn't seen from her in years. Equipped with a roster of telephone numbers, she'd made hundreds of phone calls urging union members to vote for him. When Jake brought home fliers to be mailed, she took on that job too, stuffing and licking until her hands were rough and dry.

When he won the election, Sophie was so happy she allowed herself to be lifted into a taxi so she could attend the victory party. Thank goodness, they'd finally moved to an elevator building so, at least, there were no flights of stairs to contend with. It was the first time Sophie had left the house in anything other than an ambulance in nearly fifteen years. For Jake, standing in front of the cheering crowd of union members was one kind of victory. Seeing Sophie in the audience while he delivered his acceptance speech was another.

"I know a good secretary is really important," Sophie said as Jake rinsed his plate. "I remember when I used to want to be one."

"You?" He turned around in surprise.

She looked wistful. "I always thought working in an office seemed so sophisticated. So much classier than working in a shirtwaist factory."

Jake didn't know what to say. It was the first time Sophie had ever talked about the dreams she'd had before the fire. For his own part, he tried never to think about how differently his life might have turned out if the fire had never happened. He came back to the table and reached for Sophie's plate but she shook her head.

"I can do it," she said. "You go relax." She backed her wheelchair away from the table and, with her plate balanced on her lap, rolled over to the sink.

Jake headed into the living room to look for the newspaper, found it waiting for him on the table nearest his favorite easy chair, and sat down to read. A little while later, Sophie wheeled into the living room. She flipped idly through a magazine.

"Oh," she said. "Did I tell you that Aunt Sarah stopped by today? We talked about how we kind of missed all the envelope stuffing and such."

Jake looked up from the paper and grinned. "Isn't it easier for you two to gossip without having to contend with dry envelope-mouth?"

Sophie laughed. "Remember how, at first, I used to dip my tongue in a glass of water to keep it moist. Thank goodness, we finally thought of using a damp sponge on the flaps. I do miss it though," she said. "And I was thinking..."

"Uh, huh." Jake said. He'd finally found an article talking about the confirmation hearings for Roosevelt's Labor Secretary.

"I was thinking that if I could stuff envelopes for you, I could do it for someone else. I've been reading about the Georgia Warm Springs Foundation. The place actually started out as a resort. But it has these warm mineral springs. "

Jake finished the article on the hearings and continued reading. The economic news continued to be dismal not just at home but internationally. The situation in Germany seemed particularly dire. An editorial predicted that the German Chancellor would soon be replaced, most likely by that far right-wing nut-job who was head of the National Socialist Party.

"The President actually went there," Sophie said.

Jake looked up from the paper. "The President actually went where?" he asked.

"To Warm Springs," Sophie said. "And it helped him. It strengthened his leg and hip muscles. So he bought it with his own money and turned it into a facility to help other people who are paralyzed from polio. Now he's trying to raise money so that even more people can be helped. I was thinking that maybe I could do something like that."

Jake looked at Sophie's hopeful face. He hated to burst her dreams. But she must know that being in a wheelchair as a result of polio was entirely different than being in a wheelchair because one's legs were crushed. He spoke as gently as possible.

"I don't think your situation is exactly like the President's. Maybe you shouldn't get your hopes up about this Warm Springs place being able to help you."

Sophie closed her magazine and looked at him with an exasperated expression. "Jake, you haven't been listening to me. I didn't say I wanted to go there. I said that maybe I could help the President's foundation with fundraising. I could stuff envelopes for them or make calls or something."

"Oh," Jake couldn't hide his relief. "That's a wonderful idea."

"You wouldn't mind? If I spent time doing something like that?"

"Of course not. I think it would be great. Especially now. I'm going to be crazy busy for a while. It would be nice if you had something to occupy yourself."

It was perfect, he thought. Knowing that Sophie had some busywork would make him feel less guilty about the long work hours he would be putting in and the many business trips he anticipated making. Envelope stuffing was as good as anything else he could think of. Heck, she could even do it while still listening to those soap operas on the radio that she loved.

In the months that followed, Jake dealt with the union's immediate financial woes by persuading a few donors to lend sizable amounts of money at low interest rates. He traveled all over the country, forging alliances with other unions, believing there was strength in banding together. In the nation's capital, he met with Senators and Congressmen to lobby in support of the pro-union legislation. As time went by, the economy slowly improved and he was able to negotiate better working conditions and small pay increases. By 1935, union membership had quadrupled and, with more dues coming in, there was more than enough money to pay off the loans. After that, Jake persuaded the executive board to use some of the union's new-found wealth to open health clinics for members and to fund educational scholarships for their children.

Amid all these successes, the one negative note was the Mafia's continued attempts to make inroads into unions all over the country. At the annual meeting of the American Federation of Labor, Jake proposed banning known mobsters from holding office. The proposal was voted down and, immediately afterwards, a well-known mobster named Big Sal Fanzini was elected to the AFL's executive counsel.

Fanzini was widely suspected of murdering Al Steichorn, a long-time unionist and friend of Jake's who'd been speaking out against mob infiltration for years. That made Fanzini's election an especially bitter pill to swallow. Now, Jake supposed, *he* was on Fanzini's hit list.

But, on the day before the union's national convention, not even concerns about the Mafia could get Jake down. That afternoon, he met with the executive board and gave them a preview of his keynote speech. The state of the union, he told them, was excellent. Fortunately, the meeting didn't run too late, which was a very good thing because it was Sophie's birthday and she had agreed to go out. Aunt Sarah and Uncle Lou were cabbing it with her and Jake would meet them at the restaurant. Carl Rasmussen, a reporter for the New York Herald Tribune and a good friend for many years now, was joining them.

Entering Mahoney's, Jake didn't see his party at first. The restaurant was a popular place, which, despite its name, served top-notch Italian food and was always crowded. He finally spotted them in a corner and, after greeting Tim Mahoney, who was tending bar, with a nod, he made his way over to the table them.

"I'm sorry to be so late," he said as he sat down next to Sophie. "My meeting ran a little long."

Uncle Lou laughed. "If you wouldn't be late, it wouldn't be you, Jake," he said. "Anyway, now I have an excuse for having a big appetite."

Carl, a solidly built guy with a crew cut and a high, broad forehead, wasted no time. "How did the executive board meeting go?"

Jake grinned. "Can't stop being a reporter for even one second, can you?"

Carl chuckled. "Well?"

Jake shook his head. "Let's at least order first. I'm starving and, clearly, Lou is too. Some people need actual food to feed off of."

"Okay, okay." Carl relaxed back in his chair.

Jake had been to Mahoney's so many times, he didn't need a menu to order. But he pretended to glance through it to give himself a minute to decompress, then signaled the waiter. As soon as their orders had been taken, Carl pounced.

"So, let's hear about the meeting."

Jake shook his head. "I don't think anyone besides you wants to hear about that. Anyway, this is supposed to be a celebration."

"Jake's right," Aunt Sarah chimed in. "And doesn't the birthday girl look beautiful? Look at your wife Jake. She's a movie star."

Jake smiled at Aunt Sarah. "She sure is."

Next to him, Sophie said, "You don't think the new hat is too much?"

Jake swiveled. He hadn't noticed the hat before, but now couldn't imagine how he'd missed it. It had a startlingly large brim and was so sharply angled that one side virtually covered Sophie's left eye while the other swooped up towards the ceiling. It seemed unspeakably ostentatious to him. But it was nice to see Sophie making an effort with her appearance. She seemed to be finally coming out of her shell, at least a little bit.

He remembered when she'd been unwilling to leave the apartment even for a special occasion. Now, venturing outside was something she did on a regular basis. She often entertained him at dinner with stories of the gossip she'd heard from the neighborhood women as she sat chatting with them in front of the building while their children played nearby.

The other day, he'd come home early and, from far down the block, caught a glimpse of the back of her wheelchair. Someone must have said something funny because she'd suddenly thrown her head back and peels of laughter had come trilling backwards. The other women laughed too and he'd found himself grinning. He'd forgotten how contagious Sophie's laugh was.

One of the other women evidently noticed him and told Sophie because she turned her chair around. Only then did he see that there was a small curly-haired toddler perched on her lap. Sophie had one arm across the child's belly holding her in place. Suddenly, the child began squirming, throwing her arms up and arching her back, until she slipped down Sophie's legs, twisted away, and ran back to her mother.

The smile on Jake's face faded. Poor Sophie. Forever consigned to borrowing other people's children. He didn't know why she tortured herself. She should just do what he did and avoid situations that rubbed salt in the wound.

He realized that he had never answered Sophie's question about her hat. Fortunately, Aunt Sarah saved him from having to come up with something complimentary about it.

"Of course it isn't too much," she said firmly. "You look just like Joan Crawford in that hat, only more beautiful. You tell her Jake."

Jake nodded. "Yes," he said, smiling at Sophie. "Aunt Sarah's right. Just like Joan Crawford."

He could tell by Sophie's crestfallen face that it was too late. He'd already blown it. Once by not complimenting her as soon as he arrived and a second time by not picking up on the opening Aunt Sarah had given him. He searched for something to say to make up for his earlier lapses. "Your dress is very pretty too," he said. "Is it new?"

"Yes," Sophie said quietly. "Thank you for noticing."

There was a lull in the conversation that Jake somehow felt responsible for. Unable to think of what else to do, he turned to Carl. "So, I know you're dying to know about the meeting" he said. And he proceeded to fill him in.

Fortunately, as the dinner went on, Sophie seemed to enjoy herself. Jake ordered wine for the table, and by the time they finished the main part of the meal, they were well into their third bottle. It was a good time to cut away for a minute.

"Will you all excuse me? I'll be right back. If the waiter comes by for dessert orders, I'll have a cup of coffee and a slice of cheesecake."

190

"Do you take cream in your coffee?" Carl asked.

"He likes it black," Sophie said.

"That's right," Jake said. He caught Sophie's eye and gave her a smile, hoping he was forgiven for his earlier husbandly bumbles and was rewarded with a wry grin that told him he was out of the doghouse. Then he left to make his way to the men's room.

By the time he'd finished and was on his way back to the table, Mahoney's was more crowded than ever. He threaded his way around tables carefully but, even so, accidentally bumped up against someone.

"Sorry," he said.

"Hey, what the fuck—?" the man he'd bumped into whirled around, stopping abruptly when he saw Jake's face. "You!" he growled. "What're you doin' here?"

It was Fanzini, the mobster who'd just been elected to the AFL executive board. Jake took a deep breath. This was not the time or place to start anything.

"I'm just having dinner," he said, and moved past Fanzini toward his seat. But a hard jab against his back almost made him lose his footing and he whipped around.

"You got alotta nerve comin' here," Fanzini sneered.

Jake willed himself not to react before he'd assessed the situation. Once upon a time, his fists would have flown without a second's thought. But he'd become more disciplined over the years. The fact that the mobster was at least a head taller than him didn't factor into his thinking at all. He had never walked away from a fight in his life. And he knew that if you didn't put these guys in their place the first time they started with you, they were only emboldened. On the other hand, he didn't really want to bust up Mahoney's place nor did he want to ruin Sophie's birthday dinner by taking the fight outside. He spoke just loudly enough so Fanzini could hear.

"In deference to the surroundings, I'm going to ignore that comment for now." He made sure to pause for emphasis before adding the "for now."

Turning away, he again headed toward his table. He had just reached Sophie's side and put his hand on the back of his chair when he heard Fanzini's voice just behind his ear.

"I said, you gotta lotta nerve comin' here."

Jake turned around slowly. "Look Fanzini, why don't you just go about your business and save this crap for another time."

"Yeah?" Fanzini's face was flushed. "Well, no fuckin' bastid who tries to get me and my buddies kicked outta the AFL is gonna tell me what my business is or when to go about it."

"Hey," Jake said softly in an almost friendly voice save for its dangerous undertone, "I don't appreciate language like that when there are ladies present. So either put a smile on your ugly mug and apologize to my wife and her aunt or get ready to have your butt kicked to the other side of the room."

Fanzini barked out an ugly laugh. He took a step closer to Jake so that the difference in their heights was more pronounced and looked down at him.

"My butt ain't too worried right now," he said.

Jake shook his head slowly. "That's understandable because your butt is just as stupid as the rest of you."

"Yeah?" said Fanzini. "Well, at least I ain't married to some cripple."

Beside him, Jake heard Sophie say softly, "It's okay, Jake." But, it was too late. Jake rammed his head into Fanzini's chest. The bigger man was thrown off balance and crashed to the floor with a solid thunk. Fanzini scrambled to his feet, but Jake was ready. As soon as Fanzini was upright, Jake's fist met his face with a solid uppercut. Fanzini spun around but didn't go down.

Around them, chairs scraped back as other patrons scrambled to get out of the way. Fanzini landed a punch to Jake's jaw that was going to hurt a lot for several days. But Jake ignored it and continued to let fly one blow after another. His final punch connected solidly with Fanzini's nose. There was a crunching sound and Fanzini's hands flew up to his face just as the blood started spurting out. At that point, Mahoney and a few of his waiters stepped in to "break up" the fight, although it obvious to everyone that it was already over. One of the waiters handed Fanzini a napkin and he hurriedly pressed it to his streaming nose. As the napkin became soaked with blood, Fanzini shook off the waiters' hands and pointed furiously at Jake.

"This ain't over," he said.

Jake stared back, his face impassive. Fanzini made for the door, pushing patrons who had already stepped back to clear his path. As soon as the door had closed behind him, Jake turned to Mahoney.

"I'm sorry. I should have taken it outside right from the beginning. Send me a bill for the damage?"

Mahoney nodded. "You gonna need a steak for that jaw?"

Jake shook his head. "Thanks for the offer, but I'll take care of it at home."

Mahoney headed toward the bar and Jake turned back to the table. Carl and Uncle Lou had re-taken their seats. Next to Aunt Sarah, Sophie had gone waxy pale. Even her lips had lost their color. Her eyes were rounded with fear.

"Who was that?" she asked. "Why was he attacking you?"

"He's nobody. Just a punk," Jake said as he sat down. "Forget about him."

"He said it wasn't over," Sophie persisted. "What else is he going to do?"

Jake took a sip of his coffee and set the cup down carefully on its saucer. "Don't worry about it," he told Sophie. "I promise it's nothing to be concerned about."

"But why did he start up in the first place?" The color had come back into Sophie's face and she didn't look scared anymore, just upset. "Why was he so angry with you?"

Jake took a deep breath. He really didn't want to talk about it, now or ever. "I said not to worry about it," he repeated, trying to keep his voice steady. "So please let it drop."

"Stop it," Sophie said.

"Stop what?" Jake asked, startled.

"Stop treating me like I'm a child. I'm not a child. I'm your wife and I want to know the truth. Who was that man?"

The table had grown silent. Uncle Lou, Aunt Sarah, and Carl were all looking down at their plates.

"Alright," Jake said finally. "You asked, so I'll tell you. He's a mobster. But, he's just a punk. Nothing to be concerned about." He looked at Sophie with level eyes. "I promise this is nothing to worry about. Have I ever broken a promise?"

Sophie stared at him as the seconds ticked by. Jake didn't blink. Finally, she shook her head. "No, you've never broken a promise."

"Okay then," he said, letting out his breath. "Now, did anyone order me a piece of cheesecake or do I have to do everything around here?"

Beside him, Carl started chuckling.

"What's so funny?" Aunt Sarah asked.

"I was just thinking of my headline. What do you think of this: Mayhem at Mahoney's."

Jake shook his head, but he was grateful for Carl's attempt at levity. "Is that what you were thinking about the whole time he was trying to bash my head in?"

"Of course not," Carl said. "Well," he conceded with a laugh in response to Jake's skeptical expression, "not at the very beginning."

There was forced laughter from them all, but the celebratory mood had seeped out of their party.

By the time they got home, Sophie looked exhausted. Jake helped her change into a nightgown and got her settled under the covers. He sat at the foot of the bed and pulled his shoes off. Had it only been that afternoon that he had presided over a euphoric executive board meeting? It seemed much longer ago.

"Jake," Sophie said in a small voice, "are you angry with me?"

He twisted around and looked at her. "No, why would I be?"

"Because I accused you of treating me like a child."

"Of course I'm not angry about that." He stood up and went over to his chest of drawers, loosened his tie, and laid it on top. "Anyway, I'm the one who should ask if you're angry with me."

"Why?"

"Because I ruined your birthday celebration." He removed his cufflinks and placed them in a wooden tray.

"You didn't ruin it."

"Then because I made you feel like I was treating you like a child. I'm sorry if I've been doing that. I don't mean to."

"You don't. It's just that . . ." She hesitated.

Jake looked at her. He knew how hard she tried not to complain. He often thought it would be better if she did now and then. At least it would be honest.

"It's alright," he encouraged her. "You can say it."

"Well, it's just that, I know I'm not the same girl I was."

"Sophie—"

"No, let me finish. I know I'm not the same girl I was in the photo you have in your wallet. And don't look at me like that. I wasn't snooping. I saw it one day when it fell out. Anyway, I may not still be that girl, but I'm also not the same girl I was for so long after the fire.

"In case you haven't noticed," she continued, "I don't sit inside all day anymore feeling sorry for myself. You've been traveling so much that I haven't had time to tell you everything I've been doing. I'm not just stuffing envelopes for the Warm Springs Foundation anymore. I've started volunteering for the National Society for Crippled Children. I go around the neighborhood and sell envelope seals to raise money for them. I've already raised over five hundred dollars."

Jake stared at her. He couldn't believe he'd been so stupid as to still keep that photo of Lena in his wallet. Thank goodness Sophie hadn't guessed the real reason he carried it and didn't know that he still looked at Lena's picture now and then when he was feeling really low.

"Jake?" Sophie said. "Have you been listening to me? Have you heard anything I've said?"

Sophie looked upset again, but he wasn't sure exactly why. What was it she had said? Something about not being the same girl she'd once been? But, of course, he was well aware of that. Was it still about him treating her like a child? He didn't mean to, but as he looked at her with the blanket drawn up over her withered legs, she looked as small as a child and as helpless.

"Don't *look* at me like that," Sophie said.

"Like what?" Jake asked, bewildered.

She sighed. "Never mind. I'm going to sleep."

She maneuvered herself onto her side, and, after a moment, Jake went back to getting ready for bed. He couldn't understand why Sophie was so upset with him. He knew he wasn't a perfect husband, but he provided and cared for her as best he could. He took pains to be gentle when it came to lovemaking. He'd never been unfaithful, not even once. What more did she want?

He pulled on a clean white t-shirt and a pair of striped pajama bottoms and went into the bathroom to wash up. In the mirror over the sink, his jaw was a purplish yellow. Despite what Sophie said, he knew he'd ruined her birthday celebration. And it wasn't just the fight with Fanzini. It was the way he'd treated her. He needed to try harder to notice what she was wearing and to give her little compliments. All women needed them. Maybe that's what she'd meant about him treating her like a child. Maybe she just needed to feel like he thought she was pretty once in a while. And he could bring her flowers. Even when it wasn't her birthday. He would start tomorrow.

The next morning, he woke up feeling stiff. His muscles ached. He didn't remember that jerk Fanzini getting many punches in.

Back in the day, a dust-up like last night's would have left him no worse for wear. But, then again, he wasn't as young as he used to be. Moving slowly, he went into the bathroom. The bruise on his jaw looked even worse than it felt. He touched it gingerly, toyed with the idea of skipping his morning shave, but went at it after all.

He felt better after a hot shower and, emerging from the bedroom, caught a tantalizing whiff of frying eggs coming from the direction of the kitchen. It was a reminder that the fight with Fanzini hadn't been the only contentious moment last night.

After getting into bed the night before, he'd reviewed the whole evening in his mind and felt worse than ever about the way he'd behaved. It couldn't be easy for Sophie to suffer the indignities and curious stares that were the price she paid for going out in public. In fact, it took courage. Which meant that *if* her accusation was correct and he had been treating her like a child, he should be ashamed of himself. As he walked towards the kitchen, he remembered his resolution from the night before and determined to make good on it.

Sophie was stirring something on the stove, wearing a pink silk robe that he didn't remember having seen before and a matching pink ribbon wound around her hair. He stopped in the doorway to inhale.

"Mmm. Something smells wonderful in here."

She smiled and said, "It's my new perfume. I call it fried eggs and onions. You like?"

Jake raised his eyebrows. He wasn't sure what he'd expected from Sophie this morning, but this light-hearted banter wasn't it. He didn't know what to make of it, but he was pleased and grinned.

"I love it. In fact, I think you should try to figure out a way to bottle it and sell it."

"I'm working on it. And I've already got my slogan."

"What's that?"

"Eau d' fried eggs. Because everyone knows the best way to a man's heart—"

"Is through his stomach," Jake finished, smiling. Remembering his vow, he said, "That's a very pretty robe. Is it new?"

The smile faded from Sophie's face and she turned back to the stove. "No," she said.

Jake was confused. Already he'd said something wrong and he had no idea what it was. He tried again. "I really like it."

"Thanks." Sophie slid the eggs onto a plate, put the plate in her lap, and wheeled herself over to the kitchen table. "Here you are," she said. "Toast will be ready in just a minute."

She wheeled over to the toaster, waited for it to pop up, pulled the slices out, and plopped them on the waiting plate. Jake watched as she glided back to the kitchen table, slid two pieces of toast onto his plate and took one onto her own plate at the place she'd set for herself opposite him. He waited until she had finished buttering her own slice before reaching over and touching her free hand.

"Sophie," he said.

She looked at him, toast in hand. "Yes?"

"You look very pretty this morning."

She looked back at him unblinking. "Thank you. And thanks again for the robe. I guess you don't remember that you gave it to me for my birthday last year."

"I'm sorry. I should have remembered." He tried to catch her eye. "But Sophie, doesn't it matter at all that I said you look pretty in it?"

Sophie gave a sad smile. "Sure Jake," she said. "Thanks again. Now, eat your eggs before they get cold."

CHAPTER TWENTY-SEVEN

1940

"I HAVE TO ADMIT IT," LENA SAID TO WILL FROM BEHIND THE NEW oak desk he'd chosen for her. "Moving my office here to Monticello along with the rest of the business is working out better than I thought. I still don't feel as comfortable here as I did working out of the house. But it's a nice sunny space. And I think that after I bring in a few plants and some pictures and maybe a rug, it'll be fine."

"Of course it'll be fine," Will said, smiling. "I just hope in the future, you'll have a little more faith in me."

"I have faith in you," she said mildly. "But this move was a pretty big decision. I still wish you hadn't gone ahead and actually signed the lease before I agreed to it."

"I wouldn't have had to do that if you hadn't been so stubborn," Will was still smiling, but his smile had become strained.

Lena frowned. "I wasn't being stubborn. I had good reasons for wanting to keep my office where it was."

"I know you weren't trying to be stubborn, honey," he said, the "honey" sounding forced. "It's just that you tend to think with your heart, not with your head. It's not your fault. Women are naturally more emotional than men. It's what makes them good mothers. But it's no way to run a business. A business isn't a baby."

"I know a business isn't a baby," she said, struggling to keep her voice even. "I'm the one who started this company, remember? I've worked pretty hard to get us where we are and I'm still at it."

"I've been meaning to talk to you about that," he said. "About the hours you've been putting in. I realize that with Rachel nearly grown up you don't have anything to focus your maternal instincts on. Maybe if that doctor could figure out what's wrong with you and you became pregnant again, you wouldn't make the business into a surrogate child."

"Excuse me? Are you implying that women only go into business to fulfill some maternal need? Let me remind you, Will, that I started this business when Rachel was only eight years old and still needed plenty of mothering and I was also working for Grossman's at the time. So, I certainly didn't undertake this enterprise to fill up either my time or some kind of emotional vacuum."

"No, of course not." Will looked distraught. "That's not what I meant at all. It's just that sometimes I think maybe the reason I'm putting in so many hours is to fill up the time I'd ordinarily be using to roughhouse with a son or throw around a baseball. It's like I'm doing extra work to take my mind off the fact that we haven't any children. I just thought maybe you were doing the same thing. I wanted you know that I understood if that was the way you were feeling."

Lena sighed. "I'm sorry. I shouldn't have accused you like that."

"It's alright."

"No. It's not alright." She shook her head. "I'm really sorry. I know how much you want children. And Will," she shrugged helplessly, "even though Doctor Garber never found anything wrong with me, if you want me to go to see some other doctor, I'm still willing to do that."

"I don't want to talk about it while we're at work," Will said, looking uncomfortable. "Anyway, I have to go over to the bank. There's some paperwork they want me to take care of. I'll be back in a little while."

"Do you need me to go with you?"

He paused in the doorway, his back to her. "No. I'm going to talk to them about that loan we discussed and you know the bank doesn't like dealing with women. It's why we agreed to put most of the business in my name."

"Alright. I'll see you later then?"

"Sure. I'll be back in a little while."

As she watched him walk out, she tried to figure out how the conversation had ended on such a sour note. It happened so often these days and usually ended with her apologizing while wondering who was really to blame. Probably both of them, she thought. And since Will wasn't going to change, she would have to try harder. If only she could give him the child he so desperately wanted. Maybe she *should* see another doctor. But, no matter what Will said, she didn't believe that her working was interfering with her ability to get pregnant.

Sitting at her desk in her new office with her paperwork spread in front of her, she tried to put all that out of her mind as she went over the sales figures. The little business that she had begun fourteen years ago had grown exponentially. It wasn't just monogrammed gloves and handkerchiefs anymore. A year after her first advertisement, she'd expanded her offerings to include belts and handbags, with monograms done in brass instead of embroidery thread. When those items sold like crazy, she took another chance and added signet rings, cuff links, and blazer buttons, all of which could be personalized for a small additional charge.

Rather than take out more and more ads, she decided to print a small catalogue and, almost on a whim, included a few small household items, towels, sheets, and even aprons and potholders. These, too, proved hugely popular. Keeping an eye out for new products was fun. She began adding a few new ones every year while dropping from the catalogue those items that didn't sell well.

Now, as she looked at the sales figures, she saw that they were up significantly for virtually every product. The only items for which sales had gone down were monogrammed gloves. Women simply weren't wearing gloves as much as they once had. Perhaps it was time to drop them from the Lena K catalog. Joe was no longer her glove supplier anyway. He had given up selling gloves and gone into the clothing business with his friend Arnie Sims. They were a good team. Arnie did all the designing and Joe ran the manufacturing end of the business.

People said a depression was a strange time to start a new business. But Joe said it was the perfect time because there was nothing to lose. He must have been right because Rothman Sims was doing very well and so were Joe and Arnie. They had moved into an apartment together and Joe had never looked happier. As far as Lena was concerned, if Arnie made Joe happy, that was enough for her and what two grown men did in private was no one's business.

Lena decided she would talk to Will about whether to drop the gloves as soon as she had a chance. The catalogue was going to the printers in a few days and any changes to the product line-up would have to be made by then. She moved the sales figures to one side and went on to the next task on her list. This time it involved a new product. She'd come across it at the county fair last month. The clever homemaker, who had won a blue ribbon for effort, had taken a blanket and added sleeves to the front of it, so that a person could cover themselves with the blanket but still have the use of their hands to knit or darn socks or hold a book.

These days, everyone was trying to save money on their heating bills and using blankets to keep warm enabled one to use less coal. A blanket with sleeves was a bit of a gimmick, but Lena had a feeling it would sell well if it was marketed correctly. She had taken the homemaker's name and phone number and told her that she would get in touch with her soon.

Her thought was that they could pay the woman for the idea and then find a manufacturer to produce the sleeved blanket for the Lena K catalog. Joe might even be interested. He was not averse to doing some manufacturing for other lines and she'd rather give him the business than give it to someone else. She made a mental note to talk to Will about that too before putting the paper with the homemaker's name and phone number to one side. She was about to start going through her mail when there was a knock on the door.

"Come in."

"Mrs. Kerner? I'm sorry to bother you, but I was wondering if you had a few minutes."

"Hi Jeannie. You're not bothering me. Have a seat."

Jeannie Berlin was only twenty-five years old, but with her hollowed eyes and thinning brown hair, she looked nearly twice that. Her husband, like too many men, had lost his job at the start of the depression and found solace in alcohol. Though the economy was much improved now and jobs in greater supply, he'd not found his way back to sobriety yet. With four children under the age of seven, Jeannie had her hands full.

"How are you?" Lena asked.

"I'm alright."

"Good. And your children are all well?"

"They're a handful, but they're good kids. The oldest one started school this year and I keep telling her that if she studies hard, she might be able to go to college someday like your daughter. Of course, I don't expect my Luanne is smart enough to go to a school like Vassar, but maybe some other college."

"If Luanne takes after you, I'm sure she's plenty smart enough to go to Vassar."

"I hope so. Is your daughter almost finished with school?"

"She's graduating in June."

"I bet you'll be happy to have her home again. You must miss her."

Lena smiled. "I do miss her, but I don't think I'll be having her back home again. She's got her heart set on getting a job in journalism and wants to move to New York City."

Jeannie looked shocked. "My but times are changing. When I was her age, my folks would never have let me move away to New York City."

"Times are changing. But, you know, when I was even younger than Rachel, I left my home and my family in Europe and traveled two weeks by ship to come to New York. Of course, my brother Joe was waiting for me." She smiled at the memory, adding, "And Joe will be there for Rachel too when the time comes."

"New York City." Jeannie shook her head in wonder. "I've never been there. What's it like?"

Lena glanced away as she tried to think of how to describe the place where she had spent such a short but eventful time. Images filled her mind: walking to work with Sophie in the pre-dawn dark as Hester Street's crowded pushcart market came to life; shopping for new clothes in the vast and comprehensive environs of Macy's Department Store; sitting across from Daniel at a tiny table in Meltzer's, the waiter bringing them cup after cup of tea; standing on the stage at Cooper Union Hall and holding Jake's hand aloft while the crowd went crazy and her insides turned to mush; going afterwards to Katz's where the Yiddish spouting waiters and sweet smelling blintzes brought back memories of home. And there was so much more: the exoticism of the narrow Chinatown alleys, the strange but delicious food they'd eaten at the subterranean restaurant, and the whirling colors and syncopated beat of the dance at the Settlement House.

Places and people and experiences were interwoven together in her mind and she knew she could not extract from her memories a description of the City that would do it justice. So all she said was, "It has the best of everything and the worst of everything and it's unlike any other place I've ever been."

"Oh my," Jeannie said.

"Jeannie?" Lena made her voice gentle. "Was there any special reason you wanted to talk to me today?"

"Actually there was. I... I wanted to...." She licked her lips and looked down at her lap where she was massaging the thumb joint of one hand with the thumb of the other. "Um, me and the other employees wanted to ask if you and Mr. Kerner would maybe reconsider the wage cut."

Lena stared at her. "Wage cut?"

"Yes. I mean, we all understand what Mr. Kerner said about the economy still being bad and sales being slow and all. But it'll be tough to get by on less than we're making now. If you could maybe reconsider cutting our wages or maybe cut them a little less...." Her voice trailed off and she looked up at Lena with pleading eyes.

Lena could not believe what she was hearing. She sat very still, pressed her lips together, and breathed slowly, not wanting to speak until she had decided exactly what to say. She was angrier than she had been in a very long time, but she didn't want to take it out on poor Jeannie. She nodded her head and tried to smile reassuringly.

"Yes. Thank you for coming to me. I'll have to... I'll have to get back to you about that. Please tell the others that I will get back to all of you about that."

"Thank you, Mrs. Kerner. And you aren't angry at me for asking?"

"No, no. I'm not angry with you at all. In fact, I'm grateful to you." *Grateful for bringing my husband's actions to my attention.* "I always want my employees to feel free to come to me with any concerns. Thank you Jeannie."

Jeannie gave a tremulous smile and rose. "Thank you again, Mrs. Kerner," she said.

The minute the door closed behind her, Lena began to breathe faster and harder. He's done it again, she thought. Just when she thought they'd agreed to discuss the matter further, Will had gone ahead with the very action to which she'd already raised an objection. More and more, he seemed to be completely disregarding her opinion. Acting as if the business was his alone.

But this was the worst of all because this had to do with the treatment of their employees. Unfair treatment in her opinion. Will had lied to them. Sales weren't down, they were up. There was no need to cut salaries. Why had Will done this behind her back? What had happened to the grand words Will had spoken when he'd proposed? Words about their being partners in life and in business. What kind of partnership could it be if he disregarded her opinion and did whatever he wanted the minute her back was turned?

At dinner, Will was in a cheerful mood. "This chicken is delicious." He shoved another forkful in his mouth. "Another recipe from Bess?"

Lena nodded. "I finally figured out how much one of Bess's handfuls is and what she means by a pinch. Now I should be able to make some of the other dishes you like."

"Wonderful." Will beamed. "Be sure and find out how she makes that stuffed cabbage."

"Alright. Would you like some more potatoes?"

"Nope, I'm stuffed."

He pushed his chair back and stood up. Lena decided she would give him until she finished washing the dishes to bring up the matter of the staff pay cut. When she'd finished putting everything away, she went to join him. Will was reading and didn't look up. She moved around the room, straightening the painting that hung over the fireplace, pausing to look at the framed photograph of Rachel on the mantle, and finally coming to a stop next to the Philco radio that was Will's pride and joy.

Will glanced up. "Is it time for the Lone Ranger already?"

"No. Not yet. In about ten more minutes."

"Oh." He went back to reading.

"So, how did your meeting at the bank go?" she asked.

"Very well," he said without looking up.

"Will, when you've done with reading the newspaper," she tried to keep her voice light, there are a few things I want to talk to you about."

This time Will lowered the newspaper to his lap. "That's alright," he said. "I've already read enough." He flicked the newspaper with the back of his hand. "It's enough to make a person sick. There's not a single area of life that's safe from Government interference anymore. That dictator in the White House is going to ruin this country for good. So," he folded the newspaper in half, and put it on the table next to him, "what did you want to talk about?"

Lena toyed with the idea of responding to Will's "dictator" comment, but decided that arguing about the President wouldn't be a good start to the conversation she was determined to have. She began with what she thought would be an easy topic.

"There's this new product I want to run past you. I think I already mentioned it. It's a blanket with sleeves so you can cover yourself and still have the use of your hands. I saw it when I went to the county fair and I think it could be a big seller for us. Everyone's trying to save coal money and this -"

"Darling," he interrupted her. "You know I don't like to discuss business when we're home.

"I know. But we haven't been in the office at the same time in several days. And it's getting awfully close to the deadline for deciding on the final items for the catalog."

"Well, I really don't wish to discuss that right now. I've had a long day and this is my time to relax. There's nothing we have to talk about that can't wait until tomorrow."

"Well, there is one thing."

"What's that?" Will asked, raising one eyebrow.

"There's the matter of staff salaries. We never really settled anything and we can't discuss it in the office because there's always a chance someone might overhear us."

"True," Will agreed, "which is why I've already taken care of that matter."

"What?" Lena said, hoping she sounded surprised. "What do you mean? We hadn't finished discussing it yet. Don't you remember I suggested that we institute profit sharing?"

Will smiled and shook his head. "Darling, I know you weren't serious about that idea. Why would I, a business owner, want to share my profits with my employees?"

"Because the employees help us earn that profit," Lena said evenly.

"True," Will agreed. "And that's what I pay them to do. But the employees aren't the ones risking their capital to build up this company. Profits are my reward for taking that risk."

"But sharing those profits is just another way of paying employees," Lena pointed out. "And it's a way that makes them want to work even harder for us. President Roosevelt explained the whole thing during his radio address last week."

"Even if I were inclined to consider it, which I'm not, just knowing that that anti-business socialist-leaning dictator is in favor of it would be enough for me to be against it. It's bad enough that he's already ruining the country with this social security crap and unemployment insurance, both of which are costing us a fortune in profits."

"But Will, profit sharing isn't just good for our employees, it's good for us too. It helps build company loyalty."

Will laughed. "I don't think I need to worry about employee loyalty when jobs are so scarce. Where are they going to go if they quit?"

Lena stared at him. She did not want to let him see how upset she was. She knew from experience that that would only prompt Will to end the discussion permanently out of a supposed solicitousness for her well-being. So, she said nothing, and took a few quiet breaths, hoping she would soon feel calmer. Will got up and knelt in front of the radio, fiddling with the dials.

"Will," Lena said, making her voice as relaxed as she could. "If you don't agree to reward our employees with profit sharing, then we'll have to reward them with raises."

Will, his hands still on the radio dials, swiveled part way around and looked at her. For a few seconds, he said nothing whatsoever. Then he shook his head.

"No," he said. "We don't *have* to do anything. Anyway, I've already told them that they're not getting raises this year. I want to embark on a big expansion and I need money to bankroll it." He swiveled back to the radio. "Why don't you bring in the coffee now?" he suggested. "That way you won't miss any of The Lone Ranger."

Lena couldn't help it. Tears of anger and frustration welled up her eyes despite her best effort. "Will," she said, "why did you tell them that they were getting pay cuts when you and I hadn't finished discussing the subject of their pay yet?"

Will stood up and walked over to her, putting his hands on either side of her shoulders and looking at her with a concerned expression. "Honey," he said in a soothing tone, "there's no need to get upset. I know you're just a softy when it comes to the help. That's why I took care of it. You wouldn't have wanted to be the one to break it to them would you? That's why it's better for me to handle these things. You just keep coming up with those good ideas for the kinds of products women like to buy and I'll take care of everything else. Now, why don't you go get the coffee? The show's about to begin."

"Look, Will -" Lena began.

From behind Will came a crackling sound and then the announcer's voice. "It's starting," Will said. He hurried over to sit on the edge of his chair, his eager face extended toward the radio.

Lena knew she would get nowhere while Will was thus engaged. But to herself, she made a vow. This subject was far from closed. She would bring it up again at the first opportunity.

For the next few weeks, Lena felt like a coward. She could hardly look Jeannie or any of their other employees in the eyes. The problem was that there never seemed to be any time to discuss the topic of employee pay with Will. During the day, he was hardly around because he was still hammering out the loan details with the bank, although she had no idea why it was taking so long. In the evening, he insisted that he wanted to relax and get away from shoptalk.

Today, Will had promised to stop in her office when he was through at the bank. With the catalog due to go to press in two days, they could no longer put off final decisions about what items would be included. Once that topic was done, Lena decided she would just have to find some way to bring the conversation around to employee salaries. The telephone rang and she reached for the receiver.

"Lena K Enterprises," she said.

"Lena, is that you?"

"Oh Bess, yes, it's me. How are you?"

"I'm fine. But what about you, stranger?" Bess sounded more concerned than annoyed.

"I'm fine. Busy, but that's no excuse. I'm sorry I haven't called."

"The not calling I don't mind," Bess said, her approach as straightforward as ever. "It's the not seeing. Where have you been? We haven't seen you and Will in nearly a month of Sundays."

"I know. I'm sorry." Lena said again. There was a reason she and Will hadn't been to Grossman's in a while, but it was not Bess's fault. The last time they'd gone for dinner, they'd eaten in the kitchen just like in the old days. Sam and Bess's children, David and Esty, had been there too. David, at twenty-six, was very much like his father with the same easy warmth emanating from his gentle brown eyes and sweet-natured smile. Esty was as much of a spitfire as ever. Both were now actively involved in running the hotel.

During dinner, Bess, as usual, spent the entire time hustling back and forth from table to stove delivering mountains of delicious food. Esty performed imitations of some of the guests with David acting as her straight man. And Lena couldn't remember when she'd last had such a good time. It was comforting to see that no matter how successful Grossman's became, some things never changed.

Of course, many other aspects of Grossman's had changed since Lena had worked there. Indeed, Grossman's had grown phenomenally these last few years. With times as hard as they were, people who had jobs were more interested than ever in getting away from it all and the Catskills were still a comparatively inexpensive way to do that. Some of the smaller hotels in the area had been unable to make it through the leanest of times. Their misfortune had been Grossman's gain.

More importantly, the Grossmans had made wise decisions about where to invest the profits. They'd built a golf course, a swimming pool, and a gymnasium that David had, somehow, persuaded the heavyweight champ, Al Campanolo, to train at. The press trailed after Campanolo, stayed out at the hotel and reported on both the training and the hotel's amenities. After that, the hotel became more popular than ever.

Despite all their success, however, Sam and Bess were still just Sam and Bess, as down to earth as ever, modest, warm-hearted, and kind. Sitting with them at dinner, Lena thought that nobody looking at them would guess they were the owners of a fabulously successful business. Unfortunately, the same could not be said about Will. To Lena's embarrassment, Will had gone on and on during dinner about how well Lena K Enterprise was doing; how they would soon be hiring more employees, and how the bank obviously recognized a successful business when it saw one. Squirming inwardly, Lena had barely been able to hold her tongue until they'd gotten into the car to return home. Then she'd blurted it out.

"Why did you have to go on and on like that?"

"What are you talking about?" Will said, looking completely surprised.

"I'm talking about you telling everyone that Lena K sales are up and that the bank can't wait to lend us more money."

"Why shouldn't I want to share good news with the Grossmans?" Will asked. "I'm sure they're happy for me, just like I'm happy for them. Do you think they begrudge me my good fortune?"

"No. That's not what I'm saying." Lena sighed. "It's just that, the way you talk about it, it sounds like you're bragging."

"I don't know what you mean." Will had that wounded look again. The thing was, she knew he was being honest. He really didn't know what she was talking about. That was part of the problem. Or maybe she was just overly sensitive. After all, there was nothing inherently wrong with sharing good news with good friends.

"Never mind," she said. "Maybe I'm just being silly. But please promise me one thing. Next time we go there, please don't grumble about not eating in the dining room."

"But I don't know why we can't eat in there," Will said. "I don't like eating in the kitchen. It reminds me of when we worked for them. We're not the hired help anymore. They should invite us to eat in the dining room with the other guests."

"The paying guests," Lena reminded him.

"Well, if it's about the money," Will said stiffly, "I'm sure we can afford to pay for our own dinner."

"It's not about the money," Lena said exasperated. "It's about being treated like family. Besides, it brings back good memories."

"Good memories?" said Will. "Of your days as a toilet scrubber?"

"Yes," Lena said. "Not the scrubbing toilets part, but all the laughing and joking together. And Rachel growing and Joe coming for visits. Being part of one big happy family."

"Well, that part I can understand. I miss having a big family around too. I grew up with that, you know. Always thought I'd have the same thing. But I know it's not your fault that you never got pregnant again. I know you're trying."

At that point, Lena gave up. She'd known when she married him, that he had an old fashioned streak. She'd found it sweetly gallant and, back then, after so many years of being by herself, the idea of having someone to help her, to share her concerns with, make decisions with, and team up with, had been awfully appealing. But that same old fashioned streak meant that he had rigid ideas about any number of things. And, in the end, it had been easier to put off going back to Grossman's than to make Will understand what she was trying to say.

She coped with her frustration by reminding herself of all the good things about Will, like the flowers he still brought her every Friday and the little compliments he still paid to her cooking. She reminded herself that small aggravations were bound to crop up when one had been married for so many years. He was still her husband and they were still a team. As for Bess and Sam, she resolved to find other times to see them, times when Will was busy with other things. Unfortunately, such times were in short supply. She realized that she hadn't even heard Bess's last question.

"I'm sorry Bess, what was it you asked me?"

"I asked if everything was alright." Bess said.

"Yes, of course. I've just been very busy."

"Well maybe what you need is a break. Sam is going into town tomorrow and I thought maybe I'd go with him. Would you have time to meet me at the Village Tea Room?"

"Oh, Bess. I'd love it."

"I could meet you at around 3:00 p.m. Would that be alright?"

"It would be great."

"Then I'll see you tomorrow," Bess said.

"Yes, I'll see you tomorrow." Lena hung up the phone smiling and was still basking in the happy anticipation of seeing Bess when Will walked into her office a few seconds later. He was wearing a new suit and, if she wasn't mistaken, a new tie too. Will had always been a natty dresser. But lately, he seemed to be making a special effort. She felt a rush of guilt for not appreciating him more. Here he was, working hard to expand their business and she was getting angry at him just for trying to do what he thought was best.

He smiled and she felt her heart do a little flip that it hadn't done in a long time. He looked very pleased with himself. Things must have gone well at the bank. For once, she would give him credit where credit was due.

"Did you close the deal on the bank loan?" she asked.

Will shook his head. "Not yet. There are still a few more details to get through."

"My goodness. I wonder what the problem is. It's never taken this long before."

Will stiffened. "Are you suggesting that I'm not doing everything I can to get the loan?"

"Of course not. I'm not saying it's your fault. I'm saying that the bank has never been so picky before."

Will stared at her as if she had said something ridiculous. "Picky? Is that what you call it? I call it just making sure that everything's in order. There's nothing wrong with wanting to dot every "i" and cross every "t." It's the proper way of doing business. It wouldn't hurt if you were just a little more picky as you call it."

Startled by his reaction, but not wanting to start an argument, Lena told him, "I didn't mean anything critical. I was just surprised, because we've gotten loans before and they haven't taken this long."

Will looked as if he were trying to decide something. When he spoke, he sounded subdued. "Of course you didn't mean anything critical. I overreacted. Anyway, I'm sure I'll be able to wrap things up soon."

"Well that's good," she said, her voice trailing off. She paused, once again trying to figure out how the conversation had gone sour so quickly. When she spoke again, she tried to put some energy behind her words, "Anyway, I'm glad you're here today. We're really cutting it close on the catalog. Have you given any thought to adding that sleeved blanket I told you about?"

"Yes. I don't think it's a good idea."

"Really?" Lena frowned. "I think it's very clever and would sell quite well."

"I'm surprised you're so impressed with it," Will said. "It's just a gimmick." He looked directly in her eyes. "Just a dumb gimmick."

She flinched at the adjective. She was used to him disagreeing with her, even being dismissive, but not to his being insulting. She tried to keep her voice level so that he wouldn't see how upset she was, lest the discussion degenerate into an argument about Will's belief that women were too emotional to be in business.

"The blanket with sleeves may be a gimmick, but that doesn't mean it won't sell well. We've got lots of things in the catalog now that could be considered gimmicks but people still buy them. I think this would fit into our collection nicely. We could take the gloves out to make room for it. Give it a nice build-up, maybe a full page ad."

"Was there anything else we needed to talk about?" Will asked.

"There are one or two other things," Lena said, exasperated. "But with the catalog deadline hanging over us, we really have to resolve this."

"It is resolved, as far as I'm concerned."

"How can it be resolved when we haven't agreed on anything?"

"We can't always agree on everything," Will said. "Anyway, it's too late to have this discussion because I gave the printers the final catalog proofs yesterday."

"You what?" Lena stared at him. She knew she hadn't misheard him but she couldn't imagine that he'd really given the go-ahead for the catalogue to be printed without checking with her first. Over the years, Will had taken charge of more aspects of the business than she was comfortable with, but most of them had been things she'd never really enjoyed and some, like the bookkeeping, were tasks he was just better at than she was.

Selecting new products had always been her forte and her talent for doing so had been the part of the business where Will had shown the most deference to her opinion. Of course, she accepted the fact that having Will as her partner meant sometimes having to compromise even in areas where she was more insightful, but she'd never dreamed that Will would dare to cut her out of the decisions that were, in her mind, the very foundation of the Lena K business.

She tried to think of some other light in which to view his words. But she kept coming to the same conclusion and that conclusion was unacceptable. No, it was worse than that. It was outrageous.

"Will, how could you! How could you send the final proofs when we never finished talking about the product selection."

Will shrugged. "I figured that since I was never going to agree to that blanket thing anyway, I might as well send it along."

Lena had the sudden feeling that there'd been a change in the current and she was swimming against the tide. She tried to speak calmly to hide her increasing concern.

"You know, lately I get the feeling that you don't care much about what I think of things. In fact, I get the feeling that you're trying to take over this business."

"Take over?" Will looked surprised but nervous, almost like he was trying to act surprised when he really wasn't. "What are you talking about?"

"Just what I said. Lately, you seem to be acting like you're in charge of everything. Deciding things without me like cutting our employee's salaries, leasing this space, and now putting together this catalog. You can't just make decisions unilaterally, you know."

"Actually," Will said slowly. "Actually, I can."

Lena shook her head. "I don't think so, Will. Or have you forgotten. Lena K is a partnership. I'm half its owner."

"But I'm the president."

"Only because we agreed that having your name as president instead of mine would help us get bank loans, make purchases, and sign leases. It wasn't supposed to make you in charge of everything."

"Well, someone has to be in charge."

"In a partnership, both people are in charge. Like my brother and Arnie Sims. They're partners and they make all their decisions together."

Will looked outraged. "You're comparing me to that *faygele* Arnie Sims?"

"Will, that's not a nice thing to say," Lena protested. "Arnie is a lovely man. Anyway, my point is that partners make decisions together. When you proposed, you said that we would always be partners. Didn't you mean what you said?"

"Of course I did," his tone was reasonable again. "I meant that you would be in charge of running our home and raising our family and I would be in charge of the business, just like normal couples."

Lena stared at him. "You knew that I was running a business when you met me," she pointed out. "I thought that was something you admired about me."

"Yes. I did admire that. You were a single mother, with no one to support you. Of course, you had to do what you had to do. Just like my mother did after my father abandoned us. But," he held up one finger, "my mother would have given anything to have a man come along and rescue her so that she could go back to being a full time wife and mother. I just assumed you would feel the same when I came to your rescue."

"My rescue.... Will, I was not waiting for someone to rescue me from my business. I was doing very well and, what's more, I was enjoying it. I like running the business and I like working."

Will looked as if he had just smelled something very malodorous.

"You know," he said stiffly, "that's not a very attractive trait in a woman."

At that moment, Lena knew, really knew, that she had a problem. Instinct told her that she'd better protect herself or she risked losing it all.

"Look," she said, "Let's not talk about this right now. I'm supposed to meet Bess at the teashop this afternoon. We can finish this discussion another time."

"That's fine with me," Will said.

Feeling his eyes on her, Lena gathered up her purse and her coat and left.

She drove herself to Liberty, arriving half an hour before her date with Bess. The Liberty Savings Bank was just three blocks away from the Village Tea Shoppe so she had plenty of time. Entering the bank, she saw there was no line and she quickly went up to the teller's window where an attractive young woman with wavy dark hair and blue eyes was working.

"Good afternoon," Lena said. "I'd like to withdraw some money from the Lena K Enterprises account. Can you tell me how much is in that account to date?"

"One moment please," the teller said. She walked away from the window toward the office where the bank manager's office was and disappeared inside. As the minutes ticked by without her reappearing, Lena felt her anxiety increase. It was getting close to the time she was supposed to meet Bess. Finally, the office door opened and the bank manager, a portly man with a bald head and an ill-fitting brown suit, appeared with the teller. Together they approached the window where Lena waited.

"Is there a problem?" Lena asked.

"Well," the bank manager looked uncomfortable. "There is a problem because only authorized people can make withdrawals."

"I know that," Lena said. "I am authorized to make withdrawals from this account."

"I'm afraid that's not the case," the bank manager said. "There's recently been a change to this account and your name is not listed as an authorized individual." To his credit, the man seemed a bit embarrassed by the whole thing. The teller, on the other hand, had a strange smug expression on her face.

With a sinking feeling, Lena told the manager, "There must be some mistake. I own Lena K Enterprises."

"Do you have any proof of that?" the manager asked.

"Proof?" Lena's mind started racing frantically. This was insane. She could not believe she was being denied access to her own money this way. "I can get you proof if that's what's necessary. But I want to know how this could possibly have happened. How could my name be on the account one moment and taken off the next. Who took my name off anyway? Can you tell me that?"

"I'm not at liberty to divulge that information," the manager said.

Lena's heart started racing. She felt like she was caught in quicksand and was sinking deeper with every passing moment. She forced herself to calm down.

"Well, if you can't tell me who took my name off the account, can you at least tell me whose name is still on the account?"

"I'm not at liberty—"

The teller broke in just then. "William Kerner is the name on the account."

Lena stared at her and she looked impassively back. There was something about the young teller that bothered her. She wasn't sure exactly what it was. She glanced at the woman's nametag: Elaine Macy. It rang a vague bell, but she couldn't remember where she'd heard it before.

At least the teller had confirmed her suspicions, she thought. So, Will had already changed the account to his name only. What else had he done? She was almost afraid to find out. Glancing down at her watch, she saw that it was time to meet Bess. Good thing, because she was feeling awfully desperate to see a friendly face. She would have to finish with the bank later when she could come back with some proof of her ownership of the business.

In the Village Tea Shoppe, she spotted Bess already seated at a table and hurried over, praying she wouldn't lose her composure on the way. She managed to hold on, but Bess's welcoming hug almost did her in.

"Hey you," Bess said. She stepped back from their embrace and studied Lena's face. "What's wrong?"

"Plenty, but I need a cup of tea first."

As soon as the waitress had taken their order, Bess looked up expectantly. Lena didn't know where to begin. She thought she might start crying before she could get a single word out. Bess must have sensed how she was feeling, because she started the conversation.

"How is Will these days?"

Lena shook her head. "He's... I don't know. He's acting very strangely. I don't really know why or what to do about it."

"Strange how?" Bess prompted her.

"He's started to take control of the business. He acts like I should have nothing to do with it anymore. Like I should just stay at home, make his dinner, clean the house, and wait to get pregnant."

"Have you talked to him about it?"

"I've tried, but he hasn't been around much. He's been spending a lot of time at the bank." Her tone turned bitter and knowing. "And now I realize why."

"You do?"

"Yes." Lena explained to her what had happened when she'd tried to withdraw some money from the Lena K Enterprises account. "We've always put a lot of things in his name because you know how banks and landlords can be. They don't want to do business with a woman. It was just easier having Will be president and having him sign most of the documents. He's my husband so I never worried. Why would I?"

She continued, "Now, I don't know... He's so different from when we first met. I always knew he was old fashioned, in a charming, gallant kind of way. But now, he seems to be regressing to the point where.... He acts like he expected our marriage to be completely different than it is. Like he expects *me* to be completely different than I am." She shook her head, more to herself than to Bess, then went on.

"I don't think I can be what he wants me to be. I don't even *want* to be what he wants me to be. And I don't know what to do about it."

Bess said nothing for a moment, Her face was full of compassion. Finally, she said, "You could get a divorce."

"Well, that's a pretty drastic response," Lena said, shocked. "Not," she admitted, "that it didn't occur to me during the walk between the bank and this place. But nothing Will's done is grounds for divorce. And without grounds, I wouldn't get too far."

"There's always adultery," Bess said.

"I already had one affair," Lena said dryly. "And look how well that turned out. I don't think I'm interested in another, not even to provide grounds for divorce."

"I didn't mean you," Bess said.

"Will?" Lena was incredulous. She shook her head. "No. Will may be many things, but he's not an adulterer. His sense of gallantry wouldn't allow it."

"You did say he'd been spending a lot of time at the bank," Bess said slowly. She hesitated, then went on. "When you were there, just now, did you notice a young teller? Dark hair, blue eyes? Pretty attractive? Name's Macy?"

Lena frowned. "What are you saying?"

"That I didn't just happen to be coming into town with Sam today. I wanted to see you so I could tell you something. Sam thought we should wait because we didn't really have proof. But I thought otherwise. And, in the end, he agreed."

"Bess, what's going on?"

"Sam was in town last month and you know how he talks to everyone, finds out all the news. He's really nothing but an old gossip," Bess's voice was full of affection for her husband. "Anyway, he heard a few rumors about Will and the new bank teller. She's actually the daughter of the bank's owner. And Will has been seen around town in her company. I mean, it could be just business, but then why would they be together outside of the bank?"

Lena let the import of what Bess was saying sink in. Little by little, she began feeling that it made sense. She thought of Will's frequent visits to the bank, his prickliness on that subject, and his recent pains with his appearance, not to mention the new suit and ties he'd been sporting. It was still hard to believe him guilty of adultery, but then, she would never have believed Will capable of the deceit in which he'd obviously been engaged when it came to the business.

She looked at Bess. "Even if I do have grounds," she said slowly, "there's still the business to consider. He's put so much of it in his name. If we get divorced, how will I ever prove what's mine? What if the court gives the whole thing to Will just because he's the man. You know that could happen. I don't want to lose everything I've worked so hard for. What do you think I should do?"

Bess took a long sip of her tea and swallowed. "I think you need a lawyer," she said.

And just like that, Daniel's name popped into her mind. How silly, she thought. It had, after all, been over fourteen years since she had heard from him. He had sent his regrets in response to her wedding invitation and then not been heard from again. No books, no letters, no communication at all. She had taken the hint.

Yet now, when she needed a lawyer, he was the first one she thought of. She didn't even know where he lived or worked. When she'd last heard from him, he'd been in Albany with the Roosevelt administration. But Roosevelt had moved on to the White House and so, perhaps, had Daniel. Even if she could track him down, there was nothing to make her think that he would want to help her.

She looked at Bess. "Do you know any lawyers?"

Bess was thoughtful. "We have so many guests who are lawyers. Let me ask Sam what he thinks. I'm sure we can find someone."

Lena nodded, but the full impact of Will's betrayal was beginning to hit her. It was hard to think straight; hard to breathe. She felt shaky. She needed to get control of herself. She needed to stop trembling, stop letting it get to her.

Despite Bess's presence, she felt very alone. Hurt assailed her. She felt vulnerable as a child. A spasm of sorrow squeezed her chest and her eyes filled up with tears. She felt blindly in her handbag for her handkerchief and seized it just in time to muffle her sobs against it. The cloth, roughened from smoke, repeated washings, and the passage of time, grew soft again as it absorbed her tears. Bess laid a gentle hand on her arm and, after a while, she became calmer. She wiped her damp face and, finally, gaining control, folded the handkerchief gently. It had been through so much with her, she thought and, while it might not be as white or as silky as it once was, it was still strong. It was still strong.

She took a deep slow breath and another and another. Then she nodded to herself. She would do what she needed to do.

"Joe?" Lena said into the telephone a few hours later. "Say something. Anything."

"I don't know what to say. I'm just so, so very sorry."

"Thank you." She paused. "I feel so stupid."

"What? Why?" Joe sounded more upset about that than anything else she'd said so far. She'd called him the minute she'd gotten home. As soon as she'd gotten her brain to function again, she'd realized she was not without resources. She had good friends, Bess and Sam to start with, but there were others too—the women from her voting rights classes and her employees. And she had family.

"You're not stupid," Joe said. "There was no way for you to know. You trusted your husband. That's what a wife is supposed to do. It's what a wife is supposed to be able to do. And who ever would have suspected that Will, uptight, old-fashioned Will, would have an affair?"

"You know what the sad thing is? I actually feel so much worse about the possibility of losing the business than about losing Will."

Joe snorted. "Well, that's understandable. But you haven't lost the business yet. We'll get you a good lawyer. You can win this."

"Bess said Sam may know a lawyer. And I guess I have grounds for divorce. But with all the business papers in Will's name, I don't think there's much hope of ending up with my fair share."

"Well, we'll see. Meanwhile, what will you do once the dust settles? Have you given any thought to that?"

"I haven't even thought as far as dinner tonight."

"Well, I have some thoughts about it. Will you hear me out?"

"Of course."

"I think it's time for you to come back."

"Come back?"

"To the city. To your family. You know how much I've missed you all these years and, heaven knows, Arnie loves you like a sister. Now Rachel will be here too. She's not so grown up that she doesn't need you anymore. And it makes sense from a business perspective. If you do get control of Lena K Enterprises, I can help any way you need me to. And, if the worst happens, and you lose the business, you'd have a place with Rothman Sims if you want it. We could really use you. Business is going through the roof. It's not so easy to find people with your talents and abilities."

"Or," he continued, "if you'd prefer to be on your own, I can help you get started. Lend you money and whatever else you need. But one thing you don't need is that jerk husband of yours. You never did. You started Lena K without him and, there's not a doubt in my mind that the success of that business is due to you."

Joe's voice lost its sales pitch edge and softened. "You and I always did make a great team. Remember when we were growing up? How we always depended on each other? We work well together. Anyway, enough time has gone by. It's time for you to come home to New York."

Lena's eyes filled up with tears and for a minute, she was too choked up to speak.

"Lena? You're not saying anything. Will you at least consider it?"

It took another minute, but she regained her composure, swallowed the lump in her throat and said, "Yes, I'll consider it. If Arnie says yes, then I'll consider it."

Joe grinned. "Oh he'll say yes. I guarantee it. He's been waiting for this day for almost as long as I have."

"Okay. And, in the meantime, thank you Joe, for... well, everything."

"Don't be silly, that's what brothers are for." There was a pause and then, in a voice choked with emotion, he added, "I love you baby sister."

"I love you too."

Replacing the phone on the receiver, Lena felt like weeping with relief. Thank goodness for Joe. Always there for her throughout her life no matter what the circumstances. And she knew she could count on Bess and Sam too for emotional support and even financial help if she needed it.

Once upon a time, she'd dreamed of finding that perfect helpmate, lover, husband, and partner, with whom she would work to achieve great things. What fantasies she'd indulged in, first in her imagination and then with Jake and then Will. What a fool she'd been not to see that she'd had that perfect support all along.

CHAPTER TWENTY-EIGHT

1940

RACHEL FLOPPED ON HER DORM ROOM BED AND LOOKED OVER AT HER roommate. Susan Shephard was sitting Indian-style on her bed opposite Rachel's, her blond head bent over her psychology text-book. Since it was exam week, Rachel knew it was unfair to in-terrupt her friend's studying, but she felt about to burst.

She sprang back up and stalked around the room, stopping to glance at the collection of framed family photographs atop Su-san's chest of drawers. It was easy to tell which of her parents Susan looked like. She had her father's height, his cornflower blue eyes, and his high Nordic cheekbones. Rachel couldn't get over the strength of the resemblance between father and daugh-ter. She looked at herself in the mirror above Susan's photo dis-play and tried to imagine a male face similar to her own, but her imagination failed her.

Still restless, she prowled on. She paused at her own desk where there was a half-finished letter to her mother but she was in no mood to complete it. Behind her, she heard Susan close her book and took it as her cue to whirl around. Her roommate was looking at her expectantly, her mouth twitching with barely sup-pressed laughter.

"Well," Susan said. "What is it? You may as well tell me. I'm not going to get anything done with you bouncing off the walls this way."

"I'm sorry. It's just that if Ellen Crosby says one more word about the job she has lined up with Doubleday, Dorn Publishers I'm going to spit."

Susan laughed. "Why do you let her get to you? You know she wouldn't have gotten the position if her father wasn't one of their senior editors."

"Well, then she shouldn't make it sound as if she got hired on her own merit. She just likes to rub my face in it because she knows I'm trying so hard to get a job in publishing. Not all of us are lucky enough to have Daddy in a position to hand over a job on a silver platter."

"True. But, you know," she said mildly, "not all of us are lucky enough to have parents who are willing to let us move to New York City after graduation. My parents won't hear of it. My mother says an unmarried woman has no business living anywhere except with her family."

"I will be living with family," Rachel reminded her. "I don't think my mother would let me move to the city if I wasn't going to be living with my uncle."

"And that's another thing," Susan said, taking her hairbrush from the nightstand.

"What?"

"Your uncle." She pulled the brush gently through her blond hair so as not to disturb her Veronica Lake style waves. "I mean, I have uncles too. Four of them. Three are bankers and the fourth is a stockbroker. But your uncle owns Rothman Sims. I just love their clothes. I saw a picture of Joan Crawford wearing a Rothman Sims original to the premiere of "Of Human Bondage." She looked divine. Is everyone on the Rothman side of your family as talented as your uncle? And what about your mom's side of the family? Is there any talent there too?"

"Uncle Joe *is* from my mother's side of the family," Rachel said, as she plopped back onto her bed. "He's her brother. And, he's not talented—at least not in the artistic sense. He's a very good businessman, but Arnie Sims is the design half of Rothman Sims."

Susan stopped brushing and frowned. "Then why does he have the same last name as you?"

"Who?"

"Your Uncle. I mean, if he's your mother's brother, he should have a different last name than you. Because, I mean, your mother's last name must have changed when she married your father."

"Oh that," Rachel shrugged. "My father and mother were actually distant cousins. It's part of the reason they met in the first place. I don't know all the details, but I know that had something to do with it."

Susan sighed and went back to brushing her hair. "And that's another thing. I mean, your family is so much more interesting than mine. My mother and father grew up next door to each other and everyone assumed that someday they would get married. And what do you know? That's exactly what happened. But you! That whole story about your parents and their whirlwind courtship and marriage. How they fell in love, decided to get married, and right afterwards, he gets drafted into the army and killed in his very first battle. It's so sad and so romantic."

"Yeah," Rachel said. "It's really great when you never have a chance to meet your father or know anything about him."

Susan blushed. "I'm sorry. That was a really stupid thing to say."

"No, it's alright," she sighed. "It is a romantic story. At least what I know of it. My mother doesn't like to talk about anything having to do with my father and it's really frustrating. I look at that photo of you and your dad and I can see right away where you get your blue eyes and blond hair. And then there's stupid Ellen, bragging about how she gets her writing talent from her dad. I just wish I knew what I got from my dad or, at least, a little more about what kind of person he was. All I know is that he was born in Russia."

"Isn't there anyone you can ask besides your mom? What about your Uncle?"

"I tried to ask him a couple of times when I was younger. But he wasn't any more talkative than my mother."

"Maybe he thought you were too young to discuss stuff back then. You should try asking him again."

"Maybe." Rachel fell silent as she slipped into a daydream. She imagined going to Russia and finding her father's family, an aunt or an uncle, and recognizing something of herself in their blue-gray eyes. Maybe she would meet a handsome young Marxist and, together, they would fight Stalin and restore worker's rights. Or maybe....

"Rachel? Are you listening?"

"I'm sorry. What did you say?"

"I asked if you wanted to go down to dinner in about half an hour."

"Sure." She nodded. "That would be fine."

She stood up and walked back over to her desk. She still didn't feel like finishing the letter to her mother. What she really wanted, desperately wanted, was to find out more about her father. Maybe Susan was right. Maybe, now that she was older, it would be different if she approached Uncle Joe with her questions. The more she thought about the idea, the more reasonable it seemed. Yes, indeed, perhaps a little trip to New York City was in order. She whirled around and headed for the door.

Susan stared at her, hairbrush mid-air. "Where are you going?"

"Change of plan," Rachel told her over her shoulder. "I'll meet you at the dining hall. I've got a call to make." She closed the door behind her and took the stairs two at a time. She just hoped the telephone in the parlor would be free.

Standing in the main terminal of Grand Central Station, Rachel paused to get her bearings, as women in broad-shouldered suits and dapper businessmen in wide-leg trousers streamed past. Everyone seemed to know what they were about and where they needed to go. She longed to be one of them and couldn't wait to move here after graduation. As she started on her way, she quickened her pace to match that of those around her, lifting her chin, and clicking her heels snappily on the floor.

She spotted Uncle Joe standing in their usual meeting spot next to the Chock Full O' Nuts coffee shop and waved. His round face broke into a welcoming smile like a happy jack o' lantern. What a dear he was. In his rumpled suit, he hardly looked like the owner of a fabulously successful clothing company. Indeed, she suspected that if Uncle Arnie had seen him leaving the house, he would have had a fit.

"Uncle Joe!" She threw her arms wide and was enveloped in a huge bear hug.

"Oy—what is this?" He said laughing. "Or should I say, who is this? This beautiful woman can't be my niece."

"I'm so happy to see you," Rachel said smiling. "And thank you for meeting me on such short notice."

"Of course, bubbuleh. From you, I don't need advance notice. Are you hungry? Because Arnie cooked up a storm and he'll be very disappointed if you don't eat some of it."

"I knew he would. Stuffed cabbage?"

"Yes stuffed cabbage. And noodle kugel and kasha varnishkas. All your favorites."

"I love it," Rachel said. "Who would ever guess that Arnie Sims, designer to the rich and famous, cooks like a Jewish grandmother."

"It's just one of his many talents. Come sweetheart. My driver is waiting. We can finish catching up on the way."

Rachel had already decided that she would work her way gradually into the topic that was the real reason for her trip. So, she didn't say anything about it during the car ride to the Upper East Side. Instead, she told Uncle Joe funny anecdotes about her roommate and other friends at college.

In the foyer of their elegant Park Avenue apartment, Rachel hugged her Uncle's partner in business and life. Uncle Arnie looked as boyishly suave as ever in a double-breasted blue flannel suit, his fair hair brushed back from his brow and gleaming . He waited until Uncle Joe had taken her coat, then crossed his arms, pursed his lips, and inspected her from top to bottom.

"Too thin as always," he said in mock disapproval. "Come and eat before the food gets cold."

He led the way down the hall to their high-ceilinged dining room. The glossy black walnut table was covered with platters. Bagels, a generous block of rich cream cheese, the salty lox she loved, as well as herring in cream sauce, stuffed cabbage, and, best of all, her favorite sweet noodle kugel made with raisins and three kinds of cheese.

Over lunch, Rachel told them how frustrated she was with her lack of success at lining up a job for after graduation. Like two mother hens, they clucked with sympathy. Uncle Arnie, sitting with one leg crossed elegantly over the other, leaned back and took a drag on his cigarette.

"You know," he said, blowing out a ribbon of white smoke and looking at Uncle Joe. "I bet Douglas McCullough has some contacts in publishing."

"That's true. I hadn't thought of him."

"Who's Douglas McCullough?" Rachel asked.

"He's in charge of our advertising account at J. Walter Thompson," Uncle Arnie explained. "He has contacts with all the major publishers. Maybe he knows someone who's hiring. It's worth a try, anyway."

"That would be wonderful," Rachel breathed. "Do you really think he would be able to help me?"

"You never know until you ask. I'll get in touch with him Monday morning."

Rachel beamed. "You're wonderful. And I promise I won't be forever asking for favors once I move here."

"Then you'll be eliminating one of the great pleasures of my life," Uncle Arnie said smiling back.

"He's not kidding," Uncle Joe said. "I can see it already. I'll probably gain ten or fifteen pounds after you move in because Arnie will never stop cooking."

Rachel laughed. "*I'll* probably gain fifteen or twenty pounds. Seriously though, I really appreciate your letting me live with you. It won't be forever, just until I can get myself established and persuade Mama to let me live on my own."

"Bubbeleh," Uncle Joe said. "You take as long as you want. We've got plenty of room here."

Rachel made her voice sound as innocent as possible. "Maybe it will bring back memories of when Mama lived with you when she first came to America. How long did you two live together anyway?"

Uncle Joe shook his head, chuckling at the memory. "Not long at all. Only two days."

"Two days? I thought -"

"Yes, well, we were supposed to live together, but I didn't have so much money in those days. And my landlady didn't like her boarders to have women visitors."

"But she wasn't just a visitor, she was your sister," Rachel said.

"We couldn't convince her of that. She said that either your mother went or we both went."

"So what did you do?"

"Well, luckily, your mama had made a friend at work on her very first day. And that friend happened to have an extra bed in the place where she lived. So, she invited your mama and it all worked out."

"That *was* lucky," Rachel said. "What was her friend's name?"

"Sophie Friedman." He grinned. "Oy, what a spitfire that one was."

"Did Mama live with her for long?"

Uncle Joe thought about it, but the question seemed to have reminded him of something and he suddenly looked uncomfortable and shook his head. "You know bubbeleh, I actually don't remember very well. It was so long ago." He stood up and began clearing the dishes from the table.

"You really don't like talking about this stuff, do you?" Rachel said slowly. "I'm not even asking about my father, but you don't want me to know anything about my mother's life before I was born."

Uncle Joe stopped and looked at her. Rachel stared back fiercely. She was not going to let him off the hook this time. "I'm not a baby anymore," she said. "What's the big deal? Why does everything have to be such a secret?"

Uncle Joe lowered his eyes. Next to him, Arnie was studying his fingernails.

"It's not my place -" Uncle Joe said.

"Mama doesn't tell me anything," Rachel interrupted him. "And I don't pester her out of consideration for her feelings. But I have feelings too."

"Bubbeleh." Uncle Joe sounded weary. "It's your mama's right to decide what you get to know and what you don't. When your mama first came here—it was a difficult time. Our papa, your grandfather, had just died and your mama missed him a lot. She expected to live with me and then that didn't happen. She worked all the time and went to night classes and wanted so many things for her future. And then the fire happened..."

"What fire?" Rachel demanded.

"At work. At the factory."

"Are you talking about the Northern Shirtwaist Factory fire? Was Mama there when that happened? Is that where she worked?"

Uncle Joe nodded. "I shouldn't be telling you this. But yes. She was there when that fire broke out and she escaped and lived. Thank God. But it was a terrible thing to have to go through. And, then, of course, there was the whole business with your father. So you have to understand why she doesn't like to talk about the past."

"I guess," Rachel said. "I mean, I do understand. But why can't you talk to me about it? There are so many things I want to know about my father. He was related to you and Mama, right? A distant cousin or something?"

"Yes," Uncle Joe said. "It was something like that." He went back to clearing the table. "Look, bubbeleh. I really don't feel right talking about this. But I'll make you a deal. How about if I ask your mama if it's alright if I talk to you about it. If she says yes, then next time I see you...."

Rachel's heart sank. The chances of her mother giving permission for Uncle Joe to tell her anything were slim. But she had no other choice. She'd obviously gotten all she was going to for the moment.

"Alright," she said. "See what Mama says." But to herself she thought, *at least now I know that my mother worked for Northern Shirtwaist and that she lived with a friend named Sophie Friedman. And who knows—since this Sophie was her friend, maybe if I find her, she can tell me something about my father.*

The next day was Saturday. The main library at Forty-second Street opened at 9:00 a.m. Rachel was waiting outside the building before the doors were even unlocked. She followed signs to the periodical reading room, approached the reference librarian with determination, and told him she was looking for newspaper stories of the Northern Shirtwaist Factory fire. The librarian had her fill out a request slip and informed her that it would take a few minutes for the newspapers to be brought up.

She surveyed the matching rows of long, gleaming mahogany tables on either side of the room. The morning light streamed in from huge arched windows lining the walls. Anything seemed possible in this temple of information. She took a seat facing the reference desk and waited.

Sometime later, a pimply-faced boy, his arms filled with a foot high stack of newspapers, approached the reference desk. The librarian pointed him in her direction and he brought the pile over and set it in front of her, ducking his head shyly.

There were copies of every newspaper that had been regularly published when the Northern Factory Fire occurred, including morning, afternoon, evening, and late editions from the day of the fire, the day after, and the weekend. Surely, one of them would contain some bit of information that would help unlock her mother's past and open the door to learning about her father. She began to read.

Although her American History professor had touched on the topic of the Northern fire, nothing he'd said had prepared her for the sheer horror of it. The headlines were sickening. In the Evening Sun: **One Hundred And Fifty Die In Blazing Inferno**. In the New York Herald: **Victims Hurl Themselves To Death**. In the Evening World: **Streets Strewn With Bodies; Piles of Dead Inside**.

Even worse were the photographs. There was a woman's body lying still on the sidewalk looking like so much dirty laundry dumped on the street. Another photo showed a dormitory-like row of narrow coffins, their lids removed to show the girls inside. Opposite the coffins, family members filed by searching for their loved ones. The photograph captured their numb faces as they stared at the bashed, burnt, and deformed heads of the victims, propped up to facilitate identification.

In article after article, the terror of the day and the enormity of the tragedy was made graphically clear. Rachel was torn between wanting to stop reading, stop knowing, stop imagining, and being unable to look away from the ink blotched papers. No wonder her mother never talked to her about any of this.

Several of the newspapers had published lists identifying those who had perished. She searched uneasily for the name Sophie Friedman or, really, for the absence of that name. It felt very strange to be hoping that one specific woman whom she had never met had somehow survived the tragic fire when so many others equally unknown to her had not. Some of the papers had published the ages of the deceased. "Clara Milman, 13; Catherine Vecchio, 15; Sylvia DeGarmo, 19; Ella Smith, 9." Rachel's chest felt as if something heavy were pressing against it. She forced herself to keep reading. She had to be sure.

Finally, there were no other lists. She had reviewed them all and she was sure. Sophie Friedman was not on any of them. Somehow, both Sophie and Mama had survived, a fact that was surely amazing. Perhaps, together, they had found an escape path. But regardless of how Sophie Friedman had survived, the fact was that she had. And, since she had, there was a very good chance she might still be alive. And if she was still alive, there might be some way of finding her.

Even as she felt this small bit of hope, it was impossible not to feel sick to her stomach. The names of the others, the unlucky ones, still swam behind her eyes. After three hours, she had had enough. She had neither the energy nor the heart to search for Sophie Friedman at present.

Spring break came, and Rachel left campus to go back to Monticello. Even after all these years, it didn't feel like she was going home. Home to her was Grossman's and Esty and the big warm kitchen with its round table where she had grown up eating hot latkes at Hanukah and warm blintzes on Sunday mornings. She'd never felt entirely comfortable in the house her mother and Will had bought in town.

Speaking of Mama and Will, she wondered if it was just her imagination or if they really were acting a bit strange around each other. The atmosphere at home was fraught with something she didn't understand and she found it even less comfortable than usual.

As a young girl, she'd liked Will because he brought her gifts and made her mother happy. It had been fun to be the flower girl at their wedding and she'd laughed when Will carried first Mama and then her over the threshold of their suite of rooms at Grossmans to symbolize the beginning of their new lives together.

But as time went by, she'd come to resent Will's tendency to try to control everything and everyone. From what she could tell, her mother, while grateful to have a break from doing everything herself, wasn't completely thrilled with Will's heavy-handedness either. It seemed to Rachel that Mama picked her battles, catering to Will's preferences on the domestic front while mostly standing firm when it came to business decisions.

Now, however, Rachel wondered if her mother had finally gotten tired of being treated like a lesser being. One day when Will came into the kitchen and asked Mama why she hadn't picked up his dry cleaning, her mother simply stared at him for a long moment before telling him that the dry cleaners was right next door to the bank where he spent so much time and, from now on, he could just pick up his cleaning himself, But, as usual, Mama didn't say anything to her about what was going on or how she was feeling.

Rachel spent most of her time over at Grossman's visiting Esty. Esty's older brother David was there too. He was so much more mature than the boys Rachel met at college and seemed endearingly oblivious to the fact that he was awfully cute looking.

On the last Friday afternoon of her break, she walked into the front entrance of Grossman's looking for Esty and found David working alone behind the check-in desk. He looked up and grinned when he saw her, but shook his head.

"You just missed her," he said. "She left for the station ten minutes ago to pick up a group of guests."

"Really? I thought they all arrived by car nowadays."

"Most do. But we've still got some old-timers who prefer taking the train up from the city."

"Oh," Rachel nodded. She tried to think of something to say that would make him realize that she was an adult now and not the same little girl who used to pester him to play with her.

"Hey," he said suddenly, "I was just about to go check the swing in the gazebo. One of the guests said it was swinging a little crooked. Want to come along?"

Despite his casual tone, there was something, the slightest blush on his face, a tentativeness in his gaze, that suggested the invitation was anything but casual. Now this was more like it.

She let a few beats pass before she accepted. In her experience, if you were interested in a boy and thought he might be interested in you, it was a good idea not to seem too eager.

After a few minutes of sharing the swing, it was clear there was nothing crooked about its arc and nothing to fix. Still, they lingered, talking. She learned that David had gotten a degree from the Cornell School of Hotel Administration. He was passionate about improving every aspect of Grossman's and had lots of ideas for doing it. He told ridiculously corny jokes and laughed when she told him they were ridiculously corny. And his nose wrinkled adorably when he smiled. By the time they left the gazebo to return to the hotel, they'd already agreed they would write each other after she went back to school.

It wasn't until the last day of her break that she had a chance to be alone with her mother. Will was at the office and her mother was in the kitchen making chocolate chip cookies for her to take back to school. Rachel sat at the table keeping her company. One batch of cookies was already in the oven and her mother was getting the next batch ready, spooning the cookie dough onto a baking sheet. Rachel breathed in deeply, enjoying the combined aroma of sugar, vanilla, and melting milk chocolate.

"Mmm, they smell delicious."

Her mother smiled. "These were always your favorites. Your Uncle Joe's too."

"Speaking of Uncle Joe," Rachel said, "you know I had a great visit with him a few weeks ago. Have you spoken with him recently?"

"I usually talk to him at least once a week."

"Did he ask you anything the last time you two talked? Anything in particular?"

"Anything in particular? I'm not sure what you mean."

Rachel nibbled at a fingernail. "Well, he and I had a little talk when I was there. And I told him I wasn't a baby anymore."

"Of course you aren't." Her mother stopped setting out cookies, wiped her hands on a dishtowel, and leaned against the kitchen counter, folding her arms across her chest.

"Rachel what is this all about?"

"I," Rachel hesitated. She felt that familiar reluctance to try and get her mother to talk about things that were obviously painful to her. For a moment, she felt her resolve slipping away. It would be so easy to let things go unsaid. But she knew that if she did, she would be angry with herself.

"I want to know about my father," she said in a rush. "I know it's hard for you and I don't mean to hurt you. But it's hard for me too. One half of me comes from him and I don't know anything about that side of me. Can't you tell me anything? Anything at all?"

Her mother looked at her, startled, but didn't immediately close down or cut off discussion as she usually did. As she continued to gaze, her thoughts seemed to turn inward, until it was clear she was no longer seeing Rachel at all but, instead, was remembering. She resumed placing cookies on the baking sheet, her movements slow and deliberate, and with her back to Rachel, she spoke softly.

"What is it you want to know?"

Rachel sat straight in the chair. Her heart started to beat rapidly. Now that it appeared her mother was actually going to talk to her, she didn't know where to begin.

"How... how did you meet him?"

"At a dance," her mother said.

"A dance?"

"Yes. The settlement house used to hold them every Saturday night. I went to one and he asked me to dance."

"A dance," Rachel said. So her father had gone to dances. What else could she ask? She felt giddy with success and so shocked that her mother was talking to her that she could hardly think straight.

"Was he a good dancer?" she asked, while inside she scolded herself merrily. After all this time, was that really the thing she most wanted to know about her father?

"He was a marvelous dancer," her mother said, her voice so quiet that Rachel had to strain to hear it. "He was such a strong lead that I felt like I was floating."

Laughter bubbled out of Rachel. "Did you know that you liked him right away?"

"Oh yes," her mother said, nodding to herself. "Right away."

Rachel pictured it, her tall, handsome father (of course he would have been handsome—at least, she had always imagined him so) and her mother floating in his arms. But there was something puzzling about this image. She frowned.

"So, had you met him before that? Because he was your cousin right? Or, how did you..."

Her mother shook her head. "We discovered we were cousins while we were talking. Distant cousins. His great, great grandfather and my great, great grandfather were cousins."

Rachel nodded. That made sense. "So, what, what was he like?"

Her mother's countenance softened and she smiled. "He was wonderful," she said. "Very handsome. And charismatic." She thought some more. "When he talked he had such passion. He made you care as much as he did."

"Care about what?"

"Um...." A cautious note crept into her mother's voice. "Well, all kinds of things. He thought things should be changed."

"What kind of things?"

"Well, working conditions and that sort of thing."

"So, he was kind of a rebel?" Rachel asked, her eyes round and her mouth curving upwards.

"Kind of," her mother agreed.

"Was he smart?"

"Oh yes. Very, very smart. Very quick."

Rachel nodded happily. What else could she ask? She thought of Ellen Crosby and her father, the editor. "What kind of job did he have?"

"Uh, he was... he was working in a factory." Her mother licked her lips.

"Oh." Well, of course, that made sense, Rachel thought. There was no reason for her to be disappointed about this. Most immigrants got jobs working in factories. If he had lived, perhaps he would have become something else.

As if she was reading her mind, her mother added, "But he didn't plan to do that forever."

"No?"

"No. He, ah, he wanted to go to law school. He was going to become a lawyer."

"Really?" Rachel was pleased. A lawyer was even better than an editor.

"Yes. He would have been a very good lawyer. He could out-argue anyone." Her mother grinned. "Does that remind you of anyone you know?"

Rachel laughed. "I guess that's where I get it. So, when did you decide to get married?"

"Well, the war began," her mother said in a practiced voice, back on territory she had presented to Rachel previously. "Your father got the notice that he was drafted. So, we decided to get married."

The cookie sheet was full now. Her mother again rested against the kitchen counter.

"Did you have a wedding?" Rachel asked.

"A small one."

"Was Uncle Joe there?"

"Of course."

"And did... did ...my father have any family there?"

"No. He didn't have any family in America. Well, other than myself and your Uncle Joe, of course."

"Did he have any friends?"

"Oh, he had many, many friends," her mother assured her.

"No, I mean did he have any friends at the wedding?"

"Well." Again there was a slight hesitation. "We decided to keep it very small."

"So no friends came? Nobody at all? What about you? Did any of your friends come? Did your friend Sophie come? "

Her mother drew up sharply. "What about Sophie? Who told you about Sophie?"

"Uncle Joe. But please don't be angry," she pleaded. "He didn't say anything else. In fact, he said he wasn't going to tell me anything more unless he got your permission first."

"Well, he shouldn't have said anything about her. He knows better than that."

"But why? I mean it isn't like he was talking about my father or anything."

Her mother's mouth was a tight line and her brows were drawn together over eyes that were more upset than angry.

"He just shouldn't have said anything. That's all." She was shaking her head to herself, no longer looking at Rachel, and she was breathing hard, her chest heaving up and down.

"He shouldn't have said anything," her mother repeated. "He knows I...." Suddenly, she stopped talking and sniffed at the air. Her face registered dismay and she whirled around and yanked at the oven door. Thrusting her pot-holdered hand in, she pulled out the baking sheet. Blackened, smoldering lumps dotted the tray. Her eyes filled up with tears.

"They're burnt," she said. "They're just completely ruined." She stared at the charred cookies. "I might as well throw all of them away."

"It's okay," Rachel told her. "You still have the other batch."

Her mother nodded, but looked distraught. A tear trickled slowly down her cheek and she walked slowly over to the kitchen trash and angled the baking sheet so the cookies would slide off and into the bin. Nothing happened. With spatula in hand, she tried prying them off. And as the cookies fell one by one into the bin, she began to weep—softly at first, then in huge, gasping, sobs, as if her heart were breaking.

Rachel felt horrible. She never should have forced her mother to talk about things that were so painful. God knows what her mother was remembering as she bent over the smoking and de-formed remains on the baking tray. Anyone who'd lived through the tragedy of the Northern Shirtwaist fire and the loss of her husband had had enough pain in her life. She went over and stood behind her mother, putting her arms around her.

"It's alright, Mama," she said quietly. "I don't care about the cookies. And we don't have to talk anymore if you don't want to."

But her mother didn't answer her. She just kept on prying off cookies and throwing them into the trash. And all the while, she kept sobbing as if she was never going to stop.

Back at school, lying on her bed, with her arms folded beneath her head, Rachel said to Susan, "What's wrong with me that the more I find out about my father, the more I want to know? I clearly can't ask my mother again or my Uncle, so I'm just doomed to be forever frustrated."

Susan came to sit at the foot of her bed. "There's nothing wrong with you. It's perfectly natural for you to want to know as much about your father as possible. Maybe there's some other way to find out about him."

"Like how? He had no other relatives in this country and I have no idea how to get in touch with relatives back in Russia, if there are even any left."

"Well, who else knew him in this country besides your mother and Uncle? What about this Sophie Friedman?

"I don't know," Rachel said. "I don't have any idea how to find her and my mother would obviously be furious if I tried. She got really weird just when I mentioned Sophie's name."

"Well, what about his military service?"

"What do you mean?" Rachel asked.

"There must be records from the time when your father was in the army. Maybe you could write to the Government and get them."

Rachel bolted upright. "I never thought of that. I've always wanted to know how my father died. Do you think I could maybe find out?"

"I think they must keep those records forever," Susan said.

Rachel's breath quickened. "Susan," she said, "you are a genius." She strode over to her desk. "I'm going to write to them right now. I'll give them this address and my Uncle's as well, just in case it takes them a while to respond."

CHAPTER TWENTY-NINE

1946
WASHINGTON, D.C.

THE LAST THING DANIEL FELT LIKE DOING WAS GOING TO A DINNER party. If the hostess had been anyone other than Julie Danvers, he would have begged off using work as an excuse. No one would have questioned him. The newspapers were full of stories about the wave of labor strikes that had hit the country. It didn't take a genius to realize that, as President Truman's Assistant Secretary of Labor, Daniel had his hands full.

But his workload wasn't the real reason for his reluctance. He was beginning to wonder how long he could keep up the pretense of enthusiasm for a President whose labor policies he increasingly detested. There were sure to be a few members of the Administration at Julie's party, not to mention members of the press. He didn't dare let his true sentiments show.

His dissatisfaction with Truman had been growing for months. It had begun when the President had responded to striking steel and coal workers by ordering Government takeovers of those industries. Now, on the eve of a possible strike by railway workers, Truman had threatened to draft strikers into the military so he could order them back to work. The President's warning had sent shockwaves throughout the labor movement. Union leaders argued that drafting workers to prevent a strike was akin to slavery. Daniel agreed.

He turned down 36ᵗʰ street in the direction of Julie's Georgetown home. He was almost there and should have been shifting into party mode, but couldn't stop thinking about how he could change Truman's mind. He had to make him see that destroying the country's unions wasn't the way to repair the economy no matter how much pressure he was getting from the Republicans and the business community. If he couldn't convince the President of that, then maybe it was time for him to leave Washington at long last.

Daniel had come to Washington twelve years ago at then President-elect Roosevelt's request. The first few years in the Roosevelt Labor Department had been thrilling. Daniel had been proud of the small part he'd played in the passage of labor laws that protected the right to unionize, limited work hours, guaranteed a minimum wage, and regulated the employment of children.

When Roosevelt died, Daniel assumed his time in Washington was over. To his surprise, Truman asked him to stay on and Daniel agreed, hoping the new President's reputation as a friend to the working-man would prove true. When it didn't, he swallowed his disappointment and stayed on anyway so there would be a pro-labor voice in the Administration.

But drafting striking workers was a line Daniel was not prepared to cross with the President. As he mounted the steps of Julie's home and lifted the brass doorknocker, he told himself that if Truman made good on his threat to do so, then he, too, would have to take a stand.

Julie's butler answered the door and led Daniel to the salon, a room that owed its elegant and warm atmosphere to walls and ceilings paneled in rich walnut, matching red leather Chesterfield sofas, and a richly colored oriental rug. There were already at least two-dozen people milling. A liveried waiter was circulating a tray of martinis and Daniel helped himself to one. He'd just taken a sip when he saw Julie coming to greet him.

"You made it," she said, smiling. At 45, Julie was more alluring than ever. Her strong features were now striking; her self-confidence enhanced their appeal

"Hello," he said as he brushed her cheek with his lips. "You look wonderful as always."

He held her gaze for a moment, and they exchanged a wordless acknowledgement of pleasure at seeing one another. There was so much history between them. Their friendship could easily have ended years ago and he was grateful that it hadn't.

Barely ten days after their weekend at Hyde Park, a letter from Julie had arrived in Daniel's mailbox. His heart beating quickly with anticipated joy, he'd slit the envelope and, still standing, begun to read.

Dearest Daniel

I have no wish to prolong your suspense concerning the question you recently posed to me and, so, will get right to my answer. I am honored beyond all words. But I cannot accept your proposal.

Just like that, his soaring elation exploded like a clay pigeon shot mid-air. His hopes crushed and his heart in pieces, he lowered the letter, unsure whether he could bear to read any more. He'd been so sure that she cared for him and he'd felt so ready to settle down. Memories of his last rejection made this one doubly bitter. But reading on, his feelings turned from despair to shame.

I treasure our friendship greatly and would never want to hurt you. But I promised myself long ago that I would marry against my father's wishes only in the face of the deepest, truest love. I've no doubt that you're very fond of me, but it's not fondness I long for. And while I believe your proposal was sincere, it's timing—so soon after you learned about another marriage—suggests you may have been acting on impulses having less to do with me than you may realize.

If I'm wrong, and I would be happy to be so, then I apologize and retract everything I've said above. But I don't think that is the case. I hope we can remain friends and that you don't think me too cruel.

Very truly yours,

Julie

As he again lowered the letter to his lap, he realized the truth of what she'd written. His only regret was the possibility that he had hurt her and that, despite her words, he would lose her forever as a friend. And losing Julie as a friend would be a profound loss because she was kind, principled, and one of the smartest women he knew. He wrote back quickly to let her know that he, too, wished to remain friends.

Not long afterwards, she turned up in Albany for a dinner at the Stimsons to which he'd also been invited. There was only enough time to exchange pleasantries before Anna Stimson called everyone to the dining room. But as he searched for his assigned seat, he was pleased to see Julie's place-card next to his.

"I have a confession to make," Julie said with a tentative smile after they were both sitting. "I've been a bit manipulative."

Daniel raised his eyebrows. "Have you?"

"Well, maybe manipulative isn't the right word. But our sitting next to each other isn't a coincidence." She took a breath before continuing.

"You see, I requested Anna to arrange it. I know what you wrote, but I wanted to make sure. I had to know if things between us really were alright. If we really are still friends."

Daniel saw her uncertainty and he looked deeply into her eyes to assure her of his sincerity.

"How could we not be?" he said simply. "You know me better than anyone else. And there's no one whose friendship means more to me than yours."

At that moment, something unspoken had passed between them. And from that time on, there'd been a new depth and intimacy to their friendship. By the time Roosevelt was elected to the White House and Daniel followed him to Washington, Julie had married her fourth cousin, William Danvers, a prominent Washington businessman and attorney, and moved into this lovely Georgetown estate.

William Danvers was a large, gregarious man with no strong political leanings, which was helpful since his construction business benefitted from attention to both sides of the political spectrum. He was more than happy to foot the bill for the social gatherings his wife organized. Over time, Julie established herself as a hostess with a knack for bringing together fascinating and diverse groups of movers and shakers and for nurturing robust conversation amongst them. For years now, an invitation to her salon had been one of the most sought after tickets in town.

"Am I late?" Daniel asked her.

"Not at all," she assured him. "Justice Frankfurter hasn't arrived yet and neither has the Vice-President."

"A Supreme Court justice and the Vice-President in the same night? Are you planning a coup?"

She laughed. "It's just the way it worked out. I never expected them both to be available."

"Am I sitting near either of them?"

"You're at my end of the table not too far from the Vice-President. I've seated you next to Lee Richmond."

He whistled softly. "If I'd known she was coming, I'd have worn a blue tie to bring out the color of my eyes." He was only half-joking. He'd never met the former model turned war correspondent, but he'd seen plenty of pictures of her. "Is she as beautiful in person as she is in photos?"

"More," Julie told him, adding dryly. "And you two have a lot in common. She's never been romantically involved with anyone for more than a fortnight either."

Daniel laughed. "You promised you were going to let up on that subject."

"Alright. That's the last you'll hear about it—tonight. Come. Let me introduce you to her."

Lee Richmond was indeed beautiful, with high cheekbones, slanting green eyes, and glossy chestnut hair. Sitting beside her at the dinner table, Daniel found himself captivated. Her stories about covering the war were mesmerizing. She'd gotten right into the action and narrowly escaped being blown to bits several times. And she had a gift for relating details that made the soldiers and airmen she'd met come alive.

She was equally good at drawing Daniel out, asking him direct questions with a charm that was hard to resist. He found himself talking more about himself than he usually did, telling her about his voyage to the United States, his early days as a *shlepper* and the beginning of his legal career.

"So," Lee said, "what do you like best about what you do now?"

"Mediating labor disputes," he said without hesitation. "It's incredibly satisfying when I can bring together two groups who see their goals as diametrically opposed. I try to help them resolve their issues so that each side feels like they've won a lot and only given up little."

"So, you're a peacemaker."

"I guess you could say that."

"But don't you ever feel like one side is really right? Don't you ever push for the outcome you think is fair?"

"Sometimes I do encourage the parties in one particular direction or another. I lean on them a little. But it's not my job to fight for one side or the other."

Lee cocked her head. "Not your job or not your nature?"

"Both, I guess."

"So," Lee said, a hint of a smile playing around her beautiful mouth, "you're a lover not a fighter."

"There are ways besides fighting to get what you want."

"You must have the patience of a saint though. I know some of the guys you've had to deal with: John Lewis, Phillip Murray. It's not easy to make them give up anything. They're not push-overs."

Daniel grinned. "Neither am I."

Lee put down her silverware and adopted a thinker's pose, one elbow on the table and chin resting on her elegantly curled hand. She studied him for so long that he began to wonder what she was looking for and how he was measuring up.

"You're an interesting man," she said slowly. "Confident, but without the obnoxiously huge ego that virtually all the other brilliant men in this town have. You have a powerful job and all the right connections, but you don't throw your weight around. And with those broad shoulders and blue eyes, you must have women coming on to you all the time. So, tell me," she smiled, "why is it that you aren't yet married?"

Startled by the personal nature of the question, Daniel's knee-jerk reaction was to throw the question right back at her. But there was something sexy about her straightforward approach, an appealing confidence in her boldness. So, instead, he matched her frank look and, allowing a hint of his amusement to show said, "You tell me."

Lee raised her eyebrows, then nodded with approval. "Alright," she said, pausing to give it some thought, "well, it could be that you work too hard to have time for affairs of the heart." She waited for a reaction, but when he didn't respond she continued. "Or, it could be that you've had your heart broken once too often." Again she waited and again he was impassive. Or," and here she smiled, "it could be you have the same preferences in that area as Sumner Welles. But somehow," she shook her head, "I don't think so. Or maybe—" she paused, tilting her head and looking at him through her glittering, slanting eyes, "it could be that you simply haven't met the right person yet."

Daniel let the four possibilities hang in the air while he pretended to consider them. Then he focused his eyes on Lee's and held them for a few seconds. "Yes," he finally agreed. "It could be any of those things."

Lee smiled. "As a reporter," she warned, "I'm not one to stop without getting a definite answer to my questions."

"I'd be disappointed if you did."

Lee gave a low, throaty chuckle. "I think," she said, "that I would like for you to drive me home this evening."

"We haven't finished dinner yet," Daniel pointed out.

"That's alright," Lee said. "I'm not in a hurry." She smiled and her cheekbones gleamed. "Just make sure you save room for dessert."

The next morning, a streak of sunlight slicing into Lee's bedroom through an opening in her drapes coaxed Daniel awake. Rolling over, he was disappointed to find her side of the bed empty. He'd been hoping for a reprise of last night's extremely satisfying activities.

There was the sound of a door opening and Lee entered barefoot and wearing a terry robe, her hair damp and tousled. She smiled at him and he grinned back lazily propping himself on one elbow.

"I don't usually sleep this late," he said. "You tired me out last night."

She shook her head. "You can't blame that entirely on me."

"Who said anything about blame? I'm talking about credit."

"That I'll gladly accept."

She walked over to her dresser and began brushing her hair and he watched her reflection in the mirror. Even without make-up, she was strikingly beautiful. But Daniel had dated other beautiful women before, some of whom were just as intelligent as Lee. What made Lee special was that besides beauty, brains, and self-confidence, she was just damn fun.

Last night, after they'd arrived at her apartment on Connecticut Avenue, she'd mixed drinks for both of them at her small but well-equipped bar. Over very dry martinis, they'd begun by talking about some of the people who'd been at Julie's bash. As the hour got later, the party post-mortem got sillier. To Daniel's delight, Lee turned out to be an excellent mimic. Her impersonation of the Vice-President was so dead on that Daniel could barely catch his breath he was laughing so hard.

"Could I persuade you to re-join me?" he asked her now, patting the bed next to him.

"It's tempting. But you know what would really put your invitation over the top?"

"What?"

"If you had some pancakes and eggs hiding under the blankets. I'm starving. What about you?"

"Now that you mention it."

"I'd offer to whip something up, but I got in late yesterday afternoon and I fly out again tomorrow evening. It didn't seem worth it to stock up on groceries."

"No problem. I'll be showered and ready in ten minutes and then I'll be ready to take you to your favorite breakfast spot."

"And what if I have two favorites," Lee said, her eyes holding a challenge.

"Then we'll just have to eat out again tomorrow morning," he told her.

On Monday, Daniel got to the office late. He'd treated himself to an extra hour of sleep to make up for the fact that he'd seen Lee off at National Airport the night before. He'd ended up waiting with her in the American Airlines lounge until one in the morning. When she'd disappeared through the boarding gate, it was the first time they'd been apart the entire weekend. He couldn't wait for her to return.

He barely had time to review his telephone messages before he heard his executive staff members arriving in the adjacent conference room. When he entered, his deputies and assistant deputies were seated around the long table. He took his place at the head and opened the meeting by requesting an update on the railroad workers' dispute.

Tom Sanzo, who he'd assigned to oversee negotiations between the parties, was blunt. "It's not looking good," he said. "The union isn't budging."

Daniel shook his head in frustration. "Did you convince them that the President isn't bluffing? That he's really prepared to draft striking workers?"

"I think they believed me, but it didn't seem to matter."

"They better believe you," Daniel said. "Because it's going to happen. This is a showdown and the union is going to lose. Go back and tell them that they really have no choice on this one."

Tom nodded. "Will do. How much time do you think we have left?"

Daniel considered the question. "Maybe a week at the most. And Tom, I want an update every couple of hours. Alright," he said, "what else is going on?" He looked around the table.

Claude Adkins, Daniel's chief of legislative affairs, cleared his throat. "There's a lot of noise in Congress about repealing the National Labor Relations Act. The railroad strike is giving them plenty of ammunition and the mid-term elections are looking good for the Republicans. If they get enough votes they'll amend it in a heartbeat."

Daniel took a deep breath and let it out slowly. "Let's see how persuasive you can be. Make an appointment with Senator Taft's chief of staff. He's the lead on all this. Maybe we can get them to tone it down a little."

He looked down at his agenda. "What about the garment industry? Any truth to the rumor about a strike in that sector?"

Ruby Miller sighed. "I'm sorry to say that there is some truth to it. I was going to ask you if you had time for a sit down with Jake Brenner. He's in town this week and he requested a meeting."

Daniel was tempted to say no. It was ridiculous, he knew, but he still remembered that dinner in Chinatown all those years ago when Brenner had acted like an arrogant jerk. Obviously, it was wrong to hold one evening that had occurred more than twenty-five years ago against a person. It was also immature and unprofessional. Still, he had avoided coming in contact with Brenner for many years and wasn't sure he wanted to sit down with him now.

Ruby was waiting. Daniel sighed. The administration could not afford to have another major strike on its hands. A garment workers' strike wouldn't have the impact of a railroad strike, but it would affect employment rates, which was another issue of grave concern go the President. If there was something he could do to head off a work stoppage, it was his duty to do it.

"Alright. Set something up. I think I've got some time Thursday afternoon, but check with Mrs. Babbitt." He glanced around the table again. "Nothing else? Good. Then let's get to work. It's going to be a busy week."

On Thursday, Daniel worked through lunch, taking a break only to mention to Mrs. Babbitt that once his meeting with Brenner began that afternoon, she should wait fifteen minutes and then buzz him to say that the President was on the telephone. In his experience, that was usually an effective way of bringing any meeting to an abrupt end.

At 2:00 p.m, Mrs. Babbitt buzzed to notify him of Brenner's arrival. As soon as Brenner entered his office, Daniel felt his hackles rise. Brenner's hair was now a wiry gray, but his eyes were as fierce as ever. He exuded energy and power; the kind of man people would immediately assume was the leader of something. He strode over and reached across Daniel's desk to shake his hand.

"Thank you for agreeing to see me. I know it's a busy time for you."

If Brenner recalled their earlier meeting during the long ago dinner in Chinatown, he gave no sign of it. Daniel had a childish but overwhelming desire to test Brenner's memory but squelched it. He gestured for Brenner to sit.

"It is a busy time for me," he agreed, "so let's get right down to business. What can I do for you?"

Brenner sat forward on the chair, his shoulders aggressively hunched. His forearms touched the chair's arms without resting on them, his hands were curled into fists.

"You can put a little pressure on the clothing manufacturers," he began. "They're being entirely unreasonable. They're taking advantage of the political situation and trying to take back everything we gained during the last fifteen years." He shook his head. "That won't be good for my people, but it really isn't good for the country either. The United States needs a strong, financially sound middle class. You know that and the President knows that. Just because there's a flood of returning vets looking for jobs is no reason to undo the progress we've made."

Daniel nodded slowly. "If your people were the only ones threatening to strike, I wouldn't necessarily disagree with you. But the labor situation has gotten out of control, at least in the perception of the voters. And with mid-terms coming up in a few months, the President and the Democrats have to prove they have some sway over the unions or we're going to lose the election big time. If you think things are bad now, just wait until the Republicans get in power. They're going to make mincemeat out of the National Labor Relations Act."

"So what are you suggesting?" Brenner demanded. "That we just cave in?"

"I'm not talking about caving in. I'm talking about making a few concessions. Maybe working without a contract while you negotiate."

Brenner looked disgusted. "If we work off contract, we'll never get another contract," he said. "You know that as well as I do."

Daniel was silent. He did know it, but unless the President was willing to stand up and take some heat on the labor issue, there wasn't much he could do. The tiny satisfaction he was getting out of seeing the frustration in Brenner's face didn't make up for the fact that he really hated having to pressure the union like this.

"Do you like Chinese food?" he asked Brenner suddenly, his face impassive.

"What?" Brenner's face registered surprise and confusion but no understanding of the reference.

"Chinese food," Daniel repeated. "If you eat it with chopsticks, you're forced to take very small, precise bites, but you can eat surprisingly quickly."

"I don't see—"

"Go back and try again. Give up the big demands and go for the small bites this time around. You might not feel like you accomplished much. But at least you'll still be in the game."

Brenner snorted. "I don't think you're getting the picture," he said, his voice tight with anger. "Or maybe you just don't want to see it. The manufacturers are not willing to budge an inch. Small bites, big bites. It doesn't matter. The only thing that matters is whether you're willing to help us. If not, we really have no choice but to strike. We can't go back to how things were and you know it."

He continued, "I thought you, of all people, would understand, unless you've forgotten your past completely. I don't think I have to remind you of the kind of conditions we fought to get rid of, the threats to health and safety. But maybe I'm mistaken." More than the words themselves, the look on Brenner's face held a challenge. It was as if he had thrown down a gauntlet.

Daniel stared at him. Did Brenner remember him and his friendship with Lena after all? Or was it just that Brenner was aware of his humble beginnings in the garment district and his history of advocating on behalf of labor. Either way, he didn't like the guy any better now than he had thirty years ago.

He could lean on Brenner, he thought. Tell him that not only was the administration not going to help, it was going to do the opposite. Pressure him to accept the manufacturers' terms. Threaten to sanction the union. He imagined Brenner without his power, a wounded lion. It was an interesting picture.

But he couldn't bring himself to do it. Because Brenner was right. The manufacturers were being unreasonable. And the workers needed help.

"I'll talk to the Secretary," he said. "I'll see what I can do."

Brenner nodded. "Thank you. I appreciate it. I won't take up any more of your time." He stood up just as Daniel's intercom buzzed.

It was Mrs. Babbitt. "I'm sorry Mr. Cowan, but the President is on the line."

Daniel picked up his phone and put his hand over the mouthpiece. "I have to take this," he said to Brenner.

"Of course." Brenner extended his hand and Daniel rose from his seat to shake it. "Thank you again," Brenner said. "I'll see myself out."

Daniel, still cradling the telephone receiver in his hands, watched the door close behind Brenner. Now that the man had left, he felt a churning in his stomach. What was it about the guy that touched such a nerve in him? So Brenner had been a jerk one night many years ago. Why should he still feel it so keenly?

Placing the telephone receiver back on the base, he thought back to that night in the Chinese restaurant. He remembered how he'd fiddled with the chopsticks and how Lena had laughed when he'd finally steered a morsel of Chinese food into her mouth. Brenner had looked daggers at him, as if he were offended by Daniel's success, although why he should be, Daniel had had no idea. It was almost as if Brenner resented his attention to Lena, even though Brenner's girlfriend, a very pretty and vivacious girl if he remembered correctly, was sitting right next to him.

Unless... unless Brenner had been interested in Lena himself. The idea came to him out of the blue, but now that it had, Daniel had to admit that it made sense. He'd been so naive in those days when it came to male-female relationships, it would never have occurred to him that night. Now, it fit together.

And then, almost as soon as he'd completed this connection, another idea occurred to him. Lena's pregnancy. She'd said the father would never marry her. Could it be that Brenner was the father of Lena's child? No. He was letting his imagination get carried away. Lena had never said anything to lead him to believe that she was involved with Brenner.

Still, it was possible. In fact, the more he thought about it, the more possible it seemed. Agitated, he stood up, walked over to the coat stand in the corner of his office, and took his wallet out of his jacket pocket. He pulled out a faded photograph—a picture of Lena's daughter that she'd sent him years ago. Then, he'd marveled at the resemblance between mother and daughter, the generous mouth, dimpled chin, and wide-set eyes. Now, he looked at it again, searching for something different. Someone different.

And he found it. Why had he not noticed before that Rachel's eyes were not dark like Lena's? And her hair, though the same shade of brown as her mother's, was wildly curly. Yes, she looked somewhat like Lena. But she also looked like someone else. Someone who had sat across from him just a few moments ago.

Epithets jumped into his head. Words he would like to hurl at Brenner, the son of a bitch who he'd just promised to help. Of course, he couldn't prove his suspicions. He might even be completely off course. But somehow he didn't think so.

There was no way to confirm it, as he was no longer in touch with Lena. He'd not attended her wedding but he'd sent a generous gift. In response, he'd received a card thanking him not just for the gift but also for the books he'd sent over the years and for his friendship. By then, the episode with Julie had made him see things in a new light and he'd realized that friendship had its own rewards.

A short time later, he'd sent Lena a letter but received no response. So, he'd tried again. And again, there was no response. After his third attempt came back marked "Return to Sender," he concluded that either he'd misunderstood her reference to friendship or she'd decided that married life and friendship with the opposite sex were not compatible. It was just as well. He'd already learned how difficult it was for him to see anyone else while she was still in his thoughts.

The phone rang and he spun around, glancing at his watch as he did so. Damn. He was supposed to have updated the Labor Secretary fifteen minutes ago. He strode over and picked up the phone.

Mrs. Babbitt, calm as ever, came on the line. "Miss Richmond for you, Mr. Cowan."

Daniel hesitated. Much as he wanted to take the call, duty beckoned. "Thank you Mrs. Babbitt, but would you mind telling Miss Richmond that I'll have to call her back? And please take her phone number. And then would you please get me the Secretary's office?"

Minutes later, his report to the Secretary done, he was ready to make another call. This one, he would dial himself after getting the phone number from Mrs. Babbitt.

Lee answered immediately in a crisp, professional voice. "Lee Richmond, International News Service."

"Lee, it's Daniel."

"Daniel." The pleasure in her voice was unmistakable. The crispness disappeared, and her pitch dropped an octave.

"How are you?" He glanced down at the number he'd gotten from Mrs. Babbitt and didn't recognize it. "Where are you?"

"I'm fine. A bit jet-lagged, but otherwise alright. The London part of my trip didn't last as long as I expected. I got pulled from my original assignment and now I'm covering Churchill's visit to the U.S. I'm in Missouri right now. The good news is that I'll be back in D.C. sooner than I thought."

"How much sooner?"

"A week from tomorrow."

He felt a surge of anticipation at the thought of seeing her again. "Would you like a lift from the airport?"

"Does the offer include dinner? My plane gets in at seven."

"Then dinner's included. I'll make a reservation at Blackie's."

"Mmm," Lee said, the word sounding like a mix between a purr and a moan. "Did I already tell you how much I love it there?"

"No. You just seemed like the kind of woman who would appreciate a good steak."

Lee laughed softly. "You're right. I do."

"I'll see you soon."

"Good." Lee paused. "I'll be looking forward to it."

"Yes," Daniel said, nodding his head slowly, "So will I."

He hung up the phone and glanced down at his desk. The photograph of Rachel was still lying where he had placed it. He picked it up again and looked at it. He didn't know why he'd kept it all these years but there was no point in keeping it any longer. He crumpled it up and, twisting around, threw it in the trashcan behind his chair.

Blackie's was famous for three things: excellent steak, very dry martinis, and an atmosphere that offered privacy and intimacy. All three made Daniel glad he'd picked it for his first dinner with Lee in over a week. His drink had been smooth, his dinner fortifying, and now he was feeling more relaxed then he had in some time.

He and Lee paused their conversation while the waiter set their coffee on the table and Daniel took advantage of the moment to enjoy simply looking at her. Though they'd kissed at the airport, they'd been so busy afterwards collecting her luggage and finding a cab that he hadn't had time to really take her in.

If Lee was jet lagged, it wasn't evident. In the restaurant's dim lighting, her skin looked luminous. He liked the way she was wearing her hair, brushed back from her forehead to reveal her widow's peak and falling to her shoulders in thick waves.

The waiter left and Lee took a sip of coffee, glanced up to see Daniel looking at her, and smiled. "Hi," she said.

"Hi yourself." He smiled back. "Did I already tell you how beautiful you look tonight?"

"I don't mind hearing it again."

"If this is your jet lagged look, it suits you."

"Thank you. I think spending the last few days in Missouri helped me get re-acclimated."

"So what did you think of Churchill's speech?"

"I wish I could say I thought he was wrong about the Soviet Union, but I don't think he is."

"I don't either. Although the 'iron curtain' language may have been a bit more than was necessary."

"Maybe," Lee said. "But that's Churchill. He's never under-stated. What about you? How was your week?"

"Hectic."

"You look tired."

"Thanks." He laughed.

"When was the last time you took a break and got away?"

"I think it was around 1927."

"Then I'd say you were due."

"I've been thinking about taking some time off."

"Where would you go?" Lee asked. "Do you have a favorite place that you dream of escaping to?"

He shrugged. "I haven't seen that much of the world, but I can't imagine there's any place I'd love better than New York."

"What do you love so much about it?"

"Everything. Oh, I know it's crowded and dirty and the crime rate is high but, for me, the dark side of the city is more than outweighed by the bright. In fact, I think it's partly the extremes that make it as exciting as it is. Like the dark inside a Broadway theatre while you're seeing an amazing production and the brightness of the restaurants that are open long after the theater lets out. And Central Park in the winter, when it's a river of white, while buildings surround it like dark sentinels.

I love that it's got more of everything than anyplace else I've ever been. More music, more art, more newspapers, and more bookstores. More of pretty much everything that's important to me. I think it's the greatest city on earth.

"That's a very poetic description," Lee said. "But you may want to reserve judgment regarding the greatest city on earth until you've seen Paris or London. I might even be persuaded to show you those places myself."

"Now there's an offer," he said. I'd love to see them both sometime. But I doubt either of them could take the place that New York has in my heart."

Lee shook her head. "And yet you've lived away from it for so long. Why is that?"

"I'm beginning to wonder. For a while, I felt like I was really making a difference being here in D.C. But now, I think I might have a better chance of accomplishing my goals someplace else."

"And those goals are?"

"What is this," Daniel teased her, "an interview?"

Lee laughed. "If you're going to date a reporter, you're going to have to put up with questions from time to time."

"Is that what we're doing? Dating?"

"You answer my question and I'll answer yours."

"I forgot what the question was."

"No you didn't," Lee smiled, but she reminded him anyway. "Your goals?"

"The same as they always were. To improve conditions for working men and women and to fight for people who don't have the ability to fight for themselves."

"So, what would you do if you weren't doing what you do now?"

"I don't know. Maybe run for office? Maybe take on some labor law cases?"

Lee looked at him thoughtfully. "I wish you could see yourself right now."

"Why?"

"Because when you started talking about running for office and taking on cases you didn't look a bit tired anymore."

Daniel nodded. "I could get pretty excited about doing either of those things. I remember when I first started learning about democratic elections. I couldn't believe it was really possible for people to choose those who governed them. Even now, with everything I know about how politics and elections really work, I still think it's the best system in the world. And I think I could be good at it."

"I'm sure you would be great at it," Lee said, her eyes glittering.

"But, I'm not going anywhere until this railroad strike is settled. After that, we'll see." He took a sip of his drink and smiled. "Alright," he said. "I answered your question, so you answer mine."

"Now it's my turn to say I forgot the question."

"It was about us and what it is that we're doing."

Before Lee could answer, a waiter approached their table and in a hushed voice said, "I'm sorry to interrupt, but there's a phone call for Mr. Cowan. Shall I bring it to the table or would you prefer to come to the front desk?"

"Thanks," Daniel said. "I'll come to the desk." He turned to Lee, "Will you excuse me for a moment?"

"Of course. It'll give me time to decide how to answer your question."

"And don't think I'll forget," Daniel said with a grin.

It was Tom Sanzo. "We're at a dead end on the negotiations," he said. "You better get down here. The President has asked to address the Congress. He's going to draft those workers unless we can do something about it."

"I'm on my way," Daniel told him.

Returning to the table, he said. "I'm very sorry, but I have to go. I'll make it up to you."

"I'm going to hold you to that."

He escorted her to the cloakroom, collected their things, and helped her on with her coat. Outside the restaurant, he hailed a taxi for her.

"I'm really sorry," he said again as he opened the cab door.

"You'll call?"

He slipped an arm around her waist and, exerting gentle pressure on the small of her back, pulled her close and kissed her.

"As soon as I can," he said. "Now go, before I give in to temptation and get in the cab with you."

Five hours later, Daniel arrived back at his apartment exhausted. Disaster had just barely been averted. President Truman had been midway through his address to Congress when the railroad workers had agreed to go back to work. Daniel had had to fling himself in a taxicab and race over to the Capitol, where he'd given the news to John Steelman, the President's Chief of Staff. Steelman had scribbled a note and passed it to the President as he'd stood at the lectern. And Truman, with a satisfied look on his face, had announced the end of the strike to Congress.

Daniel sank into the club chair in his living room, propped his feet up on an ottoman, and sat for a moment, thinking. He reached for the telephone on the table beside the chair and dialed.

"Hello Lee? It's Daniel. Did I wake you?"

"It doesn't matter," she assured him. "What happened? Did the President draft the workers?"

"We dodged the bullet this time. They settled in the nick of time."

"I'm so glad. Congratulations."

"But I've had enough," Daniel said, feeling relieved just to have acknowledged it. "I'm handing in my resignation in the morning. It's time to go home. It's time to go back to New York."

"I'm not surprised."

"Before I do, I thought I might take a little vacation." He paused. "I was wondering...." He gave her a chance to anticipate where he was going. "Is that offer to show me Paris still good?"

There was no hesitation on the other end of the phone. "I'm already packing."

A grin spread over Daniel's face. He was feeling better with every passing moment. "Good," he said as he slipped off his shoes and loosened his tie. "Why don't I call you back tomorrow morning and we'll make some plans?"

PART III

CHAPTER THIRTY

LENA SAT AT HER DESK AND GRINNED AT HER BROTHER. HE WAS SO jazzed about his latest acquisition that he hadn't stopped pacing since coming into her office. At fifty-five, he'd developed a bit of a paunch and lost most of his hair, but he still had the boyish enthusiasm that made him so loveable.

Six years had passed since Lena had come to work at Rothman Sims, six years since she'd first walked into this building, unsure whether she had anything to contribute. At the time, her self-confidence and her energy were drained dry from the exhausting effort of fighting her ex-husband. First, there had been the long, messy, and humiliating divorce proceedings during which Will and his lawyer had done their best to portray her as a cold harridan whose withholding of affection and constant nagging had virtually driven Will into the arms of his mistress.

Then, there'd been the even longer, messier, and more extensive legal battle over the ownership of Lena K at the end of which, her snake of an ex-husband had managed to convince the judge, who was even more chauvinistic than Will, that he was its rightful owner. Although Lena had considered appealing the decision, the idea of allowing any more of her life to be consumed by dealings with Will and his attorneys was more than she could stomach. So, she'd let it go and accepted Joe's offer to come work for him and Arnie, though not without trepidation, nervous that the skills she'd developed while running Lena K wouldn't be helpful in her new job as Vice-President of Marketing. She was glad to have a place to get up and go every morning, not to mention a paycheck coming in, but she knew she would lose the self-respect she had left if she didn't actually start doing the job that her title demanded.

Prior to her arrival, Rothman Sims had attached its name primarily to the couture designs that were Arnie's forte. But since couture alone didn't pay the bills, they'd also started mass-producing an inexpensive line of ready-to-wear every-day clothes made of lesser materials and sold under a different label entirely.

After working there a few months, it came to Lena that there was a need for something in between these two alternatives to serve the needs of a rapidly expanding group of customers—working women. During the war, many women had taken jobs outside the home for the first time in their lives. Some had kept their jobs even after the war. Lena assumed that these women needed the same kind of clothes she did, outfits that were professional but still feminine. If these items could be mixed and matched, she thought, it would allow women to stretch their wardrobe budgets.

She also assumed that, like her, women wanted to wear a different set of clothes when they weren't working, clothes that were comfortable but still stylish. Women who wore overalls to factory jobs had discovered they liked the movement pants afforded. Lena proposed that Rothman Sims produce a more stylish version of women's pants, slacks that could be paired with sweaters or blouses for a casual but polished look on the weekend.

Based on her suggestions, Rothman Sims added two new lines of production under the Rothman Sims label: quality women's career and sportswear. Both lines were immediately successful. A few years later, she proposed a line of clothes for younger women that wouldn't feature the usual buttons and bows but, instead, would be a more sophisticated and polished look, but still youthful. That line too was a hit and now accounted for nearly a quarter of Rothman Sims' profits.

Now, she contemplated her brother fondly. A while ago, he'd wandered in ostensibly to discuss some manufacturing issue, but he'd yet to bring up any business related topic. A fan of all new electronics, he was waxing enthusiastic over his latest obsession.

"It's absolutely amazing!" he said "This will be the end of radio. You'll see. Soon everyone will have a television. I'm telling you, Arnie and I couldn't take our eyes off the thing. We stayed up until the Star Spangled Banner came on."

"Is that all you wanted to discuss with me?" Lena asked him mildly.

"What? Oh—No. I wanted to talk to you about JLS. I understand they were late again this month. I checked with Mike Newell in legal. He says our contract with them is up pretty soon. I think we should begin looking around for another manufacturer for the Racey line."

"They were late, but it wasn't entirely their fault," Lena said. "There was a hold-up on the materials end."

"That may be. But they've been late a few times and it's starting to be a habit. I still think we should look around for alternatives."

Lena nodded. She made a mental note to talk to Jerome Katz, the senior vice president in charge of manufacturing.

"You know," Joe said, returning to his earlier topic. "You really should get a television for your apartment. It's going to be awfully quiet at your place once the wedding is over. Have Rachel and David sent out the invitations yet?"

"They're waiting for them to come back from the printers." Lena still couldn't get over the fact that Rachel was actually marrying Sam and Bess's son. For so long now, the Grossmans had been like family. Now they really would be family.

Joe checked his watch. "I'd better get going. What time should I pick you up tonight?"

She frowned. "How long do we need to stay at this thing?"

"Don't make that face. The Jewel Ball is one of the biggest charity events of the year. And with Julie Danvers as this year's chairwoman, every society matron, trend-setter, and power player will be there, along with all of the top designers. You've gotten off easy up until now. But with Arnie sick, you're just going to have to buck up and put in an appearance."

"I hate these things."

"How would you know? You never go to any of them. You never go anywhere." He gave her a long look. "It's been years since your divorce was final. Don't you think it's time you got back out there?"

"Back out there?" Lena arched a brow. "If you're suggesting what I think you are, then you're way off course. I've told you before. I'm done with all that."

"Bubbeleh," Joe said. "You can't be serious. You're too young to spend the rest of your life alone."

"I'm not alone. I have you and Arnie and Rachel and now David. And, I'm not so young. It may not be long before I have grandchildren."

"Even when you're a grandmother, you'll still be young and beautiful to me," Joe said. "Anyway you're not a grandmother yet."

"Thank you, but I'm not interested. I know you can't under-stand because you and Arnie are still a couple of lovebirds. But my experience hasn't exactly been great. Anyway, I'm happy being on my own. Weren't you the one who told me I don't need a man to have a successful life?"

"You're taking my words out of context."

"Maybe. But darling brother, I've finally grown up and realized that all those books I read when I was a girl were just fantasies. I like my life the way it is."

"But -"

"Enough." Lena protested. "If you have any desire at all to have me accompany you to this affair tonight, you'll let this go."

Joe sighed. "Alright. What time shall I pick you up?"

"8:00 p.m.?"

"That'll work. And relax," he said as he headed out the door. "We don't have to stay until the very end."

She watched him leave, happy the conversation was over. She knew Joe meant well, but he didn't know what it felt like to be betrayed, humiliated, and robbed as she had been. She hoped he never had to find out. She would go to this thing tonight out of duty but, as for re-entering the social scene, she was not in the least bit interested.

CHAPTER THIRTY-ONE

MANHATTAN APARTMENTS WERE NOTORIOUSLY SMALL, ESPECIALLY WHEN it came to kitchens and bathrooms, and Daniel's bathroom in his Greenwich Village rental was no exception. But at least the showerhead was mounted high on the wall and the water pressure was strong. He turned the faucet as hot as it would go and, as the small enclosure filled with steam, stood with the water beating directly down on him, the assault shutting out everything else, until his heart started pounding and he abruptly turned off the tap. He reached for the thick white towel he'd hung over the shower door and dried himself briskly.

The steam had spilled out into the bathroom. He knotted the towel around his waist and opened the door to let in enough air to clear the fog from the mirror. As the reflective surface reappeared he caught sight of himself. He didn't look too bad for a fifty-two year old, he thought. He still had a thick head of blond hair and he was in good shape, with broad shoulders and a flat stomach. In fact, he'd lost a few pounds in the month since Lee had left, because he was exercising more, eating out less, and not drinking as much. Not that he'd ever been a big drinker, but with Lee, it had always been cocktails before dinner, wine with dinner, and cordials after dinner. She'd been big on dessert too, but would always beg him to share it with her, saying they could work off the calories when they got home. But that was in the past.

"You understand," Lee had said. "I can't turn it down. It's Chief of the London Bureau. There's never been a woman chief before."

And she was right. She couldn't turn it down. He wouldn't dream of asking her. Just as she wouldn't dream of asking him to give up his Congressional campaign to move to London.

He shouldn't have been surprised by her departure. Their agreement right from the beginning had been no strings. Rather than be shocked by its ending, he should be shocked that it had lasted this long. As Julie frequently pointed out, neither he nor Lee was known for long-lasting romantic relationships.

Still, he couldn't help thinking that if Lee had cared about him enough, hell, if she'd loved him, she wouldn't have gone. And that hurt. He couldn't really blame her because they'd never spoken in terms of love. Strong affection, certainly. Respect, absolutely. Chemistry, without a doubt. But not love.

Would things have turned out differently if he'd been honest about how he'd felt? He would never know. Nor did he care to contemplate the reasons he'd not told her. It was too late now, anyway. There were more important things to concentrate on, his campaign, the classes he taught at NYU, the legal cases he took for free or minimal charge, and tonight's shindig. The Jewel Ball. From the moment Julie had accepted the chairmanship of the city's premier charity event, she'd been trying to persuade Daniel that it could also serve as his political coming out event.

"Everyone who's anyone will be there," she said. "It's your chance to introduce yourself, make a good impression, start currying favor with the power brokers and the money men. You need votes to win the election, but these days, it costs oodles of money to get your name known."

Daniel was grateful for her support and her wise counsel. He hoped she felt the same about him. He'd tried hard to be a shoulder for her to lean on when her husband, William, had passed away. He'd assisted her with the funeral arrangements, then helped her make the move back to New York, where she'd quickly re-established herself in New York society. Tonight, he would be there for her again, as her official escort. And, she would do for him what she did best—make charming introductions and subtly establish his credentials amongst a group of people who, otherwise, might be suspicious of his labor oriented background.

By now, he was nearly finished dressing. The event was black tie, and he was wearing his shawl collar tuxedo with a white wing-tipped shirt and a black bow tie. It was time to go. He owed Julie so much. The least he could do was be on time.

CHAPTER THIRTY-TWO

BY THE TIME RACHEL GOT HOME, IT WAS NEARLY 9:00 P.M. KNOWING her mother was at a charity event with her Uncle, she'd grabbed a bite for dinner with a girlfriend. Now, she was looking forward to having the apartment to herself. She planned to look at bridal magazines and wait for David's call.

A couple of years after she'd graduated and started working at Random House, David had called to say he would be in town the following Wednesday. It was the first time she'd heard from him in the years since their correspondence had petered out around the same time she'd graduated. He'd wanted to know if she was free for dinner and she quickly accepted, thinking it would be fun to see him again after all this time. At the end of the evening, he'd asked if she was free again the following Wednesday. Much as she liked him, she'd told him it made no sense to begin a relationship with someone who lived over three hours away. To which he'd replied, "As long as I'm willing to come, what difference does it make where I live?"

So they'd gone out again the following Wednesday and the Wednesday after that and the one after that. After a while, Wednesdays hadn't been enough, so she'd started going to Grossman's on weekends. But eventually, even Wednesdays and weekends hadn't been enough because they wanted to be together all the time. Yet Rachel hadn't been quite ready to leave the job she loved in the city for the man she loved in the country. So they'd continued as before until one Sunday when David was taking her to the station to catch the train to the city and she'd realized that she didn't want to get on it. They'd gotten engaged immediately. Now she couldn't wait until they were married and living at Grossman's where she would begin work on the novel she'd always dreamed of writing.

She changed out of her work clothes, made herself a cup of tea, and sat down to relax. Rifling through the mail, she found two items for her: a letter from her college roommate Susan and an official looking envelope from the United States Marine Corps. Her heart started to beat with excitement. She read Susan's letter first—trying to tamp down her hopes. After all, she'd been trying for nearly seven years to get information from the military about her father. So far, all her efforts had led to naught.

The Navy, the Air Force, and the Army had responded to her inquiries with polite letters indicating that they had no record of anyone by the name of Abraham Rothman. They noted that this did not mean her father had not served with them. If she had more detailed information concerning the field level unit, company, troop or battery with which he had served, they would be happy to search again or to direct her to the proper records repository. As she knew none of those details, the Marine Corps was her last hope.

She slit open the brown envelope and pulled out a thin sheet of paper. "Thank you for your recent inquiry regarding the service of Abraham Rothman. We regret to inform you that we have no record...." Disappointment mingled with frustration. She felt a lump beginning to swell up in her throat, but she would not give in to it. There had to be another way.

She thought for the millionth time of Sophie Friedman, her mother's long-ago friend and roommate. She'd already tried to track the elusive Mrs. Friedman down. The New York telephone book had no less than twenty five Sophie Friedman's, twenty Sophie Freedman's, forty-five S. Friedman's and thirty four S. Freedman's. She had tried them all. None admitted to having known her mother. Of course, if Sophie Friedman (or Freedman) had gotten married, her name would no longer be Friedman and she might not still be living in New York. Heck, she might not be living at all.

Still, Rachel thought, she would not give up. She would check the marriage records for all of New York State if she had to. And if that didn't pan out, perhaps she could track down someone else who had survived the fire at Northern Shirtwaist Company, and maybe that person would be able to able to tell her something about either her mother or Sophie Friedman.

Once she and David returned from their honeymoon, she would go back to the public library and begin anew. Somewhere amongst all those articles about the fire and the lists of names of survivors, there had to be someone who had known her mother or Sophie Friedman.

CHAPTER THIRTY-THREE

"THIS SHINDIG GETS MORE CROWDED EVERY YEAR," JOE MUTTERED to Lena as he led her through a tight maze of ball-gowned women and their tuxedoed partners.

The ballroom of the Edison Hotel was a fine example of Art-Deco style with a black and white marble floor, chrome wall sconces, and a pyramid of geometric molding atop each of its tall windows. Under other circumstances, Lena would have enjoyed looking around. But right now, she wished she were home, curled up in bed with a book. She envied Arnie not having to be here and then felt guilty because he was really sick, yet had still been thoughtful enough to send over his newest dress for her to wear, a strapless black mermaid gown with a sweetheart neckline and matching elbow length gloves. Joe turned to give her an encouraging grin.

"I knew that with Julie as the chairwoman there would be a big turn-out. Don't worry. We'll pay our respects and, after that, we'll be free to leave whenever we want."

He made a bee-line for a tall, blond woman who was having a word with one of the waiters. Impeccable was the only way to describe her, Lena thought. Her chignon was perfect; her complexion and make-up were flawless. And despite her role as chairperson, she appeared, in her violet silk gown, as calm and cool as a lily on a lake.

"Joe, darling," Julie said as they approached. Her smile was gracious and warm. "Thank you for coming. I'm so sorry Arnie's not feeling well. It's always a treat to see him. He's the only person besides me who knows the words to every Rodgers and Hammerstein song."

"He feels terrible about missing this," Joe said. "But, I've brought an excellent substitute. Julie, I'd like to introduce my sister, Lena Kerner, Vice President for Marketing for Rothman Sims. Lena, it's my pleasure to introduce you to Julie Danvers, the organizing force behind this and many other marvelous charitable events."

Julie smiled and extended her hand. "It's a pleasure to meet you. And may I say your dress is magnificent. I assume it's one of Arnie's? The man just keeps getting better and better."

"The pleasure is all mine," Lena said. "And yes, it's Arnie's latest. But I was just about to compliment you on your dress. It's beautiful. Is it a Nan Duskin?"

"Thank you dear. Yes, I -" At that moment, her attention was diverted and she looked past them, smiled with pleasure, and reached around Lena to take someone's hand, drawing the newcomer to her side. She slipped an arm possessively through his as he turned to face them.

"Have you all met yet?" Julie asked. A note of pride crept into her voice. "Let me introduce you to the next member of the United States House of Representatives. Joe Rothman and Lena Kerner, this is Daniel Cowan."

Daniel. Lena was shocked to the point of immobility, her breath caught in her chest, her heart beating like a drum. She couldn't believe it. She was struck first by his presence and, then, by his appearance. The years had developed and burnished his handsomeness. He projected a masculinity so confident, he seemed like someone she'd never met.

"A pleasure, Mr. Cowan," Joe said amiably, extending his hand.

As the two men shook, Daniel's eyes moved over to Lena. His expression was neutral; it was impossible to tell what he was thinking or even whether he recognized her. He said nothing and Lena struggled to find the right words, or any words, to fill the awkward pause.

Finally, she extended her hand. "It's nice to, that is I'm glad to...." She faltered and swallowed. Daniel made no move to take her hand and she lowered it slowly. Julie's eyes flitted from Daniel to Lena and back again, curiosity turning from puzzlement to caution.

Lena glanced at Joe, hoping desperately that her brother would save her somehow. She still had no idea what to say to Daniel but knew that she wanted to, must, say something. Joe broke the silence.

"Julie, would you do me a favor and walk over to the bar with me? I see someone whose acquaintance I'd like to make."

Julie hesitated. "It's almost time to go into dinner. Perhaps it would be better to wait?"

"It won't take long. Please."

For a moment, Julie didn't move, clearly torn between her desire to stay by Daniel's side and her inbred manners as a good hostess. Breeding won out. She touched Daniel's arm lightly and said, "I'll be right back. Don't go in to dinner without me."

Daniel looked at Julie, his expression suggesting he had no idea what she'd just said. Still, he nodded. Reluctantly, Julie disengaged herself and, with a last glance at Daniel, walked away with Joe. Lena waited until they were out of earshot before speaking.

"It's good to see you Daniel," she said. He remained silent and she felt her face grow warm. "Congratulations on your nomination. I had no idea. I don't follow politics much...."

He shook his head. "Julie's being optimistic. I haven't been nominated. I'm just starting to campaign." He glanced down and pushed at the bridge of his glasses with his right index finger. Lena smiled at the old habit. But her smile faded quickly when he looked back up. His eyes were piercing.

"What are you doing here?" he said brusquely.

Taken aback by his tone, she said, "I came with my brother Joe."

"No—I mean, what are you doing in New York City? I thought you lived in Monticello."

"Oh, Yes. I did. But I moved here about six years ago when I got divorced."

"Divorced?!" He looked shocked then embarrassed. "I'm sorry. I didn't know."

"No. Of course, you didn't," she said quickly. "Anyway, I moved back here soon afterwards and got an apartment with my daughter Rachel."

At the mention of Rachel's name he seemed about to speak but didn't, so Lena continued, "I started working for Joe just to have something to do and then I liked it, so I stayed. Now, I have a very important sounding job. I'm Vice President in charge of marketing." She smiled, trying to show him that she didn't take her position seriously. "But, you probably don't want to hear all this."

"No, I –" Before Daniel could continue, Julie re-appeared at his side.

"Now, you two," she said sweetly. "It's time for dinner." She looked at Lena. "Have you found your table yet dear? Well, why don't you do that so you don't miss the first course."

Lena nodded dumbly. There was so much more she wanted to say to Daniel, but he was looking at Julie. She mumbled something about it being nice to see him again and hurried off to find Joe. Her brother was nowhere in sight. As she searched for her name on the place card table, Joe found her.

"There you are," he said. He smiled wryly. "Well that was a blast from the past. What an unexpected encounter." His smile turned to concern, "You look pale. Are you alright?"

Lena turned miserable eyes to him. "Not really. In fact, I'm not feeling well at all. I'm sorry, but I think I'd better leave. Would you call a cab while I get my coat?"

"Of course. But, Lena, are you sure you want to leave? I mean, I didn't remember him at first but then it came to me. He had a huge crush on you way back when. And, from the looks of it, he still does."

"What are you talking about?" She stared at him. She knew he was biased when it came to her, but this was ridiculous. "He barely said a word to me."

"He couldn't take his eyes off you."

"You're crazy."

"I know what I saw," Joe insisted.

"Or misinterpreted."

"What are you afraid of?"

"Nothing!" She couldn't believe Joe didn't see how awkward the situation was or how painful. She felt like there was a knife caught cross-wise in her throat. "I didn't want to come here in the first place and now I don't feel well. It's alright if you want to stay. But I'm leaving."

Joe studied her face. "Okay," he said. "You get your coat and I'll hail a cab."

Lena went to the coat check, handed her ticket to the girl, and waited.

"Are you leaving already?"

Her chest constricted at the sound of Daniel's voice and she turned around. He was standing with his hands in his pockets and looked very debonair. But his face was inscrutable.

"I never planned to stay the whole evening," she said, trying to keep her voice steady. "I'm not particularly good at navigating these affairs."

"I never used to be either. But I got used to them while I was in Albany and Washington. I have to say, Julie's events are far better than most. The food's always fantastic."

"I'm not really hungry."

He nodded but said nothing. After a minute, Lena couldn't stand it anymore. She had to speak.

"Daniel, I am so sorry. I know I made mistakes. I should have told you about Will before the wedding invitations went out, especially given our past. So, I understand why you didn't answer my letters afterwards. But I should have kept trying. I should have at least written to you a few more times."

"I don't understand," Daniel said, looking confused. "You were the one who stopped answering my letters. I continued sending you books after you were married. But I never got any response so I finally just stopped."

"I never received any more books. Or letters. How could—" Suddenly it hit her. Goddamn Will. She had no doubt he'd had a hand in this.

She took a deep breath. "I think I know what happened. You see, my former husband was," she tried to think of a way to describe Will and finally said, "well, he wasn't a very nice or honest man."

"I see," Daniel said.

The coat-check girl cleared her throat. "Is this yours Miss?"

"That's it. Thank you."

Daniel reached past her, took her coat, and dropped some money into the tip cup. He held her coat for her and she fumbled for one sleeve and then the other, feeling shy and clumsy around him in a way she never had before.

"Look," he said, after a minute, resuming his casual hand-in-one-pocket stance, "I know you're not hungry tonight but you do eat dinner sometimes, don't you?"

He was gazing at her intensely and she felt herself grow warm. She noticed for the first time that his eyes were more aqua than blue, like the color of the ocean in mid-summer. Her heart began beating quickly again and she felt the pulsing of it all through her body. It had been a very long time since any man had had this effect on her.

"Yes," she said. "I eat dinner sometimes."

"Good. Because it might be nice to get together one of these days. Catch up." His tone was light, but his gaze had lost none of its intensity.

"What about Julie?" she asked, her heart beating wildly. "Won't she mind?"

"Why would she?" he said. The answer gave no indication whether this meant there was nothing between him and Julie or nothing special about the invitation.

"Well, if you're sure," she said.

"Are you free on Thursday night?"

"I am."

"Where should I pick you up?"

"236 Bleecker Street."

"Will 7 p.m. be alright?"

"Fine," she said, though she felt anything but fine.

Joe returned, his footsteps slowing as he noticed Daniel.

Lena turned to him. "Is the taxicab here already?"

"It is if you still want it." Joe looked from her to Daniel and back again.

Lena nodded. "Good night," she said to Daniel, extending her hand.

He held it along with her gaze for a moment. "Good night," he said.

"You alright?" Joe asked as he climbed into the cab beside her.

She nodded, still feeling slightly dazed.

"So do you have a date?"

In the dark of the taxi, Lena's mouth twitched. "Sort of."

"Say it," he commanded.

She sighed. "You *might* be right."

Beside her, she felt rather than saw Joe's grin. But she wasn't as sure of what Daniel wanted as Joe seemed to be nor did she have any idea what she wanted from him.

CHAPTER THIRTY-FOUR

DANIEL KNEW IF HE DIDN'T LEAVE SOON, HE WOULD BE LATE PICKING Lena up for dinner. Still, he fiddled with his favorite blue tie as he checked himself in the mirror. He couldn't remember the last time he'd been this nervous about a date. It had probably been the last time he'd taken out this particular woman.

He checked himself one last time. Gray flannel suit, crisp white shirt. He looked fine. He told himself that any man who'd served in the Roosevelt and Truman administrations, and was a successful lawyer, respected law school professor, and candidate for the United States Congress had nothing to be nervous about. He reached for his fedora and overcoat and headed out the door.

The funny thing was that Lena lived only a few blocks from him in Greenwich Village. He wondered whether she had resided there ever since her divorce. It was extraordinary to think they'd been living in the same neighborhood for the last few years. Perhaps he'd walked right by her without noticing. So much of life was like that. You didn't see what you didn't expect to see.

236 Bleecker Street was a salmon-colored brick townhouse with a glossy black door and a shiny brass knocker. On either side of the entrance, was a squat clay planter filled with red geraniums. They reminded him of his earlier dilemma. He had debated at some length about whether he should bring flowers. He had erred on the side of not wanting to appear too eager. He'd learned a thing or two about women over the years. Charm was good; eagerness was not.

He rang the bell and waited. Just as he was wondering whether to ring it again, there was a muffled noise and the solid clunking sound of a lock being undone. The door was opened by a young woman. She was slim with masses of curly brown hair falling loose to her shoulders and was wearing a red blouse tucked into dark trousers that were cinched at her waist. Her wide set, thickly lashed, gray eyes appraised him frankly. She thrust out a hand.

"Hello. You must be Mr. Cowan. I'm Rachel Rothman, Lena's daughter."

Of course, he thought, *who else would you be.* "It's a pleasure to meet you," he said, adding to himself, *"at last."*

"Please come in. Mama is almost ready."

She led the way up a flight of stairs, giving Daniel only a few seconds to wonder what, if anything, Lena might have told her daughter about him. They emerged into a large living room. A handsome Persian carpet dominated by reds and golds covered the floor and in the middle of the room was a comfortable looking cream-colored sofa flanked by mahogany side tables. To the right, a large arched opening led to the dining room. To the left, a smaller arch led to a hallway. Rachel took his hat and coat and hung them on a coat rack in the corner.

"Please make yourself comfortable," she said, gesturing to the sofa. "Can I get you something to drink? I can make you a martini if you like."

"Just some club soda would be fine if you've got it."

"Club soda coming up." She busied herself at a bar in one corner of the room before bringing his drink. "Here you go." She sat in a barrel chair opposite him and waited until he had taken a sip before asking, "Did you have any trouble finding our street? Greenwich Village can be confusing."

"No. It was no trouble. In fact, I live only a few blocks from here on Waverly."

"Really?" Rachel raised her eyebrows.

"You seem surprised."

"Well, it's just that the Village isn't the likeliest place for a future Congressman to live."

Clearly, Daniel thought, *she had her mother's way of coming straight to the point. Or was it her father's way?* Aloud, he said, "Is it because the Village is too filled with radicals to be a suitable home for a Congressman?"

"Something like that," she admitted.

"Well, perhaps I'm more of a radical than I appear."

"Are you?"

He gave the question some thought. "I consider myself as radical as the founding fathers."

She grinned. "If that's your standard, then you are a radical."

"What's all this talk about radicals?" Lena said, appearing in the smaller archway. "Has my daughter been grilling you?"

Daniel stood up quickly as she entered the room. She looked even more beautiful than she had at the Jewel Ball. There was suddenly a fullness in his chest that he tried to keep from showing in his voice.

"No grilling," he assured her. "We've just been getting acquainted."

"I'm glad to hear it. But I know my daughter well. I made her promise she wouldn't demand to know your stance on every issue."

Rachel defended herself. "What's wrong with trying to be an informed voter?"

"Nothing at all," Daniel told her, happy to have something to focus on beside his racing pulse. "I wish all voters were interested in being informed. And I wish more women were active in politics, running for office or, at least, involved in some way."

"Wow. A politician who thinks women should run for office. That's not just radical for an aspiring Congressman, it's radical for a man."

Daniel grinned. "I think I've just been insulted twice."

"Not at all. I was complimenting you."

"As an exception to my sex and my profession."

"Well—yes."

Lena interrupted. "Rachel, you should be thanking Daniel, not insulting him."

"Thanking him for what?"

"When you were a little girl, he used to send you books in the mail. He introduced you to Huckleberry Finn and Little Women."

Rachel looked delighted. "I didn't know that. I still have those books. It was Jo from Little Women who first made me want to be a writer."

"Are you one?" Daniel asked.

"Not yet, but after my wedding, I'm going to start."

"You're getting married?"

"In seven weeks."

"Then I wish you the best of luck with your marriage and your writing." Feeling more in control than he had earlier, he turned to Lena. "If you're ready, we should probably get going."

"I'm ready."

"Rachel," Daniel said, "it was a true pleasure to meet you."

"Likewise."

He held Lena's coat, then opened the door and ushered her through.

The maitre'd at Christ Cella's seated them at a candlelit table in a quiet corner of the restaurant and they took a few minutes to peruse the menu. Like the question of whether to bring flowers, the problem of which restaurant to eat at had been a subject of much internal debate for Daniel. In the end, he had selected Christ Cella's for its intimate atmosphere, its exceptionally good French and Italian food, and its proximity to his favorite jazz club, if dinner went well. After the waiter had taken their orders, Lena glanced around.

"I've never been here before. It's really lovely. I'm glad you suggested it."

"It's one of my favorite places."

"Have you been here many times?"

"Well, not many times. I mean, I've been here a few times but I wouldn't say many."

"Well, I'm glad we're here." She looked around again. "It's... it's really lovely."

"Yes. And the food's very good too."

She looked around again. *She's bored*, Daniel thought. *Too many years have passed. It's just been too long. Wasn't it Thomas Wolfe who said "you can't go home again?"*

"Daniel...."

But if you couldn't go home again, then why did his heart leap when she merely said his name.

"Yes?"

"I'm so sorry."

"You needn't be. You already explained why you didn't answer my letters."

"Yes. Will is mostly to blame for that. I still can't believe he never posted my letters to you and withheld your letters to me, although I shouldn't be surprised. Your letters aren't the only thing he took from me." She shook her head. "I'll never put myself in that situation again. But I still should have made a better effort where you were concerned. I shouldn't have just presumed you didn't want to hear from me anymore."

"Why did you?"

"I thought perhaps you were upset with me. For not telling you about Will until I sent out the wedding invitations."

"I was surprised. You hadn't said a word about him in your letters. And then, all of a sudden, a marriage announcement. Was there some reason you didn't mention him to me earlier?"

"Well, neither you nor I were sharing much about what was going on in our lives at that point," Lena said. "And, I don't know. I think maybe I was trying to keep my two lives separate. My life before Grossman's and my life after. Rachel didn't know anything about my life before. She still doesn't. Then I met Will and I didn't want him to know anything about that time in my life either."

"It can't have been easy to keep Rachel from knowing anything about your life before Grossman's. Most children are curious about their parents."

Lena nodded. "You've met her so you can see how she is. She was always curious about everything and very persistent. But I never wanted her to pay for my mistakes. I didn't want her to be treated badly or to feel like she was less than anyone else just because I wasn't ever married. I never wanted her to be called a... a...." Her voice trailed off as if she'd suddenly remembered his own illegitimacy.

"So what did you tell her?" he asked gently.

"That her father was a distant cousin of mine. That he was drafted shortly after we married and that he was killed in the war."

"Your brother backed you up and no one was the wiser?"

She nodded. "I didn't tell anyone, except Bess and Sam Grossman."

"And now that Rachel is all grown up? Does she know the truth?"

She shook her head. "How can I tell her after all these years?"

"Does her father know about her?"

She sighed. "No. After I left the city, I never talked to him again."

"Why didn't you tell him when it first happened?"

She shrugged her shoulders. "I couldn't. He was...." She swallowed hard and shook her head. "He was...."

"Your best friend's boyfriend?" he asked gently.

She looked up in surprise. "You knew?"

"Not back then. And even now, it was just a guess. I saw him a few years ago when I was working for President Truman. There was something about him and the pictures you'd sent me of Rachel that made me wonder. And then tonight, seeing her all grown up. There's a strong resemblance."

"I know. It wasn't as marked when she was little, but her features have become more like his as she's grown up."

"But why didn't you ever tell him?" Daniel asked.

"In the beginning, I couldn't. Sophie was lying in a hospital bed in such terrible shape. She'd tried to save me in the fire and ended up burnt and crippled. If I'd told Jake, he'd have insisted on marrying me and I couldn't do that to Sophie."

"And now?"

"What do you mean?"

"He still lives in New York. Have you seen him since you came back?"

"No." She looked shocked at the question. "Of course not."

Daniel nodded. He was still trying to process it. He had so many questions. When had she and Jake first gotten together? Had Brenner loved her back in those days? What had she told Jake about why she was leaving the city and had he ever tried to find her? Daniel wanted to know every detail. He wanted to understand the whole situation.

"You loved him," he said. He made it a statement rather than a question, but held his breath, waiting for her confirmation. They were talking about events that had happened nearly thirty years ago, and yet, his stomach was churning so hard, he was afraid she would hear it.

She shook her head helplessly. "I don't know. I mean, I was in love with him. At least, I thought I was. But that was back in the days when I used to fantasize that I would marry a revolutionary and we would change the world. Isn't it ironic? There I was, going to those suffragette meetings and talking about equal rights but waiting for a man to come along and sweep me off my feet, under the illusion that I couldn't be happy or successful without a partner."

"Do you still think that?" Daniel asked.

"No. I don't. Do you?"

He hesitated. "I don't know. I guess I hope not, given my track record."

"It can't be any worse than mine. First, Jake. And then, my marriage to Will." She sighed. "That was a huge mistake. I never thought I could be such bad judge of people and of my own feelings. And then later, when I didn't even love Will anymore and was trying to figure out if I ever had, it still hurt terribly to find out he was going around with another woman behind my back. I felt like such an idiot."

She looked away and he thought she might be unable to continue, but she marshaled herself and went on, her tone bleaker. "And then the divorce and the fight over the business were both awful, really ugly. I lost my business, my dignity, my—everything. I never want to go through anything like that ever again." She shook her head and he could see that she was fighting back tears.

As he looked at her, the memory came back to him of that evening long ago when it had been he who had been doing the confessing and she who had been listening. Back then, he had stared at the table with the same look of abject misery that was on her face now. And what had she done? Had she questioned him endlessly? Grilled him for details? No. *What the heck am I doing?* he thought. *Why am I putting her through all this?* He reached over and covered her hand with his own, curling his fingers around it. She gripped his fingers as if she was clinging on for dear life.

"Lena," he said.

She looked at him and he saw that the wounds were still raw. He made his voice gentle.

"That's all in the past. It has nothing to do with who you are now."

"I don't know." She shook her head. "I just don't know."

"Well I do. You obviously did a wonderful job raising your daughter. And look at you now. You're a very successful businesswoman. Vice President of Rothman Sims."

"Thanks to my big brother."

He shook his head. "Don't be ridiculous. You wouldn't be in the position you are if you weren't good at what you do. Wasn't it your idea to introduce a line of clothes for young women? Wasn't the Racey label your idea?"

She looked at him, startled. "How do you know about the Racey label?"

He laughed. "I have my sources. Anyway, a wise woman once told me that the past is the past and doesn't define us in the present."

She sighed deeply, then nodded. "Yes. It's true. My life is good now. I have my daughter and my brother. I have good friends and a wonderful job. But what about you? You're going to be a Congressman. It's everything you dreamed about."

"Well there's still a little thing called the election that I have to win."

"And just like I told you," she reminded him, "I'll be the first one to vote for you."

"I'll drink to that," he said, raising his wine-glass.

She raised hers too. "To your future in politics."

"And to reconnecting with old friends."

They touched glasses and sipped their wine. Daniel savored his for a moment before swallowing. It was going to be alright, he thought. Thomas Wolfe didn't know everything. Sometimes, you could go home again. It might take some time to convince her to give love another chance, but he could be patient if he had to. Suddenly ravenous, he picked up his roll and started buttering it.

"So, he said, smiling at her, "how do you feel about jazz?"

Seven months later, on election night, a large and enthusiastic group of Daniel's supporters gathered in Julie's living room to listen to the returns on the radio. Among them were Louis and Anna Stimson, Jim and Lucy Kogan, Arnie Sims and Joe Rothman, and, of course, Lena.

Joe was sitting closest to the radio and periodically shushing everyone to announce the latest results. Daniel had led his opponent, Charles Cantwell, almost from the beginning of the evening. But, early on, with few precincts reporting, he, like everyone else, had been reluctant to get too excited. Around midnight, his lead started to widen and he began to believe that the unimaginable was actually going to happen. Still, a final result was nowhere in sight. At 2 a.m., he got up and went into Julie's kitchen to replenish the ice bucket; the butler having long since been dispensed. As he opened the freezer door, he heard Lena's voice behind him.

"How are you holding up?"

He turned around, smiled at her, and shook his head. "I'm so exhausted, I can't remember why I ever wanted to be a Congressman in the first place."

"I remember," she said.

He nodded. It had taken him a long time to get to this point. He'd been patient but determined. Patient about achieving his political goals and patient when it came to Lena. For the past seven months, he'd held back, given her time to come around. He'd heard her loud and clear when she'd told him about her ex-husband. It wasn't so much what she'd said, it was the way she'd looked. He knew she was scared—not just of getting hurt, but of making another mistake with her life.

He wanted to tell her that loving him wouldn't be a mistake. That he would be good for her. That he'd never stopped loving her and that, if she let him, he'd love her for the rest of her life. But how could he be sure that this time would be any different than the last time he'd said those things to her? Her friendship was, if anything, even more precious to him now than it had been then.

"Listen," he said, "just in case I forget to tell you, I really appreciate what a help you've been these last few months. I mean everything from the fundraiser you and Joe and Arnie threw for me to the nights you spent helping me stuff envelopes."

"Well, I have a vested interest you know," Lena said. "I do live in your district."

"Anyway," he said, as he walked slowly towards her, "I just wanted to say that -"

Suddenly there was a shout from the living room. Joe was calling and they hurriedly left the kitchen. He waved frantically for them to come over. "They're about to announce the latest returns. They've been calling a lot of the races in the last few minutes."

As the group fell silent, the voice of the radio announcer could be heard. "With one hundred percent of the precincts reporting in, WNBC is prepared to call the election. The winner in the tenth Congressional district is the Democratic nominee, Daniel Cowan."

There was a split second before anyone reacted and then pandemonium erupted. Daniel felt dazed, elated, and happier than he'd ever been in his whole life. He turned to Lena. Her eyes were bright with unshed tears and he took a step towards her. But before he could do or say anything, Julie appeared and threw both arms around his neck in a very un-Julie like gesture.

"Congratulations, darling!" she said. "I knew you would do it."

Choked with emotion, he hugged her back. Where would he be without Julie, he thought. She'd stuck with him through thick and thin, managed his whole campaign and very nearly funded it all too. He owed her everything. When they finally stopped hugging and stepped back, he could see that she, too, was fighting back tears.

"Thank you," he said, knowing words could never be enough. "For everything."

Julie shook her head, but couldn't seem to manage any words. And then, Daniel was swamped by others. They pumped his hand, slapped him on the back, and punched him in the shoulder. He looked for Lena and couldn't find her in all the chaos. But it was alright, he thought. He'd find another moment to tell her how he felt. He'd lost her once, but he never intended to lose track of her again.

CHAPTER THIRTY-FIVE

Rachel sat at the maple writing desk that Uncle Joe and Uncle Arnie had given her and David as a wedding present and looked down at the paper on which she'd written the man's name and phone number. There was no point in waiting. David was out for the evening, overseeing the early and late shows in the hotel nightclub, so she was alone in their suite. And, although she wasn't hiding anything—he knew she was planning to make the call—she thought she would feel less self-conscious if she did it alone. She reached for the telephone and dialed slowly. The phone was answered almost immediately and a rough voice barked out, "Hullo."

"Hello. May I speak with," she looked down at the paper again just to be sure, "Carlo Mastrocelli?"

"Ya speakin' tuh him right now. Who's dis?"

Rachel tried not to let the rough voice throw her. "My name is Rachel Grossman. And I think you may have known my mother. Her name is Lena Kerner now. But it was Lena Rothman when she worked at the Northern Shirtwaist Company. I—I know it was a long time ago, but I thought you might remember her?"

There was silence on the other end of the line. So much so that, after a few minutes, she began to wonder if the connection had been lost.

"'Mr. Mastrocelli?"

"Yeah. I'm still here."

"I'm sorry. I might have the wrong person. Are you, that is, did you work at the Northern Shirtwaist Company?"

"Yeah. I worked there. I ran the elevator."

"And by any chance, did you know my mother? Lena Rothman?"

There was a heavy sigh on the other end of the phone and after a second, the gruff voice again. "Yeah. Boy it's been a long time since I hoid that name. Who'd you say you was?"

"My name's Rachel Grossman. I'm Lena's daughter."

"Her daughter huh?" The man's tone was a little softer now. "How's she doin'?"

"Very well."

"That's good to hear." He made a sound that could have been either a chuckle or a snort. "She tell you I used to joke around wid her?"

"No, she -"

"Yeah. She was kind of shy when she first started at Northern, but she loosened up after a while. We used to kid back and forth. So, what's she up to now?"

"She works for Rothman Sims."

"Oh yeah?" Another short bark. "Well, I know she ain't still sewing shirtwaists."

"No. She's not."

"So you're Lena's girl. She was a looker. I remember that. You take after her?"

"Some people think so," Rachel said. "But I think I'm probably a mixture of both my mother and my father. You didn't by any chance know my father, did you Mr. Mastrocelli?"

"Your father? Nah. Lena wasn't married when I knew her."

Rachel frowned. Perhaps he hadn't known her mother as well as she'd assumed from his first few remarks. Then again, her mother might not have shared the news of her marriage with everyone at Northern even though it had taken place while she was working there. Rachel knew this was so, because she'd been born ninth months almost to the day from the date of the fire. She decided not to correct him. If he hadn't known her father, there was no point in continuing down that path.

"But you did know my mother."

"Sure I did. Like I told you. We used to joke around when she rode my elevator. I brought her up to the eighth floor every morning and back down again every evening. Her and Sophie. They used to ride my elevator every day."

"Did you say her and Sophie? Are you talking about my mother's friend Sophie Friedman? Did you know her too?"

"Sure," Mastrocelli chuckled. "Everybody knew Sophie. She was a real friendly type of gal. Fun loving. You know the type."

"Oh, yes," Rachel said, torn between the desire to hear more of Mr. Mastrocelli's recollections and eagerness to find out if he knew where Sophie Friedman was. Eagerness won out. It was really her father who she wanted to know about and, with any luck, Sophie Friedman would be able to tell her about him.

"Mr. Mastrocelli," she said, "I was wondering, do you happen to know where Sophie Friedman is now?"

"Now? I dunno. Why? You trying to track her down or something?"

Rachel swallowed, hoping her explanation would sound convincing. "Actually, I am. As a surprise for my mother. She's so sad to have lost touch with her after all these years. And I thought if I could find her, it would make her happy."

"Let me think. I remember she got married to that guy who was so big in the union. Jake something. Brenner I think. Yeah, Jake Brenner. That was his name. He was with the ILGWU. I think he's still with them. I don't have their number or nothing."

"Oh, that's alright. I'm sure with that information, I can find them. Thank you, Mr. Mastrocelli."

"Sure thing. And, hey, you tell your mama that Buddy says hi."

"I'll do that. And thank you again. Thank you very, very much."

There were no Sophie Brenners listed in the phone book, but there were four Jacob Brenners and fifteen J. Brenners. After three days, Rachel had reached nearly all of them without finding the former Sophie Friedman. There were only three names left. She dialed the first and the phone was picked up after a few rings. A woman's voice answered.

"Hello?"

"Hello," Rachel said. "May I please speak to Sophie Brenner?"

"This is Sophie Brenner. Who is this?"

Rachel's heart leaped but she forced herself to speak calmly. She still couldn't be certain that she had the right person. And, even if she did, she had to remember that, for the woman on the other end of the phone, her call was completely out of the blue.

"Mrs. Brenner, my name is Rachel Grossman. My mother's name is Lena... well, it used to be Lena Rothman." She waited, but Sophie Brenner said nothing. Rachel swallowed and plunged ahead.

"I believe you may have been a friend of my mother's a long time ago. It would have been back when she was working for the

Northern Shirtwaist Company. Does that sound... that is, do you remember a Lena Rothman?"

There was a long silence. Rachel gripped the phone with both hands. Finally, Sophie Brenner spoke, her voice low.

"Did you say that you're Lena Rothman's daughter?"

Rachel could hardly breathe. "Yes. I'm Lena's daughter. So, you remember her?"

There was another pause and then, "Yes, I remember your mother."

"Oh, I'm so glad. Because I have a huge favor to ask. Mrs. Brenner, I know you don't know me, but I was wondering if you would be willing to talk to me about my mother."

"I don't understand." There was a pause. "Is Lena... ? Did she—is she still alive?"

"Oh—yes! I'm sorry. I should have made that clear. Yes, my mother is very much alive. The thing is, Mrs. Brenner, she doesn't talk to me. About the past, I mean. It's too painful for her. And I don't like to make her talk about it. But there are some things I need to know. So I was wondering if you would be willing to talk to me. I know it's a lot to ask, but I'd really, really appreciate it."

As soon as the words were out of her mouth, Rachel wished she could take them back. Why had she told Sophie that her mother didn't like to talk about the past? She should have stuck to the story she'd told Mr. Mastrocelli about planning a surprise for her mother. She steeled herself for Sophie's refusal. After all this time, it would be a bitter pill to swallow.

"Does your mother know you're calling me?" asked Sophie, her voice cautious.

"No," Rachel admitted. "I haven't told her. In fact, she hasn't any idea that I've found you."

"How did you track me down?"

"It wasn't easy. Mr. Mastrocelli gave me your married name and I called a bunch of Jacob Brenners and J. Brenner's before I got to you."

"Mastrocelli? You talked to Buddy?"

"Yes. I found his name in an article listing survivors of the Northern Shirtwaist Fire. He remembered that you and my mother used to ride his elevator together."

Sophie laughed heartily. "That pint-sized Romeo used to joke around with every pretty woman who worked there. He had chutzpah. That was for sure." She sighed deeply; sounded serious again. "So when would you want to come?"

"Really? You'd be willing to talk to me?"

"Willing?" Sophie's voice sharpened. "Oh yes. I'm willing. In fact, I'm looking forward to it. And believe me, you won't be the only one asking questions."

Rachel didn't know quite what to say to that, so she let it go, asking instead, "I could come tomorrow morning if that would be okay."

"Afternoons are better for me than mornings. Around 3 p.m.?"

"3 p.m. would be wonderful."

"Do you know where I live?"

Rachel looked down at the directory. "Are you still at 230 East 21ˢᵗ Street?"

"Yes. In apartment 4-B."

"4-B," Rachel repeated, taking a pen from the top desk drawer and writing the apartment number in the margin of the directory. "Then I'll see you tomorrow afternoon at 3. And thank you very much. I really appreciate it."

Hanging up the phone, Rachel stared in wonderment at the spot where she'd scribbled the 4-B. She couldn't believe it. Tomorrow, she was going to meet the woman who had been her mother's friend and roommate almost from the time she'd arrived in America. Surely, if anyone could tell her about her father, it would be this woman.

The Brenner's street was a lovely one, lined with mid-rise apartments and abundant trees, leafy with new growth. As Rachel approached their building, she felt about to burst with an excitement. On impulse, she reached up and yanked her hair free of the tight bun she'd made that morning. It tumbled down in the long loose curls her mother had despaired of and David adored.

In the small lobby, the concierge asked her to wait while he rang the Brenner's apartment to announce her arrival, then told her she was expected and should go right up. Alone in the elevator, she tried to quell the butterflies in her stomach. Ever since her phone conversation with Sophie Brenner, she'd been on pins and needles. David had tried to lower her expectations, cautioning her that Mrs. Brenner might not be able or willing to give her as much information as she hoped. But Rachel could not wait to finally talk to someone who would be able to tell her something about her father, no matter how much or little it might be.

The elevator opened and apartment 4-b was right in front of her. She knocked. A woman's voice bade her to come in. With a shaking hand, she opened the door and stepped inside.

Nervousness gave way to shock. A wheelchair. She'd never thought... but why would she? How could she possibly have known? You couldn't tell just by hearing a person's voice on the phone that they were confined to an ugly, high-backed chair with a cane seat, wooden footrests, and huge, skinny, steel-spoked wheels. But she shouldn't stare. She should try to act natural. Wasn't that what you were supposed to do? Pretend that nothing was out of the ordinary? She should probably say something, thank Mrs. Brenner for agreeing to see her. She was so flustered she'd forgotten even this common courtesy. For her part, Sophie Brenner seemed to be just as speechless. She was staring intently at Rachel, her tear filled eyes taking in every inch of her.

Rachel, her initial surprise over, looked at the woman who had once been her mother's friend. Despite the wheelchair, there was no concession to invalidity. She'd clearly taken pains with every aspect of her appearance. There was a tough quality to her face in the strident arch of her drawn-on brows and the aggressive red of her lipstick. But there was a fragile quality too, in the paleness of her skin and the trembling of her chin. And there was a vulnerability in her eyes, magnified at the moment by their watery contents.

The silence between them was broken by Sophie, who rolled her wheelchair backwards into the living room, nodded at the sofa, and said, "Make yourself comfortable."

Rachel took a seat and waited until Sophie had maneuvered the wheelchair so it was facing her before saying, "Mrs. Brenner, I want to thank you again for agreeing to see me."

Sophie was still staring intensely at Rachel. Finally, she sighed and shook her head. "I still don't understand exactly why you wanted to speak to me."

"Well, as I said on the telephone, I'm hoping you can tell me a little bit about my mother's life during the time you knew her. From what I understand, you were roommates."

"Yes." Sophie nodded. "I met your mother on her first day of work at Northern Shirtwaists. We sat next to each other, and when I arrived, one of the other workers was giving her a hard time." She paused. "Back then, people weren't always so nice to the newer immigrants. We called them "greenies." They didn't yet know their way around. Your mother was trying to stand up for herself, but she didn't really know the ropes, so I helped her out a bit."

"That was very kind of you."

Sophie shrugged. "The one who was harassing her—well, I shouldn't speak ill of the dead I suppose, and God knows she didn't deserve to die in that inferno, but Anna was always something of a bitch."

Rachel's surprise must have been evident because Sophie broke into the same hearty laugh she'd displayed during their phone conversation. "You're shocked by my language? So was your mother. Except I didn't use the word "bitch" when I said it to her, I used the word *Chaleria*. But I didn't think you would know what *Chaleria* meant."

"I wouldn't have," Rachel conceded. "My mother never spoke Yiddish to me."

"Well, even if she had, she wouldn't have used a word like that. Your mother was more refined than me. Not that she was afraid to mix it up when necessary. But, well let's just say, she had a better vocabulary."

Rachel nodded. "My mother has a better vocabulary than almost everyone I know. I think it's because she reads so much."

"Yes. She was quite a reader. She couldn't wait to learn how to read English."

"So, you became friends through work. But how did you become roommates?"

"That happened on her first day too," Sophie explained. "I didn't live too far away from where Lena's brother had a room, so I walked home with both of them after work. When we got to her brother's boardinghouse, the landlady wouldn't let your mother go in, much less stay there with him. She thought they were an item. Sophie rolled her eyes, "She didn't approve of unmarried men and women keeping company in her rooms."

"But why didn't they just tell her they were brother and sister?"

"They tried, but she wouldn't listen." Sophie snorted and waved her hand at an imaginary landlady. "She was another *chaleria*. And your mama got mad." She laughed again, more softly this time, obviously remembering something in particular. "Your mama hated it when people weren't fair.

"Anyway," she continued, "it so happened that the boarder who shared my room at my aunt and uncle's house had just moved out and we were looking for someone to take her place. So, I invited your mama to move in. It was supposed to be temporary. But it ended up being a more or less permanent arrangement."

"So you lived together and worked together. I guess you got along well?"

"Oh, we hit it off right away. I had three sisters back home in the old country and I missed them terribly. Your mother became...." Sophie's voice trailed off, her eyes drifted down, and she swallowed before quietly saying, "she became like my sister."

Rachel didn't know what to say to this. She'd had no idea her mother and Sophie Friedman had been as close as that. Why, she wondered, and exactly when had they stopped being friends?

"Mrs. Brenner," she said, "when was the last time you saw my mother?"

"It was sometime after the fire. I was in the hospital, recovering from my injuries. She used to visit me every day. But this one day, she said that she was very sorry but she was leaving the city to go to work in the Catskill Mountains. I never saw or heard from her again."

"But why would she just stop talking to you? Did you have a fight or something?"

Sophie shook her head. "No. There was no fight. And as for why," she snorted, "I racked my brain for a reason for years. It was incomprehensible. That she would leave me just when I needed her most. She said she was leaving for a job. But I could never believe it wasn't possible for her to find a job in the city. And a job wouldn't explain why I never heard from her again."

"I'm so sorry, Mrs. Brenner. I can't imagine why my mother wouldn't have stayed in touch with you. Like I told you, she never really talked to me about her life before she came to the Catskill Mountains. I do know that for a very long time, she wouldn't even consider moving back to New York no matter how much my Uncle Joe begged her. It wasn't until she got divorced that she was finally willing to come back here."

"Your mother lives in New York City?" Sophie said.

"She moved back about seven years ago. She works for my Uncle's company, Rothman Sims."

"Rothman Sims," murmured Sophie, shaking her head. "Well, I'll be."

"I wish I could tell you more. But that's really why I'm here. Because I know so little. And, Mrs. Brenner, one of the things I know least about is my dad. I know he was a distant cousin of my mother's. And I know that he was killed in the war. But that's about it. I was hoping you might be able to tell me a little more about him. Anything."

Sophie looked confused. "Why would you think that I would know anything about your father?"

"Well, you were best friends with my mother when she met him. She must have talked about him at least little bit. And I thought you must have met him at least once."

Sophie stared at Rachel. It was hard to tell what she was thinking. Once she opened her mouth as if she were about to say something, only to close it again. Finally, she said, "What makes you think that your mother and I were still friends when she met your father?"

It was Rachel's turn to be confused. "Because I was born nine months after the fire at Northern Shirtwaist. So, if you two were best friends until some time after that -"

"Nine months," Sophie repeated, puzzled. "But," she began, then fell silent, thinking. Finally she said, "What else did your mother tell you about your father?"

"Hardly anything. Just that he was originally from Russia, that she fell in love with him at a settlement dance, and that I get my curly hair and my gray eyes from him."

Sophie stared again at Rachel. But this time it was as if she were seeing her for the first time. After a bit, her gaze seemed to turn inward, as if she was trying to puzzle something out. She began shaking her head back and forth and her breathing became increasingly agitated.

Suddenly, she looked at Rachel, with the same intense gaze that she'd exhibited earlier. Slowly, she nodded to herself. Then, still nodding, she closed her eyes and said, "Of course." She took a deep breath and let it out slowly. When she opened her eyes again, her expression was blank.

"I'm sorry," Sophie said. "I can't help you. I can't tell you anything about your father."

Rachel's mouth fell open in surprise, but Sophie merely turned her wheelchair around and rolled it up to the fireplace where there were some framed photographs on the mantle. She reached up and took one of them down, holding it on her lap and gazing at it, leaving Rachel to stare at the back of her chair.

Rachel would not let herself be dismissed so easily. "Why?" she said. "I don't understand. You were willing to meet with me. Why won't you talk to me?"

Sophie turned the chair around slowly. She was gripping the picture and her voice, when she spoke, was tight with emotion.

"You're not the only one with questions, you know," she said. "Do *you* know why it is that your mother left me and never came back? Do *you* know why it is that she never wrote to me or got in touch with me in all these years? I was her best friend and I was in a hospital with crushed legs, and a broken pelvis, and internal injuries for months. Do *you* know why she abandoned me?"

Rachel shook her head.

"Well I didn't know either. And I didn't know anything about your father. I," she stopped and swallowed hard, "I didn't even know your mother was pregnant."

"But how can that be," Rachel asked desperately.

Sophie's shook her head slowly back and forth again and again. Finally, she sighed deeply. But still, she said nothing. The truth slowly dawned on Rachel. Either Sophie was lying to her now or her mother had been lying to her for years. And there was no reason she could think of for Sophie to lie. Shakily, she got to her feet. Her eyes were rapidly filling with tears and she struggled to hold onto her composure.

"Thank you for seeing me today, Mrs. Brenner. I'm sorry if I've caused you any distress."

Sophie nodded. She spoke stiffly. "I'm sorry I couldn't be more helpful. Are you—that is will you be alright?"

Rachel nodded, desperate to leave. She swallowed the thick lump in her throat, turned away from Sophie, and headed for the door. "Thank you again," she said. "You've been very kind. I'll see myself out." She searched for the doorknob with eyes so tear-filled she could barely focus and quickly left the apartment.

Outside, she walked at a frenetic pace, not yet sure where she was headed but knowing that she needed to keep moving. Something was very, very wrong. Because it didn't add up. If what Sophie had said was true, that she and Lena had been as close as sisters until shortly after the fire, it didn't seem possible that her mother could have gotten married without Sophie knowing about it. Why would Lena have hid her marriage from her best friend? Rachel thought of all the times she'd been so careful not to push her mother to talk for fear of forcing her to relive painful memories. Well, that was all over. She was entitled to an explanation and she was going to get it. Without wasting another second, she stepped off the curb and shot her arm up in the air.

Maddie, her mother's secretary, smiled as Rachel walked in. "Hi Rachel. Your mother didn't mention you'd be coming in today."

"Well, she didn't know. It's kind of a surprise visit."

"She'll be thrilled I'm sure," Maddie said.

Rachel glanced at the closed door to her mother's office. "Is she busy?"

"She's on the telephone. But there's no one in there with her if that's what you mean. Do you want me to let her know that you're here?"

Rachel shook her head. "No, but can you let me know when she's done talking?"

"Sure. Can I get you anything? A cup of coffee or something?"

Rachel shook her head again. "No thanks." She turned and walked over to take a seat, felt too restless to sit down and walked back

"Rachel?" Maddie said, "She's finished her phone call."

Rachel took a deep breath and walked determinedly in to her mother's office.

"Rachel, what a nice surprise." Lena's expression went from pleasure to concern as she saw her daughter's expression. "Is everything alright?"

"No. Everything's not alright. I need to talk to you."

"Of course. Why don't you sit down? I can have Maddie bring us some coffee." Lena reached for the intercom button, but stopped when Rachel shook her head.

"I don't want any coffee."

"Well, at least sit down then," Lena implored. "And tell me what's making you so upset."

"I don't want to sit down," Rachel said. "I just want you to tell me the truth."

"The truth? Rachel, what is this all about?"

"I went to see Sophie Friedman today."

At the mention of Sophie's name, Lena stiffened. But Rachel was determined not to let anything stop her.

"That's right. I went to see her to ask her about my father. About the man you said you met at a dance and fell in love with and married. Except somehow all that happened without your dear friend Sophie knowing anything about it.

"Why Mama?" she continued, "Why didn't Sophie know about my father? Is it because it didn't happen the way you said it did?

Is it because you made the whole thing up? Why don't you try telling me the truth this time? Why don't you really tell me about my father for once in my life?"

Still Lena said nothing. She sat still as a statute, only the shallow rising and lowering of her chest evidence that she was breathing. Finally she spoke.

"You went to see Sophie Friedman?"

"Is that all you heard me say?" Rachel asked, incredulous. "Yes I went to see her."

Lena swallowed, "How is she?""

"She's fine. I mean she's in a wheelchair, but she seems fine." Rachel snorted. "Not that you would care. She told me how you abandoned her when she was lying in that hospital bed. Why did you do that?"

"Why did you go to see her?"

"I thought she might be able to give me some information." Rachel started pacing back and forth in front of Lena's desk. "I never wanted to push you to talk. I thought remembering the past made you too sad. I was trying to spare your feelings. I thought Sophie would be able to tell me about my father. But she didn't know anything."

Rachel stopped and faced her mother. "She was your best friend Mama. She said you were like sisters. How could she not have known anything?"

"We *were* like sisters," Lena said softly. "That's why she didn't know anything."

"What are you talking about?" Rachel cried, frustrated. "I still don't understand."

"I know and I'm sorry." Her mother looked up at her. "If you could just give me some time. I need to think about how to explain it."

"How hard is it to just tell the truth?"

"It's not that easy. I have to think." Lena ran her hands over her hair. "Just let me think," she repeated.

"No," Rachel said. "I've been waiting my whole life. I don't want to wait anymore. I asked you a simple question. Why didn't Sophie know anything about your marriage to my father? That's all you have to explain. Why didn't she know about the marriage?"

"Rachel please-"

"Just tell me," Rachel demanded. "Why didn't Sophie know about your marriage?"

"Because there was no marriage."

"There was—"

"That's right," Lena repeated. "There was no marriage. I never married your father. And I never told you because I didn't want you to grow up with that—that stigma." She shook her head. "I didn't want you to have to suffer because of my mistake. I wanted to protect you. I knew that people could be cruel about things like that. I didn't want you to be subjected to that."

Rachel stared at her mother. "But," she started to say, then stopped, not sure where she was heading with this. "But, why didn't you get married?"

"That's the part that's complicated," Lena said. She looked very tired and very sad. "We just couldn't that's all."

"Was he married to somebody else?"

Lena's elbows were on her desk and she was massaging her forehead with her hands. Her voice sounded muted as she said, "He was unavailable."

Rachel fell silent. *It made sense,* she thought. *At least it explained why Sophie hadn't known anything. Obviously, her mother had been too ashamed to tell even her best friend what she had done.*

"Is that everything?" she asked. "Is everything else you told me true? About him being a distant cousin? About the dance?" There was no answer from her mother. "No?" Rachel began to feel like the ground was shifting beneath her feet. This was beyond anything she had ever imagined. After the conversation with Sophie she'd suspected her mother had not been completely forthright with her, but the extent of her deception was so much more than she'd ever imagined. And then, a sudden thought struck her that wiped every other question out of her mind.

"What about the war?"

Lena was silent.

"What about the war, Mama?" Rachel repeated more loudly. "Was he even in the war? Tell me you didn't make that part up, Mama. Tell me you didn't make up the part about him being killed."

Still, there was no answer.

"You did?" Rachel asked. "You made it up?" She was crying now, but she couldn't stop talking. "All the time I was growing up and I thought he was dead, he was alive? Why, Mama, why? Why didn't you tell me the truth?"

"I couldn't," Lena murmured. She looked up at last and her face was streaked with tears.

"But why?"

"Because he didn't know about you. I never told him."

Rachel shook her head. "And what about now? Will you tell me now? Before it's too late, if it isn't too late already?"

"I can't."

"You mean you won't."

"No, I—"

Rachel shook her head. She couldn't do this anymore. "No! No more excuses or lies. I'll never forgive you for this, Mama. I'll never forgive you for not letting me know my father."

She turned and headed for the door.

Behind her, she heard her mother say, "Rachel, wait."

But she ignored her. At this moment, what she most needed was to be very far away from her mother.

CHAPTER THIRTY-SIX

JAKE GLANCED OUT THE WINDOW OF THE TAXICAB. THE AIRPORT traffic was so bad, they were barely moving. He turned to Maxine Jacobs, the union's Vice President of Legislative Affairs and shook his head.

"Next time we go to D.C., let's take the train. At least it arrives back in the middle of the city instead of out in the country."

"Queens *is* part of the city, you know," Maxine said drily.

"Not in my book it isn't." He leaned forward to get the cabbie's attention. "Hey buddy, isn't there anyway we can get out of this traffic?"

"I'm tryin'. I'm tryin'."

Jake grunted, aggravated. It was clear that he wouldn't have time to stop home first but would have to go directly to the office. This was particularly upsetting because, when he'd spoken to Sophie last night from his hotel room in Washington, D.C., she'd sounded a bit off. After all these years, he was sensitive to the slightest nuance in her voice, the tiniest difference in her breathing. It upset him that, more and more often, she seemed to be having bad days. So, although she'd said she was fine, he would've liked to see that for himself. But between the plane taking off late and the traffic from the airport, it couldn't be helped.

The taxi finally got moving. Jake arrived at the office a few minutes after his first scheduled meeting, leaving no time for a quick call to Sophie. He had lunch with the members of the executive board and by late afternoon, he was back in a taxicab headed for the Garment Workers Training Institute and still hadn't managed to phone home. Well, he would go home right after his meeting at the institute and have some time with Sophie before heading out again for the Mayor's birthday party. With any luck, she would feel well enough to go with him. If not, he would leave the party as early as possible. Unfortunately, there was no way he could pass it up entirely.

The taxicab let him off in front of the Training Institute and he hurriedly paid the driver. The institute was one of his pet projects. He'd noticed that many of the current union leaders lacked the knowledge that an earlier generation had gotten through first-hand experience. The institute held classes where union members with the interest and potential to take on leadership positions were taught the basics of organizing, negotiating, and representing employees.

Happily, Jake had been able to convince the executive board to approve the purchase of a building in midtown to house the Institute. Rose Schneiderman, who was still on the executive board after all these years, had recommended installing an after-school center for the children of union workers on the ground floor. This, too, had proved extremely successful.

As he walked in to the building, Jake realized that the neighboring grammar school must have just let out. Gangs of children with book-bags slung over their shoulders were disappearing into the front doors of the Institute. As he entered the building, he was surrounded by the shouts and laughter of the kids, as they jostled their way to the stairway that led to the basement gymnasium.

Jake loved seeing the children there. It brought back memories of the old days when he'd spent hours visiting the homes of union members. He might not have had any kids of his own, he thought, but he'd done his best to improve the lives of lots of other peoples' kids.

"Hey man," a voice greeted him near the elevators.

"Hector. I was just on my way up to see you."

Hector Menendez, the director of the Institute, had risen fast in the union's ranks. Warm and outgoing with jet black hair, thick eyebrows, and a matinee idol's smile, he was a hard worker and, notwithstanding his predilection for telling jokes that he laughed harder at than anyone else, a tough organizer who didn't take guff from anyone.

Hector shook his hand. "How you doin'?"

"Fine. You?"

"Can't complain." said Hector. "But around this time of day I need a cup of coffee real bad. Join me?"

"Sure. I could use a cup myself."

In Hector's office, Jake took a long appreciative sip from his coffee cup.

"So," he said, "how're things going?"

Hector smiled. "Everything's good. Everyone's workin' hard. There's a lotta enthusiasm in these classes."

"I'm glad to hear it. I'm afraid we're going to need a lot of help in the next couple of years to keep the union going strong."

"What're you talkin' about?" Hector said. "Our numbers have increased every year since before the war."

"True," Jake said, nodding. "But things are changing. The rest of the world is gearing up to take us on. The Japanese are willing to work for pennies and their wholesale prices are putting a lot of pressure on manufacturers in this country. Last week, Millenium Industries closed down a factory in Missouri and opened one up in Japan."

Hector whistled. "Well, we got a lot of good people gettin' ready to lead this union into the next decade and beyond."

"That's what I wanted to hear." Jake grinned.

"You still plannin' on coming next week to speak at the graduation ceremony for this year's class?"

"I'll be here," Jake assured him.

"Very good. And is the mistress gonna come?"

Jake rolled his eyes. Part of Hector's charm was his ability to beat the death out of anything he thought was funny. Calling Sophie "the mistress," was a crack Hector had made several months ago to needle Jake during a meeting that had run long. Hector had complained about the number of late nights they'd been putting in and how upset his wife was about it. Jake reminded him that they all had wives waiting for them at home.

"Not you, Jake," Hector had said. "Everybody knows you're married to the union. What you got waitin' for you at home is your mistress."

Jake had sent a furious look Hector's way but Hector had held his hands up. "Hey, don't get pissed at me because an ugly bum like you is lucky enough to have a gorgeous girl like Sophie waiting up for you no matter how late it gets."

Everyone at the meeting had laughed and, in the end, Jake had just shaken his head. Ever since that night, Hector had referred to Sophie as Jake's mistress. Now, Jake let the remark pass without comment. They spent another half hour talking about the Institute and Hector's plans. Jake was satisfied with what he heard.

"Alright Hector," he said as he rose to leave. "I've got to get going. Let my secretary know what time I have to be here next week. And keep up the good work."

As soon as Jake put his key in the door, he heard a flurry of scratching and little yips coming from the other side. He'd barely set one foot in the foyer when Tiger threw all six pounds of her furry white self at him in an ecstasy of wagging and licking. Jake had given the tiny toy poodle to Sophie as a birthday present a few years go and she usually spent most of her day curled up on Sophie's lap. But Jake was easily her second favorite person.

He stifled the desire to call out just in case Sophie was resting, carried Tiger into the living room, saw it was empty, and continued on toward the bedroom. As he got closer, he could hear voices, Sophie's and Aunt Sarah's, coming from inside.

By now, Tiger was wriggling wildly, so he set her down and she galloped purposefully into the bedroom and jumped onto the bed where Sophie sat propped up against two large pillows with blankets covering her from her waist down. Aunt Sarah was seated in a chair beside the bed.

Jake stopped in the doorway and surveyed them. "Well, this is a cozy scene," he said smiling.

"Hi," Sophie said. She did not look well. In the light of the bedside lamp, her face had a yellowish tint and her eyes had pronounced dark circles under them.

Jake quickly bent over her and gave her a kiss. He greeted Aunt Sarah, then sat on the bed to look at Sophie more carefully.

"You're still under the weather," he said, making it a statement rather than a question.

"It's just a cold."

"If it's just a cold, what are you doing in bed already?"

"I was tired and a little chilly. Getting into bed just seemed like a sensible thing to do."

There was an undercurrent to Sophie's tone that Jake found puzzling. But then again, Sophie never liked it when the attention was on her condition.

"Anything new since I left?"

"Not really. Oh, I told Julie Danvers that I would work on the March of Dimes charity ball this year."

"Your sure that's not going to be too much for you?"

"No. I'll be fine. So, how did the trip go?"

"I think it went well," Jake said, loosening and removing his tie. "Some of the new congressmen really seem interested in getting to the heart of things."

"You met with some of the new congressmen?"

"As many of them as we could."

"Did you happen to see that new congressman from New York? That Daniel Cowan?"

"As a matter of fact I did. What makes you ask?"

Sophie shrugged. "I remember him from way back."

"You mean from that time I met with him back when he worked for Truman?"

"No." Sophie shook her head. "From when he was a friend of Lena Rothman's. You must remember too. We all went out together one night."

Jake stared at her. "What?"

"I said that Daniel Cowan was a friend of Lena Rothman's. I'm sure you remember *her.*"

What was going on, thought Jake. Why was she talking about Lena? Sophie hadn't mentioned Lena for years. He knew she'd never gotten over the hurt of being abandoned by Lena. He was only too able to understand how she felt on that score. But what had made her bring up Lena's name now? And when had he and Sophie ever gone out with Lena and Congressman Cowan? He realized he had not yet responded to Sophie. He turned around so she wouldn't see anything on his face to raise a concern.

"Sure, I remember Lena." he said. He walked over to his chest of drawers, undid his tie, and laid it on top.

From behind him, Sophie suddenly switched topics, "So, how was your flight?"

"Fine," Jake said, his head starting to spin from this conversation. He turned back to Sophie and said, "You know, we should fly somewhere one of these days."

"Oh sure."

"No really," he insisted.

She shook her head. "Sure, let's just fly to Paris one of these days."

"We could," he said. He walked back to the bed, sat down and took Sophie's hand in his. "We should do it," he urged. "In all these years, we've never taken a vacation; never even left the city. Why shouldn't we go to Paris?"

Sophie looked at Aunt Sarah. "Paris," she said, "I'd settle for dinner at a French restaurant."

"What about someplace else then?" Jake persisted. "We could fly to Florida. You hate the cold weather. We could spend a week or two in the sunshine."

"The winter's nearly over."

"It's mid-January."

"Jake, please... "

"No, Soph–"

Aunt Sarah cleared her throat. "I'd better get going." She stood up and said to Sophie, "Shall I come the same time tomorrow?"

Sophie nodded. Her face was even paler than before and she looked upset.

Aunt Sarah smiled wearily at Jake. "Welcome home, Jake. I'm glad you had a safe flight. Don't get up. I think I know the way out by now."

Jake got up and walked over to his closet to select an outfit for the evening. He was furious with himself. The last thing he'd meant to do was upset Sophie. Especially when she was feeling ill. The whole conversation had been impetuous. More and more lately, he'd been thinking about how much time he spent away from Sophie devoted to union business. He'd only mean to suggest that they spend some time together. Instead, he'd seemed like he was trying to force her to do something, go somewhere that she didn't want.

From the bed, Sophie said in a low voice, "Is that what it's about Jake? You're upset because we never go away anywhere?"

He whirled around. "Upset? With you? What are you talking about?"

"I know it's been hard on you. You could travel the world if it wasn't for me."

"Hard on me? Did you think I was blaming you for us not getting away. "

Sophie bit her lip but said nothing.

"No! It's not your fault," Jake said. "It's just, well, work is so crazy all the time. I just wish I had more time for... I don't know." He turned around to face the closet. "Damn—where is my pinstripe anyway?"

"Look all the way on the right side of the closet."

"Thanks." He lifted the suit out and hung it on the back of the closet door so it would be waiting for him after he showered, then started searching for a clean shirt to wear with it. "I wish I didn't have to go to this party tonight. I'll try to leave early."

"I wish I was feeling better," Sophie said in a low voice.

"Me too. If you're still feeling this way tomorrow, I think we should call the doctor. I can go in to work late if you can get an appointment."

He pulled a suitable shirt from the closet, added it to the hook on which his suit was hanging, then glanced over at Sophie. Tiger had settled down on her lap and she was petting him with long, gentle strokes. Her long hair was loose and, to keep it off her face, she was wearing a pink satin headband that matched the pink satin bed jacket he'd given her for their last anniversary.

He knew she would never ask him to stay back from the party. She never had before. But he would be lonely at the party without her. And he would miss her company on the taxi ride home and her witty observations about all the other people at the party.

"You know," he said, "this has been a really long day and I've about had it. I'm sure the Mayor will enjoy his birthday just as much if there's one less person."

Sophie looked up in surprise. "What are you talking about?

"Nothing. I'm just not going. That's all.

"But you have to go. It's the Mayor for heaven's sake. You can't stand him up."

"I don't think he'll care."

Sophie smiled. "But you will. Tomorrow. You'll think about it and you'll wish you'd gone."

Jake sighed.

"See?" Sophie said. "You can't even say anything because you know I'm right. I'll be fine. I'm sure I'll fall asleep two minutes after you walk out the door."

Jake nodded, resigned. "Can I get you anything before I jump in the shower?"

"I'm fine. Aunt Sarah brought me a big lunch and I don't think I'll be hungry for a while. I'm just going to take a little nap while you're getting ready."

"I'll try not to make too much noise when I come out."

"Wake me before you leave?"

"I'd rather you got some rest."

"I'll fall back asleep afterwards."

"Okay."

But by the time he was done showering and dressing, she was sleeping and looked so peaceful, he didn't have the heart to wake her. So, he slipped out of the bedroom and gently closed the door behind him.

CHAPTER THIRTY-SEVEN

IT WAS GETTING HARDER AND HARDER TO GET HOLD OF DANIEL, LENA thought as she waited for him to come on the line in his office in Washington. She'd worked so hard to help him win the election that she'd never stopped to think about what it might mean for her. Even though he'd been terribly busy before leaving for the Capital, what with his teaching duties, his legal practice, and the endless demands of his campaign, at least they'd been in the same city. There'd been opportunities to see him, even if most of their time together was at campaign events. And there'd been more frequent phone calls, different in feel than the ones they shared now, because he'd been only a few miles away as opposed to hundreds. She hadn't realized quite how much she would miss him. She couldn't help wondering whether he missed her too.

There'd been times in the last few months when she'd thought Daniel had the same feelings for her now that he'd had years ago. But he hadn't said or done anything specific, so she couldn't be sure. On the other hand, if he was interested, his failure to say anything was understandable. She'd given him little encouragement along those lines.

When she'd first seen him at the Jewel Ball, once she'd gotten over the initial shock, she'd been stunned by how debonair and attractive he'd become. Then, when he'd asked her out to dinner, she'd been shocked by the depth of her reaction to him, shocked and a little frightened. She'd been so sure she was done with that part of her life. And yet, there was no mistaking the pulse quickening she'd experienced at that moment. Still, she'd already learned the hard way that acting on such feelings was not always wise. Given her history in general and her history with Daniel in particular, it seemed that the best course of action was to pretend she'd not felt anything.

After that first dinner, as she and Daniel spent more and more time together, she became even more convinced of the wisdom of her decision. She cherished Daniel's friendship too much to risk losing it nor did she ever want to hurt him again. If she couldn't be sure how she felt about getting involved with him, she was better off doing nothing. And becoming sure about her feelings seemed as elusive as predicting the future. Back when she'd been young, her heart had been easily accessible, ready and willing to take flight. But now it was less open, even to herself. She didn't know what she wanted and she was a little afraid to find out.

"Hello," Daniel said.

The sound of his voice after the long wait surprised her and, though she knew it was silly, she suddenly had an overwhelming urge to cry with relief. She choked it back and said, "Hi, it's me."

"What's wrong? You sound upset. Did something happen?"

"I'm fine. I'm still upset about this thing with Rachel. And then it took so long for you to come on the line...." She stopped. She knew she must sound like a spoiled child.

"I'm sorry about that. It's been busy around here lately."

"Don't be sorry. Of course you're busy. I'm just being a baby."

"No you're not. You're just upset. Is she still not talking to you?"

"Yes. I've asked Joe to intervene and David. I've tried calling her at home and at work. I started to write her a letter but what is there really to say? I lied to her."

"You were trying to protect her."

"I thought it was for the best, but maybe it wasn't. And now, I don't know, maybe I should tell her who her father is. But what if she tries to contact him? I don't know what to do. I've made such a mess of everything. I'm an idiot."

"Whoa. Slow down. You are not an idiot. You are the farthest thing from an idiot of any woman I've ever known. You just need to take a deep breath."

"She hates me Daniel. She said she'd never forgive me."

"She was upset. She doesn't know all the circumstances, so she can't really understand."

"If I don't explain it to her, she'll never speak to me again. But even if I explain everything now, she might still hate me for keeping her from her father all these years. And it might also end up ruining two other peoples' lives."

"You're letting your imagination run away with you. I'm sure we can come up with some way of getting Rachel to understand without ruining lives in the process."

Lena took a deep breath. Already, she felt better. Daniel was always so comforting.

"Alright," she said. "That sounds good."

"Is everything else going okay?"

"Yes. What about you?"

"Things are going well. I still have a lot to learn, but I'm starting to get the hang of things. And my staff is great. They make me look good. Did you hear about the amendments to the Fair Labor Standards Act? We managed to get in some additional protections for child workers."

She smiled though she knew he couldn't see it.

"You sound happy," she said.

"I still can't believe I'm really here."

"It's everything you always wanted."

"Just about."

"I'm so glad," she said. And she was. She just wished he wasn't so far away. She made her voice casual. "Are you coming in this weekend?"

"Not this one, but the one after maybe. I promise to call and let you know."

"Okay. And Daniel, thank you."

"For what?"

"For always taking my calls."

"That's one thing you never have to worry about," he said, which made her almost want to cry again. This thing with Rachel was really taking a toll on her emotions.

Almost as soon as she replaced the phone in its cradle, it rang again. She picked it up eagerly. "Did you forget to tell me something?"

"Excuse me?" It was not Daniel's voice but a familiar sounding female.

"I'm sorry. I thought it was going to be someone else."

"I hope you aren't disappointed. This is Julie Danvers."

"Oh Julie. Hello, how are you?" Lena tried to sound as if she were happy. The truth was that she had never gotten totally comfortable around Julie. But she was important to Daniel, so Lena tried to be friendly.

"I'm well, Julie. And you?"

"Very well."

"I'm very glad to hear it. Tell me, have you heard from our darling boy lately?"

"Yes. I spoke to him just a little while ago."

"And how did he sound?"

"Wonderful. Like he's really in his element."

"He was born for this," Julie said.

"Yes. Yes he was."

"Well, let me tell you why I'm calling, my dear. I'm chairing the annual ball of the New York Chapter of the March of Dimes. We're putting together a steering committee. I was wondering if you would be willing to be on it."

"The March of Dimes?"

"Yes. It's a very worthy cause you know," Julie said.

"Oh yes, of course."

"Now I know you're asked to help out with so many causes, but I was hoping you could find the time for just one more. I'd be so grateful."

Lena did a quick calculation in her head. She was already on the board for three other charitable organizations but this didn't sound like it would be a big time commitment. In her experience, when one was asked to be on the steering committee of a specific function like this, the organizers were more interested in your financial support and your contact list than in any real work on your part.

"When is the ball?" she asked.

"It's in a month, and most of the big pieces are already in place." As if she'd read Lena's mind, Julie added, "It wouldn't be a big time commitment on your part. Your secretary can probably handle most of it, compiling the list of invitees and so on. At most, we're talking about maybe two meetings before the ball."

"That sounds fine. You can include me," Lena said.

"Wonderful. The first meeting is at noon one week from Wednesday at my place. I'll make sure your secretary gets all the details."

"Thank you, Julie."

"Oh no, darling. Thank you!"

Julie Danver's townhouse on East Sixty-ninth Street between Park and Madison was, Lena thought, probably among the most expensive pieces of real estate in the world. As she walked up to the front door, she was unexpectedly struck by the memory of when she had gone to visit Mrs. Carter to beg for her help in finding a job. Then, the butler had taken one look at her and tried to steer her toward the service entrance. Now, she was wearing an Arnie Sims suit and a pair of Ferragamo heels. Then, she had been an unemployed garment maker. Now, she was vice-president of a clothing company that was rapidly becoming one of the most successful manufacturers of women's wear in the country. This time, she was ready to face the butler with no butterflies in her stomach. But, to her surprise, Julie answered the door herself.

"Lena, you look beautiful as always. Are those Ferragamo's? They're gorgeous. Isn't it wonderful that he's finally opened a shop in New York?"

"I'm sorry I'm late," Lena apologized. "Something came up at work at the last minute."

"Please don't apologize. You're fine. You're not even the last to arrive." She lead the way down a long hall. "We're meeting in the dining room. Come. I'll introduce you to everyone and get you settled."

An arched entrance opened onto to the dining room where about a dozen women sat around a mahogany table chatting. Julie interrupted them to introduce Lena, saw her to her seat, and signaled a maid to bring some tea. The doorbell sounded and she excused herself to answer it.

Lena had just taken a sip of tea and was getting ready to respond to her seatmates, when she heard Julie's voice and that of her companion coming back down the hall. Seconds later Julie appeared in the archway, looking taller and more elegant than ever beside her guest.

"Ladies," Julie said, "I think most of you know Sophie Brenner."

It was as if a vacuum had sucked all the air from Lena's stomach and was blowing it into her ears, so loud was the roaring there. The room and its occupants, save one, receded. She saw only Sophie. Seconds passed or it could have been minutes. Julie's mouth moved but she had no idea what was being said. She felt like she was watching a silent movie. She saw Julie gesture to the maid, who approached Sophie. There was some conversation between Julie, Sophie, and the maid, who nodded her head and left the room. Then Julie walked around to the head of the table, as Sophie rolled herself a little closer to the table.

Gradually, Lena's breath resumed. Sound returned too and, with it, sensibility. She became aware that her eyes were filled with tears and that her throat was painfully engorged with a lump of mammoth proportions. She was still staring at Sophie, unable to look away, not wanting to.

Sophie was clearly struggling to maintain her composure. Her lips were pressed together with either anguish or anger. In the end, it was she who looked away first, swallowing visibly, and turning to the woman on her left.

The meeting was called to order by Julie. People talked and Lena tried to pay attention but it was impossible. Her mind was racing with questions. Exactly what had Sophie learned from her meeting with Rachel? How did Sophie feel about her after all these years? What would she say to Sophie if these idiot women ever stopped talking and left this room so that they could actually speak to each other in private?

She took a sip of tea so that Julie would be dissuaded from asking her any questions that would reveal her complete inability to focus on the conversation. The tea was cold, but she kept sipping anyway. Surely the meeting was almost over. And then, well, she didn't know what would happen then, but she hoped she would think of something. Because she wanted to talk to Sophie very badly. And she had to assume that Sophie wanted to talk to her too.

The meeting was interminable. She felt like they would all be here all night long. These women would never run out of topics of conversation. She slid her eyes toward the end of the table, trying to see Sophie without turning her head. She seemed smaller than Lena remembered but it might have been because the wheelchair was so large. Anyone would appear tiny in such an ungainly contraption. As for her face, age had exaggerated all of Sophie's features. Her cheekbones were more prominent, her nose longer, her lips thinner, her face paler. She was not the strikingly exotic peacock she had once been. But, if youth was gone, beauty was not. In fact, Sophie was even more beautiful now than when she'd been younger. There was a dignity and strength now that had been absent then. Maturity was a much better match for Sophie's strong features than youth had ever been.

At last Julie stood up. She thanked everyone for coming and for making it such a productive meeting. She would contact them about scheduling the next meeting if one proved necessary. She was sure the ball was going to be a huge success and she looked forward to seeing all of them there.

The attendees began getting to their feet, chatting as they did. As the room slowly emptied, Sophie remained, looking for something in her purse. Lena made a pretense of finishing her tea. Julie walked out with some of the women to see them to the door. When only Lena and Sophie remained in the room, Sophie snapped her purse shut and raised her eyes to meet Lena's. Lena opened her mouth to speak. At that moment, Julie swept back into the room.

"Ladies, can I call either of you a cab?"

Sophie shook her head. "If I might borrow your telephone, I was going to call my driver."

"Of course." Julie asked the maid to bring the phone, then turned to Lena. "Do you have a driver or would you like me to arrange for a taxi?"

Before Lena could answer, Sophie cleared her throat. "Perhaps I can give Lena a lift."

"What a lovely idea," Julie said. She turned to Lena. "Isn't that kind of Sophie?"

Caught by surprise, Lena was speechless. But she saw immediately that this would be a chance for them to talk.

"Yes," she managed to say. She looked at Sophie and added. "Thank you very much. I hope I won't be taking you out of your way. I live fairly far downtown."

"That's no trouble," Sophie said. "No trouble at all."

There was a sliding glass partition between the front seat of the car and the back and as the driver pulled away from the curb, Sophie leaned forward and slid it closed. She sat back and looked at Lena silently.

Lena felt the force of long-suppressed emotions pressing painfully against the lump in her throat. She struggled to hold on, fearing that without the lump, she would explode like a volcano and loose control completely. But it was no use. The pressure was too great. It divested the lump from her throat like a cork being pushed from a bottle. And like the contents of a bottle suddenly uncorked, words erupted from her without premeditation or consideration.

""I never meant to hurt you," she blurted out.

"I know."

"You do?" Lena stared at her. She didn't know what she'd expected from Sophie, but understanding was the thing she'd most hoped for and been least hopeful of getting.

"Yes," Sophie said, her voice sure. "If you'd wanted to hurt me, you wouldn't have left New York City when you did. Oh yes," she nodded, "I figured out a thing or two after I met your daughter. I figured out that if you'd wanted to hurt me, you would have told Jake about the baby, knowing that he would have insisted on marrying you." She sighed. "And he would have insisted. He might not have left me for you otherwise, given my... condition. But he would have left me for a child." She shook her head. "I never saw a man so desperate to have a child." She took a deep breath and looked steadily at Lena. "The only thing I don't know is how you could be with him in the first place. That's the part I can't figure out."

Recovering from her initial shock, Lena hesitated. "It's hard to explain."

"Were you in love?" Sophie demanded.

Lena tried to choose her words carefully. "*I* thought I was," she said. "From practically the first moment I met him. Before I even knew who he was. But you have to believe me. I never would have done anything about it if it hadn't been for the fire."

"The fire. What did that have to do with it?"

Lena looked away. It had been so long since she had allowed memories of those days to come through. So long since she had allowed those feelings to touch her. It had been easier to wall herself off. It hurt less that way. But there was only one way to make Sophie understand what had happened and that was to unlock the memories and force herself to go back to that day, to the terror, to the screams and the flames.

"It was after we had both climbed out the window onto the fire escape," she said. "You thought we should climb down the fire escape ladder, but I couldn't do it. I was too afraid, so I climbed up instead."

"I wondered where you'd disappeared to," Sophie said.

Lena nodded. "I made it all the way up to the ninth floor where I was able to climb in an open window. The floor was deserted, except for me. I didn't know what to do or where to go, so I looked back out the window, back at the fire escape." She waited a moment, remembering it, picturing it, seeing in her mind the flimsy fire escape, the rickety railings, the narrow, slippery steps of the ladder, the platform full of women, their faces, their flailing arms.

"I was pinned in the middle of the crowd," Sophie said. "My feet weren't even touching the platform. I was so hemmed in, I couldn't so much as lift an arm."

Lena continued. "And then I saw the fire escape sway and come loose from the building." She paused, remembering how it had seemed suspended in mid-air for a long moment before plunging straight down. She closed her eyes to the sight of it falling.

"I felt weightless," Sophie said. "I don't really remember what happened after that."

"I thought nobody could possibly have survived," Lena said. She felt grief swelling up and she took a ragged breath as she looked at Sophie through bleak, stricken eyes. "I thought you were dead." She took a deep breath before continuing.

"After I got back to the apartment, Jake came looking for you. I told him what I'd seen. We were both crying, in shock, devastated. We... we comforted each other. And then," she shook her head helplessly, "things took a turn." She looked at Sophie again, pleading with Sophie to understand her, to believe her. "It was just that once, I swear."

Sophie said nothing, so Lena continued. "Afterwards, when we found out that you hadn't... that you'd survived, we were overjoyed. And horrified at what we'd done. Neither of us would ever have deliberately hurt you."

Lena took another deep breath and let it out slowly. She was almost done. The hardest part was over. She continued, too drained to speak in anything but a calmer voice. "When I found out I was pregnant, I knew I couldn't tell Jake. I felt sure he'd insist on doing the right thing. On marrying me. But that wasn't the right thing in this case. So I left." She shook her head. "I left my brother, my best friend, everything I knew, everyone I loved. And I planned never to come back."

Finished with the telling, Lena felt suddenly shaky and chilled. She clamped her teeth together to keep them from chattering as she looked at Sophie to see her reaction.

Sophie was rigid. Perhaps, Lena thought, Sophie, too, was holding herself tightly together so that she wouldn't break apart. Only Sophie's eyes, magnified by unshed tears, and her voice, soft and low, revealed her emotions.

"You never told him," Sophie said. "You never told Jake about the baby."

"No."

"And you never told your daughter either."

Lena shook her head. "How could I? I couldn't take a chance that she would go looking for her father."

"She went looking anyway." There was a bleak edge to Sophie's voice.

"Yes," Lena said quietly. "And now, she's not talking to me."

Sophie said nothing in response to this, but finally asked, "You never married?"

"I did. For a while. It didn't work out."

"Because you were still in love with Jake?"

"What?" Lena looked at her in surprise. "No. It had nothing to do with him."

"But are you?" Sophie persisted. "Are you still in love with him?"

"No. " Lena was emphatic. "That was a lifetime ago. I'm not the same person I was back then. I'm sure he isn't either."

"But you don't know for sure. You can't."

Lena looked at her nonplussed. What exactly did Sophie want her to say. Surely, Sophie must know that her husband loved her after all these years. Was she so insecure even at this late date? If she was, then there was nothing Lena could say to change that.

"This is ridiculous," she said.

"It's not ridiculous at all," Sophie said. "There's no way for you to know how you feel about Jake after all these years or how he feels about you. The last time you saw each other, you were in love. You can't know for sure how you'll feel when you see him again. The passage of time is no guarantee of anything. And not know-ing isn't good enough for me."

"All of this is irrelevant because I have no plans to see him ever," Lena said stiffly.

"Ah, but you will."

"What do you mean?"

"I mean the ball is in two weeks."

Lena stared at her. "You mean—"

"Of course. Why do you think I asked Julie to invite you to join the steering committee. And I'm sure you'll look beautiful. After all, it's a black tie affair." The car had stopped moving and Sophie knocked on the glass partition before sliding it open.

"Mrs. Rothman will be leaving us here," she said.

The driver got out and opened Lena's door. As she got out of the car, she heard Sophie's voice behind her.

"I'll see you in two weeks," Sophie said. "If you're not there, I'll know it's because you're afraid that your feelings are unchanged."

"I—" Lena started to respond, but before she could finish, the driver closed the door to the backseat and walked around to the other side. So she could only stand there and watch as the car carried Sophie farther and farther away.

CHAPTER THIRTY-EIGHT

DANIEL SAT IN A BOOTH IN THE CONGRESSIONAL LIMITED'S DINING car, his briefcase on the seat beside him, and a stack of papers spread over the tabletop. If he didn't get some work done during the ride to New York, he would fall seriously behind on his preparation for the week ahead. But he could no longer concentrate. His thoughts kept returning to Lena. He hadn't seen her in nearly six weeks and their conversations, particularly the last few, had not been reassuring.

Maybe it was his imagination, but he'd thought she'd sounded strained on the phone. She said everything was fine and it was just the fight with Rachel and pressures at work that were getting her down. But he sensed there was more to it than that. On good days, he fantasized that what he heard in her voice was loneliness, a sign that she missed him as much as he missed her. On bad days, he imagined that it was the opposite. That the thing she wasn't telling him was that she'd met someone new.

If she had met someone, he had no one but himself to blame. He'd been so caught up in activities following the election, hiring staff for his D.C. and New York offices, meeting with Congressional leaders, and finding a place to live in the District, that he'd not found any opportunity to tell her how he felt about her. Of course, if he was honest with himself, that wasn't the only reason for the delay. On a certain level, he knew that just because she had rejected him once before didn't mean she would reject him now. He was a completely different person than he had been thirty years ago. Confident, accomplished, successful. But if that was the case, why did he still feel like a gawky teenager around her?

The car door swooshed open and a conductor appeared. "Penn Station next stop. Make sure you have all your belongings. Penn Station coming up next."

Damn it. He hadn't gotten through as much work as he'd planned. This thing with Lena was starting to make him a little crazy. He had to tell her how he felt. This Saturday night after the March of Dimes Ball would be perfect. He would be wearing his best tuxedo. They would spend the evening together, dining and dancing. Then, he would take her home. Yes, he decided. Saturday would be perfect. He would not let the night end without telling her he loved her.

CHAPTER THIRTY-NINE

FOR THE FOURTH TIME IN AS MANY MINUTES, LENA LOOKED OUT HER living room window to see if there was any sign of Daniel. He wasn't late but she was so anxious to see him that each passing minute seemed to last far longer than the sixty seconds allotted to it. She was tempted to pour herself a glass of wine to calm herself down, but it would be rude, she thought, to start drinking before Daniel arrived. She'd been on edge for weeks, ever since the encounter with Sophie. Now, the evening she'd been dreading was at hand. The thought of seeing Jake for the first time in nearly thirty years was nerve-wracking enough. Knowing that Sophie was going to be watching her and Jake both for any hint of enduring feelings only ratcheted up that pressure.

Ever since the conversation with Sophie, her head had been spinning. Sophie's suggestion that she and Jake might still have feelings for each other had been unsettling. She didn't think it was the case, but what if Sophie was right? Maybe she had long buried feelings that would surface when she saw him. If nothing else, he was the father of her child.

And then there was the fact that she hadn't told Daniel any of this yet. She'd meant to, but he hadn't been back to New York for weeks and she'd not been able to bring herself to talk to him about it on the phone. Talking to him about anything having to do with Jake was difficult. His feelings toward Jake were hardly positive. Given her confusion over her feelings for Daniel, the last thing she wanted to do was talk to him about Jake.

The bell rang. She jumped and hurried to answer it. Daniel looked handsomer than ever. And he had brought her flowers. Beautiful blush colored roses.

"Daniel, you look wonderful."

"You stole my opening," he said, offering up the bouquet.

She smiled. "Thank you. They're gorgeous. I'll go put them in a vase and I can get you a drink at the same time, if you'd like. A martini?"

"Perfect."

"Back in a moment."

In the kitchen, she ran the stems of the roses under running water and snipped off the bottoms. Daniel had been extravagant, she thought. There were easily a dozen and a half. They would add a classy touch to the buffet table in her dining room. But, then, Daniel was a classy man. In a way, he always had been. She made his drink, carried it out, and sat down beside him on the sofa, her hands clasped in her lap.

"How was the train ride?" she asked.

"Fine. I got plenty of work done."

"That's good. And your week? You had a good week?"

"Good, yes, but busy. How about you?"

"Busy too," she said. She crossed one leg over the other and made little circles in the air with her ankle, first going in one direction and then in the other.

"Did I tell you," she said, "that we finally decided to manufacture the Racey line in-house?"

"You mentioned that you were thinking of it. How's that going?"

"Very well." She uncrossed her legs and re-crossed them the other way.

Daniel reached over and put his hand over hers. "What's on your mind," he said gently.

She shook her head, sheepish at being caught. "You know me too well."

"I know when you're nervous about something. Is there something you want to tell me?"

"It's about tonight," she said. "Only, I don't know where to begin."

"Take your time. Whatever it is will be alright."

She swallowed, her anxiety back in full force, her body tensing up even before she began. "You know how Julie asked me to be on the board of directors for tonight's ball."

"Of course. You told me about that a few weeks ago."

"Well, after that, there was a meeting for all the board members at Julie's place. And, Daniel, I know you won't believe this, but Sophie Friedman was there. I mean, Sophie Brenner."

"Sophie was there? Your Sophie?" Daniel's evident shock was somehow comforting. She'd known that if anyone could understand how she felt it would be him.

"Yes. I couldn't believe my eyes. I mean, you can imagine how I felt when she rolled into Julie's dining room in her wheelchair."

"Of course. What did you do?"

"I didn't know what to do. So, I just sat there. I sat through that whole meeting and didn't hear a word anyone said. All I could think about was, what would I say to her if I ever got the chance?"

He nodded, his eyes sympathetic and his voice gentle. "Did you get the chance?"

"Not during the meeting. But afterwards, she offered me a lift home in her car. She has this driver who helps her in and out of the wheelchair and transports her around. We shared the backseat and there was a partition so the driver couldn't hear what we said."

"And?"

Lena stood up and started pacing, twisting her hands as she walked. "She said that ever since Rachel's visit, she'd figured a lot of things out. She said she knew why I'd left the city all those years ago. She knew Jake was Rachel's father and that I'd never told him about her. She even said she knew I hadn't meant to hurt her. The only thing she didn't know was how Jake and I came to be together in the first place.

Lena paused to give Daniel a chance to comment, but he just waited for her to go on. So, she continued.

"I tried to explain. And I thought she understood. But then she started saying all of these things."

"What kinds of things?" Daniel asked, his tone cautious.

Lena shook her head. "She started talking about how I couldn't possibly know whether I still loved Jake or whether he still loved me. About how time didn't always change how people felt about each other. And about how I wouldn't know for sure until I saw him again."

"I see," Daniel said, though what he saw Lena had no idea. "And what did you say?"

"What could I say? I mean, it's ridiculous to think that a person could still feel the same way about another person after so many years, isn't it? It seems crazy that Sophie would even think about that. They've been married for what, thirty years already."

"Anyway," she went on, becoming more and more agitated. "I said that it didn't matter because I was never going to see him again. And then she said that of course I would see him again tonight at the ball. She said she'd suggested that Julie invite me to be on the board because that way I would have to come to the ball. She practically dared me not to come. She said if I didn't show up, she would know it was because I was afraid I still had feelings for Jake."

This last was said in a burst of words as Lena, ragged with relief at having gotten it all off her chest, waited for Daniel to say something. But he remained silent. His stillness added to her anxiety and she began to babble.

"I've been a nervous wreck all day. Sophie said she didn't tell him about Rachel, but maybe she's told him since I saw her. And what about these crazy ideas that Sophie has. I mean, what kind of marriage must she and Jake have if she thinks he might still have feelings for me? And what if he does? What if he's been carrying a torch for me all these years? What if he's still angry at me for leaving him? Is that even possible? And now Sophie's going to be watching us both like hawks, scrutinizing every expression, every gesture, looking for some indication of how we feel about each other. But maybe I shouldn't care about any of that. This whole thing is making me crazy."

Daniel looked at his watch. "You know we better get going or we'll be late.

"But what about everything I just told you? I mean, what do you think?"

Daniel looked at her. His face gave away nothing. "I think," he said, "that you'll know the answers to all your questions soon enough." He stood up and put his coat on.

This subdued reaction was not what she had expected. Not what she had wanted from him. As he helped her on with her coat, she wished she knew exactly what was going through his mind. That she didn't, only added to her general foreboding about the evening ahead.

"Welcome to the March of Dimes Ball." The doorman held the door as Lena and Daniel entered the opulent Grand Ballroom of the Plaza Hotel. The space had been totally transformed for the evening. In the center of the room, was a circular stage where the sixteen piece Count Basie Orchestra was already in full swing. Encircling the stage was a swath twenty feet wide filled with couples dancing and encircling this area were round tables

319

draped with floor length burgundy tablecloths, each topped with a different paper mache animal. After a minute, Lena realized that the orchestra stage was slowly revolving. The motion of the stage combined with the table top decor gave the room the circus-like feel of a giant merry-go-round.

The setting was so spectacular that Lena's attention was momentarily diverted from the circumstances of the evening. She had to hand it to Julie. The woman knew how to throw a party. At the place card table, she found her name and Daniel's. They'd both been assigned to the Lion table. Her eyes strayed to the "B's." The one marked Brenner was unclaimed. She waited until Daniel wasn't looking and quickly peeked at the card. The Brenners, too, were assigned to the Lion table. Like an eraser sweeping across a blackboard, the place card wiped her mind clean of everything except the thought of seeing Jake again.

As Daniel steered her through the crowd, she worked at ignoring the wild beating of her heart. People stopped to greet Daniel, shake his hand, and ask him what he thought about the latest pronouncements from Moscow and whether he believed Hollywood was really filled with communists. She smiled and nodded as if she were following the conversation until they were able to move on. They walked past rapidly filling tables topped with zebras, camels, and horses, until quite suddenly, she saw a paper mache lion striding high across a nearly full table. She could not bring herself to look at those already seated and kept her eyes averted while holding tight to Daniel's hand as he walked her around and pulled out her chair while the men at the table rose from their seats in her honor. Only when she was safely sitting down did she slowly look up.

CHAPTER FORTY

JAKE HAD NOTICED THE EMPTY SEATS ACROSS FROM THEM WHEN HE and Sophie first arrived and he's been relieved they weren't the last ones there. He was introducing himself to the woman seated to his left when he heard the scrape of chairs against floor as the men at the table stood for the last arrivals. He hastened to join them, glancing politely in the newcomers' direction. For a moment, his mind could not comprehend what he saw.

Thoughts announced themselves in bits and chunks of information. *LENA. After all these years. How? Why? Oh my God, Lena. Here at the March of Dimes Ball. And Congressman Cowan. Lena with the Congressman.*

He needed to think. He needed time to process this. There was no time. The other men at the table had already sat back down. Only he and the Congressman were still standing. Jake extended his hand and fought to make something coherent and appropriate emerge from his mouth.

"It's good to see you again, Congressman. And congratulations on the election."

"Thank you," the Congressman said, "I appreciated the union's support." Looking at Sophie, he added, "It's been a long time Mrs. Brenner. You're looking lovelier than ever."

Sophie smiled. "You have a good memory, Senator. And thank you."

The Congressman still had one hand on the back of Lena's chair and he glanced down at her before training his gaze back on Jake. "I'm sure you both remember Lena Kerner. Of course, when you knew her, she was still Lena Rothman."

Jake nodded slowly. Hearing Lena's name spoken aloud made her presence less surreal and the initial shock he'd felt upon seeing her ebbed a bit. Questions were ricocheting through his brain like a volley of arrows. But at least his ability to think in whole sentences was returning. For just a moment, he let himself look, really look at her.

She'd been compelling as a girl, more sensual than attractive, more intelligent than sexy. But she was now a beautiful woman. He remembered how, almost from the beginning, he'd been able to look at her and know exactly what she was thinking. Now, he saw a combination of emotions, including sorrow and confusion that appeared to match his own feelings.

"Of course," he said. "Of course, I remember." And echoing the Congressman's sentiments he added, "It's been a very long time."

The other occupants of the table had fallen silent, aware that something was going on but not sure what. As Jake and Daniel sat back down, Sophie sent a smile all around.

"We all knew each other many years ago," she explained, her tone bright, "but it's been ages since we've seen each other."

One of the other women at the table said, "Would you like us to move so you four can sit closer to each other."

"That's not necessary," Daniel said. "I'm sure we'll have plenty of time to catch up over the course of the evening."

"Well, it's really no problem," the woman continued.

"No," Lena said, her voice sharp. "That is, we're all so settled where we are. Please don't trouble yourselves."

The woman looked startled, but dropped the subject. And little by little, conversation returned to the table. Jake turned back to the women he'd just introduced himself to but, out of the corner of his eye, he observed Lena. She had turned to the man seated next to her. He saw the Congressman lean over and say something to them both, then rise and leave the table. Lena looked dismayed at his departure, but she stayed where she was.

The wheels in Jake's brain were whirring now, trying to piece things together. There was something about Sophie's reaction to Lena's appearance that bothered him. She didn't seem nearly as shocked as he was. The more he thought about it, the more he became convinced that there was more to this reunion than met the eye.

"Would you excuse me?" he interrupted his seatmate. He turned to Sophie. "Darling, there's someone on the other side of the room I'd like to introduce you to."

Before Sophie could answer, he was on his feet, pulling her wheelchair back from the table. He began pushing her toward the doors leading out of the ballroom.

"Who is this person you want me to meet?" Sophie asked.

He made no reply, just continued pushing until they were at the exit and then out in the hallway. He didn't stop until they were some distance from the room's entrance. Then he spun the chair around so they were facing each other.

CHAPTER FORTY-ONE

DANIEL STRODE AWAY FROM THE TABLE LIKE A MAN ON A MISSION. But other than putting distance between himself and the past, he had no idea where he was going. It was obvious to him that nothing had changed between Jake and Lena. The clear intensity of the man's feelings and the emotion plain on her face convinced him that whatever it was that had once drawn them together was still a potent force. If it weren't for his loyalty to Julie, he would have made some excuse for leaving the ball immediately. Instead, he decided to seek her out.

Her eyes lit up when she saw him. She looked radiant in an extraordinary blue silk gown, the strapless top sparkling with beads and the skirt composed of overlapping blue and green petals as iridescent as peacock feathers. Her braided hair wound in concentric circles sat atop her head like a crown. That was the thing about Julie, Daniel thought. She could always be counted on to wear the right thing and do the right thing, no matter what the occasion. She didn't throw unexpected curves at you. She didn't wait until you were ready to tell her you were in love with her and then let drop the fact that she was about to see the man she'd loved thirty years ago and, further, that she had no idea whether she still loved that man or not. When he was with her, he never, ever felt like he wasn't good enough.

He asked her to dance and she accepted without hesitation. He felt very at ease with her in his arms. Dancing with Julie was like a relaxing stroll on a pleasant day when the weather was calm. There was none of that nerve-wracking, storm-tossed, heart-beating-in-his chest feeling that he got when he danced with Lena. He told himself that he didn't miss, didn't need, and didn't want that kind of stimulation anymore. He was not a boy in the first throes of adolescence, he was a man who had survived heartbreak more than once and would again if he had to. If Lena still preferred that arrogant, over-aggressive, union bully to him, then so be it. He would not stand in her way.

He was scheduled to go back to Washington tomorrow evening but would change to an earlier train. With his schedule keeping him in D.C. more and more, there was nothing to keep Lena from associating with whomever she wanted. Julie still had her place in Georgetown and came down often. There was no urgent need for frequent trips to New York.

CHAPTER FORTY-TWO

AT THE TABLE, LENA FELT DANIEL'S ABANDONMENT KEENLY. SHE'D felt safer, stronger somehow when he'd been sitting beside her. She watched wistfully as he steered Julie around the dance floor. They looked attractive together, both so tall and blond. She felt a momentary panic at the thought that they might actually be a couple but the evening was already complicated enough without the added strain of trying to figure out what the panicky feeling meant.

She snuck a glance at Jake and Sophie. Each was chatting with their seatmate but, while Sophie appeared engaged in her conversation, it was clear that Jake was not. He looked like a man whose mind had been thrown for a complete loop. She could only imagine what was going through his brain. It was obvious that Sophie had not given him any hint of what the evening would entail.

Of course, having advanced notice had not helped her much. There was a big difference between conjuring someone up in your mind and being confronted with their physical presence; between remembering the color of their eyes and seeing those same eyes searching your own; between imagining how they might have changed over the years and coming face to face with what had changed and what had not.

Of all the emotions that had run through her during that long moment when they'd held each other's gazes, the one she'd been least prepared for was overwhelming sorrow. Looking at Jake, she had been struck instantly by how strong the resemblance between Rachel and her father was. It was no wonder that Sophie and Daniel had put the pieces together so easily. Even the arches of their eyebrows were matching. That two people could look so alike yet have no idea of each other's existence was heartbreaking.

The years that had been lost to Jake and to Rachel could never be recovered. But neither could the years that had been lost to Jake and herself. She remembered how from the very start, she had felt a physical connection to him that defied reason. It was as if by touching, they completed a circuit through which electricity flowed. It had been that way on the day they'd first met on the steps of her apartment building and it had it been that way later that same evening, on the stage of the Cooper Union Hall. The question was whether a current still ran between them or whether that circuit had been permanently broken. It was a question she could not answer at this moment.

CHAPTER FORTY-THREE

IN THE HALLWAY OUTSIDE THE BALLROOM, JAKE'S EYES PROBED Sophie's face. "Would you like to tell me what's going on?"

"What do you mean?" Sophie said, feigning innocence.

"I mean, that you obviously knew in advance about this little reunion. Why didn't you mention it to me?"

"I didn't -"

"No, Sophie." He was not going to let her off the hook so easily. "Stop right there. I know you too well, and too long. Do you want to tell me about it?"

Sophie shrugged. "Lena was on the steering committee for the ball. I ran into her at our first meeting."

"And how did she happen to be on the steering committee?" Jake asked. "Did you have anything to do with that?"

"No," Sophie said, though there was something in the way she said it that made him suspicious. "She knew Julie Danvers, and Julie asked her to be on it."

"Is that what Julie Danvers will say if I ask her?"

Sophie frowned. "I don't like being accused of lying."

"Well, I don't like being manipulated. So, why didn't you tell me that you ran into her at the meeting of the steering committee?"

"I don't know. Maybe I didn't have time because I haven't been seeing very much of you lately."

"Is that what this is about? You're upset because I've been away so much?"

Sophie looked away before she answering. "Not just away," she said. "Traveling to Washington, D.C. With Maxine."

"Maxine Jacobs?"

Sophie was silent.

"Sophie, have you been letting your imagination run away with you?"

"It doesn't take much imagination. She's an attractive woman. You're alone with her for a week."

"She's my colleague. That's all. There's never been anything between me and Maxine. You have to know that. You've met her boyfriend for God's sake."

"So, you aren't having an affair with her?"

"No," he said. "And I can't imagine why you would think I was."

"Why wouldn't I think it?" she asked, her voice plaintive. "I'm stuck in this wheelchair and you're stuck with me. If it wasn't for me, you could have traveled, done lots of things you haven't been able to do. I know you married me out of pity."

"Is that what you think?" Jake said. "After all these years, is that what you really think?"

Sophie looked down and shook her head slowly. "It's alright Jake. You don't have to pretend anymore."

"Now, what are you talking about?"

"You don't have to pretend because I know, Jake. I know about you and Lena."

Jake froze, his breath caught in his throat. Cautiously, he asked, "What do you know about me and Lena?"

Sophie's eyes were bleak. "I know what happened between you and her the night of the fire."

Jake couldn't bear the look on her face. He couldn't bear to be the cause of her pain. He swooped down and knelt in front of her, grasping her hands in his. "I'm so sorry, Soph. I never meant to hurt you. I can't believe Lena told you after all these years. I swear Sophie -"

"She didn't tell me," Sophie said.

"What?" he asked, confused again. "Then how... I don't understand. How did you find out?"

She didn't answer at once and he waited while she struggled to find the words. He rubbed the back of her hands with his thumbs and encouraged her with his eyes. Finally, she began.

"A few weeks ago a young woman came to visit me. She told me she was Lena's daughter. She said she had some questions about her mother's life. She said Lena didn't like to talk about her earliest months in America. That remembering that time was painful for her. The young woman said she especially had questions about her father. She said Lena would never talk to her about him."

"But why did she think *you* would know about her father," Jake asked. "And where *was* Mr. Kerner tonight, anyway? Why was Lena here with the Congressman?"

"Lena got divorced from Kerner about ten years ago. Anyway, Kerner wasn't this young woman's father. As for the Congressman, I'm not sure why he was with Lena tonight. I was a little surprised about that myself."

"Well, I still don't see why Lena's daughter would come to you for information about her father."

"She came because she was sure I had known him," Sophie said.

"But why would she think that?"

"Because she knew that Lena and I had been friends at least up until the time of the fire and she believed that Lena and her father had gotten married before the fire."

"Well, that doesn't make any sense," Jake said. "Why would she believe that?"

"Because Lena told her that. Apparently, Lena had to tell her that because this young woman was born nine months almost to the day after the fire."

"I don't understand," Jake said. He looked at Sophie. Tears were rolling down her cheeks, but she made no move to wipe them away. He opened his mouth and closed it. Because suddenly he did understand. He stood up slowly, turned around, walked a few steps away, then turned around again. He stared at Sophie. The look on her face confirmed it.

Words formed in his head. He had a daughter. Which meant that he was a father. To a daughter he didn't know, had not known existed. He was the father of a grown woman. It was unbelievable. It was... he didn't know what it was. It changed everything. Reframed everything.

Like a time traveler, he went back in his mind to those strange, wondrous, and terrible days when he and Lena had come together and abruptly separated. Like puzzle pieces rearranging themselves to fit, events swiftly realigned in his mind.

Of course, he thought, as realization bloomed. This was the real reason Lena had left the city so abruptly all those years ago. If he hadn't been predisposed by his mother's abandonment to assume he wasn't worthy of loving, he'd have realized Lena had lied when she'd denied being pregnant. Now, it all made sense. She hadn't left because she'd stopped loving him or because she'd not loved him in the first place but because she'd known she was pregnant. And she'd lied about the pregnancy because she'd known that if she was truthful, he would insist on marrying her and she hadn't wanted him to do that. Because of Sophie.

In the end, it all came back to that. To Sophie. His wife these past thirty years. He looked at her from across the room. She looked very small and very alone. But she was not alone and he needed to make that clear. He strode back over to her and knelt again before her.

"Let's get something straight," he said gently. "Back when all that happened, I was confused about a lot of things. And when I thought you had died in the fire, I went a little crazy. I think Lena and I both did. But it was only one night."

"Only one night," she said. "But that one night produced a baby. A child. I know how much you've always wanted to be a father. You'd never have married me if you'd known." Her voice was low. "I wouldn't have blamed you. As it is, I know you only married me out of pity."

He shook his head. "I didn't marry you out of pity. I married you because you stuck by me the way no one else ever has. My mother ran off and left me when I was twelve. My father died four years later. But you," he smiled, "you never stopped waiting for me. No matter how late I worked, you waited up for me. No matter how many times I canceled on you, you forgave me. You've always been on my side, even when it seemed like I was fighting half the world. And if that wasn't enough, no one makes me laugh the way you do. So, if you think I married you or stayed with you out of pity, you're wrong."

As he said the words, Jake realized how true they were. He may have been in love with Lena, and he may have married Sophie because it seemed the right thing to do at the time. But he'd always known she was good for him and, over the course of their marriage, she'd been more than good, she'd been probably better than he deserved.

For thirty years now, she had been at his side, his greatest cheerleader. He'd watched her go from a vibrant, energetic woman to a helpless and depressed one, then watched her overcome her disabilities and triumph. For years now, she had been a woman to admire, dedicated to her charitable causes, beloved among the neighborhood children, and still making him her number one priority. It had been eons since he had even noticed the wheelchair. Now all he saw before him was the beautiful woman with her slanting, laughing, bewitching eyes. The original reasons for his decision to marry her had long since ceased to be relevant.

By the time he finished talking, Sophie was crying. "I'm sorry," she said.

He took his handkerchief from his pocket and wiped her eyes. "There's nothing to be sorry for," he said. "I have never known anyone so full of love and life as you. And if I had it to do over again, I'd marry you in a heartbeat."

"I love you Jake," she said softly, almost shyly.

"I love you too," he told her. "And I'm sorry too. I wish we'd had this conversation years ago but I thought I was protecting you by not telling you."

"I know."

"From now on, no more secrets."

"No more secrets."

He sighed. "I'm going to have to speak to Lena," he said.

She nodded. "I know."

"But not tonight."

"No. Not tonight."

"Right now, I just want to go home with my wife."

"I'd like that too," Sophie said.

Jake leaned forward and kissed her gently. Eventually, he would have to process everything and figure out what it all meant. But not right now. Now, it was time to go home.

CHAPTER FORTY-FOUR

IT DIDN'T SURPRISE DANIEL THAT BRENNER AND HIS WIFE LEFT THE ball early or that Lena readily agreed to his suggestion that they leave as soon as dessert was served. He imagined that both Brenner and Lena wanted to be alone with their thoughts, which suited Daniel fine. Sitting beside Lena as they taxi'd back to her house, Daniel was silent. He sat erect, his muscles taut, and retreated inwards, shutting all pathways that flowed through his heart. Outside her townhouse, she asked if he would like to come in. He shook his head.

"I hope you don't mind, but I'm really tired. This traveling back and forth from Washington to New York is exhausting. In fact, I'm planning to cut back on it from now on. I've just got too much work in my Washington office to spend so much time here."

"Oh. But... , that is, when do you think you might be back?"

"Let's just see how it goes." He wasn't making any promises. "Julie will be coming down to Washington every so often. She still has her place in Georgetown. Perhaps you can come down with her sometime."

"Maybe. But Daniel, don't you want to come in for just a few minutes? Don't you want to talk a little bit?"

He shook his head. "Not tonight," he said. "I'll call you tomorrow, before I leave for Washington."

"Alright. I'll wait to hear from you."

He stayed just until she opened the door, then turned and, without a backward glance, headed for home.

Back in Washington, he immersed himself in work. He scheduled so many meetings both during and after the workday that he barely had time to see Julie when she came to town a few weeks later. He was grateful for her willingness to come to his office.

"I asked my secretary to make tea," he said as they settled themselves on a couple of chairs in a corner of his office, "but if you'd prefer coffee, I'll let her know,"

"Tea is fine." Julie smiled. "For some reason, I find it warms me up better than coffee and I could use some warming up today."

"It is cold for April."

"It's even colder in New York. But that never used to bother you."

Daniel laughed. "It still doesn't. I ordered the tea with you in mind."

"If it isn't the cold, then what is the reason you've stopped your visits to New York?"

"It's the work," Daniel said, surprised at Julie's incisive tone, which made the question seem like something other than chit chat. "I've been unbelievably busy."

"Unbelievably sounds about right."

He raised his eyebrows and pretended to be offended. "Just what are you insinuating? Are you impugning my credibility?"

"No, just your motivation."

"Julie, seriously, what's this about?"

"Just that I think you're avoiding New York for a reason."

"And what reason might that be?"

"Fear."

"Excuse me?"

Julie shook her head. "We've known each other too long to waste time pretending."

He sighed, conceding the point. "I'm not hiding," he said quietly. "I'm just getting out of the way."

"I suppose you mean for Brenner."

"Who else. I saw them the night of the March of Dimes ball."

"He's married," Julie pointed out.

"It's irrelevant whether they're actually going to do anything about it. It's how she feels that counts."

"And you've talked to her about it?"

"I didn't have to."

"Oh, so now you can read women's minds?"

Daniel's eyes narrowed. "Do you know something you're not saying?"

Julie looked exasperated. "No. Lena doesn't exactly confide in me. But she does confide in you, doesn't she? She tells you everything. And she turns to you for help. She worked like a demon for your election. And she goes out with you whenever you're in town."

"She's a friend," Daniel said. "That's all."

"Oh, Daniel." She sighed.

"What?"

"I'm disappointed in you. And don't give me that look. I know you, remember? All your life, you've fought for what you believe in. You've fought for workers' rights. You've fought for equal treatment under the law. You've fought against crime. You even took on President Truman, for God's sake. But you won't fight for this woman? What's that all about?"

"Why should I have to fight for her?" he said stiffly. "If she doesn't know by now what kind of person I am, then what's the sense of me fighting?"

"If you don't, you're a fool."

Daniel felt the heat creep up his neck. It hadn't happened to him in years. He wasn't going to let it happen now. He shook his head. "I can't believe you're saying this to me."

Julie sighed. "Daniel, you've learned a lot of things over the years, but you still haven't learned what women want." She looked rueful, like he was a student who was showing no aptitude for his lessons. "Women want to be loved and they want to be told that you love them and that you need them. If you want her, you need to go after her. Let her know how you feel. Take that risk."

"No," he said. "I took that risk once before and she rejected me."

"So? That was then. You're a different man now and she's a different woman. And even then, even back then, you didn't really fight for her, you just made her an offer. This time you're different, so act differently. You've spent a lifetime fighting for others, now it's time to fight for yourself."

Daniel regarded Julie thoughtfully. Just moments ago, she had recited a litany of facts about Lena, about how she confided in him, worked for his election, went out with him whenever he was in town, and turned to him for help when she was troubled. But

Julie, too, confided in him, worked for his election, went out with him when he was in town, and leaned on him when she needed help. He wished he could feel about Julie the way he did about Lena. But he never had and he knew he never would. He loved her dearly, but not that way. He hoped she didn't love him that way either and that it wasn't costing her too much to urge him to go after Lena. But he knew she wouldn't let any pain it might be causing her stop her from doing what was right. So how could he let it stop him.

"I'll do it," he said. "I may go down in flames, but I'll go down fighting."

Julie nodded. "Believe me, Daniel," she said. "If she's got a brain in her head, she won't turn you down."

CHAPTER FORTY-FIVE

JAKE'S VOICE WAS INSTANTLY RECOGNIZABLE. LENA REALIZED THAT, on some subconscious level, she had expected to hear from him eventually. She was glad it was sooner rather than later. She'd always thought that sight was the most important sense. But now she knew that other senses were far more potent, embedded in some deep pathway of the brain so that encountering them again catapulted one back through time.

"Lena?" he said. And just hearing him say her name made her tremble.

"Yes. How are you, Jake?"

"I'm..." He took a deep breath. "I don't know how I am. How should a man be when he finds out that he has a grown daughter he never knew about?"

Her throat constricted. So there it was. Sophie had told him after all. He didn't sound angry so much as bewildered. She didn't know what to say, didn't know where to begin.

"Lena?"

"I'm still here. I just... I really don't know what to say except that I'm sorry. I mean, at the time...." She didn't finish the sentence and the unsaid words generated memories in her more vivid than any words.

"Yes, well," he paused. "I didn't really call to talk about the past. I called because... I want to know about my daughter." He said the last part in a rush, the words tight and brittle, the word "daughter" seemingly unfamiliar and strange in his mouth.

"Of course. I'll tell you anything you want to know."

"Not on the phone," he said quickly. "That is, I'd rather talk in person. That's why I'm calling. To see if you would be willing to meet. Not this minute but sometime that's good for us both."

337

She froze. The idea of a get-together threw her mind into turmoil. But she couldn't see how she could refuse.

"Of course I'm willing," she said.

"Good." She could hear the relief in his voice and some of the brittleness seemed to melt away. "Is there someplace convenient to you?"

"There's a restaurant called the Odyssey on West 4th Street," she said.

"That'll be fine. Is next Friday alright? At noon?"

"Yes. That's a good time for me."

"Alright. Then I'll see you there. And Lena -"

"Yes?"

It was quiet on the other end but she knew he was still there. He said nothing for so long that her nerves got the better of her and she pressed the phone tight to her ear. In the silence, she felt him struggling with his emotions. Her chest became heavy with his pain and she felt his sorrow and frustration deep within her as if the telephone wires were conducting something more than just sound. Her eyes filled with tears as she clutched the telephone's spiral cord.

Finally, he spoke, saying only, "Thanks for agreeing to meet me."

She swallowed. "You're welcome. I'll see you on Friday." There was a click on the other end and she shakily lowered the receiver.

She had barely hung up the phone when it rang again.

"Hello?"

"Lena?"

Relief flooded her and the heaviness of her heart dissolved allowing it to soar. "Daniel, I'm so glad it's you."

"I'm sorry it's been a while since I've called. Things have been hectic. How have you been?"

"I've been fine."

"And Rachel?"

"I don't know. She's still not talking to me."

"She just needs time."

"I guess." She paused as she debated whether to tell him about Jake's phone call. He'd been so distant after the March of Dimes Ball. She didn't want to upset him; she didn't want to hide anything from him either. "I have something to tell her that I'm pretty sure she's going to want to hear."

"What's that?"

"Jake just called me." There was silence on the other end. "Daniel?"

"Yes, I'm here," he said. His tone was guarded. "What did he say?"

"He said that Sophie had told him about Rachel. He asked if I would be willing to meet with him to talk about her."

"What did you tell him?"

"Well, I didn't feel like I had any choice," she said and waited for him to weigh in, hoping he would agree. But he was quiet, so she continued. "I think I owe it to him and I know I owe it to Rachel. I said I would meet him. I'm not going to say anything to Rachel right away though. I'll wait until afterwards, once I see how it goes."

"So you are getting together with him." He sounded like he was processing the information.

"Yes, next Friday at noon. I wish it were sooner though. I know I'm going to be a nervous wreck between now and then."

He made a sound that could have been um hmm. She waited for him to say more. She needed him to say more. She wanted to feel his solid strength through his words and feel that she could lean on that strength. He cleared his throat.

He said, "Maybe the time will go by faster if you know you have something else happening on Friday. Something you're not nervous about."

Immediately, she breathed easier. "Like what?"

"Like dinner and a show with me."

"Really Daniel?" She felt almost like crying at the news. "You're coming to New York next weekend?"

"Yes, and I just happen to have two tickets to a new musical, *Guys and Dolls*. It's playing at the 46th Street theater just down the block from that little Italian place you like."

"Tre Colori? I love that place. And *Guys and Dolls*—how did you ever manage to get your hands on tickets?"

"Being a congressman does have *some* perks. We'll have to eat a little early to make it to the theater on time. I can pick you up at five-thirty or so."

"That sounds perfect!" Suddenly, she couldn't stop smiling.

"Then I'll see you on Friday," he said.

"Yes. I'll be looking forward to it."

"So will I," he told her. "Very much."

In the days that followed, Lena found it almost impossible to concentrate on work. By midweek, she'd just about given up getting anything constructive accomplished. She was sitting in her office trying to decide what to wear to the theater, when the phone rang.

"Mrs. Kerner?" asked a woman's voice.

"Yes."

"I'm calling on behalf of Jake Brenner. He's asked me to give you his regrets but, unfortunately, he has to cancel your lunch on Friday."

"What? I don't understand." Anger mingled with frustration. She'd been on pins and needles the entire week waiting for this lunch that Jake had asked for. She couldn't believe he was backing out on her. "Who is this?"

"I'm Mr. Brenner's secretary."

"Well I'd like to speak with Mr. Brenner."

"I'm sorry but he isn't here right now. I'm sure he'll be in touch when he's able to reschedule."

Lena had no intention of being put off indefinitely. "When do you expect him in?"

"I really don't know."

"I find that hard to believe. You're telling me that he gave you no indication as to when he would back?"

"No. I'm sure he'll get back to you as soon as possible."

Lena hung up the phone and sighed. She would so much rather have gotten her meeting with Jake over with, but there was clearly nothing she could do about it. She would just have to wait until he rescheduled.

On Fridays, Lena usually allowed herself the liberty of taking things a little slower than the rest of the week. She liked to linger over the morning paper while slowly drinking her tea. She was in the middle of doing both when Daniel called.

"I'm sorry to be calling so early," he began.

"That's no problem. Is everything alright?"

"Everything's fine. It's just that my day's gotten a little more hectic than originally planned. I'm afraid it's going to be pretty tight timing for this evening."

"Oh." She tried hard to keep the disappointment out of her voice. "That's alright. There'll be other evenings."

"We don't have to cancel everything," he said. "I'm just thinking that it might be better if I met you at the restaurant instead of at your apartment."

"Is that all? That's no problem."

"Well, it's not exactly how I was hoping the evening would go, but there's nothing I can do about it. So I'll see you at the restaurant at, say, 6:00 p.m. at the latest."

"Yes. I'll meet you there."

"Good. And now, believe it or not, I've got to run. Breakfast meetings are very big here."

"Alright. I'll see you this evening."

He was gone before she had a chance to mention that the meeting with Jake had been cancelled. It was just as well. She had a feeling that the less she mentioned Jake's name, the better.

She returned to the paper and browsed through it at a leisurely pace. She was close to being done with it, when a headline caught her eye and then her full attention. It was an obituary.

Sophie Brenner had died.

She stared at the words as if they would say something different if she looked at them long enough. *No,* she thought. *NO! It can't be true. It can't be.* Her mind rebelled. Her brain would not allow it to be true. *Not now. Not before I've had a chance to make everything right between us.* The word "no" continued to grow in her head. It became a roar. It blocked out any other sound or thought.

But what finally came out of her when she put the newspaper down was not the word no. It was a ragged sob. And then, suddenly, she was crying as if her heart was breaking.

Thirty years ago, when she'd left New York City, she had grieved over leaving Jake. But she had never grieved over leaving Sophie who she had also loved. Now the old loss melded with the new so that it was impossible to figure out where one ended and the other began. It was like a scab had been forcefully ripped off her heart, exposing a wound she'd thought had long ago healed. She didn't try to stop herself. There was no reason to. Instead, she let herself cry. She wept until, eventually, the tears naturally slowed and finally stopped.

She grew gradually calmer and tried to figure out what to do. The newspaper was still on the table in front of her. She re-read the last line. Services today at 4 p.m. at The Central Synagogue.

She took a minute to compose herself, then picked up the phone to call her office. She needed to let them know that she wouldn't be coming in today.

As she walked into the entry hall of the synagogue, she merged into the crowds that were slowly moving in the direction of the main sanctuary. She found a seat in the back and watched as the remaining rows filled up. At the front of the sanctuary, she saw a gleaming mahogany coffin with a triple beveled edge and a row of shiny brass handles. Whoever had selected it had gotten it exactly right, she thought.

After a few minutes, a rabbi wearing a dark suit and a narrow tie appeared at a podium on the raised platform at the front of the sanctuary. The crowd sounds became muted, the rustling slowed, and then ceased. A door opened to the rabbi's left and Jake entered with two short, elderly people walking on either side of him. It was Aunt Sarah and Uncle Lou. Lena's eyes filled with tears at the sight of them.

Jake helped them get settled in the front row. His attention was focused; his eyes were hooded. He looked like he had gotten a haircut that morning. His part was sharp and his hair temporarily forced into submission making him look unlike himself. He sat so that Aunt Sarah was between him and Uncle Lou.

The service began and the rabbi led them through psalms. Lena repeated the words to keep her mind from wandering. There were too many things she couldn't allow herself to think about.

Finally, the rabbi closed his prayer book and laid it down on the podium. He stepped back from his post and looked meaningfully at Jake. Lena held her breath as Jake slowly stood and walked heavily up the steps. He unfolded a paper and looked out at the expectant crowd.

A memory came to Lena of the last time she'd seen him on stage, the night of the rally at the Cooper Union Hall. Then, he had held the audience in the palm of his hand. He'd captured them with his passion; he'd captured her with his charisma. Now, as then, the audience was hushed, rapt. Even in his present state, grieving and exhausted, the lines of his face deeper than she remembered from the ball, his hair grayer, and his eyes damp, even now, he commanded attention.

"To those of you who knew Sophie well," he began, his voice resonant, "there's little I can tell you that you don't already know. You're here because you loved Sophie and admired her, and because she made you laugh or made you care or just made you feel more alive."

He glanced down at his notes, but Lena knew it was to give himself a moment's respite and not because he didn't know what he wanted to say. He continued.

"Sophie always told it like it was. She didn't care for phoniness or sugarcoating, much less outright lies. She took what life handed her and got on with it.

"You probably know," and he produced a small smile, "that she could curse like a sailor when she was provoked. She had quite a—well, let's just say she had a good vocabulary." He looked serious again. "But she had a heart as big as—no, bigger than anyone I know. And what she couldn't do for her friends physically, she made up for with time, attention, and caring."

He paused and looked around the audience. When he began again, Lena had the distinct sensation that he was looking directly at her, though she knew it was not possible for him to have spotted her so far back. His voice was softer, huskier as he continued.

"Sophie was loyal to a fault. She loved her friends, not blindly, but unconditionally. She understood that no one was perfect and she could forgive almost anyone if she knew their intentions were good and their hearts in the right place. I know that each of you, will carry a piece of her in your heart always."

A hard and painful obstruction, too sharp to be just a lump, was suddenly present in Lena's throat. She had apologized to Sophie that day they'd shared a taxi from Julie Danver's house. But had it been enough? Had Sophie realized how deeply sorrowful she was over the pain she had caused her and over the years of friendship lost? Had Sophie understood that her intentions had been good and had she forgiven her?

At this point, Jake paused and looked down again. When he resumed, his voice was brisker, as if he was hoping momentum would get himself through the next part. "Now I want to speak to those of you who didn't know Sophie; those of you who are here solely because of your connection to me." He shook his head slowly. "You should know that anything I've been able to accomplish, any success I've had, would not have been possible if it weren't for my wife." His voice caught a little on the last word as he said it and his hands tightened on the podium.

"There was a time," he said softly, "when I thought it was merely sweet of Sophie to wait up for me until whatever insane hour I came home from whatever meeting I was stuck in. I took for granted her continual interest in my work, her gentle encouragement when things weren't going well, and her exuberant enthusiasm when I was successful."

It was easy to take that kind of life-long love for granted, Lena thought. Wasn't she guilty of it too? Maybe if she wasn't so busy being afraid of making another mistake, afraid of failing at love again, she would have realized it sooner.

"It took me a long time to realize what I had," Jake began. But at that point, his voice broke and he stopped talking. He gripped the podium and stared down at it. This, Lena thought, was what it was like to see a man's heart breaking open. And, for just a second, Jake didn't look old, or middle aged, nor did he call to mind the man who had stood on the stage of the Cooper Union Hall. Instead, in that moment of naked emotion, she saw the young boy whose mother had abandoned him. She wanted to put her arms around that little boy and tell him that everything would be okay.

And then Jake regained his composure and when he spoke, his voice was strong, almost defiant. "It took me a long time to realize," he said again, "and I'm only grateful that it wasn't too late, that I would not be half the man I am today if it weren't for her unwavering devotion."

"So, for those of you who are here because of your connection to me, rather than your connection to Sophie, you should know that whatever good will you may feel towards me, you should feel toward Sophie too. And I hope that, although you may have come here out of respect or affection for me, you will leave here with that same respect and affection for the beautiful woman who shared her life with me."

His eulogy completed, Jake stared unseeing out at the audience until the rabbi glided forward and laid a hand gently on his back. Then Jake nodded, folded the paper carefully, and slipped it into his front pocket before making his way back to his seat.

Lena bowed her head, pushing the tears off first one cheek, then the other with the palm of her hand. Like a broken faucet, they did not stop their steady, drumbeat down the front of her face. She stood when everyone rose as the coffin made the journey from the front to the rear of the sanctuary and she remained standing where she was as people started trickling out of the row.

And still, the tears kept falling. It was too late now to make things right again between her and Sophie. But it was not too late to make things right with those who were still living. Sophie's death was a reminder that life was too short not to grab a chance at love when it was in front of you. She knew now, what she had to do.

CHAPTER FORTY-SIX

DANIEL ARRIVED AT TRE COLORI A FEW MINUTES EARLY. LENA WASN'T there yet, so he told the maitre' d that he would wait at the bar. He didn't think Lena would mind if he ordered a martini while he waited for her. He thought he could be forgiven on this occasion for needing something to steady his nerves.

Originally, when he'd thought he would be picking her up at her apartment, he'd planned to bring a beautiful bouquet of flowers. But when he'd had to change the arrangements and meet her at the restaurant, he'd decided to skip the bouquet. The days for wooing her with flowers and candy were long past. Words had always been his friends. So, he would fight for her with nothing more than the words in his heart.

All day long, at work, on the train, and in the taxi, he'd tried not to think about the fact that Lena was meeting with Jake Brenner that very day. He understood the necessity for their conversation, although he didn't understand why it could not have been conducted on the telephone. But it was just as well. In a perverse way, he was glad Lena was getting together with Brenner. When he said what he had to say at dinner tonight, he didn't want there to be any unanswered questions in her mind concerning how she felt about Brenner. Let Brenner have his turn. Daniel could wait. If after hearing what each of them had to say, she chose Brenner, then so be it.

At 6:15, he ordered a second martini. Lena often ran a few minutes late. Promptness was not necessarily one of her virtues. There was still plenty of time for dinner before the show began. He saw the maitre d' trying to catch his eye but ignored him. The restaurant wasn't that crowded. They could hold the table a while longer.

At 6:30, the maitre d' strolled over to ask if Daniel's dining companion had arrived. There was a solicitousness in his manner that Daniel found infuriating. But the restaurant was starting to fill up and he needed to remain in the man's good graces or risk losing his reservation. He assured the maitre' d that she would be here any minute.

At 6:45, aware that he was drinking too fast, he nevertheless ordered a third martini. He avoided the maitre'd's pointed glances. He told himself that there were a lot of reasons why she could be late. She could have gotten tied up in something at work. Or lost track of the time. Or gotten caught in traffic. Or perhaps, awful as it would be, something really serious had happened to someone she knew. This last was such a terrible thought that he was doubly angry with himself because he knew that a part of him preferred it to the other possible reason that he was not letting himself consider.

But by 7 p.m., it was obvious. She had made her choice. He'd been a fool once again. He had allowed himself to believe that she could love him when he knew that he was not the type women fell for. He had tried that with Lee and it hadn't really worked. She had left him for London. He was the friend type. He had always had plenty of women friends.

The maitre d' was approaching. Daniel stood up. A little too quickly. Three martinis in under an hour were having their effect.

"It's alright," he told the maitre d'. "You needn't hold my table any longer."

"But," the man looked puzzled. "your lady friend has just arrived."

Daniel stared at him. So, she'd come after all. Of course. Lena was too kind a person to just leave him waiting here forever. She had come to break the news to him.

"Thank you," he said.

She was waiting just inside the door of the restaurant, in fashionable black and looking lovely. She smiled when she saw him. A kind, gentle smile. He'd once read that when you were going to give someone bad news, it was a good idea to give it to them in a public place. Like a restaurant. That way there would be no scene.

Well, he was a Congressman. He could not afford to make a scene in a public place. Not that he would have made a scene even if they'd been in private. If she didn't want to be with him, he wasn't going to protest. In fact, he would tell her that she needn't even stay for dinner tonight.

On the other hand, it occurred to him, wasn't that what he always did when it came Lena? Wasn't that what Julie had said? That he gave up without a fight. Well, damn it, he thought. That wasn't going to happen this time. Public place or no public place. He was going to take a stand. For once.

"You look beautiful," he said forcefully.

"Thank you. And I'm sorry I was so late, I -",

""S'all right," he said. "You needn't explain. Anyway, I believe our table is ready."

He crooked his arm and she slipped hers through it as the maitre d' began leading them to their table.

"Daniel," she said, "are you alright?"

"Perfectly. Why do you ask?"

"I don't know. You don't seem yourself."

"Ah," he tried to smile mysteriously, "perhaps you don't know me as well as you think you do."

The maitre d' pulled out a chair for Lena and Daniel sat opposite her. They each accepted a menu.

"Daniel," Lena tried again, "please let me explain why I'm so late."

"S'not necessary."

"But I want to," she insisted. I don't know if you had a chance to read the newspaper today and it probably didn't make the Washington papers. The thing is... Sophie is... she's gone. She passed away. Her funeral was today. I had to go. I'm sure you understand."

"Of course," he said. He did understand. Sophie had been all that was standing between Lena and Jake. And now she was gone. Of course, Lena would go to Jake immediately.

"And what happened when you went?" he asked.

"What do you mean what happened? It was a funeral. There was a huge turnout. I knew there would be but I was still surprised at the size of the crowd. Apparently Sophie was involved in a lot of causes."

"I'm sure some people were there for Brenner," Daniel said meaningfully.

"Yes, of course."

"And how is Brenner?"

"About as you would imagine. He delivered her eulogy. It was very moving."

"He was always good at that. Manipulating the emotions of a crowd."

"Daniel, are you sure you're alright?" she asked, her brow furrowed.

"Sure. Why?"

"Well, that wasn't a very nice thing to say. This was his wife's funeral. I don't think he was trying to manipulate anyone's emotions."

"Nice? You think I'm not being nice?" He snorted. "I'm too nice. I've always been too nice. All my life I've been too nice."

"What's wrong with being nice?"

"It's not what women want."

"Daniel, lower your voice. You're starting to attract attention."

"Oh sure," he said. "That's just what you don't want. A scene. That's why you're going to break the news to me here."

"Break the news? Daniel, I have no idea what you're talking about."

He lowered his voice and leaned over to her and whispered loudly. "Don't you?" He was feeling very comfortable and he relaxed against the back of his chair as he knocked down the last of his martini. "Well," he told her, "I'm not going down without a fight. Not this time."

"A fight? Daniel, what's going on? Who are you fighting?"

Daniel thought about that. He wasn't really sure what the answer to that question was. He didn't want to fight with Lena. He wanted to love her. So was Brenner the one he was fighting with? His brain felt fuzzy. Maybe it *was* Brenner he was supposed to fight. Perhaps they could have a duel. With pistols. No, with swords. Or with pens. Yes, that would be better. After all, wasn't the pen mightier than the sword or something like that.

"Daniel?"

"Do you remember," he said suddenly, "how we used to take a lot of time looking at the menu at the Meltzer's after night school and then, in the end, we'd both order nothing but tea because we couldn't afford anything else."

Lena looked more confused than ever. "Of course, I remember."

"And now look at us." He smiled. "Sitting in this restaurant. This expensive restaurant. I can take you to places like this. I can show you things. Does *he* like to eat in fine places and go to theater and concerts? "

"He? Who are you talking about? Does who like to eat in fine places? Daniel please tell me what you're talking about?"

"Damn it I'm talking about us," he said. "You and me, instead of you and Brenner. I want you to choose me this time. Love me. Marry me."

Lena stared at him. "Are you asking me to marry you?"

Was he? This wasn't going the way he'd planned it. But wasn't that exactly what he wanted? Had always wanted? So why not just cut to the chase. Fight or go down in flames. Piss or get off the pot.

"Yes," he said. "I am asking you to marry me."

"Yes," she said.

"Yes, what?" he asked.

"Yes, I'll marry you."

"But -" Now it was his turn to be confused.

"You're not taking it back are you?"

"No. Of course not. But I thought… that is with Brenner being free… I thought…"

"What? What did you think? That I went to Sophie's funeral and threw myself at Jake?"

"Well… I…."

Lena smiled at him. "You know, I once said you were brilliant. But, actually, you're kind of an idiot."

He stared at her. "An idiot?"

"Yes," she said gently. "I'm not in love with Jake. How could I be? When I'm head over heels in love with you."

"You are?"

"Yes. Now are you going to kiss me or am I going to have to make a scene?"

"Um. I don't think a scene is a good idea," Daniel said. "I am a Congressman after all." He looked at her and knew that in all his life he had never been happier than he was at that moment. "On the other hand," he said, "what's the matter with a scene now and then?" Then leaning over and not caring who might be watching, he kissed her exactly the way he had wanted to beginning with the first time he'd seen her on board the Pretoria.

CHAPTER FORTY-SEVEN

"COME ON, HONEY," DAVID SAID.

Rachel looked at him. Easy for him she thought. But she knew that if anyone could understand how she felt, it was her wonderful husband. She was grateful to him for accompanying her today; grateful for the support of his arm around her waist and the love in his gaze.

She felt a flutter deep within and placed a hand on the small, but definite roundness of her expanding stomach. The kicks were coming more frequently with each passing day. Her mother had told her that during her own pregnancy, Rachel had been so active, Lena had half expected her baby to crawl out of her womb rather than coming out the usual way.

Thinking of that conversation, Rachel felt a surge of warmth toward her mother. Now that she was going to be a mother herself, it was a little easier to understand what her own mother had gone through all those years ago and the choices she had made. She still wished Lena had handled things differently and not lied to her for all those years. But she was glad they had gotten to the point where they could talk again. She'd lost so much time with one parent, she didn't want to lose any time with the other.

And she had missed her mother terribly. The more her pregnancy had progressed, the more she'd realized that she wanted her mother to be part of it and to be part of the baby's life when he or she was born. Her mother would be a fantastic grandmother. And, since her mother was going to be married to Congressman Cowan, the baby would also have an excellent stepgrandfather.

David exerted a little gentle pressure on her waist and she nodded. It was time. She reached into her pocket and felt for the handkerchief that she'd put there this morning. Only last week, her mother had given it to her, explaining its significance. Now, she curled her hand around it and gave it a little squeeze. Then she knocked on the door. From the other side, she heard footsteps. The door swung open and he was standing there looking at her.

The moment she had been waiting for all these years was finally here. She couldn't move; couldn't do anything. If she tried to speak, she was just going to lose it. At that moment, she felt the baby kick again and she smiled. Because she knew it was going to be all right.

"Hello," she said. "I'm Rachel."

"I know," Jake said. "I am very, very glad to meet you. Please come in." He stepped back to let them enter and gently closed the door behind them.

The End

SPECIAL THANKS

To Keri Culver and Diane McConkey, my friends and writers group buddies, who read and critiqued several drafts of every chapter of this novel, provided invaluable feedback, and helped me stay the course.

To my sister, Janet, who cheered me on endlessly in this endeavor (and in everything else I attempt).

And to my parents, who nurtured me in too many ways to list, not the least of which was helping me submit my first novel, written at the tender age of eight, to a publisher.

ABOUT THE AUTHOR

Hillary Adrienne Stern is an attorney for the Federal Government specializing in employment law. She currently resides in Bethesda, Maryland with her dog Darcy. When she's not busy writing, she can be found studying Italian or going on safaris in Africa.

11430725R00222

Made in the USA
San Bernardino, CA
04 December 2018